ANTHONY QUINN

Anthony Quinn was born in Liverpool in 1964. From 1998 to 2013 he was the film critic for the *Independent*. He is the author of six novels: *The Rescue Man*, which won the 2009 Authors' Club Best First Novel Award; *Half of the Human Race*; *The Streets*, which was shortlisted for the 2013 Walter Scott Prize; *Curtain Call*, which was chosen for Waterstones and *Mail on Sunday* Book Clubs and *Eureka*.

ANTHONY QUINN

Freya

VINTAGE

1 3 5 7 9 10 8 6 4 2

Vintage
20 Vauxhall Bridge Road,
London SW1V 2SA

Vintage Classics is part of the Penguin Random House
group of companies whose addresses can be found at
global.penguinrandomhouse.com

Copyright © Anthony Quinn 2016

Anthony Quinn has asserted his right to be identified as the
author of this Work in accordance with the Copyright, Designs
and Patents Act 1988

First published in Vintage in 2017
First published in hardback by Jonathan Cape in 2016

penguin.co.uk/vintage

A CIP catalogue record for this book is available
from the British Library

ISBN 9781784703127

Printed and bound by Clays Ltd, St Ives plc

Penguin Random House is committed to a sustainable future
for our business, our readers and our planet. This book is made
from Forest Stewardship Council® certified paper.

For Laura Quinn

Who is so safe as we? Where none can do
Treason to us, except one of us two.

John Donne

I
At Swim, Two Girls

I

The bus, snailing up Whitehall, had nearly come to a standstill in the crowd. On its side someone had chalked HITLER MISSED THIS BUS, which had got them swarming onto the road, cheering. They walked alongside it as proudly as marchers with a carnival float. Passengers had pressed their faces to the windows, waving, tickled to be at the centre of this exultation.

Freya had seen the bus about half an hour before, but had decided to walk; and here she was outside Swan & Edgar, on time to meet her friends. It was warm for early May. She stood in the wide doorway watching the mass of bodies swirl and eddy in front of her. She had never seen a crowd in quite this mood before, not even when she was a girl at the Coronation in 1937. Among the women, who seemed to move along in huge flocks, she detected something excitable – no, more like hysterical, as if every single one of them were just getting married. Was that why the men looked so dazed?

On and on they came, the girls in their summer dresses, as gaily coloured as the plumage of exotic birds. A gaggle had just passed her in a great wave of perfume and laughter. They had been waiting for this day like a prisoner who has heard a rumour of his release yet still dares not believe it, so often has the hope been dashed. From the high windows above, streamers were pouring down, and Union Jacks fluttered over balcony railings. Freya hadn't yet immersed herself in the euphoria. Of course she was relieved, like everyone else, and had caught the train up from Plymouth the night before in the expectation of a jubilant welcome from her parents: our brave girl, back at last! That pleasurable sense of return had lasted until the moment she let herself into her father's place in Tite Street and found – she felt it as a shock – nobody home.

The previous weekend she had telephoned her mother to persuade her up to town for the day. She came infrequently, having sold the family house in the summer of '39 and retreated to a village in Sussex. Her husband's responsibilities as an ARP warden obliged him to be in London more often than in the country. By degrees the studio in Chelsea became his home. War had given them a kind of permission to pursue their own lives, though neither had taken the formal step of asking for a separation. Freya still believed it was in her power to engineer a rapprochement, and had announced her intention to come up for VE Day in the hope that this would at least put them in the same room. But her mother must have got cold feet, and there was no telling where her father had got to.

At Swan & Edgar she examined her reflection against the dark polished glass of the door. Bothersome though it was today, the uniform lent her a certain dash. She was leggy, like her mother, statuesque and somewhat flat-chested. Her eyebrows, darker than her mid-brown hair, framed a face notable for its hollow cheeks. Her gaze projected something more challenging than was intended; she was a little short-sighted. The set of her mouth was wilful. Now, with the babble of the crowd gathering at her back, she peered more intently into the glass, as if she might read an intimation of the future there. What in the world was to become of them now that –

4

'Freya!' The voice cut through the air. It was Jean Markham, also in uniform, with girls whose faces she'd last seen at school two years ago, Sophia and Betty and Maud and Catherine P. and Catherine S. The sternest girl in her year, Jean wore her smile like an unfamiliar lipstick.

'Jean –'

'My, don't you look smart!' cried Jean in her parade-ground tone. Amid the flurry of kisses and hugs Freya glanced at the stranger among them, a russet-haired girl who held back rather awkwardly from the rest. She was tall, as tall as Freya, pale-skinned yet luminous, and somewhat ill at ease; Freya's impression was of an ungainly swan. Jean, all briskness, introduced her as Nancy Holdaway.

'Not seen her in ages and she telephoned me *out of the blue* this morning!' There was the faintest touch of annoyance in her tone to suggest that surprise telephone calls were gauche and unwelcome. Freya stared at the girl for a moment before extending her hand.

'Hullo,' she said, feeling the girl's slim palm.

'How d'you do?' Nancy replied, blushing. Freya, who never blushed, always felt a little superior to people who did.

Catherine P. said that they should start to make for Downing Street, because Churchill was going to address the nation at three. As they pushed their way into the crowds moving south, Freya half listened as Jean recounted episodes from her last two years as a Waaf, first in Inverness, later in Norfolk. She had heard some of it before in the occasional letter Jean had written, though the details had been left vague on account of censorship – you could take gossip only so far during wartime. In any case, the other girls weren't that interested in the Waaf, they were much more eager for news of her boyfriends. Jean had been quite busy on that front, and told stories about men chasing her, pestering her, boring her and (occasionally) catching her. Her candour provoked giggles and squeals of mirth, which made Freya wonder if the others were still virgins.

By the time they reached Trafalgar Square the noise and the press of bodies was overwhelming. The heat of the day and the frenzy of the mood were taking a toll. At the foot of Regent Street they had watched a team of St John Ambulance men shoulder their way out of a scrum; they were carrying a woman with blood pouring from her head. 'Only fainted,' someone called out. A bottleneck had formed at the turn to Whitehall, and Jean, raising her voice to group-leader volume, said they should stay close.

Freya looked back at Nancy, who was bringing up the rear. Jean, noticing this, leaned towards Freya's ear and said, with a conspiratorial sniff, 'School-leaver.'

'How do you know her?'

'Oh, friend of the family. My father worked with her father, years back when we lived up north. She wrote to tell me she was in London, and I forgot all about it until – oh goodness!'

Her exclamation was prompted by a boisterous conga line of revellers cutting right across their path and causing little waves of panicked jostling. It was moving with a headlong, high-spirited abandon, indifferent to the normal rules of pedestrian behaviour; some people were dodging out of the way, others were joining in. Freya still had her back turned when, without warning, a meaty arm grabbed her around the waist and pulled her into the wild to-and-fro of the swaying line. Caught unawares, she lost her bearings for a moment, jounced along by the arms of the unseen man behind her. As she steadied herself to the forced rhythm and caught her breath, she glanced over her shoulder, intending to give her waylayer a polite smile of withdrawal, just to prove she wasn't a spoilsport. His red face, sweaty and bleared with drink, indicated that such civility was

6

unnecessary. She dragged herself from out of his grasp and ducked back into the crowd.

She looked around at the roiling masses, loud, oblivious. The others were nowhere to be seen. She rejoined the heave towards Whitehall, her head bobbing from side to side as she tried to pick out Jean's blue-grey uniform in the throng; once or twice she thought she spotted her in the distance, then realised her mistake. (Short-sightedness didn't help.) Drat! She sensed the high promise of the day threatening to unravel. Jean had taken charge of entertainments and Freya had fallen into line with her bossy shepherding. A little stab of disappointment provoked her to call out Jean's name, once, twice. A few people looked around, blank-faced. There was no answering voice.

Squinting into the distance again she caught a flash of russet hair that seemed familiar. Wasn't that Nancy, the girl who'd been tagging along? She felt her steps quicken as she threaded her way through the tumult. Drawing nearer, Freya started to doubt her powers of recognition, for the girl, as far as she could tell, was on her own. And her wide-stepping, mannish walk didn't seem to fit with the callow schoolgirl whom Jean had introduced. She hesitated a moment, considering the potential scene of embarrassment.

'Hullo there?' she said, touching the girl's shoulder.

She turned round. 'Oh! Freya . . . isn't it?' Nancy's face lit up in a show of relief: she might have been her only friend in the world.

'Where are they?'

'I don't know! One minute I was right behind them, the next –' She gave a hopeless shrug of appeal. Up close Freya now noticed Nancy's extraordinary tiger eyes, an intense olive green with very dark irises. Her skin was dewy, and flushed. As the crowds flowed by on either side an uncertainty vibrated in the space between them. Cast adrift, they clung to each other like shipwrecked mariners.

7

'Well, this is a nice to-do,' said Freya with an amused half-snort. 'Looks like Jean has given us the slip.'

'Surely she didn't mean to?' Nancy asked, earnest dismay in her expression. Freya merely shook her head; it was beneath her to explain that she was joking. Just then a huge roar went up, and the crowds were sucked towards the middle of Whitehall like iron filings to a magnet. The bells, which had been pealing for hours, had stopped, and the air grew shrill with whistles and cheers. The ambling movement of bodies quickened into urgency. Ahead of them they heard a cry go up: 'It's him – he's coming outside!'

Freya turned to Nancy, whose forlorn air made her feel of a sudden responsible. 'Come on,' she said, briskly putting her arm through the girl's. 'Whatever else happens, we mustn't miss this.'

And they plunged forward, still holding on to one another.

Later they bought ginger beer at a stall and found themselves a bench in the Embankment Gardens. They had given up on finding Jean and the others. Nancy gazed out to the river, her free hand shielding her eyes against the sun. Freya, her whole body damp with sweat, peeled off her serge tunic. She had lost her hat in the crush to catch sight of Churchill.

'Well, that's one for the diary,' she said, blowing a stray tendril of hair from her face.

Nancy nodded, then glanced at Freya. 'Do you keep a diary?'

'No.'

After a pause she said, 'I'm awfully sorry about – well, being landed with me.'

'Ha. It could be that *you've* been landed with *me.*'

Nancy shook her head. 'Oh no, Jean told me what an amazing friend you were.'

'Is that so?'

8

'Yes, really! You don't believe me? *Amazing* was the word she used.'

Freya returned an archly humorous look. 'That's not the word I'm disputing. It was the "friend" part.'

'Oh . . .' The girl seemed at a loss again. 'Sorry, I thought you were friends – from school –'

'Yes, we have that in common. Oh, I've known Jean for years, and I like her well enough – we've even corresponded a bit. But I'd say that we're friendly with each other, rather than being actual friends.'

Nancy gave an anxious frown. 'I'm not sure I understand the difference.'

Freya leaned back. 'Well, I needn't have singled out Jean. I tend to keep a distance from people. At school I was *not* a popular girl.'

'But in the Wrens,' Nancy said, with a bright glance at Freya's uniform, 'I imagined there'd be such camaraderie, the friends you'd –'

'I didn't join the navy to make friends. I joined because there was a war on.' That sounded rather off, she thought, and softened. 'I had pals, of course. One or two of them I may keep up with.'

She had joined the service (she explained) aged eighteen, and did a year's apprenticeship in Greenwich, then another year to qualify as a plotting officer. At Plymouth, where she was posted, they put her in charge of a watch that received information from coastal radar stations. She and her Wren ratings would do fifteen-hour shifts, reporting the position of shipping traffic as it appeared on their screens. By the summer of 1944 she was in the Operations Room recreating a panorama of the entire sea war in the North Atlantic.

'Crikey,' said Nancy. 'What a responsibility.'

'I know. And the wonderful thing was – I was good at it. Whenever there was a captain visiting, or an admiral, I could give an assessment of the situation at any time. I

9

mean, you always knew it was bloody dangerous –' She broke off and looked round at Nancy, whose round-eyed solemnity made her chuckle. 'Perhaps I should save my war stories for another day. We're meant to be celebrating, aren't we?'

'Yes! What should we do?'

Freya stood up and put her hands on her hips in a businesslike way. 'Hmm. My own inclination would be to find a pub somewhere and get blind roaring stinko.'

Nancy met this proposal with a smile as wide and artless as a flag waving in the breeze. 'Stinko it is!'

They decided – or rather, Freya decided – to walk along the river towards Victoria, where she knew a couple of likely places. On the way they passed strolling hordes of people in paper hats, singing, laughing, cheering; the mood of the afternoon, less giddy than in Whitehall, had held its holiday brightness. Freya, with an occasional sidelong glance, mused on the moment, two odd girls making a pair. It wasn't how she had envisaged the day. And yet she wondered if this chance encounter mightn't after all be a blessing.

Nancy seemed a decent sort. And she had such an interesting face . . . Apparently she had come down to London a few weeks ago to start work at a publisher's. She'd got digs at a boarding house off the Tottenham Court Road. It wasn't very nice, but she would only be there for the summer in any event. She was going up to St Hilda's in the autumn, to study English.

'That's funny,' said Freya. 'I've got a place at Somerville.'

'Oh! I thought you were –'

'Too old?' she said with a smirk, and Nancy blushed on cue. 'I'm twenty, as a matter of fact. I applied three years ago, and they deferred the place when I joined the Wrens.'

Nancy gave a disbelieving little shake of her head. 'Oh, what marvellous luck! I won't know a soul there but you.'

'Actually, I still haven't decided whether to go or not.'

'But why would you turn down a place at Oxford?'

'After the Wrens I wonder if studying for a degree seems a bit – trivial.'

Nancy looked rather crestfallen at that, so she didn't say anything more.

As they turned away from the river towards Victoria, the streets looked gaunt and tired. There were so few cars; petrol rationing had seen to that. Bomb damage had left huge dusty gaps everywhere, and scaffolding patched the faces of buildings like screens around a fragile patient. In spite of the festival atmosphere the city felt shabby, haunted, makeshift. You couldn't imagine it ever returning to the place it once had been. Freya began to wonder if the pub she was leading them to would still be there, in any sort of repair. A cafe she used to frequent in Soho had taken a direct hit one night; she had felt it almost as a personal affront when she turned into the street and found it gone.

She felt her body tense as they turned the corner into Buckingham Palace Road, and then relax as the old Victorian pub with its fussy finials and spires sprang into view. On entering they found the place in a roar; Freya had a sense that every pub in London today would be the same. People stood three-deep at the main bar, and drinks were being passed over heads by a rowdy clientele. Off to the side a piano was accompanying a ragged chorus of voices singing 'Roll Out the Barrel'. The sawdust on the floor was damp with spilled beer.

'What'll you have?' Freya asked Nancy, once they had jostled their way to the bar.

'Erm . . . a lemonade?'

'You won't get stinko on that.'

As Nancy dithered, Freya signalled to the barman. 'Two pale ales, please.'

They took their drinks and found a place to stand by a window of rippled glass. Freya swallowed a mouthful and

11

looked around; it seemed that no matter what time you stepped into a pub you always had a lot of catching up to do with everyone else. People were tipping back the drink with a steady practised air, as if they'd somehow made it their occupation. The singers had done with 'Roll Out the Barrel' and started on 'Tipperary'. She fished out a packet of Player's Weights and offered it to Nancy who, after a moment's hesitation, took one. They lit up, and Freya watched as the girl took an awkward sip of her cigarette and puffed, without inhaling.

'You've not smoked before, have you?'

Nancy grimaced. 'Is it obvious?'

'You're not exactly Dietrich,' she said drily. 'Relax your fingers, like this. Don't bunch your hand. There – that's better.'

'If my parents could see me now . . .' Nancy said with a giggle.

Freya felt it was high time she asked. 'What *is* that accent of yours?'

'Oh, well, Yorkshire, I suppose. Harrogate – but not the smart side.'

Freya, unaware that Harrogate had any sort of 'side', let alone a smart one, gave her an appraising look. There was barely two years separating them, yet it might as well have been ten. The war had done that: she had started in the Wrens as a girl, and come out of it a woman. Nancy, in contrast, with her ingenuous gaze and gawky demeanour, was practically a child still. Not her fault, but there it was.

A little knot of drinkers next to them were engaged in an agitated dispute. Freya had overheard one of them say, 'Churchill's done a grand job of work for a man his age,' to which someone raised a dissenting voice – he was sick to death of Churchill, 'a self-satisfied windbag,' he said, who ought to stand down and let a younger man take the country into peace. This view, a bold one in the circumstances, was greeted with outraged cries of 'Shame' and 'Sit down, yer fool.' The argument gained in stridency and heatedness; alcohol, of course, was paraffin poured on the bonfire. Freya, wanting to keep a shine on the day, drained her glass and leaned her head towards Nancy's ear. 'Let's get out of here before they start a brawl.'

Outside the early-evening temperature had cooled a little. The roads were still swarming with people carrying flags, and someone was playing 'Rule Britannia' on a toy trumpet. On a quieter street they found another pub, and drank more pale ale. Nancy, becoming expansive, said, 'D'you know, when I heard someone say that the war was over last Friday, I couldn't quite believe it. I'd been out with some friends and hadn't heard the announcement, so when I got back to my digs later on – the landlady must have been away – I crept into the parlour and turned on the wireless for the midnight news, still wondering. Then I heard the announcer saying, "Tomorrow morning at 8 a.m. the war in Europe will be over . . ." I just stood there in the dark, stunned. I listened right through, until they played the national anthem. And the next thing I knew tears were pouring down my face. I couldn't stop! It was like – I don't know – like the world had been given a second chance, and we could start afresh.'

Freya was staring at her. She didn't quite sound like a girl any more. 'Did you really think that?'

Nancy paused. 'I didn't think it, exactly – I felt it. It was a sort of spasm of hopefulness, wonderful and frightening at once, like the way your stomach gives a jump when you're in a car that's going too fast! I had the most exhilarating sensation of something coming to life. Nothing could stop us.' But then she did stop, and seemed to become aware of Freya listening to her, and laughed. 'You probably think that sounds rather silly.'

13

'No, I don't,' said Freya, touched by Nancy's plain-spoken optimism, and obscurely envious of it. It occurred to her that not everyone had seen the newsreels from Belsen, the stark pictures of hundreds of emaciated corpses piled high, and the lines of blank, hollow-eyed survivors, near-corpses themselves, staring out at the camera. You couldn't tell if they were men or women. She had watched the films in a cinema on Regent Street, benumbed, listening to the moans and the sobbing of people around her. She hadn't turned away from the screen, just because other people had. For some reason she found herself hoping that Nancy hadn't seen them – not yet.

They had another couple, and then Freya became suddenly excited at the thought of a pub in Chelsea she'd been to with her father, and hauled Nancy off into the street again. When they got there the place was heaving and had sold out of everything but gin; so they drank that, large ones, and then a little band started up, and a couple of soldiers who had been giving them the eye asked for a dance. At 9 p.m. the wireless went on for the King's speech; at the end of it the whole room rose to its feet and sang 'God Save the King', and they joined in, almost shouting the words. They danced again, but stayed close to one another, and when Nancy's partner began to get too familiar Freya stepped in and detached her. Nancy by now looked rather limp, and her eyes had slowed in their blink. Another gin and she'd be under the table.

'Come on,' she said, steering through the sweaty tumult, her hand in the small of her back. Outside night had fallen, and they marvelled for a moment at the street lamps, lit for the first time in years. There would be no more sirens, no more blackouts, no more hurrying footsteps in the dark. The cool air was clearing Freya's head, yet she didn't want the evening to end.

'We could go back to my dad's place – what d'you say?'

Nancy, swaying a little, murmured her assent.

On arriving at Tite Street Freya half hoped that the lights would be on, but there was still nobody about. The mixed smell of white spirit, paint and varnish hung like a presence in the room. She decided on a whim to take down the blackouts from the tall windows. Nancy, surveying the casual disarray of canvases and oils, seemed to be in a daze.

'I'll get us something to drink,' Freya said.

Nancy followed her into the kitchen, trying to dissimulate the fact that she was tipsy.

'We've got gin, some sherry – ah, and whisky. Go and sit down, I'll bring in some glasses.'

Nancy hovered for a moment, like a bee at a window, before backing out of the doorway. Freya put the bottle of Dewar's and a heavy soda syphon on a tray, and followed her into the main room. Nancy was staring at a huge dark portrait above the fireplace.

'Your father – isn't he awfully famous?'

Freya shrugged. 'He's pretty well known. Stephen Wyley. Here –' She poured her three fingers of whisky. 'You might want to put some water in it.'

Nancy, handling the syphon as if it were a fire extinguisher, pressed the tap, and unleashed an exuberant flood all over the tray. 'Sorry, sorry . . .'

Freya sighed, and craned her gaze to Nancy's face. 'God, you're absolutely whizzed, aren't you?' She took the syphon from her and directed a squirt into both glasses. She held hers aloft. 'We should have a toast. How about – to starting afresh?'

Nancy, smiling at the echo of her own words, clinked glasses. Then she leaned back into the sofa, her eyes hooded and shrinking. Watching her, Freya wondered if she might need a little pick-me-up. Flipping through a stack of records, she pulled one out of its sleeve, and winding up the old

15

gramophone, she dropped the needle. It crackled for a moment on the scratchy shellac, then quietly began.

My love must be a kind of blind love,
I can't see anyone but you.
And dear, I wonder if you find love
An optical illusion, too?

Nancy moved her shoulders in time to the music's swaying rhythm, but after a minute or so Freya saw her eyelids start to droop. This wouldn't do at all. At the end of the song she got up and said, 'Are you ready for another dance?'

'I think so,' Nancy replied, her voice seeming to run down, out of fuel.

'Right then. I'll be back in a sec.' She hurried to her room and rummaged in her handbag for the little bottle. She tipped out a couple of tablets and swigged them down with the whisky, then shook out a couple more and returned to the studio room. Nancy had fallen into a sideways slumber.

She gave her a little shake, and handed her the tablets. 'Here, take these.'

Nancy squinted blearily. 'What are they?'

'The late show,' said Freya, holding out a glass for the purpose. 'Their technical name is Benzedrine. We used them a lot on night shifts.'

Nancy obediently swallowed them down. Freya, pierced by a little shiver of excitement, sat down at the piano and started to play. It was the same tune they had just been listening to, but she had upped the tempo to a jaunty waltz. The notes melted off her hands. That was the wonderful thing about Benzedrine, it gave you such focus and clarity – her fingers purled over the keys without her even having to think about what went where. The song was at the command of her touch . . . *Now* she was having fun!

16

You are here, so am I,
Maybe millions of people go by,
But they all disappear from view
And I only have eyes for you

Her persuasive contralto caressed the words. A shadow had joined her at the piano, and she was singing it, too. They ran through the song once more, with Nancy playing a pert counterpoint at the top end of the scale. On finishing they collapsed in laughter; then Freya had them try it once again, singing alternate lines, and finishing on a note of extravagant harmony.

And I only have eyes for you-ou-ou-ou-ou-ou!

Nancy, restored to girlish animation, said in a wondering voice, 'Those pills really are –'

'I know,' said Freya, feeling the cold, speedy glow of the drug take hold, routing the party-pooper, fatigue. 'You can go for hours without even getting drunk. Now, shall we dance?'

They moved the tall easel and the paraffin heater from the centre of the room, clearing a space on the worn-out Turkey carpet, and Freya put on a Benny Goodman record she thought might suit the mood. Then, with the same straight-backed posture she'd adopted at the piano, she lifted her arms and led Nancy into the steps of a waltz. Her body through the thin cotton of her dress felt heated, febrile, willing. It was odd, she thought, to be holding close a girl who a few hours ago was a perfect stranger to her. And odder still was how they could fit together, her angular self-possession against Nancy's wide-hipped gawkiness; yet there was somehow a current of intuitive ease between them, it wasn't just the disinhibiting effects of the Benzedrine, though of course that helped.

The little ormolu clock on the mantelpiece chimed eleven. Freya had been so lost in the dance that she hadn't noticed

Nancy's green eyes glittering with tears. She reared back in alarm. But it became apparent to her that she wasn't just crying, she was laughing, too. She had dropped her head almost to Freya's shoulder.

'Are you all right?'

Nancy nodded, her face now averted and downcast, and they continued to sway to the music. She couldn't tell if Nancy was concentrating on her steps or recovering from her minor hysterics. When she lifted her face again, the eyelashes were still wet with tears; but her voice was composed, and thoughtful.

'I want to remember this for the rest of my life,' she said, looking dreamily over Freya's shoulder.

'Well, it's that sort of night –'

'No, no, I don't mean because of the war. I mean this, here, now.'

'The Night They Danced in Tite Street.'

Again she nodded, and Freya slipped over to the gramophone to wind it up. The music returned in a soft fog of brass and strings. She presented her arms to Nancy in an exaggerated display of courtliness.

'Shall I lead?'

2

Freya awoke with a start, having slipped off the edge of a dream that had turned suddenly and vividly erotic. She felt annoyed with her failure to cling on. Outside her bedroom door she had heard footsteps in a soft shuffle of hesitation; there followed a tap, and the door creaked open in apology.

'Morning,' said Stephen, her father.

Freya didn't raise her head from the pillow. 'What time is it?' Her voice came out a gravelled croak.

'Quarter past eleven. There seems to have been drinking on the premises last night.'

She only groaned in response, hearing his quiet half-laugh.

'Who's Sleeping Beauty, by the way – on the couch?'

She had to think a moment before she understood. 'Oh. Nancy, a girl I met in town yesterday.'

She still hadn't deigned to look up. It was important to let him know – without their having an actual argument about it – that she was aggrieved by his absence the previous night. His tone of voice suggested he already did know. 'Cup of tea?'

'Mmnh.'

Stephen disappeared off to the kitchen. Slowly she elbowed herself into a semi-upright position; her head felt as heavy as a bowling ball on the slender pivot of her neck.

She winced on seeing a half-smoked cigar parked in an ashtray at her bedside: so that explained the revolting burnt *brown* taste that filled her mouth. Yeeuch. She'd forgotten their 'hilarious' idea of lighting up a couple of Stephen's Havanas as they finished off the whisky last night; also her impersonation of Churchill that had made them laugh. She wasn't laughing now.

Well, they'd had a jolly time, all right. Nancy had shown herself very game, as dance partner, accompanying pianist, drinking companion. They'd really gone to town on the Scotch . . . and the Benzedrine had worked its miracle of wakefulness again. Better get up and check on her. En route she stopped at the bathroom and almost took fright at the face she saw in the mirror; her eyes were heavy-lidded and swollen with a fatigue she hadn't witnessed on herself since the air-raid days. She splashed on some water, feeling depressed. Her mood wasn't lifted on seeing Nancy's recumbent form on the couch, *her* face rather saintlike in its quietude; annoyingly, the facetious epithet Stephen had just used to describe her contained more accuracy than humour. She sat down and gave the girl a little shake. Even the way she emerged from sleep, eyes ungluing like a child's, had an innocence about it.

Nancy looked around. She appeared for a moment unable to comprehend her surroundings. Her confusion turned to a look of round-eyed horror as the door opened and Stephen walked in bearing a tray of tea. With a sudden panicked 'Oh' she pulled up the bed sheet to cover her bare arms. Freya, suppressing an urge to snigger, said, 'It's all right, it's only my dad.'

The deep blush of Nancy's cheeks suggested it was anything but all right. Wrapping the sheet around herself like a shroud, she slid off the couch and hurried out, mumbling a scarcely audible 'Excuse me'. Stephen set down the tray and pulled a grimace of mock alarm.

20

'I was only bringing in the tea,' he whispered.

Freya answered with a sardonic smirk. 'I don't think she's used to seeing a strange man first thing in the morning . . .' She poured a cup from the teapot and ambled after her guest to the bathroom. Answering her knock Nancy cracked the door a sliver before admitting her. She was wearing a slip, a robust-looking brassiere beneath it, and a very unhappy expression.

'What's the matter?' asked Freya.

Nancy returned an incredulous look. 'I've just been caught half naked on your father's sofa, that's what! My clothes are –' she gave a hopeless wave – 'I've no idea where. And the state they're in . . . I spilt all that beer down my dress, my stockings are filthy –'

Freya had not recently encountered such fastidiousness. 'There's no need to fret. I've got spare clothes with me, you can borrow whatever you need.'

Nancy looked doubtful. 'Really?'

'Of course. In the Wrens we were always in and out of each other's rooms borrowing this or that – it's just like boarding school.'

'I've never been to boarding school,' Nancy said forlornly.

'Well, don't be a ninny. I can't promise you *haute couture* but I'm sure I can fix you up with something.' A glance told her that she might struggle for a dress – Nancy's figure had curves where she had none – but they could improvise. 'Why don't you run a bath and I'll get started? Here's some tea, by the way.'

She tripped back to her bedroom and threw open her suitcase, plucking out several likely items – a blouse, a thin woollen cardigan, a green skirt and a pair of stockings. She added, in a spirit of mischief, a pair of wide-legged slacks, as an alternative to the skirt. She gathered them into a pile and carried the lot through to Nancy. Water was thundering from the taps in the background. When she returned to the

21

living room Stephen was reading *The Times* on the rumpled couch, a cigarette on the go. He looked up enquiringly. 'How's the startled nymph?'

'In a stew of mortification,' she replied, flopping onto the chair opposite and fishing out a cigarette from Stephen's slim silver case. 'She's practically still a schoolgirl – you have to make allowances.'

Stephen lifted his chin, as though about to reply, then stopped himself. His look by degrees turned fond. 'You enjoyed yourself, then, yesterday?'

She tipped her head to one side, considering. 'Everything but the cigar.' She looked at him and said, 'What did you do?'

'Oh . . . Joan Dallington had a little party at Bury Street, mostly people from the gallery. She's planning a show of war paintings – did I tell you? Home-front stuff. Asked me if I'd contribute a few things.'

'The Blitz pictures?'

'Yes, those. Plus the army portraits. And I dare say the Churchill picture, if they can get it back from the MoD.'

'That's thrilling,' Freya said with a slow smile. Though he would never admit it, she knew her father was secretly quite proud of this last. The rumour went that the sitter had admired it, too. With this little upswing of friendliness between them she sensed it would be a moment to clear the air. 'I felt rather miserable when I got back on Monday night and found the place empty. Mum said she might be up, and wasn't – but I really thought *you* would be –'

'I'm sorry, darling,' he said, in a chastened tone. 'If you'd telephoned to say you were coming up . . .'

'Why weren't you here?'

Stephen raised his eyebrows, as though to say it was none of her business, but he too seemed to catch the conciliatory mood. 'I was out, as I said. I sometimes stay at the club, you know.'

She stared at him hard for a few moments, and then nodded, acquiescent. She wanted to ask how things stood between him and her mother, but she knew that this would entail a much longer conversation, and the possibility of raised voices. For the present, with a guest in earshot, a truce held, and they would strive to maintain the illusion of family accord.

She yawned, and took a sip of tea. How strange to contemplate such leisure! She had thought of her life as a line divided into two parts, with September 1939 as the caesura. There was 'before the war', and then everything that followed. But what about *after* the war? To wake up and know that you were not due at the Operations Room at 0800 hours, that you would not be doing another week of night shifts, that the CO would no longer be shooting sour looks in your direction. Impossible to take it in at once. She recalled now a conversation with Nancy from last night, when they were briefly serious, about the people close to them who had died, mere drops in an inconceivably vast ocean of loss and grieving. And what she wanted to know was: why had they survived when so many others had not? How had they come by such stupendous luck?

The bathroom door had opened, and they heard tentative steps padding across the hall. Stephen, ever the gentleman, rose from the sofa at Nancy's entrance and introduced himself.

'It's not the most comfortable couch, I'm afraid,' he said with a rueful chuckle.

'Oh, no, it was perfectly fine,' said Nancy, still not quite catching his eye. 'I really ought to have gone back to my digs –'

'No you ought *not*,' said Freya, and turned to her father. 'It was two in the morning and we were absolutely whizzed.'

Nancy had, to Freya's surprise, chosen to wear the slacks, and looked quite fetching in them. The blouse was a tight fit across her chest. Her face, without make-up, had a fresh and vulnerable openness. Freya found herself staring at those wide green eyes, which prompted the girl to ask, uncertainly, 'Is something the matter?'

'No, no. Those trousers – they suit you.'

Stephen said, 'So, how did you meet?'

'Jean Markham introduced us yesterday,' said Freya.

'Ah, Jean . . . the foghorn, yes?' said Stephen.

Freya stifled a snigger, and looked to Nancy. 'Dad thinks all my school friends sound like sergeant majors. It's the Paulina bray.'

Nancy nodded, and said thoughtfully, 'I suppose Jean's voice does carry rather.'

'I do beg your pardon,' said Stephen, smiling. 'That's a much kinder way of putting it.'

They drank more tea, and Stephen – at Nancy's earnest prompting – talked about his time in the ARP. (She had seen his tin helmet hanging on the back of the bathroom door.) He had been at his busiest during the raids of 1940 and 1941, when London had been savagely 'knocked about'. But then at least the engines of the German bombers gave them fair warning of what was coming. In recent months, air-raid precautions in London had been rendered useless by the V-2 rockets coming over from occupied Holland. Hitler had saved the worst till last.

'They travelled faster than sound, so they made no noise. Sirens couldn't help. You could do nothing to protect yourself. I heard one lady describe them as "bombs with slippers on".'

'You must have seen some awful things,' said Nancy with a little shudder. 'We only read about them in the paper.'

'We didn't get them as badly here as they did to the south, but it was bad enough –' He stopped himself, and looked at Nancy. 'People were brave. Quite amazingly brave. Thank heavens we won't have to go through it any more.'

24

Freya, feeling a sudden sharp pang of hunger, went to the kitchen, and returned with a downcast look. 'There's not a thing to eat.'

'Sorry, I haven't been here much,' said Stephen. 'Perhaps I could take you girls out to lunch instead.'

Nancy, at a loss, looked to Freya, who saw her chance. 'Can we go to Gennaro's? Please?'

Stephen laughed, turning to Nancy. 'Her favourite place. It's the ice cream. All right, I'll see if I can reserve a table.'

Freya let out a whoop of triumph. Before the war Gennaro's was the place the family used to go to for a treat, either on her birthday or perhaps after one of Stephen's exhibitions. Once the house was sold, however, and her mother moved them down to Sussex, the days of dining out faded away. When she joined the Wrens there was an occasional outing to a restaurant, but rationing usually meant that the food was poor and the drink in uncertain supply. Now her memories of Gennaro's were of an Elysian bounty, tender veal escalopes, or great heaps of spaghetti carbonara, or a fragrant risotto. But they were merely what you ate before the main event, which was two ravishing globes of ice cream in a silver bowl, topped with a wafer and eaten with a slender long-handled spoon.

She left her father talking to Nancy while she had a wash and dressed. In the mirror her face had managed to shed its blur of fatigue, and she spent a few moments plucking her eyebrows. Her father had left his shaving kit next to the basin, along with a bottle of Penhaligon's and an unfamiliar wristwatch, a Rolex tank; its black leather strap had the glossy refulgence of crocodile skin. She fixed it around her wrist, holding it at different angles to admire. A beauty. It must have cost him a fortune! His work was obviously selling, even in these straitened times.

She opened the bathroom cabinet and took out a bottle of Jicky. She squirted a little on her throat, inhaling its notes of vanilla and lavender – and instantly fell to thinking of her piano teacher, Madeleine, who had always worn the scent. Wasn't it strange, the way smell could put you back in a place more evocatively than any other sense? She hadn't really thought of it in years, yet just that whiff transported her back to the drawing room in Elm Park Gardens and her first faltering attempt at Chopin, Maddy next to her, tapping out the time. Where was *she* now? Long minutes passed before she woke up to herself. My God, you could drown in looking back if you weren't careful; she replaced the bottle and closed the cabinet.

Stephen said he had some errands to run, so he would meet them at the restaurant. After he had gone Freya enlisted Nancy's help in taking down the blackout curtains in the two bedrooms. As they struggled with the dusty folds of dark serge drooping over their shoulders, Nancy said with a laugh, 'It's like getting lost inside a nun's skirts.'

'Not an experience I'm familiar with,' said Freya archly. 'Were they beastly to you at convent school?'

'There were one or two it was best to avoid, but most of them were all right. And I'm grateful to Sister Philomena, and Mrs Eagle – they encouraged me to apply to Oxford.'

'Mrs Eagle? On a wing *and* a prayer, then.'

Nancy stopped, and smiled at her. 'I'd never thought of – that's so funny!'

Freya shrugged, wondering why, if it was so funny, she hadn't actually laughed. When they'd first met yesterday she was worried that Nancy had no sense of humour at all. But after last night, when they had guffawed at almost everything, she had felt an enormous sense of relief: you couldn't really be friends with someone if you didn't make them laugh.

'Your father's awfully nice, isn't he?'

'I suppose he is. What did you talk about?'

'Well, I started asking him about his work, but he insisted on talking about *me* and what I was going to do at Oxford. He said he had a wonderful time when he was there.'

'Mm. From what I've heard he just got tight a lot and chased after girls.'

Nancy let this priggishness go without comment. 'I got the impression that – well, he's rather keen that you should go, too.'

Freya nodded. 'It's partly because he feels guilty about my early education. You see, my parents sent me and my brother to a very odd school called Tipton. It's a "progressive" place where they let you do what you like, more or less. Pottery and drama and growing vegetables were the sort of things they encouraged, but if you were at all academic you were bored to sobs. I ran away a couple of times, actually, so my dad, who wasn't crazy about the place either, persuaded Mum to take me out. When I turned fourteen I went to St Paul's, though by that point I had a lot of catching up to do.'

'And yet you still got a place at Oxford,' said Nancy.

'I'd already be there if war hadn't got in the way.'

'But, well, you've done your bit, do you not think you've earned it?'

Freya was silent for a few moments. 'I suppose I worry that Oxford might be a backward step, which I've vowed never to take. And can one really live anywhere but London?'

Nancy's face indicated that she had a reply to this, but she kept silent. Freya found this agreeable as a tribute from youth to experience. With the blackouts removed the studio was rinsed with lemony daylight; motes of dust swarmed at the windows. Nancy looked around at the high ceilings, and at the walls clustered with paintings and sketches.

'It must be so glamorous, having a father who's an artist.'

Freya followed Nancy's eyeline around the room. 'Not really. It seems quite ordinary to me. Why, what does your father do?'

Nancy gave a half-laugh. 'He's an insurance broker. Honestly, you don't know what "ordinary" is.'

Freya shrugged, conceding the point. 'This is all I've known. Dad has always painted, and I don't imagine he could do anything else.'

'It must be wonderful to earn a living at something you love, though – don't you think? To create something out of nothing . . .' Her voice had gone dreamy.

'Is that what you're going to do?'

Nancy's expression became serious. 'If I can. I want to be a writer. More than anything. I've wanted to since I was about six.'

'Ah – hence the job in publishing.'

'Yes, but that's *only* a job. Writing's a vocation. I just thought being surrounded by books all day would be an encouragement.'

Freya made a doubtful moue. 'It might put you off. You'd probably find out how little most writers earn.'

Nancy smiled. 'That doesn't worry me. I'd write even if it meant having to starve.'

Freya stared at her for a moment; it was the same tone of voice she had heard last night, when Nancy had talked about the end of the war. Her sense of conviction was amusing, and faintly alarming.

She looked at the clock. 'Come on, we'd best be on our way.'

They walked north through the hung-over streets, which wore a bedraggled bank holiday air, the Union Jacks drooping from the windows like a drunkard's shirt tails. They passed people still in a daze, their beds unvisited since the excitement of yesterday. On the King's Road they chased down a number 19 bus as it slowed towards the junction with Sloane Square; Freya, with her long athlete's stride, got to the platform first and, just as the bus gathered speed, she grasped Nancy's outstretched hand and practically dragged her on board.

The bus carried them through the red-brick blaze of Knightsbridge and thence into the circling hum of Hyde Park Corner.

'So what sort of thing do you write?' said Freya.

'Oh, I've written a bit of poetry, but it was terrible rot. And I keep a diary.'

'Every day?'

She nodded. 'But I really want to write a novel . . .'

'You've had a try, then?'

Nancy shook her head, looking slightly embarrassed. Eventually she said, 'What about you? I saw there was a Graham Greene in the bathroom.'

'I couldn't write a novel. I remember as a girl wanting to be an archaeologist. That thrilling idea of digging things up that had been lost for centuries.'

'What about now, though?' Nancy pressed.

'Well . . . I like the sound of "Foreign Correspondent". You know, reporting on coups and uprisings from unstable republics. But of course a woman rarely gets the chance to do it. Have you ever read Jessica Vaux?'

'I've heard of her.'

'She's remarkable. Enlisted as a nurse in the First War, went into journalism and became the youngest news reporter on Fleet Street. She wrote her first book about the Weimar – she predicted the rise of Hitler. She was in Paris up to the last days before the Germans marched in – they say she got out with just her typewriter and a suitcase.'

'Crikey. She sounds intrepid.'

'Mm – and she's still hard at it.'

They had reached Piccadilly. Stepping off the bus they entered Soho's bustle of narrow streets, though the shops

29

nowadays looked sorely understocked and bomb damage had torn open melancholy vistas of brick and glass not seen since Victorian days. At least the Italian grocer was still there, and the market traders cawing their prices from stalls on Berwick Street. The pubs, thrashed from yesterday's festivities, looked shiftier than usual, and some had hung apologetic signs in the window, RUN OUT OF BEER.

A surprise awaited her at Gennaro's. Her father, seated at a table in the corner, was not alone. His companion was thirtyish, attractive, well dressed, chestnut-coloured hair done in the 'Forces Favourite' style of an American actress; she greeted them with a smile of dazzling affability that put Freya abruptly on guard. Stephen introduced her as Diana, and seemed quite at ease in doing so.

'This is my daughter Freya, and her friend – um – Nancy! Diana works at the gallery with Joan,' he explained.

'How nice to meet you at last,' said Diana, as though she had been longing for an introduction. She was nicely spoken, with a genial lightness in her tone. Freya kept shooting glances at the newcomer from beneath her brow. She felt relieved to hear that their connection was a professional one, though the woman's casual manner wrong-footed her. Far from meeting 'at last', she conveyed in her friendliness a suggestion that they'd met on previous occasions, and enjoyed themselves thoroughly.

'I hear you had quite a night of it, cigars and all,' Diana said.

Nancy pulled a mock grimace. 'We agreed that the cigars were a mistake. How did you celebrate?'

Diana cut an amused glance at Stephen. 'We had a little party at the gallery, in Bury Street. Joan brought out a case of claret she'd been saving since the start of the war. Very good it was, too.'

'Six years' worth of hoarding gone in one night,' said Stephen.

Nancy, craning forward slightly to examine Diana's slubbed silk jacket, said, 'That's a very smart suit you're wearing. Is it handmade?'

'Thank you, it is – though not for me. My sister had it made just before the war and grew out of it, so I was the beneficiary. I've patched it here and there since, but it's still the best thing I own. I'm fed up with Make Do and Mend, aren't you?'

'Rather,' agreed Nancy. 'I wonder how long they'll keep up clothing coupons. Actually, Freya and I took down some blackout curtains this morning, and it occurred to me they might be just the thing for a winter coat!' She looked for support from Freya, who offered only a tight smile.

Stephen, who knew her moods, became more lively in compensation. 'My suits are in a terrible state – the ones that haven't worn through have shiny patches at the elbows and the seat. And my pyjamas are so threadbare they seem to have assumed the form of *netting* – really, they're getting to the stage where they'll barely cover my despair.'

Nancy giggled at this witticism, and Diana said, 'Your idea about the blackout curtains isn't so unusual. A friend of mine recently had to go to a smart wedding, and had no coupons left. So she took down a velvet curtain and made herself a dress by tucking and pinning it. When the wedding was over she unpicked the thing and put it back up as a curtain.'

'It would be nice,' said Stephen, 'to buy some decent clothes again. We've become rather a shabby-looking lot, I'm afraid.'

Diana sighed. 'Though I've heard that men have started wearing evening dress to the theatre again, like the old days.'

'The condition my dinner jacket's in I'm not sure they'd let me enter a theatre.'

'Oh, Stephen, don't exaggerate!' said Diana. 'You looked very debonair in it the other night.'

31

Freya's ears pricked up. 'Where were you?'

'Oh, there was a reception in Whitehall for the War Artists' Advisory Committee. I suppose the Churchill portrait got us in –'

'You mean, you went together?'

She noticed Diana look sharply at Stephen, who said, 'Diana was my guest for the evening.'

Freya left a cold measured pause before saying, 'I see.'

An awkwardness briefly settled over the table until Diana said brightly, 'I don't know about you but I'm starving. Shall we order?'

Freya remained quiet throughout lunch, speaking only when obliged to and offering no assistance to the conversation. She hardly touched her spaghetti. It irritated her to see how Nancy had taken to Diana, and how charmingly Stephen behaved with both of them. She sensed her mood at odds with the others' gaiety, but she could not break through her cloud of suspicion and resentment. After a while they seemed almost to ignore her, happy to entertain one another: Diana's vivacious good humour, her father's wry self-deprecation and Nancy's eagerness to please formed a little circle of companionship she couldn't breach.

As the waiter cleared their plates, Stephen at last caught her eye and said, with a twinkle, 'I see that you've been keeping a space.'

'What d'you mean?'

He addressed his reply to Diana. 'She's half crazed for the ice cream here.'

'I don't want any,' said Freya, her voice flat and hard.

Stephen's frown was disbelieving. 'What? You're joking. The times we've been here and you've never once refused ice cream.'

'The times with Mum, you mean.'

Stephen paused, nonplussed. 'What difference does that make?'

She gave a bitter half-laugh. 'No difference to you, evidently.'

That shut them up; even Diana's gaze was downcast for a moment. Freya, aware of herself torpedoing the jolly mood, folded her arms in silent misery. The minutes passed. She listened as her father restored the social temperature by asking Nancy about her plans, and Nancy telling him about Oxford and the reading list she had to get through this summer. It was Diana who finally coaxed her into a semblance of sociability. As the coffee and grappa came round, she cleared her throat and raised her glass.

'I think we should have a victory toast, don't you? To those brave women in the services, and to our very own representative at the table.'

'Hear, hear – to Freya,' said Stephen, pushing his own glass across the table to her. Reluctant to unbend, but touched by their tribute, she took up the glass and downed it in a gulp. Relief at her dismounting the high horse was palpable; Stephen called for more drinks, and she felt the full warmth of Nancy's grateful beam.

'So what will you do now?' Diana asked.

'Well . . . I go back to Plymouth and wait to be demobbed.'

'Freya's also got a place at Oxford,' Nancy interposed, 'but she's insisting that she doesn't want to go.'

'Oh, why's that?'

She shrugged, not unamiably. 'I'm not sure I'd fit in there – after the Wrens, I mean. And London feels like my home.'

'But only think – Oxford! Such a wonderful opportunity. Stephen, tell her.'

'I've told her,' he said. 'Three years of reading and studying books. What could be nicer?'

Freya's mouth assumed a downward twist. 'You'd think twice about that when they put *The Faerie Queene* in front of you.'

Diana was shaking her head, puzzled. 'Just the place itself would be enough to persuade me. And you'll also have Nancy around for company.'

Nancy blushed at this unexpected elevation of her status; Diana plainly had no idea they'd only met yesterday. Freya, however, felt a sudden generous upsurge, and conceded, 'I suppose having Nancy there would be a reason.'

More drinks arrived, and the convivial atmosphere held until Stephen turned to Freya and said, 'If you're going back this evening I could give you a lift to Paddington.'

The convenience of being driven to the station appealed, though she said, 'That'd be an awful bore for you.'

'No, it wouldn't. Diana, what's the time?'

Diana pushed back her sleeve to glance at her wristwatch, a Rolex, its face at once familiar and its hands pointing towards realisation: not his, but hers. She felt her blood run cold.

'Your watch,' she said. 'It's very beautiful.'

'Thank you,' smiled Diana.

'Actually, I've seen it before. This morning – in the bathroom at Tite Street.'

'Oh,' said Diana quietly. She had gone pale. Stephen had averted his gaze.

'*Now* I understand why you're so keen for me to go to Oxford,' said Freya, staring at her. 'You should have been honest about it. "Such a wonderful opportunity." Yes – an opportunity to get me out of the way.'

'But I didn't mean that at all,' protested Diana.

'Oh really?' said Freya with a sneer, and now looked at Stephen. 'You haven't wasted much time, have you? Moving in this – *person* before you've even left your wife. That's nice –'

'Freya,' said Stephen in a low voice, 'stop it.'

'Tell me, though, did you think you could keep it a secret? It must have been very convenient with me being away from London all this time. Sorry to interrupt the fun.'

Diana, dismay crumpling her face, said imploringly, 'Freya, dear, that's not the way it is at all. I've been longing to meet you, truly, and we've never even thought of keeping it "secret" from you. Heavens, your father and I have only recently –'

'Shut up! Just shut your bloody cakehole,' Freya snapped. A fury had suddenly possessed her; her whole body was shaking with it.

'Freya, calm down,' said Stephen warningly. 'Stop behaving like a petulant little prig. Diana, I'm very sorry about this, my daughter seems to have taken leave of her manners, but in a moment she's going to apologise –'

'No she's fucking well not,' Freya muttered, and glared at Stephen. '*You* should apologise to me for being a *liar* and breaking up our family.'

They were stunned into silence for a moment. Diana stared down at the table, mortified. She felt Nancy gazing at her in a trance of disbelief. Stephen pinched the bridge of his nose between thumb and forefinger, then said, in a tone more of regret than rebuke, 'You can call me what you like, but I'll not have you being rude to Diana. Either you can –'

'Stephen, please,' said Diana. 'She's upset, I understand. I just want Freya to –'

'I don't give a tinker's toss what you want,' Freya half snarled, pushing her chair back from the table. The sudden jarring noise caused heads to turn. 'Don't worry, I'm going, you can get on with your lives again. All I've ever asked from people is honesty. The last person I ever imagined would deceive me was my own father. Thanks a lot.'

She stood up, dropped her napkin on the floor and headed for the door. She heard Diana rise from the table and Stephen's quiet restraining words ('Don't – just leave her'). She didn't look back. Outside, the life of Dean Street was carrying on regardless, the market men and stallholders yarning away. From somewhere could be heard the clang of church bells. She walked quickly on, feeling her eyes brim; she didn't know whether she was more angry with her father and Diana or with herself for making a scene and provoking them to pity. And for what? She knew her father had had affairs before, it had started with that actress, the one who died – but he had always kept them quiet, preserving the peace. Her mother would be none the wiser, and the family would remain intact. No more. His introducing this woman to her was the sign: his marriage was kaput.

She had been walking, head down, eyes blurred. The excitements of last night bore down on her like a weight, the drinks and the drugs, the dancing, the lack of sleep. Turning into Wardour Street she mounted the steps of the little churchyard and stopped halfway up, and sat down, exhausted. The yard was now a public garden, though the church had been bombed out. Ruins everywhere. A world of ash and dust. She felt the tears come freely now. She crossed her arms over her knees and let her head sink down.

'Freya?' She looked up. Nancy stood there, hovering uncertainly, a survivor of the crossfire. 'You were walking so quickly I nearly lost you. May I . . . ?'

Freya said nothing, so Nancy lowered herself next to her on the stone step. They sat there for a few moments, unspeaking, faces averted from one another. She knuckled her eyes dry. She wished Nancy hadn't followed her, the girl was a bit of a pest, really.

Her throat felt congested and sore. 'I suppose you're thinking what an awful spoilt bitch I am.' She felt Nancy flinch at the word. 'And what shocking language I use.'

A pause, and Nancy said, 'I've not heard "shut your cakehole" before – well, not from a girl at any rate.'

Freya stifled a snort. 'They let us swear as much as we liked at Tipton, the school I told you about. From the age of ten I sounded like a navvy.'

Nancy let a beat go, and said, 'I'm sorry . . . It must be very upsetting. But your dad probably wanted to – I don't know –'

'What?' said Freya irritably.

'Nothing, nothing,' said Nancy, dropping her gaze.

'I know what you're thinking. He's all sweet reason and graciousness, while *I'm* just a bloody nuisance who makes scenes.' She looked to Nancy for a response, and getting none she merely scowled. Then she said, 'What did you think of *her*?'

Nancy took a breath. 'Don't bite my head off, but . . . I thought she was nice.'

Freya, galled by this mildly voiced justice, continued to brood. When she next spoke her tone was calm, but decisive. 'You can only properly love someone when you trust them. And the only way to trust someone is through their being honest. It's the beginning of morality. D'you see?'

'I think so,' said Nancy quietly.

Freya shifted around on the step to face her. 'I can trust you, can't I?'

Nancy held her gaze. 'Of course you can.' The sincerity in her voice, almost pleading, made it impossible to doubt. The moment vibrated between them. Then Nancy stood up. 'Just wait there, will you? Don't move.'

She hurried down the steps and disappeared round the corner. Bemused, Freya sat there. Reviewing the events of the last hour she felt herself bristle with a confusion of anger, self-righteousness and embarrassment, this last emotion scraping an ever more insistent note on her nerves: she could foresee the dismal prospect of having to apologise. But then – why the hell should she? She hated 'having-tos'. She'd had enough of obligations. Something else had changed, and she thought she knew what it was: her father had always paid her the honour of being a co-conspirator. Now that was gone, too. Minutes passed, and she raked her

37

gaze along the street, wondering where Nancy had got to. She listened to the ambient noise of Soho, its hum of possibility and loneliness calling to her, like a summons.

Five minutes, ten minutes, she wasn't sure how long Nancy had been gone. But all of a sudden she was there, crossing the road, looking wonderfully lithe in those wide-legged slacks she had lent her this morning. She was smiling broadly, and holding up two ice-cream cones, one in each hand, as if they were torches to light their way.

3

At the lodge, the bowler-hatted porter licked his thumb as he riffled through the list of arrivals.

'Wyley . . . Wyley . . . Miss Eff – ?'

'That's me,' said Freya. She thought of trying a smile, but something about the man's bored, jowly face suggested it would go to waste, so she stayed impassive.

'Staircase 14,' he said, reaching behind for a key. No 'welcome to the college', not even a simple 'good morning'. She took the key and asked him if someone could help with her trunk. The porter nodded in dismissal.

Such gallantry. When the train had pulled into Oxford she had expected one of the many ex-servicemen crowding at the carriage door to offer his assistance; one or two of them had been eyeing her all the way from Paddington. But they had just poured out of the train with their own burdens, leaving her to struggle alone with the massive travelling trunk. It was like trying to lift the bottom half of a wardrobe. She had looked about for a station porter, in vain. Somehow she had managed to drag it off the luggage rack and shift it, crabwise, to the door, but once there it would require a feat of prehensile strength quite beyond her to lever it from the compartment onto the platform. Was there really not *one* among them who might put himself out to help?

She must have sighed aloud, because just at the instant of despair a young man, muffled up in a college scarf, had stopped at the open door.

'May I help you with that?'

She had smiled her assent, darting a glance at him. He was in his mid-twenties, tall, rangy-looking, with floppy hair of a nondescript brown. Narrowing his eyes at the problem, he had tilted the trunk at an angle and pulled it halfway out of the door, then said to her, 'Right, you push it from your end – and I'll bring it down on this side. Gently does it.'

His voice was mannerly, with the faintest burr of something northern. Between them they had succeeded in coaxing the trunk downwards before its weight took over and it slithered onto the platform with an unarguable thunk. 'Hope that hasn't damaged your crockery,' he'd said with a comical grimace. They stood gazing for a moment at the unwieldy object. He didn't appear to have any luggage of his own.

'Well, nice to know there are still gentlemen,' she'd said.

He had given a modest little dip of his head. 'I'll fetch you a porter.'

As he'd walked off, she'd thought to herself, *Crockery?* She sat down on the trunk and lit a cigarette while passengers streamed by on either side of her. The morning air felt stiff and inhospitable, and smuts were drifting off the train and settling on people's coats. Behind her a porter had arrived with a trolley.

'If you'll allow me, miss . . .'

'Oh.' She had stood up, looking over his shoulder for the man who had come to her aid. He had gone. Evidently his securing the services of a porter had excused him any further obligation. Or else he had been in a hurry himself? In which case his help had been all the more chivalrous. His disappearance was a little unsatisfying, though, because she had not had a chance to thank him. She had handed the porter a bob as he'd wedged the trunk into the vacant foot space of the taxi, and then they were off.

Freya hadn't seen Oxford in the three years since her interview. Her memory of the place had been mostly nocturnal, for her visit had coincided with the dead of winter when the city was still in blackout. The pale buildings had looked eerily beautiful with only moonlight for illumination. But Hitler hadn't bombed here after all. Now in daylight the shade of its stonework, somewhere between fawn and grey, seemed to complement the devotional contours of its architecture. The lawns of Somerville's quadrangles shone green after a night of rain.

Entering the staircase she inhaled a mixture of damp stone, coal smoke and dust. On a wooden board she saw her name painted, white on black, and felt a pleasant shiver of self-importance. The door to her rooms on the second floor was already open, and revealed, to her dismay, evidence of occupation. Nobody had told her she would be sharing. A trunk not unlike her own squatted in the middle of the living room, and a coat had been tossed over the back of the couch. A fire burned wispily in the grate. She crossed the room and opened the far door, a narrow bedroom, its twin on the other side. She knelt on the window seat and pushed open the oriel to look out on the quad; a cluster of students in gowns were ambling around the perimeter, chatting away. She sank into a trance of absorption, and wondered what people might make of the woman gazing out of the window, wearing a camel-coloured sweater and (she supposed) a look of sullen scrutiny. People sometimes told her she looked cross when, in fact, she was merely preoccupied. But then people were always assuming things about you.

She heard footsteps on the landing, and the door creaked forward. A girl came through carrying a blackened kettle.

'Oh, hullo,' she said. 'I was wondering when you'd arrive. I've just got some water to boil. Tea?'

She introduced herself as Ginny – Virginia – a short, sturdy girl who moved about the room with the confidence of one who'd been *in situ* for weeks, though it transpired she'd only arrived about an hour before. Her hair was bobbed, with a severe fringe; her eyes and mouth seemed too large for her neat, heart-shaped face. She looked at Freya with keenly appraising eyes.

'I suppose you've been in the service. Let me guess – the Waaf?'

Freya shook her head. 'Wrens. You?'

'ATS. Two years of it.' She took the kettle off the boil and began rummaging in her trunk. She fished out a couple of tin mugs and clanked them together. 'Army issue; didn't suppose they'd be missed. I gather we're meant to have brought our own crockery.'

'I'm afraid I didn't get that memo,' said Freya.

'Oh, I shouldn't worry – we can always borrow someone's. Here,' she said, handing her a mug. 'By the way, you've got some post.'

'Already?' She immediately thought of Nancy. Ginny pointed to a note she had placed on the mantelpiece: it was from Jean Markham. She hadn't seen her since their abortive get-together on VE Day.

Dearest F

Arrived yesterday and popped in to see if you were about. Call on me at Lady Margaret Hall at your earliest.

Jean

A knock came from outside, and two porters hefted her trunk through the door. One of them, a cocky youth of about her own age, blew out his cheeks in comic exhaustion and said, 'Dunno what you've got in there but it weighs a ton.'

Freya turned, and with a straight face said, 'Oh, that's just the dead body.'

He frowned at her, bemused, and with a glance at his mate backed out. When the door had closed Ginny looked at her and let out an outraged guffaw.

'*Naugh*-ty,' she said in a mock-schoolmarmish tone. 'Now, which bedroom d'you prefer? It's a choice between overlooking the street or facing the kitchens.'

Freya, not caring either way, picked the street view. She dragged in the trunk and started to unpack; most of her good clothes had come from her mother, either as gifts or cast-offs. As well as clothes here were all sorts of oddments: a candlestick holder (with candles), an ivory-backed hairbrush, a mirror, an alarm clock, her father's old tennis racket, still in its frame press, a straight dozen of his jazz records, some sheet music in case she decided to practise, a camera, a selection of Oxford World Classics, a Boulestin cookbook she almost knew would never be consulted, a smart silver cocktail shaker, an electric reading lamp, a selection of her mother's home-made jams, a tin of tea, coffee essence (*ugh*), and – her one memento from Devonport naval base – a pair of bruised, dun-coloured boxing gloves, given to her by an admiring drill instructor.

She reached into the corner and lifted out a squarish object wrapped in felt cloth. Untying the string she laid it on the bed; it was a framed head-and-shoulders oil of herself by Stephen, to mark her twenty-first. She stared at it for some moments, not yet reconciled to the bold and somewhat accusing gaze of the sitter. Is that how she appeared to him? He had got her dark eyebrows right, and the somewhat combative jawline, but the hair with its vivid flecks of red and gold seemed an extravagant touch too far. Secretly she'd hoped for something from Asprey.

'Do you have a – oh, I say!' cried Ginny, who had put her head round the door, and now craned forward for a closer inspection.

'I'm not sure it really looks like me.'

Ginny folded her arms and swivelled her large eyes between Freya and the painting in her hands. 'Who's "SW"?' she asked, squinting at the artist's initials.

'My dad. It was his birthday present to me, a few weeks ago,' she said.

'You don't sound all that pleased,' Ginny said with a whinnying laugh, and Freya sensed her own ingratitude. 'This bedroom's too poky for it. Here, let's show it some light.' Plucking the picture out of Freya's hands she reversed into the living room. She wandered around, holding it up at different heights. 'You see, it could go here –' she framed it against the wall dividing the windows – 'but it's still not getting the full benefit.'

Freya, alarmed at such exposure, even by proxy, shook her head. 'I don't think so, not in the living room. It looks . . .'

'What?' said Ginny, puzzled.

Well, it looked like swanking. 'Let's leave it for now,' she said, propping it against the wall; she could sneak it back into her room later. Ginny, thrown off the scent, went over to her own trunk and took out a circular tin, which she placed on a little table by the fire.

'Look what my mother packed,' she said, wresting the lid off and lifting out a Madeira cake. It turned out that her mother ran some kind of typing school for young women in London, and one of her well-off clients had given it to her – a regular perk of the job. Ginny cut them a piece each.

'It's awfully good,' said Freya, through a mouthful. 'How on earth – ?'

'Black market, probably – oh blast, we really will have to get some crockery,' she added, as the cake began to disin-

44

tegrate in her hand. 'And these tin mugs will have to go, too. They make the tea taste of –'

'Petrol?'

'Yes!'

They spent another hour unpacking and putting the room in order. Ginny was reading History, though she cheerfully admitted that two years in the ATS had more or less destroyed her aptitude for study. ('I could no more write an essay on the causes of the Thirty Years War than I could explain the internal workings of the combustion engine.') Freya too felt the long hiatus of the war had unfitted her for scholarly concentration. She had done a good deal of reading while she was in the Wrens – she would have gone mad from boredom without books – but the habits of library-haunting and lecture-going seemed impossibly alien to her.

She was still not certain why she had decided to come here. In the calm following the storm of lunch at Gennaro's she had examined more rationally her theory about Stephen wanting her 'out of the way' and conceded that he had no such ulterior motive – though she didn't speak to him for weeks all the same. She knew she ought to have written an apology to Diana by now. After being demobbed she spent the rest of the summer at her mother's house near Finden, in Sussex. Attlee had brought Labour to power on a landslide in July, though, maddeningly, she had missed being able to vote by a matter of weeks. She turned down her mother's offer of a birthday party, and asked only that the family should gather for a dinner on the August weekend she turned twenty-one. Her father came down from London with her brother, Rowan, who had been staying with friends before going up to Cambridge. If her father's present to her was vexing, Rowan's was severely practical: a huge salmon, caught on a fishing holiday in Scotland. It caused some puzzled laughter in the house. An eccentric boy, he alone perceived no glimmer of oddity in his gift. 'At least he didn't try to wrap it,' said Freya to Stephen privately.

This family reunion, the first since Christmas, was one in which Freya had invested much; too much. She still nurtured a secret hope that her parents' estrangement was not irreparable, that the company of their own flesh and blood might somehow revitalise their stalled marriage. But the experience of the weekend showed it to be illusory. It wasn't even that they argued, at least not in front of her. Cora, far from seeming abandoned, had taken to village life and talked happily of her neighbours. She treated Stephen with perfect civility, which he returned, a mutual show of good manners that baffled and depressed Freya. They might have been acquaintances meeting at a cocktail party. Only once did this social front wobble, when over dinner Rowan made an innocent but unmistakable allusion to Diana. (He would have been forewarned, she knew, but Rowan was no master of tact.) On passing her mother's bedroom the evening Stephen returned to London she thought she had overheard sobbing.

To break up the monotony she considered asking Nancy to stay. They had corresponded, or rather Nancy had written five long, newsy, somewhat breathless letters and Freya had replied, once, in what she felt was a more adult temper. It seemed to her that the girl wanted something more than a friend; she wanted a mentor. She sought her approval and advice, mostly about books. She would mention this or that novel she had just been reading, and was eager to know her friend's opinion, immediately. Of course it was flattering to have someone look up to you, even consider you a kind of oracle, but also a little exhausting; Nancy had paid her the compliment of assuming her to be much better read than she was, and the burden of having to formulate an opinion of an author she knew nothing about put her on the back foot. When she did write back she concentrated on writers she felt able to enlarge upon (Waugh, Henry James, Maugham), and covered her ignorance of the rest with vague generalities on which she hoped she wouldn't be challenged. It felt a bit like cramming for an exam. The prospect of Nancy coming down and seeking enlightenment at close quarters threatened to be tiresome, so she held off inviting her.

Her potential as literary adviser proved irresistible, however, and one morning about a month before the Oxford term began she received a large packet addressed to her in Nancy's responsible cursive. A covering letter explained that the enclosed manuscript comprised the first draft of a novel – *The Distant Folds* – she had written. She hadn't yet shown it to anyone. Would it be an imposition on her to have a look? Freya felt the honour of being Nancy's first reader. She had not had a protégée before. But she didn't like being surprised by its arrival. She distinctly recalled asking her, just after they met, whether she had tried her hand at novel-writing, and Nancy replying that she hadn't. It was inconceivable that she had started writing the thing after that conversation; these pages were quite clearly the product of many months – years? – of effort. So why had she not told her the truth when they had first broached the subject?

And now here *The Distant Folds* lay, 161 pages of foolscap at the bottom of her trunk, their edges curled from prolonged inspection. At first she had put it aside, until curiosity got the better of her. She had read it straight through once, then reread it slowly, inserting comments, queries and possible improvements down the margins. She had thought of posting it back, with her revisions, but by then the new term was nearly upon them, so instead she decided to bring it with her to Oxford and return it to the author in person. That felt like the proper conduct of mentor–protégée relations, with its promising hint of condescension on one side and humble gratitude on the other.

* * *

The next morning as she was getting dressed Freya heard a woman singing in the room above. By the time she had finished she heard the outer door being opened and the warbling started up again.

'Good morning,' she said to the singer, who was dressed in a housecoat and kneeling at the grate with a sweeping brush. She was fiftyish and on the short side, starved-looking, bespectacled, cheerful.

'Oh, hullo, dear,' she smiled, rising to her feet. 'I'm your scout – Miles.'

'Isn't that a man's name?' said Freya.

'Why, yes. Miles is my surname. Olive's my first name.'

'Then would you mind if I called you Olive? I've been in the Wrens for three years and I'm fed up with addressing people by surname.'

Olive blinked uncertainly. 'As you please, Miss – ?'

'Freya. So you'll be cleaning our rooms? Ginny's next door, and still asleep by the look of it.'

'I would have made tea, but I couldn't see any . . . cups.'

Freya conceded that she would have to go out and buy a few things, crockery included. She decided to get started and threw on her coat, calling goodbye to Olive on her way out. Oxford was in sunshine, though the air was gripped by a bracing autumnal cold. Trees were waving farewell to their green and gold leaves. On the Woodstock Road caval-cades of students on bicycles flowed by, gowns flapping like crows' wings. At the junction of Broad Street she stopped to let a drayhorse clop past. The serenity and steadiness of the town bemused her; after London and Plymouth it was odd to be on streets that bore no trace of bomb damage.

She browsed in a bookshop opposite Trinity, eventually hunting down second-hand copies of Empson's *Seven Types of Ambiguity* and C. S. Lewis's *The Allegory of Love*. Her tutor had recommended both of them in a brusque letter antici-pating her arrival at college. She strolled on. Turl Street she loved immediately for its high-walled, compact civility, the facades of Exeter and Jesus and Lincoln each seeming to nod to the other in acknowledgement of their likeness while maintaining their aloofness. Round the corner she entered a market, a stone-paved maze with a roof of glass and sawdust on the floor. The smell of a butcher's stall bloomed sour in her nostrils. At a grocer's she spent a week's worth of coupons on a tiny packet of coffee and a twist of sugar. At a hosier's a few doors along she dawdled before the window display, gazing covetously at a pair of cream silk pyjamas. Their price was equivalent to the funds she had to make last the whole term.

She had retraced her steps up the Turl and back along Broad Street when an instinct prompted her to stop at Balliol. Its demeanour felt monastic, rarefied. She found herself mooching about the lodge and reading the noticeboard, as if in search of a message that personally concerned her. One notice announced the revival of a sonnet-writing competition, all entries to be admitted by the last Thursday of Michaelmas. A solemn concession – 'Enjambement *will* be permitted between the eighth and ninth lines' – made her snort with suppressed laughter.

The arched walkway led out into a long garden quad around which young men in gowns and dark suits were sauntering. She was pretty certain about the number of the staircase. It had the sentry-eyed, forbidding look of a medieval tower, but she felt under no obligation to keep out. Ascending, she heard a low, discreet patter of male voices behind oak doors, that hum of intellectual life that had filled these rooms from time immemorial, its sound as even and concentrated as bees in a hive. Or perhaps it wasn't intellectual. For all she knew they may have been talking about girls or the cost of laundry or next week's football.

She was staring from the window of an upper landing when the door to her right opened and a naked, steaming youth walked out. The towel with which he was absently drying his hair had obscured his vision for the moment, allowing her a flash of his long white torso, and the flat shield of muscle across his abdomen; the bath he had lately emerged from had shrunk his cock to a pinkish mushroom. His cheeks were steamed pinkish too, and became pinker once his eyes flicked up to meet hers.

'God! What the hell – !' He brought his towel down smartly to cover his nether quarters.

'Oh, sorry,' said Freya, sounding very far from it.

'What are you – this is a men's college, you know.' Flustered, he was wrapping the towel around his waist, conscious of the eyeful she had already had.

'I know that. I'm just visiting.'

He shook his head furiously. 'Well, these are *not* visiting hours.' Having made the towel secure he had put his hands on his hips, in a posture that aimed for landowner-to-trespasser outrage.

Freya, scornful of pomposity, left a pause before she said, 'Actually, I'm here because this was my dad's college – and this, I believe, was his staircase.'

The youth seemed to wilt before her matter-of-fact explanation. It is not within the command of many men to assert their dignity with only a towel for cover. In the brief stand-off between them she took a moment to consider him. He was lean and tall (though no taller than her); the face was soft-jawed and handsome, if undistinguished, and a great swatch of dark, almost black hair fell across his forehead. Unable to scare off the intruder, he had dropped his gaze, perhaps pondering his next move.

'When was he, um, here? Your father . . .' It was weak, but civil at least.

'Just after the First War. He read History. I don't think he enjoyed it much, but he did say I should look up his old rooms.'

'I see.' Something in his eyes had brightened as he looked at her. He had come alive to the situation. It was after all not a common occurrence to find an attractive girl waiting on the other side of your bathroom door. 'Well, if you care to wait while I put some clothes on, I could show you around the place.'

'Oh, there's no need, thanks –'

'No, no, it'd be my pleasure. Just wait there.'

He bounded up the stairs, calling over his shoulder that he would be 'down in a sec'. She watched his white naked back disappear from view and smiled to herself. What an introduction. She was still at the window as he returned. The dark tweed jacket and grey trousers had been hurriedly thrown on. He had brushed his hair into a parting, though his face was still ruddy from the bath.

'That was quick,' she said, giving him the once-over.

'Oh, I don't hang around,' he said with a smirk. He was trying to be suave after his blustering start. 'I'm Robert, by the way – Robert Cosway.' He offered his hand, which she took.

'Freya Wyley,' she said, with a little tilt of her head.

'Right, let us go then, you and I!'

As they walked in step onto the quad she felt the full curiosity of his gaze on her. It was as though he had accidentally trapped an exotic bird which it now pleased him to parade in public.

'So you're reading English, then?' she asked him.

'Why do you say that?'

'Because you just quoted "Prufrock".'

He frowned in arch demur. 'Just because I can quote poetry doesn't mean I'm studying English. I've got some range, you know.'

'So what are you reading?'

He smirked again. 'Why don't you try to guess?'

Because I hardly care one way or the other, she thought. 'That's the hall over there, I suppose?'

He followed her glance. 'Ah – yes. Mm. And through here –' He walked her through a cloister and pulled open a door. 'We have, as you see, the library.'

They looked about it for a few moments, and Freya began to suspect something. She decided to put it to the test.

'And where's the junior common room?'

He stared at her for a moment. 'I can show you.' They proceeded around a curved gravel path and through another archway, emerging into a flagged enclosure. A heavy iron-studded door stood open, and he hesitated for a moment before stepping within. 'Oh, sorry, this seems to be a fellows' staircase.'

She nodded pleasantly. 'I take it you're not reading Geography either.'

He laughed, looking around in distraction. 'Erm . . .' He was no better a guide to the place than she was.

'You're a freshman, aren't you? Why didn't you say?'

He looked embarrassed. 'Sorry. I only arrived here yesterday.' Humbled, he seemed much more likeable.

'Well, that makes two of us. I'm at Somerville.' She cast a glance around the brooding ashlar walls. 'It's all very High Victorian here, isn't it?'

'I know. You half expect Ruskin or Walter Pater to be lurking around the next corner. Perhaps I should ask someone . . .'

He made enquiry from a passing student, and they presently found their way there. Robert got them each a cup of tea from the buttery. It transpired he was studying PPE, having been a scholarship boy at Manchester Grammar School. He was the only child of parents who doted on him – 'They're quite elderly,' he said, as though to justify their devotion. He asked about her own schooling, and she explained how she had deferred her place to join the Wrens. His eyes widened in astonishment as she briefly recounted her time in the Operations Room at Plymouth.

'Must have been tough work.'

'Yes, it was. But we had wonderful times, too. Lots to eat and drink, sports, silly games. And the dashing officers, of course.'

'Of *course*,' he echoed, in a drawl. 'I suppose Oxford will seem rather sedate in comparison.'

She shrugged. 'It's certainly a change. But I have a few friends here . . .'

His gaze sharpened. 'Female friends?'

She laughed at his eager expression. 'Yes – actual women.'

'It's a mighty disadvantage of this place, I tell you, the chronic lack of bir— women. So far I've seen nothing but vicars' wives or bluestockings in inch-thick specs.' He abruptly checked himself with a glance. 'Present company excepted, I mean. But really it's too bad. Someone told me men outnumber women here six to one.'

'Mm,' said Freya. 'That seems to me a very promising ratio. I should be able to have my pick.'

Robert stared gloomily into the distance. 'Fine for you. I left school with high hopes I would –' Again he checked himself. 'I suppose the best thing for it would be to throw a party. D'you think you could rustle up a posse of girls?'

This was asked with a note of yearning she felt unable to tease. 'I'll see what I can do.' She glanced at her watch. 'Better be off. I have a meeting with my tutor at twelve.'

'I'll walk you to the lodge – if I can find it.'

She smiled, and wondered; he had quickly picked up on her preference for self-deprecation over pomposity. He wasn't bad-looking in a boyish sort of way. If he could learn to dress he would be quite presentable. They ambled back towards the lodge, passing under an ancient archway. 'That's very pretty,' she said, looking up, and added, '"An arch as sweet as the drip of syrup from a spoon" . . .'

'Who's that?' he said with a suspicious look.

'Jessica Vaux. From one of her essays.'

'The woman who had the son by Henry Burnham?' He had named a famous man of letters from the early part of the century.

She looked at him crossly. 'That's *one* thing she did. She also happens to be a first-rate writer, a critic, a historian and a political commentator.'

'Oh, right –'

'And, to quote my Penguin copy, is a "shrewd and eloquent judge of human nature" – which probably came in handy when Burnham hurried back to his wife and left her to raise the child alone.'

'Yes, I'm sure,' he said, nodding and frowning.

'I recommend her book about the Weimar Republic, *Funeral Rag*. It's a classic.'

They had reached the lodge, where they rehearsed a short *pas de deux* of farewell. Robert's expression had grown anxious.

'I had so much more I wanted to discuss,' he said, rubbing the side of his head. 'How should I get in touch with you?'

'You can write to me at Somerville – Freya.'

'Yes, Freya Wyley. I shan't forget that name.'

'Well, thank you for the tea, and the tour.' She walked off, then turned to give him a quick wave goodbye. 'Watch out for those bluestockings.'

4

Three weeks into term and still there was no sign of Nancy. In the first few days, whenever there came a knock on her door, Freya was convinced it would be her. But though visitors kept calling at a steady rate, she was never among them. At first she was baffled, for Nancy's letters over the summer had contained nothing but avowals of friendship and interest; she seemed almost to be counting the days to Oxford and their reunion. Then there was the manuscript of the novel, dispatched with a letter of imploring sincerity.

She now saw that her delay in responding might be interpreted as indifference. She had assumed that Nancy would call on her at the earliest opportunity. But would it not have been more gracious on her part to pay the first call? She knew Nancy to have a good deal of natural modesty; however eager she may have sounded in correspondence, she was probably not the type to thrust herself forward in person. Nor could Freya absolve herself of the vanity that derived from a perceived superiority. Nancy's puppyish willingness to defer to her as the senior partner in the friendship had allowed her to stay aloof.

After a lecture one morning she had joined the murmuring shuffle out of the hall when a voice, pitched at an unmistakable volume, called her name. She turned to find Jean Markham striding up alongside her.

'I thought I might run into you at some point,' she said, and Freya realised with a quick stab of guilt that she had failed to reply to her note from the first day. 'How do you like it at Somerville?'

'Fine, fine. I've been meaning to call on you –'

'Yes, I wondered, *Is she avoiding me?* You've been very elusive, starting with that debacle on VE Day.'

Freya laughed lightly, though she detected in Jean's tone a reproach that was not altogether humorous. It was true that she had not kept their friendship in good repair, though all she admitted was that most of the summer had been passed at her mother's house in Sussex.

Since they were not far from her rooms she invited Jean up for tea. On the way the latter informed her of various Paulinas she kept up with around Oxford – a regular clique, it seemed – but Freya managed to change the subject when an evening reunion was proposed. Having never been popular at school, she had no desire to dredge up associations that felt almost meaningless. On entering her rooms Jean looked about like a bird, beak pecking at the ground. She paused as her eye encountered Freya's portrait on the mantelpiece. Ginny had propped it there two weeks ago while its permanent position was still being decided. The angle of Jean's neck as she contemplated it implied something less than approval, but all she said was, 'From your father?'

'A birthday present,' Freya said, mingling apology with an unconscious note of pride.

'Nancy Holdaway told me in a letter that she'd met him. She's here – did you know?'

'Yes, I did,' said Freya, covering her surprise. 'You've seen her?'

'Mm. Nice girl, though *very* young – hasn't got much about her.'

'She's just shy. And she has more about her than I did at eighteen.' She didn't feel this to be strictly true, but something in Jean's tone provoked her into defence.

Jean returned an arch look. 'I remember you at eighteen. A proper spitfire you were, and don't deny it. Certainly the first St Paul's girl *ever* to say "fuck" in front of a teacher!'

Freya's mouth made a rueful downturn. 'I blame my early education.'

'You were also the only one who knew about sex, other than the stuff that frogs get up to, I mean.'

Jean took this as her cue to enlarge upon the availability of men in the city, and which societies offered the readiest opportunity to meet them. The safest bet, she reckoned, was the University Labour Club, where earnest group discussions about 'the tasks of peace' would later give way to drinking, carousing and a great deal of what she called 'pairing off'. Freya only half listened, preoccupied by the conversation immediately prior to this. It didn't seem quite right that Nancy was going her own sweet way around Oxford without any reference to her. As she turned the matter over it occurred to Freya that her pride might be at fault: it was more pleasing to be sought after than to seek.

Jean was still going strong on the subject of the Oxford male. Her time in the Waafs had stoked an appetite for sex she saw no reason to curtail in her new career as an 'undergraduette'. The candid enthusiasm with which she related these adventures amused Freya, though she was reluctant to answer it with stories of her own success in Plymouth and London. Something in Jean's bullying camaraderie put her on guard; she didn't quite trust in her discretion.

The entry of Ginny into the room enabled her to bring this get-together to a close. Jean at last took her leave, and Freya waved her off at the lodge with promises to keep in

57

touch. In her pigeonhole she found a letter from Robert Cosway.

Balliol College, Ox.

Dear Freya,

I hope you have recovered by now from the fright of seeing that strange naked fellow on the staircase at Balliol. It seems there's quite a fashion for such exhibitionist behaviour at present and I'm only sorry that you had the misfortune to witness it. Nothing much to report from the Citadel of Male Heartiness, where yahoos and brawny ex-servicemen roam the quads and the female of the species is less spotted than a lesser-spotted grebe. Honestly, I thought Manchester GS was bad enough but this place takes the biscuit for its tragic and unutterable birdlessness (and I don't mean the feathered kind). Indeed, I'm not absolutely convinced that the young lady I ran into a couple of weeks ago was real – were you a vision or a waking dream? In order to settle this question please allow me to invite you to a party, where I may once more assure myself of your corporeality. It's on Friday 23 November at Union Lodge on the Banbury Road, and I gather that alcoholic beverages will be served. Your presence will receive a mighty welcome, yea, as water unto a wanderer lost and thirsting in the desert.

I remain, madam, your respectful servant,
Robert Cosway

PS Do of course bring along any other fair ladies of your acquaintance.

The false nonchalance of the PS caused her to smile. His primary motive was to secure a large contingent of girls, which he had disguised as a seeming afterthought. She was still musing on this when she saw her tutor approach. Mrs Bedford was in her late fifties, stout, mild-mannered, with a great bird's nest of unruly grey hair that announced the triumph of scholarliness over personal vanity. At her first tutorial, Freya had given it as her opinion that *Beowulf* was 'hands down' the most tedious poem she'd ever read. Looking over her spectacles Mrs Bedford had replied, after a pause, 'I must endeavour to raise it in your estimation.' Her forbearance impressed Freya the more on learning that she had published an authoritative critical edition of it twenty years before.

In the same understated ironic tone the tutor began, 'I'm farming you out, Miss Wyley. You'll be going to a fellow at Corpus, name of Leo Melvern, very sound. He himself is a published poet, of course.'

'I've never heard of him,' replied Freya.

Mrs Bedford blinked at this, and said, 'Perhaps wiser not to communicate that to him straight away. How are you getting on with – everything?'

'Pretty well, thanks.'

'I noticed you walking out of college the other day carrying – if I'm not much mistaken – a pair of boxing gloves. Are you a prizefighter, Miss Wyley?'

'No, that is, I've never got in the ring with anyone. But when I was in the Wrens a man taught me how to punch the bag, and I found I rather enjoyed it.'

'Really?'

'It's good for keeping weight off, too. I couldn't eat dough-nuts and ice cream if I didn't spar now and then.'

Mrs Bedford was frowning uncertainly. 'But surely you could do something less, ah, aggressive – rowing, for instance, or hockey?'

Freya shook her head. 'I'm not cut out for team sports, I'm afraid. I become exasperated too easily. With boxing it's just oneself and the instructor. It's a bit like learning to dance.'

'I see. Well, in the meantime I shall arrange for you to go and see Dr Melvern. I dare say he'll be intrigued to know he has a pugilist to teach. Perhaps he will prepare a *corner* for you. Good day, then.'

Freya liked old 'Bedders' and her sly bantering humour; she wasn't pompous or abrasive like other dons she had met, and she listened to people as though she were actually interested in what they had to say, a courtesy that Freya had not yet mastered for herself. It wouldn't hurt to show her appreciation of the old girl by devoting a little more effort to *Beowulf* when it came up next term.

A few days later the summons came from Leo Melvern at Corpus Christi. His note was typed on vellum paper with the college crest, and appointed the time of their interview with a grave Edwardian formality. Directed up a staircase on the dainty front quad, she found the door to the designated rooms ajar and walked in. A low-lit sitting room had been converted to a study, a wide cliff face of books lowering over an angled desk in the corner. On the sofa sat a delicate pixie-faced youth absorbed in a book, his legs drawn up to his chest. He looked up on Freya's entrance and gave her a vague nod. Mrs Bedford had told her to expect a tutorial partner, but it hadn't occurred to her that it would be a male.

'Is this Dr Melvern's room?' she asked him.

'It is,' replied the pixie, looking her up and down. He closed his book and stared at her.

Freya privately marked the boy down: you were supposed to stand up when a lady entered a room. (It was one of her father's sacred rules.) In the absence of their host she proceeded to wander around. She stopped at the fireplace to peer at the invitation cards crowding the mantelpiece. A framed certificate occupied the wall above.

'"The Postgate Prize awarded to Leopold Melvern for his collection *Cold Oblivion and Other Poems*,"' she read aloud. 'Putting "oblivion" in a title's rather tempting fate, isn't it?'

The youth on the sofa wrinkled his nose. 'D'you know the book?' His voice was flat and adenoidal.

'No. I don't read modern poetry. It gives me a headache.'

'What, all of it?'

She pursed her mouth consideringly. 'Bits of Auden I like. And Louis MacNeice. *Autumn Journal* is very good.'

The youth brooded on this for a moment, then said, 'What about modern novels?'

Freya gave her most insouciant shrug. 'Greene I admire. But I don't feel the urge to study modern literature.'

'Why's that?'

'Well, I suppose because I'd prefer to write it.'

She knew this was arrogant, and untrue, but sometimes she said things just to know how they would sound out loud. He gave a peeved little laugh and shook his head. 'I should remember that remark.'

He had narrowed his eyes at her, sceptically. He seemed about to continue, then thought better of it and rose from the sofa, consulting his watch. 'Hmm. Since it appears that Miss Daubney has decided not to join us, we should perhaps be getting on.'

She stared at him. 'Oh . . . so you are –'

'Leo Melvern. *Cold Oblivion* had some excellent reviews, by the way, its title notwithstanding.'

'I think you've played a trick on me.'

'I don't see how. You asked if this was Dr Melvern's room, and I replied in the affirmative. For some reason you assumed that I was – what?' His tone lightened. 'I seem to have embarrassed you.'

She wasn't embarrassed; she was annoyed by her own gullibility. He looked like a student who was playing at being a tutor, and for some reason that annoyed her, too. For the moment her only consolation was in being at least an inch taller than him. His youthfulness confounded her; he was surely no more than twenty-six or twenty-seven, had barely started shaving, and yet he was already a college fellow with high-ceilinged rooms and lofty manners to boot. She wished she hadn't talked with such bravado about modern literature; he'd said he would remember that remark of hers, and now she didn't doubt it. What a twit she must seem!

She accepted his offer of a sherry, which was cloudy and came in a glass that recalled her dolls' tea parties as a child. For the next half-hour they talked in general of poetry, and what she knew – not enough, judging by the censorious pauses he left after each reply. Whenever she offered a sally of enthusiasm for something he would stare at her for a moment before squashing it. At one point their talk turned to Kipling, and Freya quoted a few lines from 'Danny Deever', which she had always loved.

Melvern nodded, but with a knitted brow. 'It has a certain uncouth music, I agree. But doesn't it really belong in the music hall? It sounds to me more like balladry than poetry.'

'I don't see the difference. Ballads are poems, aren't they?'

'In a manner of speaking. But I don't think they can sustain serious academic enquiry – they're simply for recital.'

At this point there was a knock, and on Melvern's barked 'Enter' a blonde girl, very pretty, stuck her head round the door. Her cheeks were flushed and she sounded breathless from hurrying. 'I'm so sorry to be late. Camilla Daubney. I thought this was scheduled for three o'clock tomorrow –'

'*Did you* indeed?' Melvern cut in with a cold sneer. 'You are at this university to read English, Miss Daubney, yet it seems you are unable to make the very simple distinction

62

between Wednesday and Thursday. Hardly promises much, does it?'

Cowed by this full-bore attack Miss Daubney recoiled visibly, and said 'No' in a meek low voice.

'You'd better sit down,' he said, still scowling. The girl, her head bowed, folded herself into a corner of the sofa as though she hoped it might consume her. Melvern then reverted to the tone of donnish equability he had been pleased to adopt before the interruption. He pointedly addressed Freya, not deigning even to glance at the late-comer. Another ten excruciating minutes brought their hour to a close.

Outside, as they crossed the quad, Miss Daubney looked warily over her shoulder, as if to check that Melvern's evil eye wasn't following them from his study window.

'Golly!' she said in an undertone, her large blue eyes widening in amazement. 'I *said* I was sorry . . .'

'Well, he's new to it – the power. They relish wielding it over someone.'

The girl smiled her gratitude, offering her hand. 'It's Camilla, by the way.'

'Freya. I had my own little humiliation, before you arrived. I walked in and assumed from his sixteen-year-old appearance that he was my tutorial partner.'

Camilla's hand flew to her mouth in a show of mock horror. 'What did he do?'

'Nothing very gracious. He doesn't seem to care for any remark you make unless he can condescend to it.'

They came out onto Merton Street and found they were both heading north. Camilla was at Lady Margaret Hall, where she had briefly met Jean Markham. Unlike them she had come up to Oxford straight from school, and Freya once again sensed the weight of seniority that war had conferred on her. It was growing dark, the autumnal light shrinking a little earlier each day. A damp fog muffled the lamplights on the high street in a spectral blur. Before they parted Freya invited her new companion to the party in Banbury Road a few weeks hence; she imagined that Camilla's porcelain prettiness would be heartily welcomed by Robert and the woman-starved hordes at Balliol.

By the end of that week, when Nancy still had not called, Freya knew she would have to take the initiative. She had convinced herself they would run into one another at a lecture, but it had never happened. It chafed at her pride that in this staring contest she would be the first to blink. She considered writing her a note to arrange a time, then had second thoughts – better to surprise her and have the advantage.

She set out for St Hilda's on Friday morning with the manuscript of *The Distant Folds* tucked into an old Royal Navy document wallet. Crossing Magdalen Bridge she leaned into an unpleasant scything wind, a sign of approaching trials. (Stephen had warned her that winters in Oxford were medieval.) Withered leaves skittered along the pavement, and spindly trees looked down mournfully on their lost vesture. Having composed herself at the door, Freya was unprepared to knock without reply. She tried again, wondering if Nancy was hiding from callers. But she could hear no movement on the other side of the door.

With nothing else to do she traipsed over to a cafe on St Clement's. The room was mutterish with conversation, punctuated by the hiss of steam from a giant tea urn behind the counter. She ordered coffee and a bun, which was stale. Students arrived in packs, their entrance bringing a whoosh of cold through the door. Looking about the place she seemed to be the only person sitting alone. How did people manage to acquire so many friends? She brooded on this while she smoked, absently aware of the cafe's clientele coming and going around her. She didn't bother to look up when someone asked if the seat next to her was vacant, only nodded – and then heard the same voice say, 'Freya?'

Nancy stood there, a thick scarf muffling her neck, her pale cheeks rouged from the cold, russet hair streaming from beneath a black woollen hat. She looked like a beautiful witch. Freya rose from the table, stunned, then winded by the force of Nancy's hug. They gazed at one another, laughing their disbelief; Nancy's eyes gleamed, even greener than Freya had remembered them.

'What – what are you doing here?'

'I just called at your room,' said Freya, 'and you weren't in! I've been stooging around here for ages –'

'Darling!' Nancy cried, and with a little groan of longing embraced her again. The warmth of their reunion had attracted glances around the room – a neutral observer might have assumed these two young women hadn't seen one another for five years, rather than five months. Nancy, detaching herself from the gaggle of friends with whom she had arrived, insisted that Freya return with her to college, as though they had not another minute to lose. Once outside, they crossed the busy confluence of the Cowley and Iffley Roads and turned into Cowley Place, arm in arm. Nancy did most of the talking on the way, and Freya sensed even in these early moments how she had grown in confidence since they'd last met.

'You look very fetching in that hat,' said Freya.

Nancy beamed at her. 'I can't tell you how happy I am to see you.'

'So why haven't you called on me yet?'

Nancy gave her a sidelong glance and seemed about to speak, but only shook her head. Her room at St Hilda's was much smaller than Freya's, with a bed, bookcase, desk and chair the only furniture. Nancy set about boiling a kettle while Freya inspected the photographs and knick-knacks arranged across the mantelpiece. Her attention was caught by a small devotional portrait of a bearded man, eyes lifted imploringly heavenwards and his head encircled by a fragile halo.

'"St Francis de Sales",' she read from the inscription. 'Who's he?'

'A great man,' said Nancy proudly. 'The patron saint of writers.'

'Ah, very apt for a writer – *Sales*.'

'No, I think it's pronounced – oh, I see, you're being funny . . .'

Freya shook her head. Some things hadn't changed. Nancy, hiding her embarrassment with a giggle, went back to preparing the tea. With so much to say they couldn't help being skittish around each other, starting to speak at the same time and then holding back ('Sorry, you first –' 'No, you go!'). Freya, observing Nancy, privately reproached herself for delaying the reunion; she ought to have come round on the day she arrived, pride go hang. Intimations of something she had felt before in Nancy's company were reawakening. It was an enlivening sense of being admired, perhaps even *adored*, and in consequence a desire to justify that admiration by becoming a cleverer and wiser person than she actually was. She supposed this striving for a better self was rather like being in love, though not having experienced the condition she couldn't be sure.

'I gather you've been knocking about with Jean Markham,' she said, accepting a cup of tea.

Nancy nodded, looking thoughtful. 'Yes, a little. Though I get the impression Jean finds me rather tiresome – considers me, you know, a chit of a girl.'

Freya laughed. 'Well, I've been in the services and I find your *chittish*ness perfectly charming.'

'I suppose you've got heaps of friends at Somerville.'

'Not really. One or two. Jean's invited me to a reunion of Paulina girls I have no particular wish to see again. Have you met any nice young men yet?'

66

Nancy blushed and shook her head. 'There seem to be a lot of thirsty ex-servicemen roaming the place. I went into a pub where you could hardly move for them.'

'Don't you think this 11.15 curfew a bit of a bore? I find that the very point of the evening when things start to get interesting.'

'I suppose so. But, in all honesty, it's been quite a handy excuse when I need to get out of temptation's way.'

Freya hoisted her eyebrows and said in a suggestive croon, 'I think I'm going to have to take you in hand, my dear.'

Nancy's mouth split into the crazily wide grin that had disarmed her the day they met. It was the most artless and lovable thing Freya had ever seen. But after a moment her expression changed, became quite solemn. 'Actually, I was starting to wonder if I'd ever see you again,' said Nancy.

'What? Why on earth would you think that?'

She paused before answering. 'It was a mistake to send you my novel – I shouldn't have been so hasty. I had an idea you were so embarrassed on reading it that you couldn't bear to face me.'

'Don't be ridiculous. I'm the one to blame – I should have written to you as soon as I'd read it. But it was so near to term beginning that I thought I'd see you before I had a chance to write, and then –'

'So you weren't appalled by it?'

'Of course not!' said Freya, holding up her document wallet. 'In fact I've brought it along, with a few notes I've written in the margins. Maybe I could –'

'Oh, I'm *so* relieved,' said Nancy. 'I thought I'd driven you off forever.'

Freya had taken out the manuscript of *The Distant Folds* and squared it up on her lap, pleased to be reminded that she was its first reader. The promise of the writing seemed to her self-evident, but she was wary of misleading its author.

Better to dispense honest medicine than coddle her with useless flattery.

She cleared her throat with barely a trace of self-importance. 'The first thing to say is that the book, in its present state, is unpublishable.'

Nancy blinked in surprise, and said, in a tentative way, 'Well, I see that it would need some editing –'

'No, no, more than that; I think it needs entirely restructuring. In this first draft it just sort of *sprawls*. There are too many characters, too many points of view crowding the story. Mark Fordyce, for example, doesn't seem quite substantial, and what's-her-name – Roland's sister – is just dead weight. It needs sharper focus, and a single consciousness to hold it all together.'

Nancy's face had begun, by small degrees, to fall. 'Fordyce was one of my favourite characters in the book.'

Freya could hear the hurt in her muted tone; the honest medicine was not going down so well. She pressed on. 'You must also learn to stop explaining every little thing. The reader needs some space to inhabit – you can't just keep telling and telling in this breathless, impetuous way. Allow your reader to wonder, to question, instead of hectoring them with information. I think it comes down to trusting one's characters; once you've got them on the stage, so to speak, you should let them tell and act the story for themselves. The writer should perform a kind of disappearing act. D'you see?'

Nancy only nodded, without catching her eye. Freya sensed that her strictures were more baldly spoken than they needed to be, that she was perhaps too zealous in showing the path of artistic righteousness. But this would be important in toughening up a first-time writer. She continued a little more in this vein, riffling the pages of the manuscript as if they were the examination papers of a bright but wayward pupil. Just as she was about to conclude she spotted a note she had marked 'NB'.

'Oh, one other thing. You keep using the word "suddenly". I counted it at least a dozen times in the first fifty pages. You have to stop – I mean, *nowhere* is so terrifying and unpredictable as this. "Suddenly he spotted her . . . suddenly she realised . . . suddenly they came into view." It creates a false sense of drama, d'you see? I've marked them on the manuscript, in any case.'

She looked over to Nancy, who was staring into vacancy, preoccupied. Eventually she lifted her gaze to Freya, and said in a small, baffled voice, 'Was there *any*thing you liked about it?'

Freya pulled in her chin. 'Of course. I only thought you'd prefer my being honest about what needs changing.'

'Yes. You have been very . . . honest.'

'I'm beginning to sense that you'd rather I hadn't.'

Nancy looked into her lap and said, distantly, 'I was prepared for criticism, but I didn't imagine that "unpublishable" would be the first thing you'd say.'

Freya clicked her tongue. 'I know it may have sounded harsh, but I'm speaking to you as an editor, an adviser – someone who wants to help you.'

'In that case I'd rather you had spoken as a friend. Then at least I mightn't feel as though I'd written something incompetent.'

'I didn't say that –'

'You didn't have to.'

'Nancy, listen to me, why would I have read it twice if I didn't think there wasn't something worthwhile there?'

'I don't know,' said Nancy, shrugging; she picked up the manuscript and held it protectively against her. 'What is it, I wonder, this "worthwhile" something? You haven't said a single kind word about it, so it's hard to tell.'

Freya was taken aback by this combative tone. She had never suspected Nancy, meek, gentle Nancy, capable of such a tone, and for the first time she wondered if she had been quite tactful: the writerly ego was known to be a fragile mechanism, but it hadn't occurred to her that it applied to youth as much as to maturity. Now she had to decide whether to praise and thus appear to capitulate, or to stand her ground and allow the offence to linger. The dilemma was taken out of her hands by Nancy's announcing that she had 'an appointment' to keep – the excuse seemed the more insolent for its vagueness. She had stood up and presented a steady smile to her guest.

Feeling somewhat diminished by this turnaround, Freya said, 'I'm afraid something has gone amiss. Half an hour ago we seemed to be so – *jolly.*'

Nancy had put on her coat, and with it a polite air of nonchalance. 'It *has* been jolly,' she said, still smiling, 'and I'm very glad to see you again. But I really must go, I'm sorry.'

She walked Freya out of her room and down onto the quad, keeping up a deflecting stream of pleasantries. She even asked after her father, to which Freya replied in a distracted way, hardly aware of what she said. At the entrance to a staircase Nancy stopped and indicated, with a regretful tilt of her head, that this was where they must part. She gave a little wave (their embrace at the cafe seemed a long time ago) and disappeared within.

Freya walked on, slightly dazed by this abrupt ending to their reunion. She had an impression of being 'managed' that was both unfamiliar and disagreeable. Ought she to have used the soft pedal? But no, she wasn't going to blame herself, she had offered her advice in good faith. It was Nancy's lookout if she couldn't take it. All the same, she had never imagined such cold self-possession in the girl. It had been a little humiliating, really. A lesson there, if she only knew what it was.

5

Freya was disgruntled. In the days following she brooded on the scene of her recent encounter with Nancy, dimly aware of her own mishandling of the occasion. She wished she could play it over again, perhaps by starting with a few positive comments about *The Distant Folds* before pitching in with the criticism. Or perhaps not. For her overriding feeling was not one of remorse; the honour she had felt in being the novel's first reader was congealing into a resentment that she had ever been landed with it. Should a friend have put her under such a delicate obligation? And, having done so, turned huffy on being given an honest opinion? She reread the letter Nancy had enclosed with the manuscript and narrowed her eyes when she came to the line *the only response I can imagine being hurt by is indifference*. Huh! Not *quite* the only response, it would seem. She considered her alternatives: she must either bite her tongue and keep silent or else 'have it out' with her. Both prospects were vexing.

In the end she decided to write to her. A letter would serve to clear the air without necessitating an outright apology. It was the grown-up thing to do. She rehearsed a few phrases in her head before beginning, but she would get only so far before a sentence took an adversarial tone and checked her flow:

I do think you have taken needless offence –
I do wonder if you are too thin-skinned to be a writer –
I do feel you have wilfully misconstrued my words –

Each time the page was clawed up into a ball and deposited in the waste-paper basket. She thought of something her mother had once told her when a difficult letter had to be written: 'If you can't think of what to say just write something truthful. And if you can't make it truthful then write something kind.'

Somerville, Ox. Nov, 1945

Dearest Nancy,

I'm so sorry about last Friday. What should have been an entirely happy occasion ended in a misunderstanding, and without ever intending to I caused you distress. I don't want to revive an argument that would best be forgotten, so instead let me state for the record: You have all the makings of a true writer. St Francis de Sales, and I, and many others, are going to be proud of you.

One more thing. My mum's coming up for a visit Friday week and taking me to lunch – I thought you might like to meet her.

With my love,
Freya

She felt rather proud of her mother as she took her on a little tour of the college. Cora Wyley was tall and slender as a mannequin, still striking in her mid-forties, even if her clothes bore signs of weathering; the soft tweed jacket and silk blouse pre-dated the war, and Freya had an inkling that she might have worn the jacket more recently to do the gardening. No threads of silver could be seen in her brown hair (she dyed it) and her eyebrows were so neatly arched

72

they looked plucked. Even the tiny wrinkles that had formed around her eyes and mouth heightened her sad elegance. She let out little coos of appreciation as Freya conducted her around the chapel and the hall, but she sensed her mother's relief on getting back into the open so she could have a cigarette.

'Has your father been up yet?' she asked as they made their way towards the lodge.

Freya shook her head. 'He wrote to say he would, maybe next term. He intends to bring *Diana*.' She gave the name a tart emphasis.

Cora said, in a level voice, 'He wants you to like her.'

She found this mild-mannered acceptance of Stephen's new helpmeet unfathomable. As one who had nursed a grievance against her mother's controlling personality – it was she who had instigated her hateful education at Tipton – she imagined that Cora would put up more of a fight to keep her marriage together, and would have raged against Stephen's taking up with someone else. But she seemed determined to put a glad face on the whole business. The college tour done, they were walking down the Woodstock Road towards St Giles. Freya thought she had better ask or else go mad from wondering.

'Mum, why aren't you more upset about him?'

Cora gave her a sidelong look. 'I *was* upset at the beginning, but what good would moping about it do? It was the war, and company was valued – people had to make temporary arrangements.'

An alarm rang inside Freya's head. She stopped on the pavement and looked at her mother, and wondered how it had never occurred to her. 'Did you – have you – I mean . . . ?' She couldn't bring herself to articulate it.

A crooked smile tweaked her mother's mouth. 'You have to remember, I was alone, for a *long time*. Stephen was mostly in London getting up to who knows what, you were in

Plymouth, and Rowan was either at school or – well, you know what he's like. He's not even there when he's home, so to speak.'

'So who was – is – he?'

'It's over now, and it was no one you know. Darling, don't look so disapproving. D'you expect me to just retire from life?'

'No, no – of course not. I only wish you'd told me. You should have been honest with me.' She realised she had said the same thing to her father at the Lunch of Doom.

'Oh, you and your honesty! Why does everything have to be so personal? Choosing not to tell isn't being *dis*honest, my love. When your father first went off with someone, I didn't know about it, and frankly it wouldn't have helped if I *had*. The pain of being thrown over isn't lessened by somebody confessing it . . .'

Freya's voice went very quiet. 'Are you going to get a divorce?'

'Well, Stephen has told me he wants to marry –'

She came to a halt on seeing her daughter's face averted, shoulders in a silent judder. She was right, thought Freya, leaning into her misery. Being honest didn't always help, for there was no comfort in knowing this, the final evidence that her mother and father were parting irretrievably. She sobbed it out against Cora, her consoling murmurs briefly tautening the ache within.

'There's nothing I can do,' she said, her voice gluey, not sure if she was asking or telling.

Her mother, still holding her, sighed. 'I'm afraid not, darling. But nothing else has changed – we're still your parents, you're still our marvellous girl.'

Freya wasn't used to being vulnerable in front of her mother. Cora had been a loving parent to her and Rowan, but she wasn't soft. In the face of distress she was brusque and given to no-nonsense exhortations along the lines of

'Buck up, dear' and 'Don't be a ninny'. It had become a family joke. That she did not take recourse to those phrases now suggested to Freya how chastening this flood of emotion had been for her.

Once she had calmed down she took her mother's proffered handkerchief and dabbed her eyes. 'Sorry,' she muttered.

Her mother tutted the word away and said, 'You're not the one who should be apologising. I think what we both need is a good stiff drink.'

They had one in the bar of the Randolph while they waited for their guest. Freya also took a moment to repair her smudged eyes before the mirror in the ladies, and contemplated the prospect of her parents' divorce. Another casualty of war, as broken and forlorn as any bombsite. She gazed at her reflection, at the defiant set of her mouth, and silently vowed never to inflict that mistake on a child of her own.

Nancy arrived just as they were being seated in the restaurant. Freya, hollowed out from her crying jag, already felt light-headed with the large whisky she had bolted down in the bar. Her delight on seeing Nancy was almost possessive in its intensity; her wide-eyed gaze, her gawkiness, even the slight uptilt of her nose seemed an unconscious expression of her lovability.

'Mrs Wyley,' said Nancy, shyly offering her hand.

'It's Cora,' replied her mother. 'How nice to meet you at last.'

Nancy shot a look of uncertainty at Freya, who didn't miss a beat. 'That manuscript I was reading down in Sussex was Nancy's novel,' she explained. 'She has an amazing talent – it's like Elizabeth Bowen, only more enjoyable.'

Cora canted her head at an interested angle, and said to Nancy, 'My word, you must be good! Freya hardly ever praises anyone.'

Nancy's face was a blushing confusion of pride and astonishment. 'I think Freya's just being kind. The book needs an awful lot of work –'

'But you're going to write an even better one,' said Freya, with a confidence that seemed to embrace and exclude at once. Cora, perhaps sensing Nancy's discomfort under this fierce glare of approval, steered her towards a conversation about her studies, and how she liked Oxford. Meanwhile Freya had seized the wine list and ordered the first bottle she recognised. She looked around the room, at the waiter's retreating back, the carver with his trolley a few tables along, the anonymous couples facing one another, the dusty potted palms by the door, the limp brocade curtains, the smells of mediocre food being cooked – and felt a terrible crushing sadness. A line of poetry came to her – *Say not the struggle naught availeth*. But how mundane the struggle felt, after what they'd put themselves through, this effort to wrest back a semblance of normality; how feeble and dogged and lost we all are.

'Look, there's partridge on the menu,' her mother was saying. 'I haven't seen that since before the war.'

The waiter had returned with the wine, and Freya watched impatiently as he uncorked and decanted it. 'Would madam like to taste . . . ?'

'No, just pour it,' she said with a peremptory nod. The wine was barely in her glass before she had emptied it with great gulps.

'Someone's thirsty,' her mother said. 'So what do you girls do when you're not at lectures? There seem to be a lot of men around the place.'

'Nothing but,' said Freya. 'They're either beer-drinking ex-servicemen or serious chaps in flannels smoking pipes. Though I did meet one quite presentable fellow at Balliol . . .' Pleased to provoke their outraged laughter with the story

76

of her staircase encounter with Robert, she was spurred on to a little comic embroidery. 'When he started yarning about his scholarship I got rather fed up and dropped my gaze to what I'd just seen on display under his towel. I said, "I don't know about a scholarship, but I suppose they might have given you an exhibition."'

Nancy, over her giggles, said, 'I could never tell a story like that to my parents.'

'Nancy's a Catholic,' Freya jumped in, for her mother's benefit. 'That's why she's having the cod – fish on Friday!' She turned to Nancy. 'So you never talk about sex?'

'Freya,' said her mother, more in weariness than warning.

'Well, no,' said Nancy hesitantly, 'but it's not just that. We never really talk about anything . . . intimate. My parents wouldn't know how. Most things, they're either understood or they're just undiscussed.'

'Do you have brothers and sisters?' asked Cora.

'I have a younger sister, Miriam. She's still at school.'

'That's quite small for a Catholic family,' observed Freya.

Nancy nodded, and paused before replying. 'My mother had another child, a boy. He was still a baby, not even a year old – one morning they found him dead in his cot. I was about eight, and didn't understand what had happened. I was told that it was God's will, but beyond that they never talked about it. If someone accidentally mentioned an infant dying a sort of blind went down – so it remains this terrible unspoken thing.'

Freya kept a brief silence before saying, 'If only people could talk honestly about painful things, instead of bottling them up. Wouldn't it have been better if your parents had been open with you?'

Nancy returned a shrug. 'I think they must have talked to the parish priest about it. But I know what you mean – it might have helped us all if they'd been willing to sit down

77

and talk. Instead, when the anniversary comes round the house is plunged into this gloom, though nobody will ever acknowledge it. So it goes on.'

Freya exchanged a look with her mother that seemed to touch on their own familial turmoil: they would have to tread softly. The arrival of the food was timely, and the cloud which had been threatening dispersed. The partridge she had chosen was a bit stringy, but it was tastier than anything they served at hall in Somerville. After the relative bounty that sustained the officers at Plymouth – steaks and butter and real coffee – the return to a civilian diet had been dismal. She had forgotten how disgusting powdered eggs could be.

'Isn't it grand to eat proper food once in a while? Even that mutton they were just carving looked nice.'

'I wonder where they get it all,' mused Nancy.

Freya's mother arched her eyebrows and said softly, 'The same place most of the restaurants in London get it – the black market.'

'The last time Nancy and I were in London together we went to Gennaro's.'

'Ah, yes, I remember hearing, with your father. And I suppose you had the ice cream?'

Freya flashed a conspiratorial look across the table. 'No, I was in the most terrible bait with Dad at the time and I refused it, just out of pride. Of course it didn't bother *him* at all, so I went without for no reason.' Drink had made her voluble, and she was happy again. 'But afterwards I was sulking outside on my own when Nancy showed up – carrying ice creams for both of us! She'd only walked halfway round Soho to find a shop selling them. Now what d'you think of that?'

Cora smiled across at Nancy. 'I'd say that's the loveliest thing a friend ever did.'

Her voice was lightly amused, but Nancy, not for the first time in the course of lunch, had a stunned look, like someone who had won a prize in a contest she'd not been aware of entering.

By the time they emerged from the Randolph's dining room the dreary autumnal weather had closed in; a gauzy mist off the river had submerged the streets and the flag-stones were oily underfoot. But her mood was still flying. Nancy had gone, leaving a trail of effusive thank-yous in her wake; Freya accompanied her mother back to the railway station.

'I feel a bit tipsy,' Freya admitted.

'I'm not surprised, darling. You drank the best part of two bottles – and that huge whisky in the bar.'

Freya linked her arm through her mother's. 'What did you think of Nancy?'

'She's a dear, isn't she? Such beautiful eyes –'

'I know!' said Freya. 'That was the first thing I noticed about her.'

'It's very sweet . . .'

'What is?'

'To see how besotted she is with you – hanging on your every word.'

Freya tipped her head slightly. 'Do you think so?'

'You should be careful with her. Not everyone's as robust as you. A tear nearly came to my eye when she talked about her brother dying. "God's will", indeed. Poor thing, if *that's* all she had to console her . . .'

Freya, who was more fascinated by Nancy's Catholicism than she cared to admit, said spontaneously, 'How terrible to be God. Imagine having the whole world on Your conscience.'

Cora made a huffing sound – the sound of a stillborn laugh – and said, 'That's one way of looking at it.'

As they edged their way through the press of bodies a tune was coming from a gramophone in the next room.

Freya cupped her hand to Nancy's ear. 'I love this song!' Nancy pulled an uncertain face. 'What is it?'

'It's "The Sheik of Araby".' And she tootled along with an imaginary clarinet, swinging it from side to side to make Nancy laugh.

They had arrived at the Banbury Road party together, which in the days since the Randolph lunch was how they did most things – afternoon tea in their rooms or in the covered market, evening drinks at the Eagle and Child, bicycling up to Headington Hill, trips to the cinema or the lecture hall. On the previous Sunday morning she had even accompanied Nancy to Mass. For Freya it felt like compensation for the best friend she had never had at school. At Plymouth she had knocked around with other Wrens, and had affairs with various men, but none of them were close to her in the way Nancy was. The awkwardness over her novel had, if anything, bound them tighter together, for in those moments of hostile disputation they had both felt the warning touch of estrangement, and recoiled.

The room where the gramophone played was smoky and beery and thronged with young men, some in earnest discussion, most of them goggling in amusement at the fellow in the middle of the floor dancing by himself. Dancing was perhaps too genteel a word for it: with his elbows flailing away, his knees going like pistons and his head twitching this way and that, he seemed as one in the throes of a possession – or a fit. He was quite oblivious of anyone else in the vicinity.

Freya, after observing this spectacle for a few moments, said, 'Robert.'

The man stopped abruptly and, as if emerging from his trance, looked around. He squinted at her momentarily before a smile of recognition creased his face.

'Why, if it isn't Freya!'

'I didn't know there'd be a floor show. What d'you do for an encore?'

Robert cackled, sweeping a dark fringe of hair from his sweating brow. 'I can't help it. I love this thing.' He saw that Freya was not alone. 'Hullo there!'

'This is Nancy,' said Freya. 'Nancy – Robert, whom I last saw in –' she paused, with a little smirk – 'Balliol.'

Robert, reading the pause correctly, explained to Nancy: 'This is the second time your friend has caught me unawares. I can't tell if it's coincidence or if she lies in wait before pouncing.'

He began ushering them through to a back room where a knot of men were crowded round a beer barrel. It had been tipped onto its side and fitted with a makeshift nozzle. He called to one of the drinkers and held up three fingers, inscribing a rough halo to encompass his guests. This bar-room tic-tac soon had the desired effect: the youth approached bearing four glasses of beer on a wet tray. His hungry glance at Freya and Nancy suggested that an introduction should be the reward for his errand. Robert drawlingly obliged.

'Freya, Nancy – this is Charlie Tremayne, guide, philosopher and friend.'

'And beer carrier,' Charlie added with a little nod. He was a short, pleasant-faced boy with tortoiseshell spectacles and close-cropped, mouse-coloured hair; Freya intuited that he would be playing second fiddle to Robert.

They clinked glasses, and Robert, blowing a strand of hair from his eyes, looked from Freya to Nancy with candid interest. 'Your arrival has definitely raised the tone of this party. It's been very second-rate up to now.'

'Really?' said Freya. 'When I heard "The Sheik of Araby" blaring out back there I thought we'd come to the right place.'

Charlie blinked in surprise. 'Don't often meet a girl who knows about jazz.'

'Oh, I don't know much. I just like the stuff my dad plays – Ellington, Sidney Bechet, Louis Armstrong, that sort of thing.'

'And how about you?' said Robert to Nancy. 'Know your Basie from your "Basin Street Blues"?'

'I'm afraid not,' she said with a little grimace of apology. 'Vaughan Williams and Elgar are more my line.'

'Nancy's a wonderful pianist,' said Freya loyally. 'We spent VE night together tickling the ivories.'

'Lucky old ivories,' said Robert, waggling his eyebrows. 'By the way, you might want a bit of this.'

He had produced a hip flask from his pocket to hand around. Freya took a sip and tasted the perfumed sourness of warm gin. Ugh. Charlie followed suit; Nancy, she noticed, quietly declined it. Robert, having taken two long swigs, became lightly combative. Across the room a target had caught his eye.

'Look at that twerp. Who does he think he is – Noël Coward?'

The 'twerp' was in fact a pale-faced young man, slender as a reed, in a provocatively garish outfit of green velvet suit, gold satin shirt and buckled shoes. His blond hair, severely parted, fell over one eye, like a male Veronica Lake. He blew languid smoke rings from a cigarette clamped in an ivory holder. He made a self-conscious spectacle, though Freya suspected that what most annoyed Robert was the man's being the centre of attention: a little group had crowded around, almost gawping at him.

'He's very exotic-looking,' said Nancy. 'I think he's wearing make-up.'

'I wonder who his tailor is?'

'Someone the police are still looking for, I imagine.'

'I think he's rather dashing,' said Freya, goading him.

Robert made a disgusted hissing sound, and looked away. The velvet-suited dandy had by now twigged the vibrations of interest emanating from the other side of the room, and, discarding his circle of familiars, approached. He had a walk to match his appearance, a high-stepping lope that was part athlete, part show pony. His hooded blue gaze took hold of Freya.

'Have we met?' he said in a purring baritone.

Freya shook her head, watching him.

'Are you *sure*?' he persisted.

'I think I would have remembered a suit like that,' she said, with a quick glance up and down. 'I'm trying to decide on that shade of green – sort of . . . froggy.'

The gaze didn't move an inch. 'Chartreuse. But tell me, where might we have met before, outside of a dream?' His eyes widened saucily on the last word.

'I can't think. I'm Freya. And you are . . . ?'

Again came the considering blink. 'Nat Fane.' He offered his exquisite pale hand in the manner of a pope expecting a kiss.

Robert, who along with Nancy and Charlie had been ignored by the stranger, now interposed, 'Nat? As in the insect?'

He looked down his nose at Robert, and replied, 'As in Nathaniel.'

'Well, *Nat*, we've been asking ourselves what kind of fellow wears an outfit like yours. My money's on – a male impersonator.'

Charlie sniggered behind his hand, but Fane returned only a slow, pitying nod. 'I shall presume that's what it pleases you to call wit. To answer your question, however – I am an artist and an actor. I am a playwright and a producer; I am a writer, a critic and a composer. I am a connoisseur and a collector of beautiful things.' He paused, and in a tone of magisterial condescension added, 'I am also, for the time being, a student at this university.'

'My goodness, isn't that a lot?' said Charlie sarcastically.

'Indeed, I do wonder,' replied Fane, eyeing him like a cobra, 'how can there be so much of me – and so *little* of you?'

Freya, stepping in as peacemaker, said, 'Well, since we're doing introductions, this is my friend Nancy, and these two are Robert and Charlie.'

Fane acknowledged them with a lordly tilt of his head. He then turned his gaze back on Freya, and said in a confiding voice, 'May I have a private word?'

Freya gave a little shrug to the others, and allowed Fane to draw her aside. She was more curious than ever. He offered her a cigarette – a tipped Sobranie – which she took, and lit it with a slim gold lighter. Through a cloud of smoke he said, 'I have a proposition for you.'

She suppressed a laugh. 'What, already?'

He ignored her facetiousness. 'Do you act – I mean, have you done any acting?'

'I once played Mary in the Nativity. But it was a non-speaking role. Aside from that, no,' she said.

'That doesn't matter. To explain: I am, at present, casting my own production of *The Duchess of Malfi*. I have already auditioned several ladies for the title role, without success. It's vital that I find someone with the right face, the right voice, the right . . . *demeanour*. I have an inkling that someone is you.'

'And you can tell all this in thirty seconds' acquaintance?'

'Of course.'

Freya smiled and shook her head. 'I'm afraid your inkling is unreliable. I don't know the first thing about acting, and I shouldn't like you to waste your time trying to teach me.'

He stared at her a moment, as if amused at the idea of being turned down. 'You need a little time to consider it, I understand – the part is a challenging one. We should arrange a meeting.'

His self-confidence was impermeable. Far from hearing her answer as a refusal, he seemed to take it as an encouragement to further discussion.

'Here she is!' There was no mistaking that parade-ground voice: Jean Markham had burst through the party crush in a cloud of Yardley. She was heading up a small gang of serious-looking women. Only then did Freya remember inviting her. Fane looked at the interloper with the bristling disdain of a peacock eyeing a parrot. He nodded at Freya and withdrew.

'Jean – you've come,' she said weakly.

'Well, you said there'd be a lot of men!' Jean made a quick survey of the room, and seemed satisfied. Then, indicating with her eyes, she said, 'Who was that extraordinary boy you were just talking to?'

'Oh, he's called Nat Fane.'

'Ah, so *that's* him . . . I did wonder – they say he put on a school production of *The Merchant of Venice*, starring himself, and took it to the West End. What did he want with you?'

'I'm not entirely sure. He said he wanted to cast me in a play, but . . .' She made a comical grimace to suggest some deeper intention than this.

Jean, reading her look, demurred. 'I don't think so, darling. Surely you can see he's a roaring queen?'

Freya only shrugged – though from the glint in Fane's eye she doubted it. The party was picking up in volume; next door she could hear them chanting along to 'Minnie the Moocher'. Even Jean was having to raise her voice to be heard. Jean's gang, friends she had made in the University Labour Club, wore the unsmiling air of prison warders about to break up a riot.

Spotting Robert still hovering in the wings, she caught his eye and pulled him towards her as if with an invisible lasso. She had secured her means of escape.

'Jean, meet Robert Cosway – he's the chap who invited us here.'

Jean's eyes gleamed as they settled on Robert. As Freya slipped away she saw in Robert's glance a full awareness of his being used as a decoy; the stab of guilt was not deep enough to discomfit her. She ducked back into the roar of the party on the lookout for Nancy. After a few minutes she found her in the relative quiet of the kitchen talking to Charlie, who clearly couldn't believe his luck. He didn't even seem to mind that she towered over him.

Charlie looked over her shoulder. 'So you managed to shake off that flaxen-haired fop?'

Freya laughed. 'It wasn't difficult. Anyway, I'm told he's queer.'

'That's not what we've heard,' said Charlie. 'For one thing, he's engaged to be married. For another, he's been tupping the ladies in his *Hamlet* production.'

'Ophelia *and* Gertrude,' Nancy added.

'Ah, that's interesting. He's just asked me to be his Duchess of Malfi,' said Freya.

Nancy looked horrified. 'You don't act!'

'That didn't seem to deter him.'

She had been flattered by his attention. He attracted her, not in a sexual way – he was too epicene for that – but in his willingness to stand apart from the crowd; no other man here would have dared to wear such clothes, or to affect that languid manner of address. He was an extraordinary creature, and he behaved as one who knew it. Through the doorway she could see Robert shooting glances at her: another suitor. He was as self-involved as Nat Fane, she thought, but less assured, more bumptious; an arrogance lacking in confidence. He had practically confessed to her that he'd never had a girlfriend. His desperation rather touched her.

Another jug of beer was being passed around, and she helped herself to more. She had taken two Benzedrine on her last trip to the lav, and felt ready to go again. She grabbed Nancy's hand and led her back to the music room, where she could hear Louis Armstrong playing 'Ain't Misbehavin''. Another one she loved! Since no one asked them to dance she turned to Nancy, and by unspoken consent they improvised a quick-step waltz across the floor. It was the first time they had danced together since VE night at her dad's flat, and as she surrendered to the music and inhaled Nancy's scent and her scalp tingled with the wild silvery onrush of the drug, she fancied she saw at last the point of being at Oxford.

With her eye on the curfew Nancy said she would have to get going. Freya offered to walk her back to St Hilda's, and having extracted their coats from a heaped bed upstairs they slipped out. Hazed gaslights along Banbury Road offered illumination against the night. Behind them they heard the door open and a blast of the party echoed forth; a figure had emerged in their wake. Freya for a moment thought it would be Robert or Charlie, but the grand billow of his silhouette argued otherwise.

'Ladies, a moment please,' Nat Fane drawled. He sauntered up to join them on the drive. The billow was explained by the opera cape he had slung around his shoulders: no ex-army greatcoat for him. In the dark his face gleamed as pale as the moon. On learning they were heading for St Hilda's he asked leave to accompany them, since he was going that way too, though once they fell into step Freya had the confounding sense that they had tagged along with Fane – he had the air of one who led, not one who joined.

'So how did you become so devoted to the theatre?' Nancy asked him.

Fane made an interested 'hmm' noise before saying, 'I long for the day when someone asks: How did the theatre become so devoted to *you*? I suppose my *coup de foudre* was Olivier as Hamlet. The first time, I adored him. Second time, I studied him. The third time, I understood him.'

'And the fourth time?' asked Freya.

'There will not be a fourth time. The challenge now is to unseat him.'

'But I thought you wanted to be a playwright, or a producer?'

'Why not all three? I am a creature of ambition . . . I'm minded to regard modern stage acting as a Trinity of sorts. Irving is the Father. Olivier is the Son –' he paused, glancing at his listeners – 'and I am the Holy Ghost.'

Freya half snorted a laugh. 'You'll be founding your own Church next.'

'Unnecessary,' said Fane lightly. 'I shall make believers of you without the yoke of religion. The stage will be my Church.'

They had crossed over Magdalen Bridge and stopped at the gate of St Hilda's, where Fane took Nancy's hand and placed on it a lingering kiss. He made the gesture seem at once solemn and lascivious.

'Goodnight, then,' said Nancy, whose eyes, flicking sideways to Freya, delivered an unmistakable message: watch out. Freya quickly kissed her goodnight before she and Fane retraced their steps across the bridge.

'An interesting study, your friend – Nancy, is it? The hair is Pre-Raphaelite, but the face, the body, well . . . a *diffident Valkyrie* is perhaps the closest I can get.'

Freya thought that rather clever, though she declined to say so; he looked too puffed on praise already. 'She's my best friend,' was all she said, which induced a little moue of confusion on her companion's face. Some men, she realised, could never quite grasp friendship between women:

they imagined it a sort of conspiracy against them. She abruptly lost this train of thought as Fane grasped her arm outside the entrance to Magdalen and put a finger to his lips. Under the dim lamp in his cape and pallor he looked like an albino vampire. He silently leaned his head inside the lodge gate, then withdrew it. Without asking, he put her coat collar up and tucked her hair beneath the loose woollen beret she wore.

'The porter's off his watch. The game's afoot. If we're quick about it we can sneak in.'

'To your rooms?' It was ten minutes past curfew.

'Of course. Or do you require a formal invitation?'

She followed him through the stone-flagged lodge and thence into the inky dark of the quad. Lights glowed from high windows, but they encountered no one as they skirted another quad and entered a staircase. Fane's rooms were large, ancient and cold. He switched on a table lamp, illumining walls that swarmed with postcards, playbills and theatrical memorabilia. Everything was framed, photographs, letters, even menu cards signed by the famous to 'Dear Nat'; the room was evidently his personal museum. Above the fireplace was mounted an original poster advertising a *corrida* in Spanish, with matador and bull painted in flaring, torrid colours.

She shivered as she stood at the empty grate, though Fane made no move to light a fire.

'Do you have coal?' she asked him.

'I believe so. My scout takes care of all that.'

'And if the scout's not here . . . ?'

He shrugged, already preoccupied with his drinks trolley. Freya found a few coals left in the scuttle, and with the aid of an old newspaper lit a small fire. On the opposite wall she spied a framed black-and-white photograph of Fane onstage in doublet and hose, a crown perched jauntily on his head.

'Youthful self as Henry V,' he supplied on enquiry, shaking a silvery beaked object from side to side.

'What on earth is that?'

Fane held the object still. 'It's a silver-plated cocktail shaker in the shape of a rooster,' he drawled, as if to imply: what else? He poured out a jewelled liquid into a pair of glasses and handed her one of them. 'Old-fashioneds. Two fingers of Scotch on a sugar lump, with a dash of Angostura bitters.'

'Here's how,' said Freya, taking a long swallow. She had seated herself close to the fire, which gave out feeble pops and crackles. Fane, lighting another cigarette, ambled over in his languid way and flopped down next to her. He stared hard at the fire she had made, and frowned.

'You *are* very practical, I must say.'

'So you wouldn't bother doing it yourself?'

He returned an arch look. 'I only play with fire. I leave others to set them.'

The line sounded like something from a play – a play he himself had written and regarded with enormous satisfaction. Freya had the curious impression of being addressed not as a person but as an audience. She wondered if he expected applause. Of small talk he had none, which may have explained the abruptness with which he had shifted his weight and plumped his mouth upon hers. Before she could react she felt his long tongue sliding inside her mouth, over her teeth, like a seal squirming over rocks. She allowed him a little more of this oral exploration before she drew away.

'Is this your casting couch, then?' she said, patting the chesterfield they sat on.

He had fixed her with a searching look. 'That's one of its uses. Now would you care to take your coat off?'

'It's bloody freezing. And by the way, regarding the part of the Duchess, the answer's still no.'

His expression changed; he now looked rather sly. 'Is that why you think I brought you up here?'

'Isn't it?'

He shook his head slowly. 'The play is immaterial. As I said, I'm a collector of beautiful things.' He took that as a cue to resume the kissing. This went on for some time, with Fane trying to extend the scope of intimacy netherwards – and Freya humorously resisting him. Then something else occurred to her, and she disengaged herself.

'Is it true you're going to be married?'

Fane allowed himself a bark of laughter. 'What a question – and what an extraordinary moment to ask it.'

'Well?'

He sighed. 'There was a brief engagement, some months ago. I asked the lady in question to be released from it, and she assented. Would it have made any difference if I still were?'

She considered for a moment. 'I don't know. Probably not.'

'Well, then. Are you ready for a little game? It will require the removal of all but your underclothes.'

Freya tucked in her chin. 'You may have noticed I've still got my coat on. My teeth are chattering. Unless you've got firewood I'm not removing anything.'

Fane looked at the fire with bored disapproval. He stood up, cast his gaze around the room and strode over to the wall they were facing. He took down one of the larger paintings and, using his letter knife, began prising the canvas away from its heavy frame. After several protesting snaps the wood had been reduced to spars, which he placed upon the fire. It seized upon this luxurious fuel, and soon flames were dancing in fierce delight around the splintered fragments.

Fane, gesturing at the blaze, said, 'Just drop your things on the rug. I'll be back presently.'

After that extravagant show of resourcefulness Freya thought it would be poor form to back down. She was also intrigued to know what 'game' he had in mind. She threw off her coat and, still shivering, removed her cardigan and blouse and skirt. She hesitated over her stockings, then (not to be a spoilsport) peeled them off too. Fane, who had withdrawn to his bedroom, now reappeared in a scarlet-and-black silk dressing gown, carrying what looked like a small racket.

'Bit late in the evening for tennis, isn't it?' she said.

'It's a squash racket, actually,' he said, handing it to her. He took in her semi-clad form and gave an approving nod. Then he began rearranging the furniture, pushing the table and sofa back and turning the leather club chair by the fire right round so that its back faced the room. She couldn't guess what he had in mind, but hoped it wouldn't be anything too energetic: the Benzedrine was wearing off. He swept back his floppy blond quiff from his forehead and surveyed his handiwork.

'Room for a good swing,' he muttered with a thin inscrutable smile. He proceeded to bend himself forward over the chair and flipped his dressing gown up to reveal his bare buttocks, white and vulnerable as a pair of fresh eggs.

Not quite the game she had envisaged.

Looking over his shoulder Fane said, 'I thought I'd be a gentleman and give you first whack.'

6

A few days later Freya was in her room when an inquisitive double tap came at the door.

'It's open, Nance.'

'How did you know it was me?' said Nancy, entering with a grin.

'From your knock. It sounds . . . friendly. Your timing is excellent – I've just made some tea.'

She sensed Nancy fidgeting with curiosity. Since the Banbury Road party other commitments – essay deadlines, a visit from Nancy's aunt and uncle – had kept them apart and thus delayed a full debrief on her after-hours adventure with Fane. Mischief prompted Freya to prolong the anticipation, diverting her guest's attention to the second-hand tea set she had bought in a junk shop. 'Just one tiny chip on this cup here – apart from that it's perfect.'

'Lovely,' said Nancy.

'And how was it with your aunt and uncle?'

'Very nice.'

'Take you for dinner?'

'Yes, yes, that restaurant in St Aldate's –'

'I know the one. The shepherd's pie there –'

'Freya, please, don't keep me in suspense. What happened?'

'Oh. With Fane, you mean? It was *interesting* . . .'

'Did you –' Nancy's voice dropped to a whisper – 'make love?'

'Not exactly,' she said, lowering herself gingerly onto an armchair. This was going to be painful. '*Ow* . . .'

Nancy's voice rose a scandalised octave. 'Oh my God, what did he *do* to you?'

'That's what was interesting.' She proceeded to relate, with jokes and demonstrations, the swishing entertainment initiated by Fane. At the end of it she lifted her skirt to give a flash of her bruised haunch and laughed at Nancy's horrified recoil.

'But . . . why?'

'Because that's how he gets his thrills –'

'No, I mean why did you *let him*?'

Freya gave a half-shrug. 'Well, I suppose I was curious – and we'd been having a jolly old time. He's terribly clever, and funny, and a great talker.'

'And a sadomasochist! He hurt you, and enjoyed it.' Her expression suddenly froze. 'Did *you* enjoy it?'

Freya pursed her mouth ruminatively. 'For the first ten minutes I couldn't stop laughing. Then when he started on me . . . No, not really. I'd rather just have gone to bed with him. Instead I walked back with a sensation that my bum was on fire.'

'Oh, the swine,' said Nancy with feeling.

'No, he's not. Nance, he didn't force me. Don't get huffy about it.' When Nancy didn't say anything she continued. 'What about you? You seemed to be getting on with Charlie.'

'Yes, he's very sweet . . .'

'But . . . ?'

Nancy paused, looking down at her hands. 'I prefer Robert.'

'Ah.'

Behind that syllable lay a complex of feelings, foremost among them a wish that Nancy preferred someone else.

Freya had a strong intuition that Robert wouldn't be a good match – Nancy was altogether too thin-skinned, too gentle-souled, for him. She couldn't bear the thought of such a girl entrusting herself – *surrendering* herself – to someone as immature and abrasive as Robert. Nancy needed a man who would look after her, not some wild boy desperate to dip his wick.

And yet she could not banish a low nagging note of self-interest in her desire to keep the two apart. Despite Nat Fane's making a dead set at her she didn't regard his pursuit quite seriously; he was too much bound up in himself to seek after another's heart. Robert, on the other hand . . . He had something about him, something tender and troubled that spoke to her. Of course his manners weren't wonderful, and he had no idea how to dress. Compared with Fane he looked and sounded gauche. But still she couldn't deny an attraction to him. That this was apparently shared by Nancy gave it an unsuspected – and unwelcome – twist.

'So,' said Nancy, with an uncertain smile, 'd'you think I should invite him to tea?'

The first peacetime Christmas in seven years ought to have been joyous, but with food still clamped in the mean jaws of rationing Yuletide cheer was thin on the ground. And for Freya it was a momentous one for entirely the wrong reason: their first Christmas as a 'broken' family. She spent it with her mother and brother down in Sussex, while her father was off somewhere in Scotland with Diana, whose name in conjunction with Stephen's now seemed unavoidable. In reparation he sent her a notably de luxe present – a beautiful silk-and-wool cardigan in sage green – which she left in its tissue paper the entire holiday.

A heavy cold confined her miserably to bed, where she read *Great Expectations* and dealt with her correspondence: letters from Nancy, from Robert, and one whose envelope written in mauve ink she knew instinctively was from Nat Fane. His handwriting was, in common with everything else about him, studiedly flamboyant, all fancy curlicues and extravagant ascenders. The only slight incongruity in it was the address at the top of the page. *The Ferns, Pinner* seemed too workaday for one of his airs and graces. 'I was a changeling,' he had said, straight-faced, when she expressed surprise at his provenance. 'I ought at least to have a manor house and a few hundred acres. But fate decreed *Pinner* as my place of birth.'

Fane's was a long letter that rarely strayed outside the necessary span of his own moods, fancies and tastes, a self-obsession that should have been tedious but in his case was leavened by a style that switched without effort between charm and light-voiced mockery. No mention was made of their night together, though Freya had the impression that this was not on his part a discreet avoidance of the subject; he merely had other things on his mind. He wrote about the two or three plays he had seen since returning to London, at such a length and with so many considered aperçus and bons mots that he might have been rehearsing a column for a newspaper. But if he took for himself the role of headline performer he was also quick to appreciate a correspondent capable of entertaining *him*. Freya's reply brought, to her astonishment, another letter from his pen by return of post.

. . . I confess that I stand, or rather, lounge-on-an-unmade-bed, corrected – it had hitherto been my conviction that the only English letter writer of note under the age of twenty-five was myself. Then your last arrived and lo! I was of a sudden bewitched, my pulse set racing by the *furioso tempo* of your epistolary vim. Strange to say the most brilliant of your paragraphs were those to which, philosophically, I felt least sympathetic; to wit, your sustained assault on our beloved seat of learning, the

96

city of perspiring dreams, that modern Arcadia – Oxford, by any other name. I much enjoyed your disobliging reflections on its somnolence, its smugness, its want of excitement, but then – as you admit – the pace of Life Itself has fallen off since war ended. For my own part I'm with Hazlitt: 'We could pass our lives in Oxford without having or wanting any other idea.' Like a stick of seaside rock I am stamped OXON all the way through. I came to the place from the dismal oubliette of school, you see, not from war service, and thus feel the beautiful privilege of it more keenly.

Now, apprised of your disillusion, I shall endeavour next term to show you its Elysian delights, for I can't bear to think of you unhappy there, in tears amid the alien Cornmarket . . .

She found herself rereading this passage several times. Habitually suspicious of praise, she was tickled to be thought capable of 'epistolary vim', indeed of 'brilliant paragraphs', and not just by anyone but by Nat Fane, who was already being feted as a stylistic dandy. This seemed to her an imprimatur far more valuable than anything her tutors could bestow. As for Oxford, she envied Fane his besotted devotion to the place. He had perhaps hit the nail on the head in contrasting their pre-university lives. To her the undergraduate routine felt becalmed after the frenetic rhythms of wartime; she missed the perilous excitement of being always on call in the Wrens. Rising for a ten o'clock lecture on Chaucer's Pardoner was no match for being woken at five and summoned to an emergency meeting in the Ops Room at Plymouth while German bombers droned overhead. It was not the war she wanted back but the sense of a shared endeavour, of knowing her own role in the grander scheme and being good at it. Back then you couldn't help feeling there was something always *at stake*. But what could be at stake in this city of hushed cloisters and bicycles and Latin grace at dinner?

It also disheartened her to realise that the age-old assumptions of male superiority had not been eradicated by war – merely displaced. In the Wrens a kind of meritocracy had been established *faute de mieux*; a woman was trusted to do a job usually because there wasn't a man at hand. By degrees the woman would prove herself just as capable of playing her part, perhaps more so for having assumed it in adversity and been hardened in consequence. In her own experience as plotting officer she had gone head first into the unknown, but determination, mingled with pride and fear, had seen her through. She had kept her nerve because to do otherwise was unthinkable. By the end she had secured the respect of her superiors simply by being as efficient and reliable as a man.

Oxford didn't operate on those egalitarian lines. Of course it had been a redoubt of male privilege since twelve hundred and whenever it was, back in the days when women counted only as childbearers and chattels. Even the advent of women's colleges had made barely a dent in the ramparts. Winning her spurs in the Wrens carried little weight here. Amid the bovine atmosphere of collegiate maleness she was just a skirt with a library book.

And she missed boxing. Denied access to a boxing gymnasium she took to practising in her room. If Ginny was about she would get her to hold up a cushion while she pummelled away at it – a duty that Ginny soon tired of. Craving exercise she went for long walks, to the north as far as Woodstock and Blenheim, or south to Boars Hill and Bagley Wood. Most times she took Nancy or Ginny along on a footslog and they hiked through water meadows and fields and dripping copses where rooks cawed in the treetops.

One Saturday at the end of January she and Ginny crossed Port Meadow to a pub in Binsey, the Perch, and stopped for a sandwich and a pale ale. The saloon bar was in a competitive roar of braying voices, but they managed to find a table in the back offering quiet. Ginny, who was beginning to get the measure of her friend's restlessness, suggested she look for something to occupy her time.

'Really, there are so many hobbies besides boxing.'

Freya clicked her tongue in reproof. 'Boxing isn't a hobby, it's a sport – maybe not even that. I don't want a "hobby" in any case. That conjures up flower-arranging and model-aircraft-making. There has to be something more.'

'I agree,' said Ginny, peeling back the sandwich and wrinkling her nose. 'Spam again.'

But Freya was pursuing her own line of thought. 'The problem – our problem – is that we've done it the wrong way round. Going out into the world, having all that responsibility, that should have come after university. But we did the serious thing first, because there was a war on! No wonder Oxford feels so tame.'

Ginny was gazing off at a group of young men in duffel coats and college scarves crowding the bar. 'I don't know – seems all right to me.'

'Really – can you imagine three years of this? What are you going to do with yourself?'

Ginny's attention was still directed over Freya's shoulder at the drinkers. 'I can think of a few things,' she said. 'Not everything's on the ration, you know.'

Freya smiled back at her. Perhaps I'm the exception, she thought, the malcontent in Lotusland. She wished she could be like Ginny, so gregarious and relieved to be free, but she wasn't; she felt something inside her had stalled. Writing an essay a week wasn't much of a stimulus. At twenty-one she never suspected there would be so much time to fill.

She noticed Ginny giving her an odd look.

'I think one of those chaps is giving you the eye.'

Freya turned round, but her short-sightedness made her struggle to pick out an admirer. They had chatted on for a desultory minute or two when a figure loomed up beside them. His face, with its chiselled features and dark eyes, seemed familiar to her.

'Hullo there. I think we've met before . . .'

'Yes, we *have*,' she replied, in a tone that was eager to make it true, though she still couldn't place him.

'You had the trunk – at the railway station.'

The clouds parted. 'And you helped me with it. Of course!' She made a reflexive gesture that invited him to join them. 'I'm Freya, this is my friend Ginny –'

'Alex McAndrew,' he said, shaking their hands and taking a seat. She recalled now the faint Scottish burr in his voice. The college scarf he wore was also familiar to her.

'You're at Balliol?'

He was indeed – a Greats scholar. He spoke with a smile at once modest and becoming.

'D'you know Robert Cosway?'

'I know the name – we haven't been introduced.'

Alex was originally from Edinburgh, where his mother still lived. Like them he had deferred his university place for the war effort, working the last four years for the government in an unspecified 'intelligence' department. But he didn't want to talk about that, he wanted to know about them, and so out came their war stories – the institutional rivalries, the carpetings, the friends lost and found, the triumphs, the mistakes, the great escapes. Ginny kept pressing him to 'spill the beans' about his department, and he, with perfect good humour, kept swatting her away. It made Freya wonder if he had actually been involved in something too difficult to explain. All he would admit to was a relief that he had got through it 'unscathed', the implication being that certain of his colleagues had not.

'And to go from that to *this*,' he added, his hand wave seeming to encompass the Oxford life entire.

Ginny's expression was wry. 'Would that everyone were as grateful!'

Alex saw that Freya was the target of this jibe. 'You don't like it here?'

The gentle note of concern in his voice awoke a sudden remorse in her: she *was* ungrateful. 'It's not that . . . we were just talking about how different it's been from wartime. Oxford feels like – I don't know – an irrelevance. An anticlimax.'

'Time hangs heavy after the Wrens,' Ginny explained.

By now the cluster of men with whom he'd been drinking at the bar had started to circle their table, like sharks, obliging Alex to perform some introductions. Ginny proved very amenable to this extra company, and Freya, though she would have preferred a tête-à-tête with Alex, mucked in with the rest. Later, when they had been turfed out of the pub, Alex made a point of accompanying her and Ginny back to Somerville. Freya, happening to peek into the basket on the bicycle he was wheeling along, noted the spines of several library books. She picked one of them out.

'Henry Green? I thought you were reading Greats.'

'I am. That's research – a piece for *Cherwell* on the war in modern British fiction. Not quite the commission I was hoping for.'

'So you want to be a journalist?'

He blew out his cheeks. 'I dunno. I should have been hard at it this afternoon – due first thing Monday and I haven't written a word!'

'Just like a journalist. I suppose you've read the latest Waugh?'

He shook his head.

Ginny, who'd been listening, said, 'That's one you were reading last term, wasn't it?'

Alex's voice turned supplicating. 'You know it? Oh! This could be the saving of me.'

Freya wrinkled her nose. 'I'm not sure I'd be of any use.'

'Freya, dear,' Ginny interposed, 'if I'm not mistaken you're in this fellow's debt over a certain immovable object he helped *you* with . . .'

She studied his face, the noble cheekbones and sad-spaniel eyes reminding her for a moment of a Renaissance martyr. You could sense something almost erotic in that banked-down yearning gaze. *Almost*? Who on earth was she trying to kid? 'I could probably spare you a couple of hours tomorrow,' she said, feigning a note of concession.

'Just a florid, cringing, self-indulgent book about nobs,' said Robert, with a savage little jerk of his head. 'Not enough that they're spoilt and stupid, they have to be *Catholic* too, so that Waugh can moon about what sensitive souls they are. And as for his treatment of the common man –'

'I imagine the common man will get along fine with or without his book.'

'– the snobbery of it is breathtaking. I'm amazed at you, Freya. I can understand your reverence of Jessica Vaux, she's a real writer, but *this* stuff – I thought you had more taste.'

'Sorry to let you down,' said Freya pleasantly. 'Though I believe I've the advantage of you in having actually *read* the book.'

Nancy stuttered out a laugh. 'Robert! Why are you so resentful of a thing you don't even know about?'

'It hasn't held him back before,' drawled Freya.

The three of them were drinking tea in her room the week after she had given Alex the emergency 'tute' on *Brideshead*. She had spent Sunday afternoon coaxing him through the entire fiction piece, of which the passages on Waugh she had more or less written herself. Alex had been grateful to her, though he hadn't responded to her flirtatious promptings with quite the degree of commitment she would have liked; when, for instance, she had tipped her head to one side in a way that other men had found irresistible, he had merely beamed at her and knitted his brows again over Charles Ryder's infatuation with the Flyte family. He was of that charming, and rather maddening, type who hadn't the smallest idea of how attractive they were.

'So how far did things go with this *Alex* fellow?' asked Robert, narrowing his eyes.

'As a matter of fact he was a perfect gent. He didn't lay a finger on me.'

'You sound disappointed. Was it your plan that he should?'

'He *is* terribly good-looking,' said Freya, making it sound a matter of philosophical certainty.

Robert, now properly nettled, said, 'I must say, your taste in men –'

'Ah, my taste again – first it's writers –'

'– quite mystifies me. Fane's a ridiculous narcissist, but he at least has a sort of glamour. Alex McAndrew, though, *really* – he looks effete even in his rowing kit. And he's bloody Scottish to boot.'

'What's wrong with being Scottish?' asked Nancy.

He gave out a *tsk*, ignoring her. 'I don't understand it. Of all the men you could have . . .'

'Oh yes? Who did you have in mind?'

Robert responded with a silent scowl. Freya's eyes flicked to Nancy, who had been watching their little sparring match with guarded interest. An emotional minefield was opening before her: she could tell Nancy's feelings for Robert were gathering strength, but so far she could detect no reciprocal interest from him. As his display of petulance had indicated, Robert's romantic affinities seemed to be tending if anywhere towards herself, which was gratifying in its way.

'Anyway, the *Cherwell* literary editor thought Alex's piece so good he commissioned another – on why the Great War poets were so much better than those of our war.'

Robert, the sulk still in his voice, said, 'I'd have thought the answer to that was obvious.'

'Oh. Why?'

'Because a good half of our lot managed to stay out of it. Whatever else you say about the '14–'18 war, everyone mucked in, the intellectual classes and the workers alike – so in the trenches you were as likely to meet a poet as a postman. That didn't happen in '39.'

'Are you saying there were more shirkers?'

Robert made an equivocal expression. 'Let's just say there were a lot who managed to save themselves by staying put.'

'Hmm. I'm not sure Alex would care to pursue that line, given what he did in the war.'

'What *did* he do?'

'Something in intelligence. He was a bit mysterious about it.'

'That rather proves my point,' said Robert. 'Bright chaps who would have been scribbling away on the front line first time round got themselves office jobs in the second. Much safer.'

Freya squinted at him, and said coldly, 'I dare say Alex gave as much blood, sweat and tears as anyone else. The last war required sacrifices too, they were just of a different kind. It's one thing to talk out of your arse, Robert, but your insinuating that he tried to avoid the fighting is *pretty low*.'

Robert coloured at this. 'I wasn't insinuating anything. I don't give a stuff what he did in the war –'

'Easy for you to say,' said Freya, her blood up.

'I was at *school*, for God's sake.'

'Yes, and you sound like you've never left.'

Robert got to his feet, and straightened in a show of dignified hurt. 'I don't see why I should sit here and take this.'

'Why not?' she retorted. 'You might learn a thing or two.'

A brief daggered silence followed as Robert seemed about to match her taunt. But he only glared at her, before shaking his head and leaving the room.

Nancy, who had been half hypnotised by this altercation, said, 'Should I go after him?'

Freya pulled a face. 'Why?' Of course, she knew why, but objected on two counts; first, that Robert's ruffled feathers deserved no smoothing, and second (what she couldn't mention), that it was imperative to thwart a potential intimacy between them. Robert seemed careless of her, and she couldn't bear the thought of Nancy blundering in and getting hurt. Friends needed protecting, especially the ones who didn't know any better.

Nancy was watching her with a hooded look. 'You enjoy provoking him, don't you?'

'I suppose I do. He rises to the bait every time.'

'You should take pity on him. He's half in love with you.'

'What? Did you not just hear him deploring my "taste in men"?'

Nancy nodded slowly. 'Yes, and you could tell what was behind it – he only made a fuss about Alex because he wants you himself.'

'I don't think so,' she replied, with a laugh more cavalier than she felt. It disturbed her that Nancy was so astute in reading between the lines; she too had sensed the possessive undercurrent in Robert's personality. Strange, she thought, how very different men could be. There was Nat Fane offering sexual perversion at the drop of his pants, while Robert could only express his attraction through the heat of argument. As for Alex, the most obviously desirable of the three, she hadn't yet got his measure: he'd been so eager to get her to his rooms, only for them to spend the whole afternoon *working*.

As they said goodbye, she felt Nancy's eyes fixed upon her in mute enquiry. Freya had batted away that theory of hers about Robert, but could tell she wasn't convinced. Nancy understood her better than people who'd known her for years – really, it was almost spooky. Outside the afternoon was darkening as she collected the tea things and emptied the loaded ashtray; another drab Oxford evening lay ahead, with dinner in hall the only diversion. Perhaps she ought to go out –

A knock came at the door. She presumed it was Nancy, come back to collect something she'd forgotten, but she opened it to find Robert. He looked subtly altered from when he had exited the room half an hour ago; he seemed no longer enraged, though his brow was troubled and his gaze downcast. He had the resigned air of a defendant preparing to be sent down.

'Oh, it's you,' she said. 'Did you just see Nancy on her way – ?'

He shook his head. 'I was hiding round the corner. May I come in?'

She stepped aside to admit him. He slouched into the room, seemed about to sit, then moved to the far window, facing away from her.

'I've just cleared away the tea things, but I can . . .'

'No, thanks,' he said, his face averted. 'I only wanted to – You know, it's strange, I think I must have some terrible instinct for self-sabotage, because even when I'm in the company of people I like I feel a compulsion to aggravate them, alienate them, usually by talking a lot of –'

'Balls, my liege,' she supplied. Now he did look at her.

'Yes – balls. It's just to get a reaction out of people. It's a fault in me, and I apologise. I didn't mean to cast aspersions on Alex, or his integrity. I'm sure he's a good egg who's done his bit. But what I can't bear is the thought that you like him *more than me*. Really, how is that possible?'

She laughed, not unkindly. 'Robert, don't be silly. I hardly *know* him. I've spent a single afternoon in his company talking about bloody Evelyn Waugh. And I don't know what you mean about liking him more than you. It's not a competition.'

'It's always a competition,' he said, unsmiling.

She sighed, and moved towards him. 'It's nice of you to apologise. It shows honesty. I like that in a friend.'

He reached out and clasped her hands in his. 'Is that all you want – honesty?'

'It's one of the things,' she replied carefully. His eyes were fixed in earnestness upon her while his grip on her hands tightened. Oh dear, she thought, he's going to turn this into a Big Moment.

'Freya, I do want you –' his voice had gone husky, almost hoarse – 'to be more than a friend. If I have to get on my knees and beg –'

'Oh, please don't do that,' she said, stifling another laugh in the instant before he nearly winded her with the force of his embrace, and she realised that asking him not to beg could be construed as a sort of licence for him to do something else. Suddenly his face was blocking the light and he had clamped his mouth upon hers. It was not suavely done, but she had at least prepared herself for his spring; she could feel the hormonal fury pouring off him. He reminded her of a young American pilot she had been out with a few times at Plymouth, the heat of him, the sinewy strength of his arms and the needy questing hands on her body. The difference was that back then it wasn't the first time for either of them; what they had done together felt more like a transaction, hurried and unsentimental in the wartime way, but friendly withal. Here, with Robert, there was the pressure of responsibility, and it devolved mostly on her: he was a virgin, and she wasn't.

They had tumbled onto the ancient horsehair couch, and in between kissing her he was emitting low urgent grunts that she supposed were meant to indicate overmastering desire but sounded more like a bull preparing for a charge. It was not unpleasant to have his weight on top of her, pinioning her, but the noise was not to be borne.

'Robert. *Robert*,' she repeated sharply.

He raised his head to look at her. 'You want me to stop?' he said, and he looked so forlorn that her heart turned over. Yes, this would be the moment to take the bull by the horns, so to speak – but her initiative had snagged on a spike of pity.

'No,' she said, holding his face steady in her hands. 'Only stop making that noise, would you? We can get along very well without it.'

Afterwards they lay there, stupefied, half listening to voices raised in the quad and the occasional muffled footstep on the staircase. She could feel a dampness pooling on her stomach from where she'd managed to pull him out at the critical moment. Robert propped himself on his elbow to look at her, the edges of his face blurred in the early-evening gloom.

'You know what's great about you?' he said in a tone of post-coital gratitude.

She blinked up at him. 'Do tell.'

'You're not just a woman – you're a right good chap, too.'

It wasn't a compliment to set the heart on fire, but she could tell it was kindly meant. 'Er . . . thank you.'

Ginny would be back any minute, so she told him to look sharp. She watched him drag his clothes on while he chattered about some film he wanted them to go and see next week. He had never sounded so cheerful. She realised, with inward self-reproof, that she had allowed something to be set in motion, and it was neither sensible nor kind.

'Robert, listen to me. One very important thing,' she said, with an emphasis that stopped him in his tracks. 'Nancy mustn't hear about this.'

From his expression she could see he had no idea why.

Next day she found a note at the lodge addressed to her. It was from Alex, who turned out to have news of an appointment at *Cherwell*.

. . . in fact so short-handed have they been that – *mirabile dictu* – I've somehow landed a minor position in editorial, with a brief to commission articles, reviews &c. You're probably laughing your head off, and I wouldn't blame you. I'm aware that I owe this preferment to you – nearly all the best bits of that War in the Modern Novel piece were yours – which is why I hope you'll agree to write something for the paper under your own name. It can be about anything, really, so long as it's vaguely connected to the arts. We've got a theatre issue planned, and an idea for a profile is being bandied around. Have you by any chance heard of a chap called Nathaniel Fane?

7

Fane is the Spur
by Freya Wyley

His name is a typo, he said: he really ought to have been Nathaniel Fame, 'since that is my calling'. At the age of 19 he is already on the way to being notorious. On the grey streets of Oxford, spring 1946, Nat Fane stood out like a harlequin at a convention of undertakers. That was him, tall and rake-thin, wafting through town in a purple velvet suit, yellow silk shirt, polka-dot handkerchief foaming at his breast pocket and chisel-toed patent leather shoes. He turns heads wherever he goes. Other favourite accoutrements include an opera cape lined in scarlet silk and kid gloves the colour of buttermilk. On the morning I met him he was dressed, with comparative restraint, in a white shirt, high-waisted grey slacks and a fawn-coloured top coat slung, film-producer-style, over his shoulders. This was his 'working attire', he explained, brushing an invisible speck off his sleeve and lighting his first cigarette of the day.

As we walked down Beaumont Street towards the Playhouse, someone hailed him from across the road. 'I wave a gloved hand, and they cheer,' he said with an imperious lift of his arm. The line was pinched from Oscar Wilde, an earlier legend of Magdalen College to whom

Fane is the natural heir. Like Wilde, he has an affinity for the theatrical and a challenging line in instant self-mythology. On the night I was introduced to him, at a party, he declared himself to be 'an artist, an actor, a director, a writer, a critic and a collector of beautiful things'. He is an athlete as well as an aesthete, if his sporty swing of a squash racket was anything to go by. And, also like Wilde, he is apt to get other people's backs up. It is often the fate of the man brave enough to set his face against the forces of orthodoxy that he will be sneered at as a mountebank, a flibbertigibbet, a poseur. In Fane's case the outlandish exterior – those clothes, that make-up – will only stoke the flames of indignation. He has not yet been 'debagged' and dumped into Mercury, but were that sentence pronounced on him one may imagine the eager young bullies queueing to take the job.

If he were only a monster of conceit his reputation around town would be neither here nor there. Yet Fane is possessed not just of a giant ego but of an outsize talent. It was apparent from a young age. Born in Pinner, he was educated at a minor public school ('I forget where') whose drama club furnished him with the means to indulge his precocity. At fifteen he put on two interlinked plays, *King* and *Country*, written by, directed by and starring himself. That they won golden opinions from all quarters wasn't enough for the young playwright, who wrote an anony-mous review of the production and managed to get it published in the local newspaper. It praised the author's 'magisterial accomplishment'. No opinion, it seemed, has quite the goldish lustre as the one he holds of himself. Since then he has taken major Shakespearean roles in his stride – Hamlet, in his most recent production, Henry V, Iago, Benedick, Mercutio in *Romeo and Juliet* ('I wasn't considered pretty enough for Romeo,' he added in a baffled aside). There will be more to follow.

I had been accorded the privilege of witnessing a rehearsal of his latest production, *The Duchess of Malfi*, at the Playhouse. The first night was coming up fast, yet Fane showed no sign of nerves as he greeted his cast good morning and settled into a canvas chair with a cup of pungent black coffee. Fane initially observed the actors in silence, his posture concentrated, still, hawkish. He barely gestured – then of a sudden he swooped into action, seizing on a line and shaping it precisely. At one point in the play Ferdinand, the mad brother whose incestuous desire will doom the Duchess, says, 'I am to bespeak a husband for you.' Fane stopped the actor and asked him to replay the line as an unconscious fluff, so that it became, 'I am to be – er, to bespeak a husband for you.' He has a seemingly infinite capacity for taking pains. 'Any fool can put on a play,' he said later. 'But to me there is no satisfaction in merely entertaining. I want a play to immerse the audience, to plunge them into something strange and disconcerting. I want to grab them by the throat and not let go.'

The company broke for lunch, and I accompanied Fane for what I assumed would be a sandwich and a cup of tea at Fuller's. Instead he insisted on going to the restaurant upstairs at White's, where we dined – rationing be damned – on shellfish, trout *à la meunière* and a bottle of Puligny. Restaurants are his natural element, appealing both to his epicurean tendency and his gregarious instincts. Waiters here fussed around him; they seemed to believe he was a 'personality' of some kind. Uncoiling from the tensions of the rehearsal room, Fane enlarged on his personal ambition as actor, producer and impresario. Next term he is to play the title role in a modern-dress version of *Macbeth*, another part he considers to be his destiny: 'I *am* Fane of Cawdor,' he remarked, straight-faced. He has no use for modesty – false or any other kind – outlining a 'sacred Trinity' of British stage actors: 'Irving is the Father. Olivier is the Son. And I am the Holy Ghost.' He said this with the tiniest glint of mischief. It is on occasion difficult to know if Fane believes such grandstanding or if he merely seeks to provoke his listeners. One cannot rule out the possibility of it being both. His conversation is all high-denomination banknotes; quotation is his loose change. Even over lunch he could not help performing, and the entertainment was gold standard.

He looked at the pudding menu and discarded it, but he decided that we must have another drink to send us on our way. His tipple of the moment is Brandy Alexander, though he claimed not to have heard of Anthony Blanche, the witty exquisite of Evelyn Waugh's recent novel *Brideshead Revisited*, who in one memorable scene drinks four of them in quick succession. Blanche becomes to the narrator, Ryder, a near-mythical figure, a brilliant dandy who is also the story's inadvertent truth-teller. In him one may discern something of Nathaniel Fane, the marvellous boy who seemed to arrive in Oxford a fully-formed man, innocent yet sophisticated, forward yet elusive. Just as in that rehearsal room, he hovers on the edge of proceedings while simultaneously focusing them. He is, in every sense of the word, egregious: standing apart from the flock, an outrageous foe of propriety, and a caution. Fame, one senses, is hurrying towards him.

'It's . . . wonderful!' said Nancy, lifting her face from the new issue of *Cherwell*. She wore a look of grave admiration. 'You've got him completely, the manner, the talk. And it's *funny*, too.'

Freya, with a little uncertain laugh, said, 'D'you think so – really?'

'To be honest, I didn't know you were –' She stopped herself, and blushed.

113

'Capable of it? Nor did I! But it was a stroke of luck to have Nat for my first assignment. I may never be as entertaining again.'

They were occupying their usual places in her rooms, Freya lounging on the couch, Nancy in the armchair, cross-legged and leaning forward. It was a fresh spring morning towards the end of Hilary term, and Nancy had brought a bunch of daffodils as a present. Freya, skittish about the reception of her debut in print, felt in her friend's verdict a grateful shock of relief. Before Nancy arrived she had placed the paper at a carelessly discarded angle on the floor that gave no hint of herself having read the thing over and over again. To contemplate her byline at the head of the page became in itself a near-erotic delight; it was as though she had never really *seen* her name before, with the pleasing visual rhyme of its three 'y's, kicking their legs sideways like chorus girls. Freya Wyley: it sounded so authoritative, so mature, a byline that knew what it was talking about and would tell it straight. From the moment it seized on her eye she realised that *this* was what she wanted to do. It wasn't even that she had an urgent message for the world: she knew only that she must write.

'Has *he* read it yet?' asked Nancy.

'I don't know. He asked to have a look at the piece before I filed –' she was picking up the terminology – 'but I refused, told him no journalist would let a subject read their copy before it went to press. Alex said the editors were delighted and want me to do more.'

'I should think so,' said Nancy with reflexive loyalty. She allowed a beat to pass before changing her tone. 'Have you made any progress with him – I mean Alex?'

Freya shook her head. 'The game's up. I did a bit of digging, all quite innocent-seeming, and it seems that he's got some girl up in Edinburgh. I'm not sure how serious it is, but . . .'

'That's bad luck,' Nancy replied, somewhat preoccupied.

'How did your evening with Robert go?' said Freya lightly.

Nancy's brow creased in an unhappy frown. 'OK, I suppose. We had a few drinks in the White Horse. He's very easily distracted. Every time an attractive girl passed by his eyes came out on stalks.'

Freya made a commiserating gesture. 'You know how men are. Do you think he's – ?'

'Keen? No, not really. I mean, he's charming company, and he paid me some nice compliments. But I get the impression he has his sights fixed on someone else.'

'Did he say anything?'

'Not exactly. I think something's happened, I can almost hear it in his voice, but he won't tell me what.'

Freya nodded, and said quickly, 'He does get distracted, you're right. I'm not sure he'd be terribly trustworthy as a romantic prospect.' She had to be careful, she knew; if Nancy were to find out about her and Robert this line of conversation might not reflect well on her.

'What have you done about the novel, by the way?' She was aware of raising another awkward subject between them, though in the diversion to a matter of literary uncertainty it felt much the safer of the two. She sensed Nancy's sidelong glance to be a touch sharper than usual.

'I've put it away. I can't bear to reread it at the moment.'

'Oh. I hope it's not because –'

Nancy gave a little shake of her head before saying, 'Once I'd thought a little more I realised you were right about certain things – the need for a single narrator, for instance. But I don't think I should waste any more time on it.'

She spoke of that criticism with a dispassionate calm that both impressed and embarrassed Freya, contrasting as it did with Nancy's generous estimation of her own venture into writing. 'Nance, I do think you have a true talent –'

She looked at her directly. 'I know I do.' The steely note of self-assurance gave Freya a start – this was not the first time she had felt this disjunction between Nancy her friend and Nancy the would-be writer. 'Which is why I've started a new one,' she continued. 'Only this time I must hold off showing it to you. I don't think I can bear that much honesty.'

She concluded this with a rueful little laugh, which seemed at once to absolve Freya of undermining her and to assert that she would never do so again. There was a warning there, and it caused her an odd double spearing of her conscience. With justice might Nancy allude to the pain her friend's 'honesty' had caused – and yet was it not, conversely, the very absence of that virtue that would damn Freya in the light of what she and Robert were doing?

The following day she answered a knock at her door to find the porter toting a riotous, and somewhat ridiculous, bouquet of spring flowers.

'There's a note attached,' he said, laying the flowers in her surprised embrace. 'He must be some admirer!' he called in retreat.

For a dreadful moment she thought they had come from Robert, but a glimpse of the actressy handwriting on the envelope reassured her as to the sender.

Dearest Freya,

I was going to write that your *Cherwell* profile humbled me, but lacking as I do 'modesty of any kind' let me say only that it pleased, piqued and provoked its subject. This floral tribute is but a token of my admiration. *Quand même*,
Nat

PS Are you a member of the Union? If not, allow me to invite you to a forthcoming event with a certain theatrical lion, with myself in the part of tamer.

PPS *Very* amused by ref. to squash racket!

116

She looked for somewhere to put his flowers; the one vase she owned already held Nancy's daffodils, which she was reluctant to displace: though modest in comparison, they seemed to her the more authentic gift. She found her scout's tin bucket in a cupboard on the stairs and dunked the bouquet in it.

Her post had included a note of congratulation from Alex, who enquired as to what she was going to write next for the paper. She felt somewhat disappointed that this time he stopped short of suggesting a drink to discuss it. She wondered now if his revelation of a girlfriend back home was meant to warn her off; perhaps he had picked up in her manner a vibration of something beyond the orbit of friendliness – the gaze held a moment longer, the smile that was a little too winsome. Yet she felt herself to be caught in a maddening bind. She didn't want to be seen gaining a foothold at *Cherwell* by ingratiating herself with one of the editors – she would get by on merit. But how could she prove her professional integrity if the rest of the time she was helplessly making eyes at him?

Later that week she did something she had vowed not to do and let Robert into her bed again. Even as she did so an inner voice chided her, scaldingly aware of at least two reasons why she ought to have resisted. First, she felt her betrayal of Nancy redoubled. There had been no explicit agreement that either one of them had prior claim on him. But there didn't need to be. It was simply that Nancy had declared a liking for him, so for Freya to jump in ahead of her, in secret, would be both underhand and disloyal. The other reason, less serious but more immediately demanding, was Robert's swain-like intensity. Now that he had 'breached the sacred portal' (he found this faux-courtly language much funnier than she did) he was becoming determined to gain

117

exclusive access. There had been an early warning sign when, some days after they had first slept together, she had been at dinner in hall. One of the white-jacketed serving staff had sidled up to her and asked shyly, 'Miss Wyley, is it? There's a gen'elman outside –' he gave a quick backward glance as if worrying that he'd been followed – 'says he knows you. A Mr Cosway. Guests who aren't on the list, you know . . .'

'Yes, of course,' said Freya, rising. 'Thank you.' She felt several lifted gazes pierce her as she walked the gauntlet of the humming hall. She found him skulking in the stone-flagged entrance, and was irritated to see no hint of apology clouding his face.

'There you are,' he said, smiling apparently in relief. He moved towards her, but she deflected his attempt at an embrace.

'Robert, what are you doing here?'

'I was going crazy looking for you – in your rooms, in the library –'

'I'm having *dinner*,' she said, frowning hard. 'What on earth is the matter?'

He looked rather offended by her tone. 'Well, you didn't reply to my letter, for one thing. I also thought, given what we'd done in your room –'

'Shh, for God's sake,' she hissed, aware of pricking ears in the vicinity. 'You want the whole bloody college to know?'

He bristled visibly. 'It's of no consequence to me who knows.'

'Well, it is to *me*,' she snapped, wincing at her own volume. This would not do. She couldn't very well go back into hall, but she didn't care for a set-to in public with Robert, either. Her brusque manner had reduced him to silence, and seeing his hurt expression she relented. With a toss of her head she led him off around the quad and into a shadowed staircase, deserted at this hour. This furtive setting evidently gave

118

Robert the wrong idea, for once hidden from view he grasped hold of her and pressed his mouth on hers.

Having struggled to free herself she pushed him away. 'Robert, *please* –'

In the grainy gloom his face had lost definition, but the wounded edge to his voice was unmistakable. 'Why are you being so unfriendly? Have I done something wrong?'

'No – no. But you can't just come barging in here any time you please.'

'I wanted to see you! And it was only the other night you seemed quite happy to see me –'

'Yes, but that was – We did something on the spur of the moment that probably wasn't a good idea.'

'What do you mean?'

She sighed. 'I don't want to hurt people – Nancy.'

He snorted in disbelief. 'That's ridiculous. This isn't *about* Nancy, it's about you and me.'

'She's in love with you, Robert. And she's my best friend.'

'Bit late to worry about that, wouldn't you agree?' A silence fell between them, and she could sense from his brooding that he had spotted a different angle to the problem. When he next spoke his tone had become judicial. 'I don't think you're doing this to protect Nancy. It's because you're involved with Alex, isn't it?'

Freya gave a mirthless laugh. 'Oh, I wish –' That tore it. She heard Robert give a little gasp of surprise, and knew she had blundered.

'I thought so,' he said coldly. 'He's turned you down, I suppose.'

'No, he hasn't. He doesn't even know I –' She wasn't going to spell it out.

'Sorry, but I – I'm baffled. How can you prefer him to me?'

'You've asked me that before.'

'So give me an answer.'

He had pushed her, pestered her, to speak honestly. And since that was her governing principle she would let him have it. 'I prefer him because I just do. He's charming, and he's kinder than you are. And he would never ask me a question like the one you just did.'

Robert stared at her as though she had slapped him. There was a little catch in his throat when he said, after a moment, 'You're a bitch, you know.'

He turned on his heel and stalked off into the night.

A week went by, then most of another, without any word from him. That was fine by her, still mindful of his unpleasant parting shot and the look of disgust as he delivered it. More troubling was her obligation to keep up appearances in front of Nancy. Robert had been such a frequent caller on both of them that a sudden break in his visiting pattern would naturally arouse suspicion. When the subject came up between them Freya was quick to make a show of indifference as to his whereabouts.

'Maybe he's snowed under. You know how he moans about being worked so hard. Have you sent him a note?'

Nancy nodded. 'Last week. It's odd, he's usually so prompt to reply. It may not be work, of course . . .'

'What d'you mean?'

She couldn't keep a forlorn note from her voice. 'Well, you know what he's like – *cherchez la femme.*'

'I'm not sure. He'd very much *like* to play the Lothario, but he's not especially good at it – you can feel the desperation underneath.'

'Can you?' said Nancy quietly, her eyes averted.

Freya sensed her subtle misdirections being baulked. Nancy didn't like the idea of Robert as a skirt-chaser, but she was too kind-hearted to derive satisfaction in thinking him, on the contrary, a sexual failure. All might be well if Robert could only see Nancy for the amazing catch she was and sweep her off her feet, thus releasing Freya from the treacherous position she had connived at. But even for this fantasy to stand a chance would require a basic commitment on her own part – namely, to detach herself from Robert. She would have preferred to effect this in a civilised way, with an agreement to stay on friendly terms. In the event he had aborted that possibility on the night he called her a bitch and stormed off – but at least the break had been made, and a distance of days put between them. Pride alone was enough to keep her silent; now she was also fortified by a moral purpose to resist any reconciliation.

Their estrangement might have continued indefinitely had not Freya chosen to have a quick half at the Lamb & Flag one evening with Ginny. She was putting her coat on when the door of the saloon bar swung open and Robert walked in. He was on his own, and looked as taken aback by the coincidence of their meeting as she was. It was a quiet night in the pub, with few other patrons around, so they had no way of pretending not to have seen one another. There is also a charm about such happenstance, which seems to unite the chance-meeters as beneficiaries in the mysterious scheme of the universe: fate has fingered them, and to deny its spell would be churlish, and possibly ungrateful.

Ginny, who knew something of the imbroglio with Robert, shot Freya an uncertain look, to which she replied, 'I'd better catch you up.'

Once Ginny had gone they had a drink together, and another argument. But this time they finished it in bed.

8

Freya got down to some serious work during the Easter vac, for fear of embarrassing herself at mods next term. (Dr Melvern had already been on the warpath about her lack of application.) Accordingly she thought it best to stay put at Somerville rather than risk being distracted either at home with her mother or in London at her father's. Perhaps Stephen had interpreted this as a snub, because the letter she'd received from him that morning was all conciliation and flattery – he thought her *Cherwell* profile of Nat Fane most entertaining (she had proudly sent him a clipping) even if her subject did sound 'terribly full of himself'. He was sorry not to have managed a trip there yet, he wrote, though his favourite time to see Oxford was Trinity term anyway.

In fact (he continued), they should set a date soon, because he would have to plan it around a big commission that had just come his way.

I'm sure you've read about the trials still dragging on at Nuremberg. The War Artists' Advisory Committee has agreed to send me as part of a group to document proceedings. I'll be there for two weeks, possibly longer, and depending on courtroom access I should be able to get up close to Goering, Hess and the rest of them.

Rather disconcerting to think of oneself in the same room as the men responsible for millions upon millions of dead and dispossessed. Can there be any defending them? Of course one imagines this lot as the very epitome of evil, but from the photographs I've seen they appear to be just tired, plain-faced, middle-aged men – they look more like bank managers and tax inspectors than war criminals. Maybe that's what is so disturbing about them . . .

Two weeks before the end of the vac Nancy returned to keep her company, and in the quiet studentless streets, with the town opening its face to spring, she had what she would remember in years to come as the most enchanted period of her Oxford life. They went walking arm in arm through the Botanical Gardens, had beer and sandwiches at the Trout along the river, took tea in the covered market and read aloud to each other in the evening as swallows wheeled and swooped outside the windows. They talked of Robert, but briefly and without consequence, as if they were spies reluctant to betray one another, hoarding their own supply of information. She knew that Nancy had exchanged letters with him – he was gadding around up north somewhere – but apparently they hadn't seen one another in the interim.

One evening the conversation turned to Alex, who had been on holiday with his mother in the Highlands. Freya had received a letter from him that morning stamped with a distant island postmark.

Nancy said, narrowing her eyes as if to conjure his image, 'I like Alex, but he's ever so private about things. Whenever I mention something personal he just changes the subject. Has he ever talked to you about his father?'

'A little bit. He walked out on them when Alex was small – never heard from him again. I think that's why he's close to his mother.'

'And what about the mysterious girlfriend – anything in the letter?'

Freya made a downward twist to her mouth. 'Not a thing. Most of it was just *Cherwell* gossip and what he's reading at the moment. Oh, that reminds me –' she leaned over to her bedside table and picked up his letter – 'he quoted this tiny poem in it, by Catullus, clearly assuming I have Latin, which I don't. Can you make it out?'

She passed the page to Nancy, who recited it.

Odi et amo. quare id faciam, fortasse requiris?
nescio, sed fieri sentio et excrucior.

'It's quite famous, I think. "I hate and I love. Why do I do that, perhaps you ask? I don't know, but I feel it, and I am tortured."'

Freya stared at her for a puzzled moment. 'What on earth does he mean by that?'

'Well, it's a poetic conundrum, he's divided in his feeling –'

'I don't mean Catullus, you nit – I mean, why has Alex quoted it?'

Nancy shrugged. 'Maybe he loves his girlfriend and hates her, too. I suppose you'd have to ask him.'

'Or maybe he loves and hates *me*,' suggested Freya, only half joking. Could she possibly have elicited such extremes of feeling in him? It seemed unlikely, but as Nancy said, he was so private you couldn't tell. She had tried to draw him out on a few occasions, and failed. In matters of the heart he was a clam.

Nancy, frowning at her, said, 'Why would anyone hate you?'

She laughed and made a mock-simpering expression in reply. 'You're terribly sweet, aren't you?'

But Nancy gave a little shake of her head, as if to say sweetness had nothing to do with it.

The old boy came in at a shuffle, supporting himself on a silver-knobbed walking stick. Stout and red-faced, he wore a checked tweed suit and an expression of disdainful amusement. A monocle glinted over his eye. Nat Fane, with whom this gentleman had just been sparring in a stage conversation ('Whither a National Theatre?'), danced attendance on him in a mixed spirit of obsequiousness and impudence. Freya was among the guests at a private party in the Oxford Union bar. Fane, ushering the illustrious personage to the centre of the room, called for quiet.

'Ladies and gentlemen, we have been blessed this evening. Our guest in the debating chamber is not only the most renowned drama critic of our day, he is a speaker whose coruscating personality has ornamented this evening with flashes of incomparable brilliance and erudition. He is, if I may –' he shot a sideways glance – 'the monocle of all he surveys – Mr James Erskine.'

A thunder of clapping burst forth as the critic offered a bow and a smile which suggested that this outpouring of appreciation was simply his due.

As they watched Fane steering the old man around the room, performing introductions, Nancy turned to Freya. 'Nat's like a dog with two tails, isn't he? I think he'd die of happiness if Mr Erskine only patted his head.'

Freya smiled. 'Ah, it's not his *head* that interests him. Nat told me that in the taxi on the way from the station Erskine put his hand on his knee and said, "Dear boy, may I ask whether you're a votary of Greek love?"'

'You mean – he's queer?' said Nancy in whispery, wide-eyed surprise. 'I'd like to see the look on my father's face

125

if he heard that. He's read Erskine's column in the *Chronicle* for years.'

'Would he stop reading him once he knew?'

'Oh, he'd stop reading the *Chronicle*!' said Nancy, and they both laughed. Alex, who was returning from the bar with drinks, asked them what was so funny.

'Just talking of the "coruscating personality" over there,' replied Freya. 'We were speculating on the shock it would be to his readers once they found out he was *not as other men*.'

'A poof, is he?' said Alex, wrinkling his nose in disdain.

Now it was Freya's turn to be surprised: it was so unlike Alex to disparage anyone, let alone a whole 'type'. When she looked at him some moments later his features had returned to their amiable ease, and all was well. She wondered again how she'd stopped herself making a dead set at him. A few days into the new term she had mentioned the Catullus poem he'd quoted in his letter, hoping to tease out the ambiguity of *odi et amo*, but he stonewalled her completely, claiming only that he had had the poet 'on the brain'. She could almost believe him.

They were about to settle at a corner table, she and Nancy, when Nat approached, Erskine at his side, like an eager courtier leading on his bored monarch.

'Jimmy, would you allow me?' he said, in his most purring tone. 'Here are two young ladies who've been *longing* to meet you.'

Freya, whelmed in a cloud of cologne and smoke from Erskine's cigar, hadn't been 'longing' at all, but for Nat's sake she decided to play the game and baste the old bird with a juicy compliment or two.

'That was an extraordinary performance,' she said.

Jimmy fixed her with an odd look. 'You know, they are the very same words I'd use when I had to go round to flatter some halfwit actor after a show. "Extraordinary" was large enough to appease his vanity and ambiguous enough to keep my self-respect. The other thing I used to say was "I don't know how you do it, my dear". It sounded like a tribute but of course it hid a little dagger!'

'Well, I can't *imagine* how you do it,' said Freya pertly.

His eye sharpened behind his monocle. 'Ah. Very good.' He turned to Nat. 'You could cut yourself on this one.'

'Quite,' agreed Nat with a smirk. 'She's already a star writer on *Cherwell*.'

'That so? What d'you say your name was?'

'Freya Wyley. And this is my friend Nancy – she's going to be a writer, too.'

Jimmy nodded like a man who had heard it before. Nancy was too shy to say anything, so Freya jumped in again. 'Do you perhaps have some advice for young aspirants?'

'Advice . . .' he said, clamping the cigar in his mouth and taking a draw. 'The danger is in giving advice to people who only imagine themselves to have talent. You may be doing them a disservice.'

'So how can you tell –'

Jimmy anticipated the question: '– if your talent is base metal or the real thing? Of course one never can, not absolutely. Doubt is intrinsic to the artist's calling. And the greater the artist, the greater the doubt. Only the talentless have perfect confidence.'

Now Nancy did find her voice. 'Then . . . how did you become convinced you were a writer?'

'Ha! You may well ask. I started out fancying myself an actor, until the company manager told me, firmly, that I wasn't good enough. Crushing at the time, but I afterwards found that I had something else – a voice. What I needed was an opportunity. I'd been writing theatre notices in my twenties, and decided to submit one on spec to the editor of the *Post*. He printed it, and kept on printing 'em – they got sackfuls of mail from people, some of it very disobliging.

But they all read me. A few years later the *Chronicle* made a bid for my services, and off I went. Now –' Jimmy paused, gathering himself for the next flourish – 'you may think "he was bloody lucky", and I would agree, luck played its part. So let us imagine that the first editor who took me on was a dolt incapable of distinguishing between my prose and that of the butcher's boy, but gave me the job just because I was available. That would be luck. But when *another* paper's editor comes along offering more money and a bit of a fanfare, well, that's not luck any more. That's talent.'

'But you've worked at it, too,' said Nat shrewdly.

'Certainly I have. I'm not a genius,' he said, pausing for a moment in case someone cared to object. 'Only Hazlitt and Shaw among theatre writers deserve that honorific. For the last thirty-seven years at the *Chronicle* I've worked ten hours a day, not counting the time I've spent attending the plays and reading the books for review. A writer must always be working at his craft, refining it. Flaubert said, "Prose is like hair – it shines with combing." That is the way to succeed. But mark all the hundreds of ways one can fail – by being inattentive, lazy, slapdash, weak-willed. By not taking pains. By settling for the notion that "this'll do". One could also mention the temptation –' here he turned pointedly to Nat – 'to overegg the mixture. The boy Fane here can write, damnably well when it pleases him. His error, he won't mind my saying, is the old one of showing off. Use one or two quotations and you pique the reader's appetite; use one *hundred* and he'll reel away from the page sickened. And keep your punning in check, too. "Monocle of all he surveys" indeed! That's vulgar, I'm afraid, like cheap jewellery.'

Nat, far from being offended by these strictures, smiled and bowed and said, 'I shall in all my best obey you, madam.'

Jimmy let loose a snort of laughter, and wiggled his empty glass. 'Dry old do, this. Will someone please fetch me another brandy and soda?'

By now he had plumped down on a little sofa, where a knot of students had congregated around him. Once someone had hurried over with a bottle of cognac he proceeded to entertain the company with a daisy chain of theatrical and literary anecdotes that stinted nothing in name-dropping, rival-bashing and self-aggrandising. He had met nearly every British theatrical personage of note in the last forty years and could recall, apparently verbatim, whatever conversation he'd had with them: 'As Gielgud once confided to me . . .' was a characteristic overture. Freya watched him hawkishly; like the rest of them she was mesmerised. Everything about Jimmy Erskine was prodigious: his conceit, his memory, his appetite for talk, his will to amuse. So too his ability to drink, though he was one of those boozers who put it away without being much affected beyond a reddening nose; the bottle of Martell which the youth had obligingly set before him was down to a quarter two hours later, and the old boy hadn't slurred a syllable.

Freya, wondering where Alex had got to, was about to go off in search when someone piped up with a question about Nazi Germany and war reporting. Whom among the press did he rate? Jimmy's answer was unhesitating.

'Greatest of my generation is Jessica Vaux, or Jecca Beaumont as I knew her back in the twenties. A remarkable woman, and terrifying once she had the whiff of cordite in her nostrils. Did you know she kept a loaded revolver on her bedside table? Ha! I like a woman who can defend herself. Had it been me in those squeaks I'd have scrambled to the nearest shelter and prayed for the cavalry. She never did.'

'Do you see her still?' asked Freya.

'Oh, not for years. She moves about a lot – lived in Paris for a while. I heard somewhere that she's gone to Nuremberg for the *Tribune*. I wonder if it bothers Goering that he will now be only the *second* most frightening person in the court-room.'

While the rest laughed, Freya felt sparks fly off the cogs and wheels grinding inside her head. Nuremberg: Stephen would be there at the same time. What an opportunity for him – he must introduce himself to her, who knows, he could even ask to paint her, in which event . . . She was still making these calculations when Nat stood and asked them, 'before the curtain falls', to give their guest of honour a send-off. Erskine inclined his head to acknowledge this second round of applause. He had talked for longer in the bar than he had on the stage. How exasperating, Freya thought, that he'd revealed his acquaintance with Jessica Vaux just as he was about to leave – she had so many things she wanted to ask him.

Nat had gone down to the street to whistle up a taxi; Jimmy had been left on his own on the sofa, absently twiddling his cane. A sudden wild initiative pierced her, like an electric charge making her skin prickle – she'd thought it an opportunity for Stephen, but that wasn't right. Almost mechanically she forced herself to join him, perching at a respectful edge on the couch. His expression was one of glazed indifference, and she decided to cut straight to it.

'Mr Erskine –'

'Jimmy, my dear,' he drawled.

'– I've been thinking about what you said – about how you took your opportunity. Well, this is Jessica Vaux's first time in Germany since 1938. I have an idea of arranging an interview with her while she's reporting from Nuremberg. Would you be able to help me place it, at a newspaper?'

She thought his monocle might pop out, but he only squinted at her. 'Hmm, I might have known it would be you . . . . At the risk of being shredded in your jaws I must decline. I'm bombarded by requests from people all the time – please read my play, read my novel, read (God help me!) my book of poems. Dozens in the post, every day. If I dealt with one I'd be obliged to deal with 'em all. So I refuse. It's safer that way.'

'I'm not asking you to read anything. The article I'd write would be good enough for print – I only need a berth for it.'

'Then try the berths and deaths column,' he said, turning away.

She was prepared for his rudeness, and parried the thrust. 'I don't believe you never make an exception. And I am, after all, only taking my cue from a master – I just need the bit of luck *you* got.'

Jimmy dismissed the flattery with a sardonic snort. 'At such moments I find myself thinking of a line from Charlotte Brontë's *Villette*. It goes: "I now signified that it was imperatively necessary I should be relieved of the honour of her presence." Isn't that a wonderfully elegant way of saying "Piss off"?'

Freya nodded. 'And yet – I'm still here.'

He sighed. 'Tenacious as well as impertinent. Listen to me, your scheme is quite hare-brained. First of all, Jessica Vaux hasn't been interviewed in years – unlike some of us, she doesn't enjoy the attention. Second, at Nuremberg she'll be in the courtroom all day and writing all night. You'd never get a spare moment with her. Third, she'd eat you for breakfast.'

Freya gave an insouciant shrug. 'Maybe. But I *will* get to meet her – I have an "in", you see.'

'Really. And what might that be?'

'My father is Stephen Wyley. He's been commissioned to do courtroom sketches for the WAAC at Nuremberg. He'll be in the press gallery with her.'

Now Jimmy did come to attention. 'Wyley? I wondered, when I heard your name . . . He was going to do a portrait of me, years ago, but nothing came of it. Talented feller.' He paused, remembering, then looked more closely at Freya. 'This idea of yours – what's wrong with doing it for *Cherwell*? Fane said you were a star writer.'

'It's a good paper,' she replied, 'but this story is bigger than *Cherwell*. And besides, I want to have lots of readers.'

'Don't we all. I suppose I should applaud your enterprise, though I also think –'

'"What a bloody pest she is,"' Freya supplied in an unillusioned tone.

He chuckled, and with his cane gave the floor a meditative tap. 'I have an old friend at the *Chronicle* who may be interested –' he raised a finger to check her excitement, and repeated, '*may be*. His name's Barry Rusk. I'll let him know there's an impudent young pup at Oxford who thinks she might get a scoop on Jessica Vaux. The rest will be up to you.'

Without being able to stop herself she clapped her hands together. 'Thank you – really, *thank you*.'

He waved away her show of gratitude, but then seemed to be diverted by something over her shoulder. She followed his eyeline to catch Alex skulking in the entrance hall; he had absented himself for the post-event performance. A goatish gleam had brightened Jimmy's eye.

'That dark-browed Adonis over there. You know him?'

Freya, exhilarated by her recent negotiation, called over to Alex, who saw what was afoot and approached slowly. She wondered where he had got to: it was a mysterious habit of his to disappear without warning. She introduced the two of them, sensing a lack of enthusiasm on Alex's side. He mumbled a few words of appreciation nonetheless.

'So kind,' Jimmy said, staring candidly at him, 'but where have they been hiding *you* all evening?'

Alex looked shifty, and laughed. 'I had to nip out for a while.'

'Well, I'm sorry we didn't meet,' he said, and Freya couldn't help hearing the warmth of his voice in pointed contrast to his dealings with her.

'Alex is an editor at *Cherwell*. He gave me my first opening,' she said.

Jimmy gave a wicked smirk. 'Perhaps you might give me one, too.' At that point Nat poked his head round the door to tell Jimmy that his cab was waiting. The old man leaned towards Alex and said in a confiding tone, 'You should keep an eye out for this one. She'll have your job if you're not careful.'

Alex, glancing at Freya, again laughed uneasily. 'It was nice to meet you.'

'Likewise!' cried Jimmy. 'Goodnight to you.' He was addressing Alex, but almost in afterthought he looked at Freya, and tipped his hat. Then, with Nat holding the door, he waddled off, and out.

The secret thrill of it was swelling in her chest: it felt as though the *Chronicle* editor had personally invited her to submit a contribution. But it *had* to be a secret, for the time being: she didn't want to set herself up for a fall, and she thought that Alex might be offended if he found out she'd been putting the bite on Jimmy Erskine to advance her career. It might look like she was getting above herself, whereas she felt only an impatience to be getting on.

Nancy had already gone, obedient to the 11.15 curfew, so Freya had taken the opportunity to have Alex walk her back to Somerville. She had discovered a little-used tradesmen's door on Walton Street for passing back and forth after hours, and by this means now smuggled him into her rooms. Out of consideration to Ginny, in bed at this hour, she raised a finger to her lips, and their conversation dropped to an undertone. The candle she lit on the chimney piece thickened the furtive mood, throwing butterfly shadows on the wall each time they moved.

'I suppose you found his flirting rather repulsive,' said Freya, lighting a cigarette and throwing herself on the couch next to him.

Alex pursed his mouth. 'I'd hardly call that flirting,' he said leniently. 'He was just some old man –'

'– dreaming of handsome young boys,' laughed Freya, quite aware of her transferring tactic.

'What had you two been talking about?'

'Jessica Vaux mostly. It seems he once knew her. He'd also met my dad.'

Alex nodded, and with a little giggle said, 'What did he mean by you "having my job"? Is a *Cherwell* coup imminent?'

Freya shook her head. 'Not that I know of. He was just teasing me – seems to think I'm very pushy.'

'Oh. Are you?'

She turned to face him, searching his face. 'When it suits me,' she said, placing her hand, with infinite lightness, on his chest. She could feel his heartbeat picking up the pace. Alex covered her hand with his own, holding it close, warming it – and then, slowly, regretfully, releasing it. She stared at the hand, returned to her lap, and nodded.

'Ah.'

Alex seemed to wince at her disappointment. 'I'm sorry. I'm very sorry.'

'I thought you might – that you perhaps felt – what I feel about you –' She stopped, hoping he might jump in, but he didn't. 'D'you *know* what I feel about you?'

He was still silent, and she suddenly felt a dispiriting little drag on her heart. Had he ever really signalled a romantic interest in her at all?

'Freya, you're a wonderful girl. Truly, you're not like anyone else I know –'

The sincerity in his voice was painful to her. 'But you're in love with this girl back home – is that it?'

He looked away, sighing heavily. He was shaking his head, as though it were a pity beyond all telling. 'I wish I – I don't want to mislead you –'

'What's her name?'

Alex, who had been looking away, shifted himself to face her. Misery had congested his features. For a long time he said nothing, and she wondered for an absurd moment if he'd forgotten it. 'Jan. Janet. Please don't ask me to tell you about her –'

'I won't,' she said unhappily. 'I don't really want to know. I suppose at least I can stop making a fool of myself –'

'Freya, you're nobody's fool,' he cut in. 'I mean it. In another life I would – Oh Christ!'

An anguished silence intervened. Eventually Freya said, 'Where did you go this evening, by the way?'

He shrugged. 'Nowhere in particular. Why?'

'It's a habit of yours – you just vanish, suddenly, and nobody seems to know where. Did you see a friend?' She was watching him, and a sudden movement of his head told her she had hit a nerve. The connections were starting to click. 'You did, didn't you?' she said. 'I think I know what's happening. You've met someone else and you feel guilty.'

In his stare was weariness yet also, she thought, a glimmer of admiration. He seemed about to say something, but stopped himself.

'So – you've got another girl here, in Oxford, and Janet doesn't know. You can't bring yourself to tell her –'

For answer he stood up and retrieved his coat from the chair. She felt a kind of sadness in the way he buttoned up and tied his scarf, though she couldn't tell if she felt sorry for him or for herself. Standing there, his shadow wavering against the wall, he seemed to radiate loneliness. If only he could be honest with her! He had started towards the door.

'Alex, wait. I'm not angry with you. Just tell me I'm right – about this.'

When he turned, she could no longer read his expression, though she could hear something cold as ashes in his voice. 'You have no idea.'

He left the room without another word.

9

'That's a preposterous idea,' said Stephen, a thin brush poised in his hand, like a conductor about to tap his baton.

He was standing on a little parallelogram of light that had fallen across the parquet floor at Tite Street. He had been distractedly dabbing away at a canvas while Freya, long legs scissored over an armchair, was laying out her scheme to meet Jessica Vaux at Nuremberg. In the days since she had first conceived it she had assessed the practical nature of her plan and realised, with a dizzying sense of possibility, that it could be done. She had taken the train to London specifically to tell him, and Stephen's first response had been to laugh. His second, once he realised she wasn't joking, was to dismiss it as 'preposterous'. Freya clicked her tongue in annoyance: she hated not being taken seriously.

'Listen, she's the greatest foreign correspondent of this century. I'll never have a better chance to interview her, or a more dramatic setting for it. Why would you not want to help me?'

'My wanting or not wanting to help is beside the point. You're a student, you have exams coming up. How would you explain it to your tutors? "Sorry, just off to Germany for the war trials!" It can't be done.'

'But it can! I only need to take a week off to do it – I can work around the exams. Dad, please, there'll never be another opportunity like this, ever – her returning to the country whose doom she predicted. Her escaping from Paris in '39. The story's too good to miss.'

Stephen stood listening, one hand on his hip, slowly shaking his head. 'From every conceivable angle it's – What about money? Flying there will cost you. What about identification papers, working permits, letters of recommendation? You know, security in Nuremberg will be so tight you won't be able to cough without getting a doctor's note. The whole city is under military rule. How do you propose getting around the place?'

'But that's just it. I'll be with *you* – as long as you're a legitimate presence there so am I. If it means carrying your paints or brushes or your entire *bloody luggage* I'll do it. *And* I'll be in uniform – they're not going to make trouble with an officer from the Wrens.'

Down below they heard a woman's light steps on the porch and the front door opening. Freya looked up at Stephen enquiringly.

'Diana,' he said. 'She sometimes drops round to make lunch.'

'Oh fucking hell,' Freya muttered beneath her breath, though loud enough for him to hear. She wondered if she only swore in front of Stephen to remind him of his error in sending her to Tipton: how did he expect her language to be ladylike after that?

Yet if she was going to pursue this plan she would have to make herself agreeable to him – no sulking, no sniping at the mistress, no swearing. At the sound of the door opening in the hall she marshalled her features into a semblance of graciousness. Diana came breezing into the room and almost reared back at the unexpected sight of her.

'Hullo,' she called, remaining in her insolent posture across the armchair.

138

'Freya, hullo!' Diana said brightly, recovering her composure. She was carrying a brown paper bag, which she held up for inspection. 'Just bought us some sandwiches – are you peckish?'

It had been nearly a year since their one meeting, that terrible lunch at Gennaro's. It had escaped her notice back then that Diana was beautiful. She carried herself with a confidence that seemed lit from within. Where most complexions looked pasty, hers looked creamy. While she busied herself in the kitchen Freya and Stephen resumed their dispute, at a less combative volume.

'Jessica Vaux is a rather grande dame these days. She's probably not the type to put herself out for a journalist from *Cherwell*, with all due respect –'

'I'm not intending it for *Cherwell*. I've bigger fish to fry. I met James Erskine at the Union last week –'

Stephen looked astounded. 'Jimmy Erskine?'

'He said he knew you, years ago – you wanted to paint him.'

'Correction: he wanted me to paint him, and pestered me for months. But I managed to elude him.'

'Why?'

'I didn't like the cut of his jib,' he replied mildly. 'But I did do a portrait of his friend László – d'you remember it? The face in the convex mirror?'

'The froggy one – that was Jimmy's friend?'

'Now there was a lovely man. I wonder if he's still around . . .'

'Anyway,' continued Freya, reverting to the matter at hand, 'he promised to help me place it at the *Chronicle*.'

Stephen acknowledged the dig. 'Well, that's nice of him – but Erskine can promise what he pleases. Unlike me, he doesn't have a personal interest in your safety or your education.'

'You seem to think I'm still *twelve*, but I've actually served this country in a war, Dad.'

At this point Diana reappeared carrying a plate of sandwiches on a tray. Seeming to twig the unsettled vibration in the air she gave a little nervous laugh before saying, 'Is everything all right?'

'Yes, of course,' said Stephen wearily. 'Just a small difference of opinion. Freya wants me to act as her liaison officer in Nuremberg while she interviews Jessica Vaux.'

Diana tilted her head inquisitively. 'So Jessica Vaux is reporting on the trials? I remember reading her as a student – that story about –'

'She's there for the *Tribune*,' Freya cut in. 'I've always longed to meet her, and this would have been my chance. But I've been thwarted by the one person who could arrange it.'

'Don't be melodramatic. I take to heart my parental responsibilities, that's all; you'll understand when you have children of your own.'

Freya had to throttle back her temptation to laugh out her scorn: if he took his 'responsibilities' so seriously why had he left his wife and broken up the family? What hypocrisy! But she couldn't bear a reprise of those hysterics – it was too exhausting, even for her.

'Have you informed the lady herself about your plan?' asked Diana. 'Maybe she would help if you explained it to her.'

'I wrote to her publishers about a week ago. I've heard nothing.'

Diana looked thoughtful. 'Perhaps you should try her agent. Do you know who that is?'

Freya shook her head, noticing Stephen's look of wounded surprise: Diana's show of interest in the matter wasn't lending much weight to his own authority. She picked up a sandwich and took a bite; Spam, as usual. The talk turned to other things. Diana wanted to hear about Oxford. Freya found herself staring at her open, ingenuous face. As for Stephen, he seemed happier than she'd seen him in years, despite today's contretemps. Resignedly, she realised she might even learn to like the bloody woman.

Later, as the glum back elevations of Paddington's terraces slid by the carriage window – she had caught an early-evening train back to Oxford – the fact of Stephen's refusal to help jangled on her nerves. She knew it had been an ambitious plan. Her own inexperience, Jessica Vaux's forbidding character, the unlikeliness of finding the time or the money to spend a week trailing her in Nuremberg – the obstacles to success were quite apparent. And yet the idea still inflamed her. It seemed unjust that she had spotted the potential of the story only to be thwarted by practical considerations.

On returning to college she found a note from Robert in her pigeonhole, asking to see her, 'on a matter of urgency'. Her heart experienced a dismal moment of frustration as she guessed what it might be. When they met the next day at the Eagle and Child, he was seated on his own, smoking in the furtive way of a witness called to the station for questioning. He wore a brown checked jacket and an open-necked shirt, possibly in deference to her avowed dislike of his bow ties. He offered a cigarette, which she took and lit.

'Is that a new case?'

Robert nodded, gazing at the cigarette case with a slightly sheepish air. 'It's from her,' he said, unsmiling.

'Nancy? Oh, *Christ*.'

'Yeah. You should have seen the look on her face when she presented it to me. The hopefulness . . . I wanted to shoot myself.'

'Shouldn't you have refused it?'

Robert sighed, and opened the case again for her inspection. 'I would have done, until I saw this.' On the sprung metal band the initials R.C. had been lovingly engraved. 'She said it was an early birthday present, so I couldn't really give the thing back then, could I?'

Freya stared at the gift despairingly. She had wondered whether Nancy still held a torch for Robert, and now she knew: it burned all right. How hateful, how truly ghastly her behaviour would seem once it got out that she and Robert had already . . .

'I was on the verge of telling her,' he continued, as though reading her thoughts.

'No, you mustn't. If anyone's going to it's got to be me.'

'"If"? I thought you were sick of us skulking behind her back. I'd rather hoped in any case that you'd do it, well, for me as much as for her.' There was a faltering humility in his tone that took her by surprise; she *did* owe it to him. She reached out to take his hand.

'I need to find the right moment, and I will,' she said, searching his face for reassurance. 'Please – please don't make me regret doing it.'

He shook his head. 'I won't. But what about you? I thought you might still be sweet on Scotland the Brave.' He gave the last three words a humorous Caledonian burr.

'If you mean Alex – no. I'm not.' She spoke with conviction, for she knew it would serve neither of them to admit that Alex had given her the brush-off.

'Good – cos he doesn't deserve you.'

She gave him a level look. 'And you do?'

He nodded so boyishly she couldn't help laughing. 'We'd better drink to it. You and me, Freya – for keeps.'

She kept finding ways to defer a meeting. The obligation she felt to Nancy persisted, but her conscience was not robust enough to bring the matter to a head: there would be time, the right moment would present itself . . . Seeking delay, she busied herself by writing to Jessica Vaux's literary agent in London, though the Nuremberg plan seemed to be up in smoke. She had overreached herself.

Conscious of avoiding Nancy, she had also kept her distance from Alex. On finishing her latest piece for *Cherwell* she was on her way to the offices to deliver it when she realised the likelihood of running into him. She dismounted from her bicycle and wheeled it along the pavement, lost in thought. After their last encounter in her rooms, coming face-to-face would be awkward. Or maybe it would only be awkward for him, taken by surprise at her unscheduled appearance. By the time she had nerved herself for this performance she had reached the *Cherwell* building, and felt she had no choice but to go through with it.

He wasn't there. The girl sitting at Alex's desk said she hadn't seen him for a while, though she was welcome to leave a message. Freya, at once frustrated and relieved, said that that wouldn't be necessary. She was about to hand over her copy when, on an afterthought, she took out her pen and wrote across the top of the first page, *Just one of those things – Catullus*. She didn't quite understand what she meant by it, but she had a strange idea that he would.

Telephone calls to the porter's lodge were accepted only in emergencies, so she felt a lurch in her chest as she picked up the receiver the following evening.

'Freya?' It was her father's voice, though she heard no anxiety in his tone.

'Dad – what's happened?'

'Nothing at all. Darling, I had to tell the porter it was an emergency or he wouldn't have sent for you. How are things?'

'Fine – now that my heart's stopped hammering. What's so important?'

She heard a snuffling laugh at the other end. 'I was wondering how far you'd got with your plan – if you'd heard from Jessica Vaux.'

'No. She's in Germany, and I don't imagine her agent will be desperate to forward post from undergraduates.' She kept her voice level, with the merest hint of reproach.

'Ah. So you're no longer interested in coming out to Nuremberg?'

'Don't joke about that.'

'I'm not joking. I've got rooms at some villa just outside the city; it's where the press are staying. The WAAC have made provision for an assistant. If the college will allow you to take the time off then all's well. You'll have to arrange your own flight – I can lend you the money if you haven't got it.'

She felt her hands tremble as she held the receiver. 'Oh, Dad, Dad . . .' She heard herself laughing, exclaiming, the words falling out of her in a breathless gabble, really, honestly, she just didn't *know* how to thank him . . .

'It's not me you should thank,' Stephen said, 'it's Diana. She's been on at me all week – quite as bad as you are, actually.'

'Diana – why?'

'Because that's the sort of woman she is. She could have come out with me, but she insisted you go instead.'

'Now I feel . . . bad,' she said, hardly able to speak for happiness. 'I'll write and thank her, I promise.'

'Yes, you should.'

But a sudden terror had seized her. 'D'you think I can pull it off, really?'

'What's this? Last week it was "Nobel Prize or bust"!'

'I know, I know, but – what if the whole thing's a flop?'

Stephen laughed, but his voice was kind. 'No use thinking like that. As the poet said, a man's reach must exceed his grasp, or what's a heaven for?'

They talked for a while longer about practical arrangements, though she was too giddy to absorb much of it. Stephen was due to leave the day after tomorrow, so the next time they'd meet would be in Germany. When she rang off, she emerged from the telephone cubicle in the lodge and stood at the edge of the empty quadrangle, looking up at the sky's darkening blue distances. An ordinary Oxford evening towards the end of May, and she scorned its tranquillity, its complacent calm. She felt she had stolen a march on the place, by knowing something it didn't.

She had decided to keep it a secret; the fewer people who knew about her little venture abroad the smaller the chance of the college authorities getting wind of it. Almost a secret: there was one person she couldn't resist telling. Hurrying over to St Hilda's the next morning she darted about in search of Nancy. After getting no answer at her room Freya had a notion of where she must be – the swot! – and, remounting her bicycle, pedalled furiously in the direction of the Bodleian. She had just parked opposite Blackwell's when she spotted Nancy's tall figure, bag in hand, walking quickly along Catte Street. She called out her name, but Nancy gave no sign of having heard, veering off down Holywell Street. Freya decided to give chase on foot, and when she came within hailing distance called her again.

Nancy turned. She had a distant air that Freya had occasionally seen before. Her smile was the giveaway: so broad it would animate her whole face, today it seemed constrained, and the light in her eyes seemed more a matter of will than a reflex. Freya thought it might be tiredness – Nancy was the most hard-working of all her friends – which would require only the tonic of her own company to banish. They continued along the street.

'Nance, I've got the most exciting thing to tell you.' As she recounted her news she felt the contours of her plan take on a renewed brilliance. Even if it failed it would surely be marked for sheer imaginative endeavour: a tyro journalist travelling to Germany in search of the doyenne of twentieth-century war reportage.

'That *is* exciting,' said Nancy quietly. 'I'm sure you'll get front page on *Cherwell*.'

'Oh, no, this isn't for *Cherwell*. I'm going to try for the *Chronicle* – Erskine said he'd help me place it.'

Nancy stopped, puzzled. 'And what does Alex think about that?'

'I don't know. I haven't told him.'

'Ah.' Something knowing in Nancy's intonation of this syllable put Freya on guard. She glanced curiously at her friend.

'You think I should tell him?'

Nancy shrugged, and resumed walking. 'Alex gave you your first chance as a writer. He might be rather hurt to find out you're aiming for Fleet Street.'

'I don't see why. I think I've repaid his faith in me. This story's much too big for a student newspaper in any case.' Nancy only nodded, and Freya felt some of the shine being knocked off her excitement. Was it so wrong to have ambition? She added, a little resentfully, 'Well, if you think I should consult my conscience –'

Nancy, with a little snort of sarcasm, said, 'That would make for lively hearing.'

'What d'you mean?' said Freya, feeling her heart go bump down the stairs. No reply was offered. 'Nance, I'm not sure what –'

'I know all about it,' said Nancy with a catch in her throat. 'Jean Markham told me, in case you're wondering. Spotted you both in a pub. Of all the men you could have had – why *him*? You always spoke so slightingly about Robert, I sometimes imagined it was your way of diverting suspicion. But

146

then I thought, Freya's not like that, she's my friend – she wouldn't sneak behind my back –'

'And I wouldn't, I swear, it just happened. The whole thing took me by surprise – before I even had a chance to consider your feelings we were just . . . in it,' she finished weakly. She dared a sideways glance at Nancy, expecting tearful distress, but her eyes were dry; all she could read in them was wounded pride. Nancy was standing close to the wall, distractedly poking a loose bit of brickwork with her shoe. When she next spoke there was more wonder than indignation in her tone:

'You said something, a while ago, about Robert being untrustworthy as a romantic prospect. You were probably right. But it never occurred to me that you were the same. You're the one who's always judged others by their honesty – it was one of the first things that impressed me about you. It was almost frightening, that complete unforgiving certainty you had. But this . . . How can I ever believe you again?'

Freya, stung by the question, had to defend herself. 'But you don't want me to be honest! Look at what happened with your novel. When I dared to give you an honest view you took offence. Now, when I withhold something for fear of your being hurt, you tell me I'm not honest enough. You can't have it both ways.'

Nancy shook her head, eyes half closed in disgust. 'That's balls. It's one thing to hold back your opinion of a book – who cares, it's just an opinion – but it's quite another to conceal a *fact*, in this case the fact of your hopping into bed with a man you knew I was crazy about. You demand honesty of other people, but for some reason you think you can pick and choose when it's demanded of you. The truth is – you're a hypocrite. A wretched hypocrite.'

A colour had risen to her cheek as she spoke, and for a moment she looked shocked by her own vehemence. Freya, outflanked, belatedly snatched up a shield of injured rationality. 'If I'd told you about it, what then? How would it have helped to know that he was in love with me and not you? I didn't ruin anything between you and Robert – all I did –'

'I know what you did. You allowed me to keep hoping, when you knew there was no hope. You made a fool out of me.' Nancy gave an unhappy laugh. 'I thought the one thing I could depend on, whatever else might happen, was your being a friend. But it looks like I've been deluding myself about that too.'

Freya, aghast, took a step towards her. 'Nance, please – please don't say things like that. If there'd been a way not to hurt you –'

'There's always a way. You choose to hurt or you don't. Just be honest with yourself, Freya.'

Nancy held her gaze for a moment, and started to walk away. Freya watched her back retreating along Holywell Street, head down, and with a heavy, almost swooning air of remorse she turned in the opposite direction. Well, she had known it would be bloody, once it came out, but *that* had exceeded her gloomiest imagining. She had underestimated Nancy once before, when she had criticised her novel. That was a chastening moment. But this was something far more serious, because it touched on the integrity of her character. Nancy's appraisal had been very thorough: she was untrustworthy, she was sneaking, she was a wretched hypocrite. *Be honest with yourself* . . . She huffed in annoyance as she wheeled her bicycle back towards college. No one had ever spoken like that to her before. Or was it that she'd never really listened? Her habitual response to criticism was one of airy indifference, since it usually came from people not qualified to give it.

She was aware of owing something to Nancy. She had understood Freya instinctively, knew how to accommodate her moods, shared her enthusiasms, forgave her occasional brusqueness. They were real friends – *best* friends! Now she wondered if they'd both got it wrong: perhaps theirs was not a friendship so much as an infatuation between leader and acolyte. Something had broken between them. But completely – irrevocably?

Back at Somerville she stood irresolute in the lodge. By an unfortunate coincidence this was also the day she had been girding herself for a flagrant violation of honesty – a stupendous whopper indeed – but one that couldn't be avoided if she was to pull off her plan. She'd realised that in applying for a week out of college it would be simple naivety to disclose the actual reason, so a fiction would have to be concocted in its place. The standard she had run up the pole for honesty was beginning to look pretty ragged.

It was the appointed hour. At her knock a voice invited her to enter, and there was Mrs Bedford, cosy and bespectacled at her hearth in a manner that made Freya think of Mrs Tiggy-Winkle.

'Miss Wyley, welcome. Come and sit here,' she said, gesturing at the sofa by the fireplace. 'I don't usually light a fire in May, but today has been unseasonably cold.'

It was maddening that Bedders created such a force field of amiability. If she had been a scold or a nag it would have felt very much easier to perpetrate a deception upon her. That her tutor had been friendly and encouraging gave a painful tweak to the guilt amassing within. Once they were settled with their tea Bedders enquired as to how she was getting along with Leo Melvern at Corpus, whether his tutorials on Chaucer were much to her liking. Freya wondered if Melvern had made an official complaint about her essay work, but since Bedders made no reference to it she assumed he hadn't.

'And all else is well? How's the boxing?'

'It's rather fallen by the wayside,' replied Freya. 'Women aren't admitted to the university boxing club.'

'Then I dare say the men have had a narrow escape – I'm sure you would have given them what for.'

Freya smiled, and in the little pause that followed she modulated her tone towards the confidential. 'I have something to ask you. Um, my mother is about to have an operation – I gather it's quite serious. She's coming out of hospital next week and will need a good deal of rest and recuperation. Someone will have to attend on her, which is difficult, since she lives in a remote part of Sussex. Naturally I feel the responsibility is mine, so I'd like your permission to take the week off.'

Mrs Bedford frowned her concern. 'I'm very sorry to hear it.' She hesitated a moment before continuing. 'Forgive me, I understood that your father is still . . .'

'Yes, he is,' said Freya, drawing her features into a grave expression, 'but my parents are – separated. He's abroad at the moment, working. I have a younger brother at Cambridge. Other than that there's no immediate family who can help. We're quite close, my mother and I, and she'll appreciate my being with her.'

'Of course, of course,' the tutor replied. 'It is perfectly natural that you should be at her side, and I'd be very willing to give you leave for the week. My only concern is that it's so very near your examinations. What if your mother's convalescence requires a longer commitment of your time?'

'Oh, she has a good friend coming down from London the following week. It's only because she was unavailable next week that I'd like to volunteer to help. As for the exams, my mother's place will be quite conducive to study – it's very quiet, so I should be able to work without interruption –'

'Apart from tending to your mother.'

150

'Yes – apart from that.'

Bedders went to her desk and arranged the necessary paperwork, reminiscing the while upon similar missions of mercy she used to undertake for her ailing father, the unavoidable nature of filial responsibility and the often disobliging behaviour of the patient. Eventually a college exeat was in Freya's hands, and another obstacle had been dislodged. She had been surprised, in the end, by how fluently she could lie: that whole business about the friend relieving her after a week had been made up on the spot.

'I'll inform Dr Melvern of your absence,' said Bedders as she held open her door. She gave Freya's arm a maternal pat. 'Such a troubling time . . . Perhaps you could write to let me know if there's anything you need.'

Oh, just a couple of airsickness tablets and a map of Nuremberg, Freya thought – that should see me right.

10

The ground below loomed up towards the plane, at first the same relentless flat fields, russet-topped villages and placid grey rivers winding on, and on. A forest would break up the monotony and then vanish. The next time she glanced out of the tiny window they were directly over an ashen necropolis, a wilderness of ruins from which it seemed no phoenix should ever rise. The plane banked abruptly, as though it had just glimpsed the devastation for itself and made an instinctive lurch away. Freya flinched too: had she just seen all that was left of Nuremberg?

Ten minutes later they had landed on a strip flanked by a dreary cluster of grey and green outbuildings, not so much an airfield as a makeshift shanty town where planes were received and unloaded and turned around like so many pack mules. The place was swarming with military personnel, most of them American, all in a frenzy of toing and froing and none taking the smallest notice of the new arrivals. Freya, in uniform and carrying a small suitcase, felt herself to be invisible amid the vast, hurrying scrummage. She wanted something to drink, but the only sign of commercial activity was a long desk from which a quartermaster was selling American cigarettes. Freya asked for a packet of Chesterfields.

'Only sell 'em by the carton, ma'am,' the man drawled.

'I don't have any German marks,' she said.

'Be no good to me if ya did. Got sterling?'

She bought two cartons, and asked him where she might find transport; but he only shrugged. After another brusque exchange with a passing mechanic she found herself on a little concourse at the edge of the airfield. The noonday sun was turning up the heat, and she felt sweat prickling beneath her serge tunic. Two GIs, bareheaded, were lounging next to a dusty jeep, one of them wiping the back of his neck with a handkerchief. Both were drinking from a jerrycan. She approached them and put her suitcase down.

'May I please have some of your water?'

They stopped talking and turned blank bovine gazes upon her. The senior of the two looked at the jerrycan he'd been drinking from, and put it aside. From the back of the vehicle he lifted an identical one out, unscrewed the lid and handed it to her. She thanked him and took long gulping draughts, too eagerly; the water spurted down her chin and onto her front. Finished, she swiped her wrist across her mouth and handed the can back, suppressing a small belch. She asked them if they knew a place called the Schloss Vogelsong. Yup, they did, it was a huge old villa about three clicks away – the press had taken it over.

'Is there a bus or something I can get there?'

The pair exchanged a swift look that Freya read as *Is she kidding?* The one who had given her the water muttered something to his pal, who nodded and pushed himself off the bonnet where he'd been leaning. They performed a laconic little ritual of parting.

'I can drive you,' the water-giver said, turning back to Freya.

'That's awfully kind,' she said quickly, which he answered with a soundless chuckle and threw her suitcase onto the back seat of the jeep. Without a word he opened the passenger door for her to climb in. Replacing his helmet he

153

got in and drummed a little tattoo with his fingers on the wheel. Then, as if remembering the civilities of another time, he extended his hand. His name was Richard Caplan, a first lieutenant who'd been stationed at Nuremberg since the Allied forces had taken the city in the final month of the war.

'I've just seen it from the plane,' said Freya. 'There didn't seem to be much of it left.'

Caplan nodded slowly. 'We bombed that place and then some. January '45. I guess three-quarters of the city got wiped right there.' Even after that, he added, the fighting had been street by street, and at times house by house.

They were driving through flat countryside, all but deserted. An occasional convoy rumbled past them. When he took his helmet off again Freya made a sidelong study of him; she was fascinated by the bullet-shaped outline of his head, the scalp shaved so close he wore merely the rumour of a haircut. His ears seemed tiny against the slabbed skull. The tendons in his neck stood out, and his jaw worked a piece of gum with stoical indifference. Yet when he turned out of profile his face, far from brutish, contained almost a schoolboy delicacy, with a ridge of freckles across his nose and a dimple at his chin. He asked her questions – where she was from, what she was doing in Germany – and listened carefully to her answers, though offered no comment of his own. She had an idea that in civilian life he had been well mannered.

On the horizon she spied a small white-walled castle, fussily gabled and turreted, set on rising ground and girded with mature trees.

'What's that place?' she said, pointing.

'Where you're headed. That's the schloss.'

Freya blinked her surprise. It looked like a palace out of a Grimm fairy tale. As the jeep turned down a drive into a shrub-lined park Caplan turned to her, shaking his head.

154

'This is where the grounds start – can you believe it?' The schloss was still at least a mile in the distance. As the grandeur of the place bore down on them Freya wondered aloud at the wealth that could have financed its construction.

Caplan said, 'A guy told me the family owned the biggest pencil factory in Germany.'

Freya replied, after a pause, 'I never knew there was that much money in pencils.'

'Me neither.'

Up close, the Schloss Vogelsong was almost grotesque in its extravagance, a fantasy of turret windows, heraldic arches and flyaway spires. It was the sort of building a megalomaniac opera producer might have conceived in a dream, and laughed about on waking. Caplan parked the jeep and, perhaps out of curiosity, followed her into the marbled entrance hall. A grand staircase spiralled upwards, echoing the clamour of voices within; but those voices didn't belong to the schloss's usual guests, corseted ladies with their pet dogs and corpulent gentlemen who talked of nothing but money and hunting. Now it was home to journalists whose instinctive reaction would be to scoff. They stood about in huddles, some in urgent converse, others in casual groupings redolent of a cocktail party. Smoking seemed to be their competitive sport.

The lieutenant, by way of taking his leave, pointed out a makeshift sign that read REGISTRATION. Freya wondered if she could engage him to drive her into Nuremberg one day, but thought better of it: he might be offended by the presumption.

'Thanks for the lift,' she said.

'Glad to help,' Caplan replied, and gave a little mock bow that was his first and last indication of a sense of humour. Then he said, 'So long,' and turned back out of the entrance hall. As she watched him go she felt a stabbing regret that she hadn't asked him the extra favour. The vaulted corridor down which she stepped would not have been out of place in a national art gallery. Arriving at the office for registration she presented her passport, visa and letters of transit. She asked the clerk behind the desk whether the place was always this busy.

'Oh, this is only a quarter-full,' said the clerk. 'The rest of them are at the courthouse. They finish at five.'

She was handed a pass and a key to the women's quarters. This was not the schloss itself but a large Victorian villa in the grounds, which she found at the end of a winding gravel path. The caretaker was a local hausfrau who may have been any age between fifty and eighty. Having inspected her pass, she took her up to the main bedroom, which was now a dormitory: camp beds had been squeezed into every available space. The woman shook her head and explained in broken English that there was no room. Freya replied that she absolutely must have a bed, and held the woman's gaze until she appeared to capitulate: on the next floor, she was shown a smaller room holding six cots, all recently slept in. An exhausted mattress lay in one corner, and from somewhere the woman found unused linen, indicating that this would be her resting place. She went off, muttering to herself in German.

The warmth in the room oppressed her, and she opened a window. It overlooked an orchard and, beyond that, a forest of pines. She surveyed her cramped quarters: even at Plymouth she had always had her own bed. Heaped ashtrays, suitcases flung open, a frowsy smell of bodies. There was something sad about the way a sudden influx of strangers could transform elegance into slovenliness. She made a little tour of the building, and found that every room, without exception, was crammed to bursting with travel cases, clothes, cameras, newspapers. In a bedroom along the corridor from her own she saw a young woman sitting cross-legged on a bed, furiously clattering away at a

156

typewriter. She lifted her head on sensing Freya's presence, smiled distractedly, and bent again to the keys.

At five o'clock she walked back to the schloss and came across, in its cavernous recesses, exactly the thing she was looking for. She might have known that no gathering of journalists would have countenanced digs that didn't include a bar. It was already filling up. She had brought a book to occupy her during the wait, *Pavilions of Smoke*, an early collection of Jessica Vaux's essays she hadn't read before. The stock photograph of the author, reproduced opposite the title page, had always fascinated Freya. It showed Vaux in her mid-thirties, a dark-haired woman whose uptilted gaze seemed of a piece with the stern, unyielding tenor of her prose.

The bar, run by Americans, was bountifully stocked, and she had just ordered a Martini when Stephen appeared in the doorway. He was wearing one of his sober navy suits from Huntsman, with a thin black tie. His tired face creased into a smile on seeing her.

'I could do with one of those,' he said, nodding at her drink and planting a kiss on her cheek. 'When did you arrive?'

'Oh, a few hours ago. And there was nearly no room at the inn. I've got a scrubby old mattress in a room with six others.'

'It's the trial of the century. Half the world's press are here.' He gestured at the high corniced ceiling. 'Quite a place, isn't it?'

She nodded. 'You look like you've come from a funeral.'

'It's rather like one – a funeral they don't know how to end. Odd thing is, everybody in that courtroom seems bored to extinction, the judges, the lawyers, the guards, the interpreters – even the defendants, if ghosts can look bored. Really, the trial's dragged on for so long you can actually see people yawning through it.'

Freya made an exclamation of disgust. 'How *dare* anyone be bored?'

'They've been through the evidence, mountains of it. Now the lawyers are having their turn, which means a great deal of nitpicking. Some argue that the court has no legal validity – that's Goering's line.'

Stephen had completed a few sketches, which he showed to her. They were variations on the Nazi hierarchy seated in two rows, some of them slumped, faces turned away, some staring dead ahead. Freya leafed through them, and shook her head. 'They all look so . . . insignificant.'

He nodded agreement. 'You should see them in the flesh.'

'What are the chances of you getting me into the court-room?'

'Non-existent. I told you that in London. You'd never get past the security.'

Freya paused, brooding. 'So . . . was she there?'

'It's a very full gallery. And to be honest, I'm not sure I'd recognise her.'

She stared at him in disbelief. His vagueness was some-times unfathomable. She opened her copy of *Pavilions of Smoke* to the page with the photographic plate and held it out for his inspection. He squinted at it for a moment.

'Ah . . . I did wonder. The hair's gone grey, but yes – she's been there.'

'Has she got a room here, too?'

'I haven't seen her around. She may have rented some-where.'

That would be just like her, Freya thought, to keep herself apart from the press camp. The woman had spent her whole life going it alone, shunning friend and foe alike. But here she was, in Nuremberg, and Freya was damned if she were to be thrown off the scent now. She considered her options. If Jessica Vaux wasn't staying at the Schloss Vogelsong, and her lodgings couldn't be discovered, the only thing for it would be to intercept her outside the courthouse and positively demand her attention.

Stephen, frowning, said, 'So you squared all this with the college?'

'They were fine. My tutor gave me an exeat.'

'Decent of them, to let you go like that.'

Freya nodded. Her father's vagueness could also be played to advantage. If he was willing to believe that the college would give her time off to travel abroad, just before her exams, she wasn't about to disabuse him. Tomorrow she would accompany him to the city's Palace of Justice, and prepare herself to waylay Jessica Vaux. Such a plan showed initiative, she thought, something that would appeal to the writer's maverick personality. And yet it also smacked of desperation, like a stage-door Johnny waiting to pounce on a famous actress. She might just as easily tell her, in the words of Jimmy Erskine, to piss off, and nobody would blame her.

The next day, a Tuesday, she was back in uniform and on one of the buses that took the journalists into town each morning. The Palace of Justice, with its imposing multi-windowed facade, had been one of the few public buildings in Nuremberg to have survived the Allied bombing. Up the steps swarmed the functionaries, the gowned judges, secretaries, interpreters, lawyers, soldiers, journalists, all overseen by the unsmiling guards, their faces harassed with boredom. Freya found that she was permitted to enter these vast municipal precincts and mill about with other interested parties in the antechambers and corridors. But, just as Stephen had warned her, there was to be no admittance to the sanctum of the courtroom without a pass.

Wednesday and Thursday followed the same pattern. She got off the bus with Stephen, stationed herself in the palace forecourt and searched the incoming crowds for a glimpse

159

of Jessica Vaux, without success. Returning to the schloss, she occupied the daytime with revising Chaucer and reading *The Allegory of Love* until Stephen returned in the evening. Worryingly, he had not seen Jessica Vaux in court all week. On the Friday morning Freya got to her waiting post an hour earlier than usual, reasoning that her quarry might be timing her arrival to avoid the crush. But once again there was no sign of her. Rather than mope all day she decided to explore, catching one of the shabby streetcars that took her into the heart of the old town. From the air the bombed streets had appeared uninhabited, scoured of life. But once off the tram she encountered little pockets of activity, women trundling prams laden with a few pathetic possessions, grey-faced pensioners shuffling along broken cobbled roads, or standing in doorways of blackened shops. There was nothing to buy, anywhere, though there was fuel to scavenge: in an alleyway two young women were breaking up rotten window frames for firewood.

People stood watching her as she continued along the streets; they were perhaps wondering what she had come for. She felt set apart from them, physically, a healthful alien among hollow-eyed spectres – an emissary from the land of the living. Black skeletons of trees peered down on her. What *was* she doing here? In the distance she spotted a church with a twisted spire, its stained glass mostly holed, and she started towards it. Mounds of rubble blocked the way. Her shoes weren't quite up to the task, and she kept slipping on the jagged tumble of pulverised brick and masonry. She soon became aware of a terrible stench rising from the ground, a mixture of disinfectant and something else just below it. She took out her handkerchief and wrapped it around her mouth and nose, like a cattle-rustler in a Western. But the putrid reek had already permeated her nostrils. She gagged a couple of times, and kept clambering, testing for footholds among the chaotic ranges of debris. Perseverance carried her back to level ground, and thence to the bombed-out church.

She walked around the side to its doorless porch, and stepped through onto a carpet of cinders, brick dust and brittle leaves. A solemn stillness held amid the dereliction. The wide nave had been denuded of pews – more fire-wood? – while the altar and chancel had likewise lost most of their ornamentation. The vaulted roof showed patches of daylight here and there, and a pigeon circled in a frantic flurry on sensing the intruder below. The plaster walls were streaked black where rainwater had seeped in. The tiled floor crunched with every step she took. Turning up an aisle she saw, part hidden beneath fallen brick, a devotional portrait of a saint. Its frame was intact, but the cloudy glass had been cracked to smithereens. She picked it up and shook out the glinting shards; it wasn't even a painting, just a print, but the face of the saint, or whatever he was, reminded her of the picture of Francis de Sales Nancy kept on her mantelpiece. The imploring upward gaze transfixed her: it was a look that asked, humbly, not to be ignored.

The place was dank and rotting. At the end of the aisle a door led into a side chapel; on entering she reared back in surprise, for slumped on a stone bench (one that couldn't be broken up) was a man in a long greatcoat, dozing. Around him were strewn a few tokens of homeliness – a horse blanket, a tiny oil stove, a battered cushion. Raising himself slightly, he smiled a sort of greeting towards her. He dipped into his coat pocket to locate a pair of wire-rimmed spectacles, and put them on. He stared at her for a moment, and said something in German; Freya shrugged in apology.

'*Amerikanische?*'

She lowered the handkerchief muffling her mouth. 'English.'

'Ah!' he said, with a rueful laugh. 'This being a house of God I will not say "Welcome to my home", for you would think me presumptuous – or mad! But it is my – what do you say? – *dwelling place*, at present. Please . . .'

He beckoned her forward. He was perhaps in his forties, somewhere around her father's age. His refinement of speech was at odds with his dishevelled appearance: his hair and beard were matted, and the sheen of his coat, she could see on drawing closer, was almost iridescent with layers of grime. Intelligent curiosity danced in his eyes. He introduced himself as Rainer, and asked her about the uniform she wore. She told him, explaining that she had come to Nuremberg with her father, on official business at the Palace of Justice.

'The trial, of course . . . The final reckoning for Hitler's henchmen! And do you think in these circumstances that "justice" will be served?'

'I should hope so,' said Freya. 'It would be a shocking waste of time if not.'

Rainer absorbed her reply with an abstracted nod, as though the question didn't really concern him, and returned his gaze to her. He wanted to know about London; he had once had a week there with his wife. '*Goodbye Piccadilly, Farewell Leicester Square!* I remember we sang it.' He whistled a few bars, and laughed to himself. Then, softly, 'By chance do you have a cigarette?'

Freya produced her pack of Chesterfields, and shook out two, one for him and one for her. When she lit a match he briefly cupped his hands around hers to catch the flame. He sank back and voluptuously inhaled a lungful of tobacco. Up close she could see his face was quite handsome beneath the unkempt beard; his eyes were a disconcerting greyish blue. After some moments of companionable smoking she asked him how he had come to speak such immaculate English. He had been a teacher before the war, he explained, at a school not far from this church. His wife had been a teacher also; she had been killed in their home during an

162

air raid. After being conscripted into the vast war machine he had been sent to fight at the Eastern front, where he experienced 'many horrible things'.

'Most of my comrades did not return to Germany. But luck was with me. I was spared!'

Freya looked at his forlorn surroundings. His wife was dead; his home blown to atoms; his city in ruins. His own survival notwithstanding Rainer didn't appear to have enjoyed a great deal of luck. And yet this refusal to lament his fate moved her. If only she could find words of consolation.

'Would you like to teach again?' she asked suddenly. 'Surely the country needs people like you?'

Rainer made a soundless rocking motion: ironic laughter, she guessed. 'People like you! You mean derelict and forgotten? I am sorry for the generation coming after us. Look at what they inherit – a country dragged into the abyss, a race of people we tried to destroy, a legacy of shame that will not be absolved in, I don't know – a thousand years. Tell me, what might I presume to teach children after all that has happened?'

She looked at him, facing down his despair. 'That it mustn't happen again?'

He gazed off into the distance. 'Yes. Perhaps that.'

'You don't sound very convinced.'

'Ha. Those men in the dock today – our masters – will be found guilty and hanged. Of course! But they are a mere speck in the colossal crime of a nation. They gave the German people a licence to pursue their wildest instincts, their grossest appetites. And the people took it. They hunted down their enemies like wolves and tore them to pieces. Do you believe that by ridding the earth of these men the Fatherland will be created anew, washed clean of its sins? Execute twenty men, fifty – five hundred! – it will not cure a country.'

163

There was a ferocious gleam in his eyes that Freya shrank from. His voice, level and precise to begin, had descended to a growl. His mouth quivered from the vehemence. She said, after a pause, 'Maybe there are more people like yourself than you know. If good men do nothing –'

'– evil will reign. *Ach.* The verdict on us is already passed, it's written. *Schuldig.*'

On pronouncing the word, whatever it meant, he leaned his head back against the wall. He suddenly looked exhausted, and ill. She thought about the empty shops, and wondered if he had eaten anything recently. Opening the bag slung on her shoulder she took out a bar of chocolate she had bought that morning in the schloss. 'Will you have this – ?'

Rainer observed it with indifference. She placed it on the stone bench, like an offering at an altar. Then she remembered Caplan telling her that the only currency of any use here was cigarettes. She felt for the packet of Chesterfields, just over half full, and put them down next to the chocolate. He was still looking away, still not speaking.

'Well . . . goodbye, then,' she said, and, on an impulse, held out her hand. She didn't really want to touch him, he looked so dirty, but she felt that this odd encounter needed something final, a gesture of amity between strangers – or was it between victor and vanquished? Having seen him ignore the chocolate and cigarettes she was prepared for him to ignore this, too. Instead, he rose to his feet and reached for her hand, enclosing it with his own, which was gritty and calloused. He shook it with solemn deliberation, holding her gaze. Then, to her surprise, he tightened his grip and pulled her hand quite roughly to his cheek, to his mouth. She tried to pull away, but he held tight, her hand clamped to his lips. He had closed his eyes, inhaling the scent of her flesh. She tensed herself, ready to fight him. He looked frail and enervated, but she also sensed in his grip

164

an animal desperation – a last crazed will to overpower and possess.

His breath was hot against her hand, his eyes still closed, in a world of his own. He wasn't letting go of her. The intense expression on his face reminded her of the time she had been at Mass with Nancy and watched people at prayer, hands clasped to their mouth; a look of silent petition. She counted to ten, and said, 'Rainer.'

After a moment he opened his eyes, like a man woken from sleep. She had spoken his name in a way that asked him to release her. Slowly, he relaxed his grip, and she pulled away. He nodded, as if at something mysteriously understood. Freya took a step backwards, raising her hand in silent farewell. His eyes seemed to droop a moment, and he said, very quietly, '*Auf Wiedersehen.*'

Outside the ruined church, she tied the handkerchief, highwayman-style, across her face, and started back over the mounds of stinking rubble.

At the schloss that evening Freya found Stephen in the bar. The news from him was not good – he had been in court all day and seen nothing of Jessica Vaux. He had asked a couple of journalist friends about her, but they didn't know where she had got to either. By now Freya was becoming resigned. Five days gone and she had not managed even a sighting of the woman. She would have to return to Oxford this weekend in time for the start of her exams on Monday. The writer's legendary elusiveness had defeated her.

As the bar began to fill up she left Stephen in the company of his colleagues. The evening was still light, and a walk in the grounds of the schloss might drive off the dismal mood that had settled on her since her venture into the old town. Here was bucolic calm, a world away from the mangled ashen disorder of this morning. Long shadows projected from the trees that lined the estate's multiple pathways, and the decorous sloping parkland called her onwards. She had been strolling for a quarter of an hour or so when she came across a greenhouse, as large as any she had visited at Kew. Its domed roof glinted under the setting sun. On trying the door she found it unlocked, and stepped inside. A riot of foliage confronted her, and a flagged path which curved in opposite directions. She took the left-hand fork, presuming that it would lead her in a circuit back to the entrance. A bitter dusty odour of vegetation and garden mulch pervaded the air. A parked wheelbarrow and watering can indicated recent efforts of maintenance.

Turning another corner she found herself in a long nursery garden of potted plants. At the far end another visitor, a lady, was keenly examining rows of vivid white-petalled flowers; she was so absorbed in her inspection that Freya was nearly alongside her before she noticed she wasn't alone. In the seconds it took her to recognise the woman Freya experienced a shock of disbelief.

The woman, surprised by her presence, locked eyes with her. She was fiftyish, silver-haired, straight-backed, with eyes that glared a gelid blue – 'the glare of the Gorgon', as someone had once described it.

Freya heard herself say, 'Oh – you're Jessica Vaux, aren't you?'

'Who are you?' she replied sharply. Her voice, rasped by cigarettes, was patrician, metallic and unfriendly. Freya introduced herself, adding that she was here visiting her father while he was on assignment. When she mentioned Stephen's name Jessica gave a quick nod of recognition.

'The painter. Somebody told me he was here.' She took in Freya's uniform at a glance. 'So you're in the Wrens.'

'I was. I've since gone up to Oxford.'

Jessica nodded, then turned back to the plants she had been studying. 'Look at these wonderful things – lilies, climbing roses, and here, these beautiful cyclamens. What

I'd like to know is – in a city where they can barely feed themselves how can anyone manage to grow such flowers?' She pronounced this last word *flarze*. 'Native resilience, I suppose,' she murmured, answering her own question.

Freya kept a respectful silence until the lady seemed content with her study. Then she said, 'I thought I might see you at the Palace of Justice – I know you're reporting for the *Tribune*.'

'I've been indisposed all week – a wretched cold. You've been at the trial?'

'No. To be honest, I've only come to see you.'

'What do you mean?' she said, frowning with suspicion.

Freya guessed that the lady was not susceptible to flattery or exaggerated deference; but there were still forms to be observed, and a due must be paid to experience. Jessica Vaux listened with sceptical amusement. She did not appear impressed by Freya's quixotic journey, nor by absenting herself from college.

'Doesn't say much for the supervision provided at Oggsford nowadays.'

'Well, I wasn't quite truthful with them about my reasons.'

Jessica scrutinised her for a moment, then gave a little pout of regret. 'I can't help you, I'm afraid. I stopped giving interviews about ten *yairze* ago when some idiot journalist printed the most outrageous lies about me. I sued his newspaper and won, but the satisfaction was diminished by dint of the money I lost in defending myself and the time I wasted in court doing so. I would sooner submit to the bastinado than go through that again.'

'I've no inclination to publish lies about you. I just want to nudge the public's memory, given the war and how long you've been out of the country.'

'I don't believe the public has forgotten me,' she said haughtily.

'I'm sure they haven't. Perhaps I should say, I'd like to reintroduce you, like – I don't know – royalty returning from exile.'

'Oh, you're very kind, my dear,' she said, smiling at this blandishment, 'and I appreciate your coming all this way. But I really *can't* oblige you. My interests, you see, have always been outward-looking – countries, wars, people, places. I've never wanted to be part of the story I was telling. Some of my colleagues can't understand it, but I'm quite content with just my byline – that, and the *cheque*.'

Freya cast around for a more persuasive argument, but she could tell from her tone of casual command that Jessica Vaux wasn't going to yield: she didn't want to, and she didn't have to. She was a woman who knew her own mind, which was something enviable in itself. They walked the remainder of the circular path, pausing here and there when Jessica, a keen plantswoman, wished to inspect some bit of flora. She talked about Paris, where she'd lived with her son prior to the war, and about her peripatetic life thereafter; she had lived on the coast of Cornwall, with brief stops in Brighton and the Isle of Wight, before settling in Lisbon, her home for the last few years ('I prefer places on the edge of things'). Her son, now grown, had gone to live in London, where she herself was now minded to return.

'I was there for a few weeks last year. It looked awf'ly knocked about.'

'It still does,' said Freya. 'Though look what we did to this place . . .' Her mind's eye had lingered on her excursion to the old town this morning, the charred landscape, the skeletal trees, the hollow-cheeked denizens. The terrible despair in Rainer's voice. She suddenly turned to Jessica. 'I wonder – do you know the word *schuldig*?'

'Of course. It means "guilty". Why do you ask?'

'Oh, I was just wandering about the old town today and met a man – a soldier, more or less destitute. He said that

Germany could not atone for its shame in a thousand years. His English was excellent, but then he used that one word at the end, and I didn't know what he meant.'

Jessica was staring at her in astonishment. 'Do you mean to say you went into the old town *on your own*?'

'I didn't have anyone else to go with.'

'My dear . . . that was most foolhardy of you. Or perhaps brave. The place is swarming with black marketeers and scavengers. The Americans won't go in without protection. This soldier you met, he might easily have –'

'Yes, there was one moment I thought I might be in trouble . . .' She described Rainer's grabbing her hand and pressing it to his mouth. In recollection the gesture had only pathos in it, but Jessica looked askance.

'I imagine he'd have liked to chew it off! You do know they're starving, don't you?'

They had just emerged from the greenhouse into the cool of the evening. The shadows had lengthened since they had encountered one another inside. They began heading back towards the schloss. The clipped hauteur of the lady's earlier manner had dissolved, and the harsh edge had come off her voice. They talked about Oxford, and journalism. Freya didn't flatter herself that Jessica's interest in her was unique; but what did strike her as wonderful was that the so-called grande dame behaved as if they were two fellow writers. It didn't matter to her that Freya was a nobody. In refusing to condescend she paid her the best compliment of all.

'So you met Jimmy Erskine,' Jessica said with a grin. 'How is the old boy?'

'Pretty well, I think. He spoke very admiringly of you. Is it true you keep a gun under your pillow?'

'It has been known,' she said drily.

They had reached the forecourt of the schloss. Freya would have liked to talk on, but Jessica had already informed her she was due to have dinner that evening with 'high-ups' from the British delegation a few miles away – she had been staying there, in fact, rather than mucking in with the other journalists.

'I suppose you think I'm being rather grand,' she said.

Freya shook her head. 'No, not really. You need to work, and you like your own company. It's probably what I'd do, to be honest.'

Some of the old beadiness had returned to Jessica's appraising look. 'Freya Wyley. You're a quick study, aren't you?'

'Am I?' said Freya with a half-laugh.

'Look, I'm away for the weekend, but I'll be back Sunday evening. If you're still here I'll meet you for dinner and, well – maybe you can get a piece out of it. What d'you think?'

Freya, dizzied with shock, took a moment to steady herself, and her voice. 'I'll still be here.'

I I

Freya was at a refectory table sipping the last of a bitter Bavarian coffee. It was now Wednesday morning – Jessica had persuaded her to stay on. Around her journalists were finishing breakfast prior to departing for the trial's morning session. She was terribly hung-over. She really hadn't felt this rough since the morning after VE Day when she and Nancy had got stinko.

She braced herself at the sight of her father entering the room and looking about in agitated distraction. She knew what was coming. Stephen planted himself squarely in front of her.

'Freya, I have just had the most – I'm in a state of shock. Please tell me what the hell's going on.'

She looked up and smiled. 'And good morning to you, Dad!'

'I'm not joking with you,' he said. 'I've just had an emergency telephone call put through to me – *from your mother*. She's been frantic with worry, crying. Your college tutor telephoned her at home yesterday enquiring after your whereabouts – some cock and bull about you taking the week off to look after her while she "convalesced". Then she wanted to know why you hadn't turned up for your exams! Of course poor Cora had no idea what they were talking about – and frankly, nor do I.'

171

'All right, calm down –'

'No, I won't bloody calm down,' Stephen cut in, furious. 'You just lied to me – to us. D'you think I would have agreed to let you come here if I'd known you were due to sit exams this week?'

'Of course not. But it was the opportunity of my life and I had to take it, even if it meant lying to you. I'm sorry, Dad, I understand why you're angry, but if I hadn't done this I knew I'd regret it forever.'

Stephen was staring off, the shake of his head slowing from rage to regret. 'Shameful of you to use your mother like that. Can you imagine how upset she was, realising that nobody knew where the hell you were? Why would you put her through that?'

'You *know* why, I've just told you. I've managed to get an interview with a writer who hasn't talked to the press in over ten years –'

'And what about Somerville? You know they could send you down for this.'

'I thought it was a risk worth taking.'

Stephen, sinking onto the bench along from her, was silent. Presently, he said, 'I don't understand you. Really. Quite apart from the disrespect to your tutors, I don't understand why you would chuck it all in – an education at a great university, in a beautiful city – on the chance that you might, *might*, get a break in newspapers. I mean, you could try for that anyway in two years' time. What's the hurry?'

Freya studied the dregs of her coffee cup. 'I don't know. I never felt sure about Oxford in the first place. The war, the Wrens – it felt like I had a life and then I put it on hold to do something that didn't really matter. I don't care about essays and Anglo-Saxon and the fucking *Faerie Queene*. The only thing I've done that seems like an achievement is that first piece I wrote for *Cherwell*. I'm sorry if that disappoints you . . .'

He looked at her now. 'It's your life, Freya, not mine, and I know you'll go your own way no matter what. But it pains me that you could show such a disregard for others. You've always made a thing about being honest, and yet you've duped the people who've always loved and trusted you.'

'Dad, I can't –'

'I don't want to talk about it any more,' he said, standing up. 'I've got work to do. You should telephone your mother.'

She watched him walk away.

The court had just adjourned for lunch as she arrived. Queues had formed at the row of telephone booths installed for the press, and white-helmeted military policemen drifted about like inmates in a prison yard. Robed prosecutors sauntered in twos and threes around the vast entrance hall. Translators, stenographers, court officials likewise stretched their legs, seeking distraction, their expressions all seeming to ask the same thing: How much more of this?

Amid the emerging throng she spotted Jessica, who broke off talking to a courtroom colleague and approached. She was wearing a smart gunmetal-blue trouser suit, with a girlish slide in her hair. She betrayed no sign of the previous night's heavy drinking, which confounded Freya.

'So you're going off already?' she said, eyeing the suitcase at Freya's side.

'Yes, I've been, um, called home. The college has been getting anxious about my return.'

'I seem to recall drinking an awful lot last night.'

'We did. I feel a bit deathly.'

Jessica narrowed her eyes. 'May I give you a little advice, my dear? Go easy on that Benzedrine. In fact, stop it altogether. I've seen it ruin people. They used it first as a pick-me-up, like you, and then they found they couldn't do without it.'

Freya didn't think it had been noticed, but very little was lost on this woman. She began to make some vague conceding reply, but Jessica cut her short.

'I want you to promise me. No more.'

Had it been almost anyone else Freya would have taken pleasure in snubbing them. But she sensed she had met her match. 'No more. I promise.'

Jessica responded with a sharp emphatic nod, as if they were shaking hands on it. There was an awkward pause as Freya prepared her farewell. 'I wanted to thank you for being so –'

'No need for that, dear. You can thank me by writing something marvellous – I don't mean about me!' she laughed throatily. 'I mean, something that will enthral your readers, so that they'll want more.'

'I'll try. Really I will.' Then she thought of something and began to rummage in her shoulder bag. 'I wanted you to sign my book . . .'

Jessica shook her head. 'Freya, darling, you *must* have been blotto. I signed it in front of you, last night.' She allowed herself a quick smirk at Freya's confusion, then bent her head to kiss her on the cheek. 'Goodbye, dear. And good luck.'

Freya had by no means forgotten everything from the night before. On the way to the airport, as the fairy-tale spires of the schloss receded in the car's back window, she retraced the events of her last evening. Having wangled dinner with her on the Sunday evening and then a lunch yesterday, Freya didn't want to push her luck by presuming on her interviewee's patience. But Jessica, who was au fait with whatever passed for society in Nuremberg, had then invited her to a party at the Grand Hotel, hosted by an eminent American prosecutor she knew. Freya, a little star-struck, didn't have to be asked twice. The hotel, wearing its pre-war grandeur as sadly as an old lady sporting the jewellery of her youth, seemed startled by the abrupt influx of so many guests, and so much foreign largesse.

She had begun with Martinis. The place was heaving with servicemen, but there was also a contingent of luminaries from the British and American press, many of them in plain awe of Jessica. Some sought her opinion as if she were the Sibyl herself, but she only shrugged and delivered a resonant sentence or two in her throaty drawl. 'Of course the man's a fool,' Freya overheard her say of one well-known lawyer, 'which wouldn't alarm me if he weren't so utterly *sincere*.' Men seemed especially mesmerised by the authority of her voice (women were not expected to hold forth in this arena). Freya mostly listened, though at one stage she felt a distinct thrill when Jessica turned and said, apropos of some matter, 'Perhaps we ought to consult my companion here – what *do* young people think of this?' She had somehow become Jessica Vaux's junior adviser.

One drink led to another as she basked in the reflected glow of celebrity. During a hiatus when briefly separated from Jessica she wandered into the hotel's smaller bar. Someone tapped her on the shoulder.

'It's Freya, right?' said a young well-built officer. 'Richard Caplan.'

She was glad he had saved her from the embarrassment of forgetting his name. They shook hands, and he smiled in a distant way. He seemed more relaxed – more human – than on the day he had driven her to the schloss. 'Can I get you a drink?'

'Sure,' she said, unconsciously slipping into the local vernacular. She stared at the side of his shaved head. His ears looked so delicate, like tiny snails on a slab of rock. 'So this is the place you come when you're off-duty?'

'One of 'em. Parties are pretty good here.'

They settled at the bar over their drinks. The good manners she had discerned on their first encounter were stiff at the edges, like his uniform. He was perhaps a touch wary, or else she was too forward, for he answered questions about himself with a stranger's laconic politeness. Home was a small town in Massachusetts, about two hours from New York. His father had been in the service during the First War; his mother was a schoolteacher. He was the oldest of five, three sisters and a brother.

'Three sisters! You're lucky – I always wanted a sister.'

'Uh-huh?'

'I've got a younger brother, but he's, well, quite odd. I always thought a sister would be like having a best friend, only closer. You know, like Lizzie and Jane in *Pride and Prejudice*.'

Caplan only nodded; the reference had gone over his head. She asked him whether he had any plans after the army, which he thought about for a few moments. One thing he'd been crazy about as a kid (apart from baseball) was painting, he said; he'd taken it up quite seriously just before he enlisted. He wasn't sure if he was any good, but a landscape he'd done had won third place in a local competition.

'My father's a painter,' said Freya. 'He never rated his talent that highly but he's made a very good living out of it.'

'That so?' said Caplan, properly interested at last. 'Is he famous?'

'Hmm . . . he's quite well known in London, as a portrait painter. Stephen Wyley. He's here. I should introduce you.'

Caplan smiled. 'I don't think he'd be interested in anything I've done. It's pretty basic, really. I guess I'll just follow my old man into the business.'

'What does he do?'

'Sells cattle feed,' he said, with a funny-sad resignation that pierced Freya. It was the thought of someone with an artist's temperament but not an artist's talent. Perhaps there were many such. What assurance did she have that she was going to be a writer? Only this: she *would* be one, or die in the effort.

Just then they heard a commotion out in the corridor, a thump of footsteps and raised voices, foreign accents. A negotiation seemed to be in progress; this gave way to the entrance of four young officers in a uniform Freya didn't immediately recognise. She turned to Caplan.

'Russians,' he supplied, studying them from beneath his brow. 'And drunk by the look of 'em.'

Freya stared for a moment. Only one of them was drunk, for certain, and talking too loudly; the others, humouring him, were just drinking. 'Ought they to be here?' she asked sotto voce.

'They've as much right as anyone, I guess. In this place you get to mix, the British, the French, us. But not the Russians. We just – don't have anything to do with 'em.'

They talked for a while longer, and Caplan, glancing at his watch, said the music was scheduled to start. Would she care –

'Would I ever!' said Freya, almost jumping off the bar stool. She hadn't danced for ages. Propelled by drink and the light pressure of Caplan's hand at the small of her back, the evening started to speed up. When they had a break from dancing she introduced him to Jessica, who seemed to approve of his grave American manners. The trouble started when she was returning from a trip to the ladies and found herself waylaid by the roistering Russian officer who'd been in the bar. His fellow officers affected not to notice him. Up close he was square-faced, handsome in a loutish way, with light blond hair feathered by inebriation. Even to Freya he reeked savagely of alcohol.

He asked her, in slurred English, if she would care to dance. Freya excused herself, joking that her dance card was full. The officer, bleary-eyed, plainly didn't comprehend anything she said beyond the implied refusal.

'Why not?' he importuned her.

Seeking a more straightforward reason she said, 'Because I believe you're even drunker than I am.'

'No no no,' he said, wagging his finger and grabbing her arm.

He jostled her forward to the dance floor. She sensed a reckless determination in his grasp even as she tried to break free. One of his comrades called out something – a warning? – but he ignored him, seeming to hear only the beat of the music. He had just started moving her about when a shadow fell between them, and Caplan was prising his hands off her. He moved his head to within inches of the Russian's face, his jaw moving urgently: she couldn't hear his words, she could only tell they weren't friendly. The sight of an American squaring up to their comrade drew the others into a menacing cluster, but Caplan held his ground. As she watched him negotiate she felt grateful: other men might have opted for a show of force, trying to impress her, but Caplan wanted only to defuse the potential unpleasantness. The scene was abruptly concluded on the arrival of two unsmiling military policemen, who hustled the Russians out of the room.

'Thanks,' she said, as he led her out of the knot of onlookers.

He looked at her and shrugged. 'I didn't like him bothering you.'

Even that, his lack of fuss, pleased her. They rejoined Jessica's table, and she immersed herself in the talk and the laughter and the steady supply of drinks. Only when she stood up and the room suddenly tipped sideways did she notice how tight she was. Caplan was looking at her.

'Are you OK?'

She thought she was, but when the room continued to list like the deck of a ship she decided to make for the exit, with Caplan in wary attendance. Once outside she drank in the cool night air, and felt a little better.

'I think I should call it a night,' she said, with a grimace of apology. She had used up her supply of Benzedrine, so there would be no quick antidote to her wooziness. Caplan, nodding, told her to wait at the entrance; he'd collect the motor and drive her back to the schloss.

'You're such a gentleman,' she said with a flirtatious tilt of her head.

'Yeah,' he replied, with a chuckle, 'a regular Mr Darcy.'

Her laughter hid her surprise: she had underestimated him. Riding shotgun in the open-topped jeep she felt the onrushing wind whip against her face, jolting her back to sobriety, or at least a possible imitation of it. Caplan drove quickly down the empty winding roads, casually assured at the wheel, talking more freely now that he was away from the hotel and its constricting pressures to socialise. She sensed he didn't care for parties, that he preferred the company of one or two friends he could be honest with. He had a watchful gravity about him that might shade towards haughtiness; perhaps he *was* a bit like Darcy.

Along the road the tops of old trees shivered and swayed. Looking up she picked out stars glinting from the vast blue-black sky, and felt a sudden leap of exhilaration within her. It didn't matter that she was still drunk; she was seized by an almost electric feeling of her potential, not just of her inchoate talent as a writer but of what she knew to be her force of personality, that unsought gift of bending people to her will. As they drove up the interminable tree-lined avenue, tyres crunching over the gravel, she wondered how it would be to exercise this power on Caplan, who might be expecting her to make a move in any case. Wasn't their chance reunion this evening an indication that fate had

179

planned it for them? By the time he turned the jeep into the darkened forecourt and parked against a shadowing wall she was fully alive to the possibility. Robert need never know, she could hide it from him; but then hadn't she already steeped herself in dissembling and lying? She had deceived Nancy, to her shame; she had deceived her father and the college just to enable this trip to Germany. She must not allow the convenience of lying to overwhelm her.

Caplan had switched off the engine. He was looking across at her, perhaps in hope, she couldn't tell.

'You've been so nice to me,' she said, leaning in to kiss his cheek. The chasteness of it felt unsatisfactory to her, and when he reached out to stop her drawing away and kissed her on the mouth she wasn't surprised. The kiss, dry but prolonged, seemed intended as an overture to something else. The euphoric feeling of just before still lingered, and as he pulled her closer to him she was jolted by a wild spasm of sexual urgency. She could feel the powerful bunched musculature beneath his shirt, and the quickening of his breathing. Why shouldn't they, after all? Caplan muttered something against her neck, which she didn't properly hear.

'I said, we could go somewhere.'

She paused, agonised. Robert would be the easiest of all to dupe – and the easiest to hurt. Which made it imperative that she resisted the temptation. She wondered if thinking about him now, at this moment, rendered her a true romantic; wouldn't a cynic just grab the opportunity when it came along? And yet she *did* want to grab it, she was right in the mood, and so was he.

Caplan blinked, and angled his face downwards. 'You've got someone – at home?'

'I'm afraid so. And I'm not sure I can face lying to him.'

He stared again at her, but she wouldn't meet his eye in case it broke her resolve. It really was that fragile. The silence

180

between them extended, until at last he gave an exasperated groan and shook his head. His tone, when he spoke, was wistful. 'He's a lucky guy.'

She got back to Oxford the following afternoon, having stopped off in London for the night at Stephen's flat. Now that the news of her delinquency was out she saw no reason to hurry. Her mother had been furious with her on the telephone, bemoaning her fright at the college's enquiry coming out of the blue, and her subsequent mortification once it emerged that Freya had led them a dance. 'How on earth did you think you'd get away with it?' she asked, and Freya didn't bother explaining that she almost *had* got away with it – if she had succeeded in meeting Jessica Vaux that first week in Nuremberg instead of chasing shadows she might have achieved her objective without anyone noticing her absence.

At Somerville the ghost of dissipation hung about her rooms. Smeared glasses, loaded ashtrays and empty bottles indicated that Ginny had been entertaining, but there was no sign of her. She was probably out celebrating the end of her exams. On the mantelpiece Stephen's portrait had been knocked askew. As she straightened it she thought of his disgusted scowl the last time they had spoken. She hadn't said goodbye to him before leaving yesterday. Heaving her suitcase onto the bed she began to unpack, before it occurred to her that this might be a short-term stay. Wedged into a side pocket was her copy of *Pavilions of Smoke*, which she took out and opened to the title page. There, in a serene Edwardian hand, was an inscription:

For my fearless inquisitor Freya, who tracked me down!
With my best regards,
Jessica Vaux
Nuremberg, June 1946

She felt that 'best regards' was rather stiff, a bit prim – after all the talking and drinking they'd done had she not earned 'with affection', or even 'love'? Perhaps the sensibility was Edwardian, too; the lady was not born of a demonstrative generation. She did like that 'fearless inquisitor', though.

Down at the lodge she checked her pigeonhole, thinking there might be something from Robert. She had written to him while she was in Nuremberg and had heard nothing back, which was almost certainly due to the chaotic postal service. The only letter awaiting her was from the college principal, summoning her to an interview tomorrow morning.

Restless, she left the lodge and walked down St Giles. Sunlight glinted off the dusty leaves of trees, and the air was muffled with the high sweetish scent of blossom. She knocked at Robert's door in Balliol, without reply. On Broad Street she passed clusters of begowned students, grinning their relief at the end of schools. She thought of her first morning here alone, back in October, and wandered into the covered market as she had then: still the same smell of hanging meat and sawdust. Brown's cafe was packed, but she found a table at Fuller's on the Cornmarket. The end-of-term mood around the place, and her recent truancy in Germany, had a dislocating effect. She could find no purchase on Oxford's cliquish insularity; there was at its centre something smug and unyielding that repelled her.

She had been staring into the middle distance so intently that she failed to notice the figure ghosting up to her table.

'My dear, look at you! I haven't seen such expressive melancholy on a face since Falconetti's Joan of Arc.'

Freya smiled up at Nat Fane. 'That's funny, I was just trying to think of the very few things I'd miss about this place, and there you are.'

'Madam, your servant,' he replied, taking a seat. He was wearing a cornflower-blue summer suit, co-respondent

182

shoes and a floppy bow tie of cream and brown. 'But this alarms me – are you intending to quit our lovely groves?'

'Perhaps. I may have no choice.' She told him the story of her German adventure and its likely consequences. It sounded in her retelling hardly plausible. Nat listened with an expression of amusement and mingled envy, as though he wished he'd thought of doing it himself.

'My word. Chivvying out Jessica Vaux – in Nuremberg! That's a feather in your cap – an entire Apache headdress, one might say.'

'Actually, I have you to thank, for introducing me to old Erskine that night. It was he who told me she was going to be there, and then I sort of pestered him to help me.'

Nat squinted at her. 'Do you really think he will?'

'Well, I did – up until this moment,' said Freya dubiously.

'Oh, I'm sure you're right – it's just, from what I know of Jimmy he's quite a tricky character . . .'

Takes one to know one, thought Freya. She wondered if Nat was deliberately trying to unsettle her. 'Maybe I've been naive. I'll find out soon enough.'

Nat's expression had changed. It was the appraising, foxy look he had fastened on her the first time they met. She stared back at him, frowning. 'Is there something on your mind?'

'There is *always* something on my mind,' he said, raising his eyebrows. 'Such a pity you were never inclined to the stage! Girls like you aren't so common any more. You know, I've a strong intuition you will one day make someone properly unhappy.'

'I'm sorry about that,' she replied. 'Are you going to be in London for the summer?'

'I am indeed. I'm putting on another play at a theatre in Hampstead. You must come along. But wait – the college won't run you out of town, will they?'

'I honestly don't know. I think they're pretty angry with me.'

Nat's face darkened. 'Dear, dear Freya. What should we do without you?'

'"Think, and die,"' she said, and they both laughed.

'Well, *before* we do that, you must come to the Union tonight – end-of-term bash. I'll put your name on the list.'

She wrinkled her nose in demur, but when he started to plead she shrugged her assent. It surprised her to realise that she might even matter to him.

She was wearing one of the summer dresses that had not been crushed in the packing of her suitcase. The string of tiny pearls she fixed around her neck had once belonged to Stephen's mother – her Jewish grandmother. It was the only bit of jewellery she owned of anything more than sentimental value. She put a packet of Chesterfields in her pocket and opened her medicine box. To arm herself with Benzedrine prior to stepping out for a night had become second nature. She wondered if they really were as addictive as Jessica had said; she was almost tempted to swallow a couple in defiance. But no – that was a promise she must keep.

She could hear the noise from the party before she had even entered the Union. Upstairs she found herself in a dense current of people surging around the main bar. A jazz band was tootling through 'Stompin' at the Savoy', hardly in the Benny Goodman class, but not bad. She spotted Nat at a table, entertaining his coterie of disciples. He was entwined with a girl of doll-like prettiness; they looked good together, but she could tell from the doll's adoring glances that Nat wouldn't suffer her for long. Freya thought of going over, and stopped herself. This afternoon he had begged her to come, and now they would probably not exchange a word. But she didn't mind. Withdrawing into the crush she wandered around, until a friendly bespectacled face loomed in the distance, hailing her.

'Freya! Haven't seen you in ages.' It was Charlie Tremayne, Robert's friend, sweatily bedraggled from his exertions on the dance floor. She had forgotten he was a jazz nut.

'Hullo. Rather good, aren't they?' she said, nodding in the band's direction.

'Smashing! I thought I was getting somewhere with a young lady a moment ago, but she's disappeared.' He pulled a comical woebegone face. If he weren't so short she would have offered to dance with him herself. Instead, she straightened his tie which had been pulled wildly askew.

'Have you seen Robert at all?' she asked him. 'I've been away.'

Charlie hesitated a moment, then said, 'Now and then. We don't knock around much any more. To tell the truth, I was pretty fed up with the way he treated Nancy.'

'You mean . . .'

'Well, I think he played her along, and all the time he was seeing some other girl.'

'Did Nancy tell you this?'

'Some of it. She didn't say who the girl was – if she even knew.'

Freya swallowed hard. 'Have you – any idea who she is?'

Charlie shook his head. 'I imagine he'll bring her along here tonight. But surely you've heard all about it from Nancy?'

'Like I said, I've been away . . .'

He gave her a rueful look. 'It was awkward, you know, with me being rather sweet on her. I stopped calling, once I realised there was no chance.'

She squeezed his hand in sympathy. 'I'm sorry, Charlie. You'd have been a good thing for Nancy, I'm sure.'

'That makes me sound like medicine. I'm afraid we don't fall for people because they're "good for us", do we? Attraction is just a thing that happens, like the weather. You can't force yourself to feel something.'

She only nodded, not trusting herself to speak. Charlie, oblivious to her guilty mood, suggested they have a drink. As they waited at the bar he said, 'How did your exams go?'

'They didn't,' she replied with a half-laugh.

'Oh dear. You flunked them?'

'No, no, I mean – I didn't show up for them.'

Charlie looked aghast. 'What?'

'It's a long story. Entirely my own fault. I'm due at the principal's office, eight thirty tomorrow morning.'

'Crikey. Bad luck. Last cigarette and a blindfold!' He laughed, but then seemed to regret his levity. 'Sorry, I didn't mean –'

'It's all right. They can do what they like.'

He stared at her for a moment. 'You know, if it were anyone else I'd worry for them. But you – you're quite unafraid. I remember Robert saying as much the night we first met, at that party. "A real hard case" – that's what he called you.'

'Did he?' The thought made her smile. Charlie handed her a gin, and they clinked glasses together.

'Talk of the devil,' he said, and she followed his eyeline across the room to where Robert had just appeared. After what they'd been talking about Freya didn't relish the timing of this reunion: it would become apparent to Charlie that the girl Robert had been seeing behind Nancy's back was herself. Too late, he was waving him forward in invitation. But as Robert approached through the press of bodies she became aware of someone, a girl, trailing in his wake; she was young, with blondish-brown hair and a delicately featured face. Robert's half-embarrassed expression, and the girl's proprietary closeness to him, conveyed the way things stood a split second before Freya grasped the inconceivable truth of it for herself. She felt her whole body go into a sudden tremble.

'We were just talking about you,' said Charlie, unaware of the awkwardness he had just initiated.

'Really?' said Robert, not catching Freya's eye. It was impossible to go on without an introduction, and equally impossible that Robert would make one. Freya turned to the girl. 'I don't think we've met . . .'

At that, Robert seemed to collect himself. 'This is Cressida – my friends Charlie and Freya.' *Friends*, then. The girl gave a twitch of a smile and nestled a little closer against Robert, who had taken on the unnatural expression of someone who had deliberately turned his face from a traffic accident.

Freya said to the girl – Cressida – 'Have you two known one another for long?'

'Oh, no, just a few days.'

Robert, aiming for safer ground, said to Freya, 'I gather you've been away.'

'Yes,' she replied. 'Just a few days, as a matter of fact.' The ironic echo could not be mistaken, though only Robert knew its meaning.

'You missed schools, didn't you?' he said.

'I was in Germany. I wrote to you. Did you not get my letter?'

Robert shook his head. 'Why didn't you tell me you were going?'

She shrugged, and fixed him with a sceptical look. 'Would it have made any difference?'

Charlie had picked up the tension crackling between them, but showed no sign of guessing its cause. 'Freya's up before the beak first thing tomorrow morning.'

'Which is why I hope you'll excuse me. I'm going to have an early night,' she said, swallowing the remainder of her gin. She was still trembling. She had to leave now or else risk having a fight. Her 'goodnight' was cursory, and directed mainly at Charlie.

She was out of the building and onto the street, vituperative curses spilling mutely off her tongue. Of all the treacherous *fuckers*! After all the begging and cajoling he'd done, the bastard had just thrown her over. 'Don't make me regret this,' she'd said to him that day, knowing that a showdown with Nancy would be unavoidable. This was how he repaid her. Oh, the cold-hearted, viperous fiend . . .

Behind her she heard footsteps, close behind her, and she kept going. If the fiend tried to stop her, if he *laid a finger* on her, she would punch him so hard she'd break his jaw. She tensed as the footsteps caught up with hers, and felt her fist closing in readiness. He was going to get the fright of his life – She half turned, and a man walked past her, hurrying on. He wasn't Robert; he wasn't anyone. She stopped, and felt her own agitated breathing. Her jaw was clenched, her heart drumming fast, but there was nothing and nobody to vent herself against. The trace of something uncompleted, of a scene unplayed, lingered in her body hours later. Robert had not come after her. She was alone on the street.

12

The morning was overcast, and a fine drizzle was already spotting the pavement. Freya, in a daze of preoccupation, walked along Merton Street. People were passing by her on either side, but she didn't look up. She had just been to see Leo Melvern at Corpus and was feeling rather winded from the interview. She had been told to apologise for her failure to attend schools, and though she had done so with due humility it was clear that Melvern meant to take her truancy as a personal affront. He did not invite her to sit down, and scowled in the manner of a petulant schoolboy as she confessed the deception she had played on Mrs Bedford. She had hardly got the story out before he launched himself into an indignant reproach of her behaviour, the like of which he had *never encountered* in his time as tutor – which must be all of about four minutes, Freya was minded to reply, but did not. He then widened his field of fire to include her character, which he deplored as arrogant, devious and unprincipled . . . She waited there, taking it, like a commuter standing calm on the edge of a platform while the express roars deafeningly past. When he had finished, his lip still curled, she said, in a neutral tone, 'Will that be all?' He flinched at that, as if from a blow. He narrowed his gaze, disbelieving. 'My God, you've got some nerve.' It was not admiringly spoken. She faced him, saying nothing, until he dismissed her.

She was halfway along Merton Street when she looked up from her brooding and saw Jean Markham about to pass her. She called out her name, and Jean, with a curious veiled look, checked her step.

'Oh, it's you,' she said, unsmiling, and Freya only then realised that Jean had been intending to ignore her.

'How are you?' she said, making an effort at friendliness.

'Fine,' said Jean, flatly. 'Not seen much of you this term. I gather you've been stepping out with that boy from Balliol – Robert.'

'I was. Not any more.'

'Oh. I supposed you were keen on him, I mean, after going behind Nancy's back –'

'It wasn't quite like that.'

'Wasn't it?' Jean couldn't keep the distaste out of her voice. 'I'd call it a strange way to behave to a friend, and I'm pretty sure Nancy thought so, too.'

'What did she say when you spoke to her?'

'Nothing against you. She's too nice a girl to start mud-slinging – though I wouldn't have blamed her if she had.'

Freya had had enough of this. 'Is there something wrong, Jean? I can't help feeling I've offended you.'

'Really? I'm surprised you've noticed. You're so wrapped up in yourself it's as though other people don't *exist*. When we came up here the first thing you did was drop all of your school friends – you thought you were much too good for us, didn't you, knocking about with Nat Fane and that set.'

'What are you talking about? I barely know them. As for dropping my school friends, I don't see how that's possible – apart from you I don't *have* any fucking friends from school. And to judge from the way you're behaving I'm not sure I can count on you any more.'

190

Jean was shaking her head. 'I was your friend, until you decided to cut me off. Do you think I'm so stupid I didn't notice? No – you're too arrogant to care.' It was as though Jean had been listening in on her recent interview with Melvern and picked up where he'd left off.

'I'm sorry you feel that way,' she said in a conciliatory voice. 'I certainly didn't mean to cut you off.' She searched Jean's face for some relenting twitch of forgiveness or understanding. There was none. They stared at one another for a few moments longer before Freya gave a little shrug and said goodbye.

It confounded her to think she had offended Jean – stolid, impervious Jean with her loud voice and her barging confidence. But the contempt in her tone just then could not be doubted. *Had* she behaved badly? Freya had always thought of her own personality as something fierce and bright and unbending, perhaps 'difficult' in some degree, but essentially benign. Now the repeated accusation pressed her towards some unglimpsed reality: she was arrogant. It was true she had avoided Jean when it suited her. But she had never thought it had been noticed.

Her step along the pavement – she had come to Magdalen Bridge – was tentative and chastened; she wasn't sure she could take another rebuke in such quick succession. And the difference now was that *this* would really hurt her. When Nancy answered the knock on her door Freya met her enquiring look with a mixture of inhibition and defiance.

'I hope you're not going to send me away,' she blurted. Nancy, hearing this self-abasement, pulled back the door in invitation, and she entered. She said 'Please' to the offer of tea, and not knowing where to stand or how to proceed she loitered around her bookcase. Its contents had become more interesting since the early days: the stiff parade of course textbooks had admitted intruders into their ranks, insolent orange-spined Penguins and contemporary novels that seemed to announce their owner's free-thinking seriousness. Nancy herself seemed changed, more assured in her movement and the way she dressed. She was growing into a woman.

As she handed Freya the tea Nancy said, 'I thought I might see you at schools; then somebody said you weren't there.'

'I was still in Germany, on my mad mission . . .'

'So did you find her?'

Freya nodded. 'She gave me an interview.'

Nancy's head jerked back in surprise. 'That's wonderful. You must – You'll send it to the *Chronicle*?'

'Once it's written, yes,' she said with a conceding little laugh, and put down her tea. 'In the meantime it's become rather more urgent that they accept it, too.'

'Why?'

'I've burnt my boats, I'm afraid. I saw the college principal this morning and –' Freya kept her tone light, she couldn't bear to be self-pitying – 'and they've sent me down.'

Nancy's face seemed to crumple in stages. She just managed to get out 'Oh, Freya, *no*' before her voice broke and tears sprang to her eyes. She was so distraught that Freya instinctively put her arms around her, and whispered fragments of consolation in her ear. If she had ever required proof of Nancy's enduring tenderness, here it was.

As she felt the flood of distress start to clear, Freya said, 'Shouldn't I be the one in tears?' She felt another convulsion in Nancy's shoulders that was somewhere between a sob and a laugh. She raised her smudged face to Freya's and said, 'Can't you appeal against it – surely you've got someone there who'd defend you?'

Freya shook her head. 'Bedders was kind. She said I'd shown enough promise to be given a second chance. But the others didn't think so – and once they'd handed down my sentence I realised I didn't really *want* a reprieve.'

Nancy turned her head away, swallowing hard. After a moment she said, 'I can't bear the thought of my life without you in it.'

Stunned by this simple avowal, Freya said hesitantly, 'Even after what I did? How I hurt you?'

'Yes, you did hurt me. But you're still my dearest friend.' She said it almost as a matter of fact. Then her expression stiffened slightly. 'I suppose you've told Robert.'

Freya's laugh was abrupt and unhappy. 'You haven't heard, then? I saw him last night at a party. He was with someone else, a pretty girl called Cressida. So maybe I've got what I deserved.'

'That's not what I think,' said Nancy.

'I know. You're kind – altogether too kind.' She felt her own eyes reluctantly moisten. A tear rolled down her cheek and she impatiently brushed it away. 'I don't know what I'd have done if you hadn't –'

'He's not worth crying over, Freya.'

Freya shook her head. 'It's not just Robert. I ran into Jean Markham this morning, someone else I seem to have mortally offended. The look she gave me . . . Honestly, Nance, I know I've behaved badly, but – I'm not *such* a bloody cow, am I?'

Nancy smiled, and took hold of her hand. 'If I said something like that you'd tell me to stop being a ninny. Now drink this tea before it gets cold.'

Freya sank into an armchair, and drank the cooling tea. The light through Nancy's windows was pearly from the rain. As they looked at each other through tear-stung eyes she felt a kind of exhilarated sadness. She didn't care about being sent down – the shame of it didn't weigh a feather for her – but she feared what would happen now to her and Nancy. Oxford wasn't far from London, of course, they would only be a train journey away from one another. Only she knew that she had no staying power when it came to friendship; before Nancy she had made and shed friends as steadily as a tree its leaves. It had been her proud conviction that she was nobody's fool. But she had wondered, in moments of alarm, if she was nobody's friend, either. She looked around the room, at the hopeful little tokens of domesticity with which Nancy had furnished it – a vase with summer flowers, a new cushion, the devotional portrait of St Francis de Sales.

'God, I've just remembered,' she said, rootling in her satchel. 'Here, a memento from Nuremberg.' It was the picture of the saint she had picked up from the rubble of the church. She recounted to Nancy the story of how she had found it. The thing was creased and torn at one corner, yet its damage made it seem more precious.

'You took it from a church?' Nancy said doubtfully.

'Well, from a church that was bombed to ruins. It had been trampled on the floor, as I said – I'd hardly call it looting.'

Nancy frowned, and said, 'I suppose it was more like rescuing it.'

'Exactly,' said Freya, propping it on the mantelpiece next to St Francis. 'There, now old Francis has a companion.'

She stared at them for a moment, lost in thought. In the end what you had was the present. It was all any living person had. The stories which accumulated about yourself and about others were the past, they were smoothed and refined in the telling, over and over. They became thinner, fainter, a shadow at your back as you pushed on. They would signify no more than the painted faces of saints. The present was where you had to live. The future called her on; it was free, but it was empty.

She knew she could only bear it by doing something.

194

From the *Chronicle*, August 1946

Witness to the century's pageant of blood

by Freya Wyley

Man's most remarkable talent, according to the writer Jessica Vaux, is for ignoring death. 'We live in the knowledge of our permanent extinction, and yet we go about our everyday business in a haze of ignorance – as in ignoring – which I suppose is the necessary condition of life itself. Even in this place, one can see in men that fundamental resistance to what is staring them in the face.'

'This place' is Nuremberg, a city that has experienced an intimate and traumatic proximity to death for several years. Towards the end of the war its citizens lived through the imminent prospect of destruction from the air as Allied bombing intensified. Then, in the final months, the old town was almost obliterated after two SS divisions sealed themselves within it and had to be blasted to atoms by American artillery. 'Ghost town' does not quite convey its desolation, for trees still stand, trams still run, people still scavenge for a living in its ruins. Walking through it one morning in July I became aware of a curious stench rising up from the rubble, so thick and enveloping one could almost taste it. When I asked about this, Mrs Vaux explained that the Nazis did not dig out their dead after air raids. The rubble over which I had to scramble concealed more than thirty thousand corpses. 'All German towns stink on hot summer days like this. The lit lanterns you can see on the debris have been placed there by mourners who are marking an anniversary. Another cruelty the Nazis visited on their people – they wouldn't even give them a proper burial.'

And now Nuremberg is the site of another struggle, less violent but possibly as momentous. At the city's Palace of Justice the trial of twenty-one leading Nazis has entered its ninth month, an unprecedented effort to bring to book the perpetrators of an unprecedented crime. It has not been a straightforward prosecution, and never could have been – though it is unlikely that anyone foresaw the way legal complications would baulk the process and sink the courtroom into a grinding deadlock. 'A citadel of boredom,' was how Mrs Vaux described it. She has been reporting on the trial for the *Tribune*, and her accounts of its tortuous proceedings reveal undimmed her unique combination of strengths: her quick understanding, her journalist's instinct for the vital detail, her almost musical ear for phrase-making.

Her picture of the defendants has offered a veritable *galère* of grotesques. She has likened Goering's appearance, for example, to that of 'the madam of a brothel . . . his professional mask enacting a cold struggle between geniality and calculation'. Or Hess, bearing 'the frightened air of an asylum inmate, his deranged personality scoured of every clue to his past'. Or Schacht, whose stiff posture reminds her of 'a disobliging corpse that has belatedly refused to fit himself into his coffin'. Yet the prolonged trial of these men, as Mrs Vaux observed, may exert a paradoxical effect. While the monstrousness of their crimes demands the gallows, their pitiable humanity cries out for mercy. 'Even murderers can touch the conscience of their judges,' she has written. 'Subjected to scrutiny day after day, the man inside the murderer will out. And it is hard to stare for long at a man one means to destroy.'

In her own life Mrs Vaux has been on close terms with death. She was born Jessica Beaumont in 1897, the middle daughter of a lawyer with a practice in London. Her mother was a renowned illustrator of flowers. An idyllic Edwardian childhood in Surrey was suddenly upended when her father dropped dead of a heart attack at Victoria Station. A beloved older brother, Louis, was killed at Mametz on the first day of the Somme offensive in July 1916. She volunteered as a nurse in the same year, and tended the horrific suffering of men returning wounded from France. 'Their cries at night were dreadful,' she said. 'I still hear them.' After the war she recounted some of her hospital experiences in an article for the London *Evening Standard*, her debut in print, and quickly established herself as a journalist of exacting principles and wide-ranging interests. In the early 1920s she wrote angrily about the plight of the industrial poor, and wittily about the vanities and pretensions of London society. Restless in England, she landed a job as foreign correspondent on the *Sketch*, and while in Berlin wrote her first book, *Funeral Rag*, about the Weimar Republic. It became a best-seller.

One reason she had abandoned England was the continual besmirching of her name by the gutter press on account of her affair with a married man. Bad enough that the man in question was the novelist Henry Burnham, seventeen years her senior; she then further inflamed the scandalmongers on announcing that the child she had borne a year earlier was his. (Burnham initially denied his paternity – 'which I'm afraid was characteristic of him,' she said.) She did not allow motherhood to cramp her ambition, however, and took her son on her travels, to Berlin, Prague and Budapest. In Spain during the Civil War she reported on the strife among the International Brigades, and narrowly escaped with her life after a bomb half destroyed the hotel where she was billeted. Her son was at boarding school back in England when Mrs Vaux, then in Paris, felt the windows of her apartment vibrate from the German guns approaching in the summer of 1940. She boarded one of the last trains out of the city with only a typewriter and a suitcase for company.

Her life has always cleaved to this precarious and provisional course; she cheerfully admitted that, since leaving London in 1926, there is nowhere she has ever felt settled – no place that she could not leave behind at an hour's notice. And no one, apart from her son: she was married to Philip Vaux, a civil servant, for six years before she began to chafe at the routines of domesticity, and walked out. It was not a decision she was proud of, she said, though when a Fleet Street columnist ran a story that she had separated from Vaux because of an affair with another man, she sued the newspaper and won. (This is the first interview she has given about her life in the ten years since.) She is, essentially, unbiddable, and the fact that she knows who she is has made it easy for her to understand others. A publisher recently offered her 'a great sum of money' to write her memoirs, but she declined it without regret. 'My life isn't a story I wish to tell – I don't want to be looking back when there's still so much ahead.' How would she feel about someone else writing her biography? 'I would resist it while I'm alive. The thought of somebody clambering around my private life is abhorrent.' Potential biographers should beware: Mrs Vaux has been known to sleep with a loaded revolver under her pillow.

In Nuremberg she has been feted by her comrades in the press as if she were royalty returning from exile. Her voice, cracked and drawling, is somewhat grander than her suburban background, though she herself is without snobbery. She seems (I suggested to her) as comfortable talking to a waiter as she does to a writer. 'Waiter, writer – it's quite often the same job. Scribbling on a pad, watching people, endless late nights. *Waiting* is what a writer does a lot of.' She writes in pencil, lying on her bed for hours at a time. She produces reams of copy which she then compresses into a piece. 'I can only operate properly if I can write it down; that's the way I discover what I think about something.' Are there any advantages, I wondered, to being a woman and a writer? 'None whatsoever,' she replied crisply. 'You could have a good time as a woman in this job, and I certainly have. But you'd have a much better one as a man. A woman must be always justifying herself. She has to fight her corner all the way, whereas a man does as he likes just by virtue of being a man.' She speaks with authority: in the Fleet Street of the 1920s she was sometimes the only woman in the newsroom.

Her forthrightness is legendary. She has denounced Churchill for his treatment of refugees from the Eastern bloc, sent back to their own country to face certain death. Of politicians on the left and right she is disdainful – 'the imbecility is remarkable on both sides' – yet she would never decline to vote. She talked a little of an admired older cousin who became a suffragette. 'She was force-fed at Holloway for months and lost her health because of it – nearly lost her life. After what she and others went through I think it would be disrespectful – shameful, actually – not to vote. But one does despair of the people we are obliged to elect.' At the Palace of Justice she cut an imperious figure; her famous gaze, piercing as Medusa's, is rightly feared. When she learned that I had not been inside the main courtroom (the security has been intense) she insisted on showing it to me, and remonstrated with the young military policeman on guard with a few choice words. We were allowed through: such is her force of personality.

Of the trial's outcome she has refused to speculate, though according to those on the inside it seems likely that all, or nearly all, the defendants will be condemned to hang. 'Whatever happens,' she said, 'we have learned what they did, beyond all doubt. That is the crucial achievement of Nuremberg.' It is fitting that Mrs Vaux is present at this, a turning point in the century's bloody pageant of cruelty. And yet one terrible doubt remains, the one that returns us to where we began. She has looked too long at those men in the dock not to feel misgivings about the death penalty: more blood on our hands. However vile the crime, can we justify hanging the criminal? 'I don't suppose there can be anything more appalling than to rob someone of life,' she said, and pondered this for a moment. 'Or maybe there is one thing – to rob them of hope.'

II

The Public Image

13

A dishwater light seeped beneath the curtain, which drooped three inches short of the sill. Freya, lying in bed, resented that gap and its call to premature wakefulness. She had been meaning to fix it since the day she'd moved in. The house had no heating, and on a February morning the miserable chill bit deep into the bones. She felt herself starting to shiver, and no matter how tightly she pulled the blankets around herself she couldn't stop.

Fed up with this she got out of bed and groped her way from the bedroom onto the landing. On the floors below nothing stirred in the low dawn light. Her bare feet on the wooden floorboards made the smallest creak. She was never sure how many other tenants lived in the building at any one time; from her vantage on the top floor she only heard the occasional muffled voice, or the clanking of pipes when somebody was running a bath. Looking east you could see the steady backs of the mews terrace that ran parallel: blank uncaring windows, ancient guttering, a shooting gallery of chimney pots. From somewhere on the street she heard the modest clop of the milkman's horse.

She gave a one-knuckle tap on the door across the landing and sidled into the darkened bedroom. Adjusting her eyes to the curtained gloom she could tell from her stillness that

203

Nancy was asleep. Her mass of auburn hair was spread over the pillow; in sleep she always looked perfectly composed, like a model about to be painted by Millais or Rossetti. Lifting the bedclothes Freya climbed in and, shivering still, moulded herself around her slumberous form. The warmth from her body was blissful in its relief. Nancy stirred blearily, and said an unintelligible something to a phantom of her sleep. They had both been stunned by the cold of the house.

'Ouf,' whispered Freya. 'Like blocks of ice.' Nancy's feet were the only part of her that would never warm. The first winter she had got chilblains.

Their rooms were on the top two floors of a house on Great James Street, a long Georgian terrace on the fringes of Bloomsbury. Freya had spotted it in the 'For Rent' columns of the *Standard*, and they had moved in, like a couple of excited newly-weds, three years ago. It was a 'respectable' address, reflected in the carved door hood and glazed square fanlight. Only gradually did the place disclose a hidden multitude of shortcomings, including a roof that still leaked from bomb damage, a temperamental gas meter, splinters from the uncarpeted floors, and windows that rattled in the winter gales.

The location was its principal advantage. Both of them could walk to work from the house, Nancy to the publisher's offices in Bedford Square, Freya to the magazine she worked for near Fetter Lane. And if the gas was off, or they were tired of tinned soup, there was a good fish and chip shop round the corner. It was here that Freya had called for her supper yesterday evening after working late. She had taken a cod fillet back for Nancy, and they shared it companionably huddled on the sofa, in their coats.

An hour or so after crawling into Nancy's bed she woke again on hearing the thump of the letter box. Her inclination to collect the post was offset by an extreme reluctance to forsake the warmth of the bed. She could tell from the change in her breathing that Nancy too was awake.

'The temperature's dropped to minus forty,' said Freya, raising her head. 'I'm just going outside, and may be some time.'

Receiving no reply to this announcement, she got up and quickly put on a dressing gown over her pyjamas before tiptoeing downstairs. The post had brought two letters for her and one for Nancy. She made them each a cup of tea before getting back into bed.

'Here, for you,' she said, handing over her letter, which Nancy fixed with a narrow appraising look.

'I think I know what this is,' she said, and opened it. Freya watched her face while she read its contents, and guessed it was not good news.

'Well?'

Nancy folded the letter away. 'They've turned *Double Personal* down. Said that it showed considerable promise, blah blah, but it's "not suitable for our list", whatever that means.'

Double Personal was Nancy's latest novel, or rather her latest attempt to get a novel published. Since coming down from Oxford six years ago she had written two others: both had been rejected.

'I'm sorry, Nance. I really thought this was the one,' said Freya. She had read all of her friend's novels and reckoned *Double Personal* – an unsettling story of two rivalrous cousins – to be her best by far. An agent had been hawking it around publishing houses for a few weeks now.

'It *is* the one,' said Nancy, still absorbing the blow. Freya heard in her voice more defiance than deflation. Odd, she thought, the way ambition was an anaesthetic as well as a stimulant. A writer will endure the cruellest whips of humiliation so long as the prospect of success stays in view. She gave Nancy's shoulder a little jiggle of encouragement.

They lay there for a few moments, lost in thought, until Freya said, 'D'you mind me parking myself against you like this?'

'No,' she said, simply. 'Saves us from dying of hypothermia, anyway.'

'Did I ever tell you about the time I sneaked in here – it was absolutely freezing – and I was literally about to climb in when I saw that *Stewart* was lying right next to you?'

Nancy spluttered out a laugh. 'That might have been interesting! Stewart sandwiched between us. Mind you, knowing him . . .'

She didn't complete this afterthought, and they both sniggered. Nancy had been courting Stewart, off and on, for a couple of years. He was a lanky, well-spoken fellow who worked as something at an advertising agency. Some of his spindly architectural drawings were strategically placed around Nancy's bedroom walls. Freya considered him pleasant but dull, and found his spaniel-like devotion to Nancy faintly irritating.

'Not seen the Stewpot much lately,' she said, fishing.

Nancy turned on her side, head resting on her elbow. 'No. I'm afraid I've been avoiding him.'

'Oh. Why's that?'

Nancy seemed about to explain, and checked herself. Then: 'I don't think one should have a boyfriend with the same hair colour, do you? It looks rather . . . narcissistic.'

'I've always regarded Stewart's as more, um, ginger. And at least you're the right height for one another,' Freya added, careful not to sound enthusiastic. Neither of them had much use for short men.

'Anyway –' Nancy shook her head in dismissal of the subject. 'What was in your post?'

'Oh, just an invitation to a private view.' She handed the stiff card to Nancy.

'"*The Public Image* – photographs by Jerry Dicks – Villiers Gallery". Is he the one who does those sinister portraits?'

'Yeah. He photographs everyone to look like they're going to prison. But he also does glamour work for *Vogue*. I want to write a piece about him.'

Nancy continued to stare at the invitation. 'Hmm. I'd rather like to see this myself . . .'

'Then you *shall*, my darling,' said Freya in her clipped Noël Coward voice, and sweeping aside the blankets rose from the bed. The temperature had climbed a notch since she had joined Nancy, though it was still raw. In the bathroom she could actually see her own breath! A wash would have to suffice this morning. Having dressed and buttoned up her winter coat to the neck, she put her head round the door to check on Nancy, who was still in bed, brooding.

'I'm off,' she said, and Nancy looked up from her reverie. 'Nance, it will happen, you know. I believe in you.'

Nancy gave a rueful smile, and waggled her fingers in farewell.

Freya walked down Gray's Inn Road deep in thought while the morning rush-hour crowds swarmed around her. She had kept a tactful silence in front of Nancy about her other bit of post. It had come from the offices of the *Envoy*. The editor wanted to discuss a possible 'opening' which had cropped up. She had heard of this man, Simon Standish, and was flattered that he had 'followed her career for some time'. When she heard things like that she immediately wondered why it had taken him so long to tell her.

This promising development, however, hot on the heels of Nancy's latest setback with the novel, was awkward in its timing. Nancy, she knew, would be pleased for her, even as it highlighted the faltering progress of her own writing career. Freya would point out that she had the advantage of a head start, having arrived in London two years before

Nancy. Her profile of Jessica Vaux had cracked open a door at the *Chronicle* through which she had eagerly darted. In the week of her twenty-second birthday she was taken on as a junior reporter, and though the hours were long and the work unglamorous she never showed herself less than willing. More profile work came her way. Her steely line of questioning sometimes got her into trouble – 'insolence' was the usual complaint – but her copy never came up short for spirit. Her editors knew they had a good thing. This arrangement continued for just over four years until she happened to get wind of how much a colleague of hers (male, less experienced) was earning. Stunned, then indignant, she applied to her bosses for a pay rise, and was refused. She bided her time, and when a call came from *Frame* magazine offering her a job she exited the *Chronicle* at such a speed that – the joke went – she left scorch marks on their carpet.

The arc of Nancy's career had not enjoyed the same flourish. She had gained a first at Oxford, and was offered the chance of pursuing postgraduate work at another college. Instead, she decided to take a job at a publishing house in London, a handy stopgap, it seemed, while she worked on her next novel, the one that would finally be published and catapult her into the literary firmament. Except that none yet had. Why this was so Freya couldn't understand. She admired her talent, and was even a little unnerved by it, perhaps because the friend she knew seemed so different from the writer. 'Her' Nancy was a smiling, open-hearted, sweet-tempered girl. The other Nancy, as expressed in her novels, was sharp-eyed, incisive and morally unsparing; the diffidence of the person vanished in the prose.

'Parky, innit?' said the receptionist on seeing Freya, coat collar buttoned up to her nose. *Frame* had recently moved offices to a swanky new building, a sure sign in industry lore that its fortunes were on the slide. The magazine, launched in 1935, had been a byword for all that was slick and modern in photojournalism. It had scored its great successes immediately pre- and post-war, selling upwards of a million copies per week. When television came along it had weathered the initial alarm, but now that sets were sprouting in front rooms all over the country its black-and-white pictures, for all their quality, had come to look pedestrian. Uncertain in the face of this revolution the management had started to panic, adopting gimmicks and steering *Frame* ever further up the side roads of irrelevance.

She could see the flowers on her desk as soon as she stepped out of the lift. They formed a large bouquet, mostly made up of white lilies; their sharp intrusive smell made her want to sneeze. She looked over to her colleague, Elspeth, frowningly absorbed in a long screed of copy.

'Where did these come from?'

Elspeth peered over her austere horn-rimmed spectacles. 'I'm sure I don't know, darling. They were here when I arrived. Isn't there a note?'

Freya looked beneath the wrapping and found an envelope pinned to the slender stalks. Elspeth noticed her sniffing with distaste.

'Awful pong, haven't they? Makes me think of ladies' lavs.'

'Makes me think of death,' said Freya, tearing open the envelope. She blinked in surprise at the card. Its letterhead was in a distinctive font, one she had very recently seen, from the *Envoy*. There was a single line, typed:

Welcome aboard the paper!

It was unsigned. She immediately thought of Simon Standish, whose letter of this morning she had in her bag. But his was a polite invitation to her to come in and talk; she hadn't

209

even replied to him yet, so why would he already be welcoming her? Premature, to say the least.

'So who is he?' asked Elspeth, interested now.

'No one,' she said, with a dismissive toss of her head. 'The silly arse didn't even sign it.'

'Ooh. A secret admirer.'

Could it be? She knew hardly anyone at the *Envoy*. Perhaps Standish had made a mistake – a mix-up with his secretary, who had pp-ed the invitation letter and may have accidentally dispatched the flowers along with it. Except that one was addressed to her home, and this little lot to the office.

Marie had just stopped at their desk. 'Editorial meeting in ten minutes, ladies. Hope you've got some good ideas!'

'Yeah,' said Elspeth, under her breath, 'pack up and start looking for a new job.'

Freya laughed. 'Come on. It's not as bad as all that.'

Elspeth hoisted her eyebrows. 'Seen this month's sales? They're down again.' Her quip about a new job, Freya realised, had a shiver of doom to it.

In the conference room pots of coffee were being handed around the table, Marie was counting heads and a couple of the men were placidly smoking their pipes. The editorial team numbered sixteen. It was divided, uniquely on *Frame*, between photographers and writers: the two worked on a story in tandem, a chummy arrangement that came with its own anxieties, as Freya discovered. Credit was apportioned equally, but so was blame. If you came back with the wrong pictures, or if the reporting was deemed inadequate, both of you got carpeted. What appealed to Freya at first was the variety of work. One morning you could be at a fashion show, or a dog track; the next you could be tootling down to Eastbourne for an old trouper's farewell turn at the pier, or off to Basingstoke to interview a mother who had just had quads. The stories went high and low, between coming-out parties for debs or dances at a working men's club. As she became more adept in the job she was entrusted with racier stories about strip joints and nightclubs. The camaraderie it fostered was much to her liking, and if the late hours and the deadlines left her little time for a personal life, that too was fine.

When everyone seemed settled the deputy editor, Jocelyn Philbrick, called the meeting to order. He was a lean, well-groomed fellow of about forty whose silver mop of hair contrasted with a still-youthful demeanour.

'The editor's running late, so we'd better press on. First of all, there's been grumbling about our news reportage, and I have to admit we're starting to look a little . . . slow.'

'There's no "starting to" about it, Jocelyn,' said Viv Compton, the women's editor. 'Compared with television we *are* slow. As a weekly we can't compete with TV and newspapers. So we should concentrate on what we do best – human-interest stories with wonderful photographs. Instead of trying to cover *all* the news we reduce it to a digest. That way we still look on top of current affairs without the effort of cramming everything in.'

'Television's going to destroy us anyway,' said Bob Denny, a grizzled senior photographer, and the office curmudgeon. 'We may as well go down doing stuff we believe in rather than compete against *the monster*.'

'Very cheering, Bob, thank you,' said Jocelyn, with the courteous irony of one who had fielded such pessimism many times over. The debate continued around the table for some minutes until Marie leaned over and muttered something, to which Jocelyn nodded responsibly. 'Yes, indeed – we must get on. Bright ideas?'

Elspeth spoke up. 'I thought we should prepare something to mark the end of rationing. So we visit a housewife in Frinton, or wherever, see what groceries she puts in her basket now, then compare it with what she'll buy in July, when meat and butter and what have you become available.'

'If not affordable,' someone put in.

Jocelyn nodded. 'Yes, good. I see it – The End of Austerity.'

'Photograph the family at dinner – "all smiles,"' said Bob Denny, unsmiling.

'Farewell Spam fritters – hullo Roast Lamb,' said Terry Flint, another photographer, his hands modelling the air to enclose the caption.

Marie was looking down the editor's 'forthcoming' list. 'We have to arrange an interview with Dirk Bogarde for his next picture – first go at comedy.'

'Really?'

'He plays a dashing doctor, it says here.'

'Bogarde in a comedy? That won't fly.'

'Doesn't matter. He'll look good on the cover,' said Jocelyn. 'We should send one of the girls to do him, I suppose.'

Bob Denny said, 'I reckon he'd prefer one of the boys . . .'

Tuts and sniggers greeted his little jest. Jocelyn only sighed. 'We also have to line up that piece on Alf Barry's missus. Anyone fancy that? Freya – haven't heard much from you.'

Jolted from a haze of preoccupation, Freya said, 'I'm not doing another footballer's wife. Sorry.'

'Why not?'

'Because the last one almost bored me to extinction.'

Jocelyn lifted his chin. 'I see. Poor Mrs Barry – seems such a nice lady. Do you have anything to offer instead?'

'As a matter of fact I do,' said Freya. 'Jerry Dicks. He's got an exhibition coming next month. I'd like to do a profile, explain how he went from being this anonymous jobbing smudger to the most original British portraitist of today. We could use a selection of his own pictures – they'll look beautiful.'

212

There was a brief silence, which Bob Denny broke with a protesting gasp. 'Original British *what*? The only Jerry Dicks I know is a vicious little queen who hangs about Soho cadging drinks and pissing up walls.'

'Maybe. But he also takes brilliant photographs,' said Freya with a tight smile. She had always sensed that Bob disliked her. She turned to Jocelyn. 'I don't think we should rule out a man just because of his "disreputable" character. The artist as ruffian is more compelling anyway. Look at Caravaggio, or Christopher Marlowe.'

'True enough,' said Jocelyn, tipping his head. 'Dicks is certainly out of the common run.'

'That's one way of putting it,' muttered Bob, flaring his nostrils in distaste. 'Personally I don't rate his stuff. You can't talk of him in the company of Parkinson or Beaton, for instance.'

Freya laughed and shook her head. 'That, if you don't mind my saying, is balls.'

Bob's expression darkened as he sat up in his chair, and Jocelyn, alert to the sudden crackle of antagonism, raised his hands like a referee separating two prizefighters. 'Ah-ah, let's keep it civil. Freya, there's no need for that. Bob was only giving his opinion. That's fair, isn't it?'

She arranged her features into an impression of equability. 'Of course. Bob can believe what he likes, as long as I'm allowed to estimate his critical capacity at approximately zero.'

Bob, thrusting back his chair, stood up. His face was angrily flushed. 'You should learn some respect, missy. Think you're so smart with your degree from Oxford and your foul mouth.' His northern accent had thickened with his disgust. He turned to Jocelyn. 'I'm not going to sit here and be insulted by . . . *juniors*. Get your staff in order, man.'

He stalked out of the room. The ruffled air he left in his wake created an embarrassed pause in proceedings. It wasn't

213

that the others liked Bob much – he was a legendary moaner – but they tried not to provoke him. Into the silence Freya said, 'I don't have a degree from Oxford, by the way.'

They carried on for a while, suggesting ideas, assigning pairs to this or that story, but the wind had been knocked out of the meeting's sails, and soon Jocelyn steered it to a close. As they were filing out of the room he asked to see Freya in his office.

'That was neither wise nor kind,' he said, shutting the door behind her. 'I know Bob can be a pain in the neck, but he does deserve a measure of respect.'

Freya stared at him. 'Why? He's never shown any respect to me.'

'Come on, Freya. Even if you don't think you owe him, you owe it to me. It's part of my job to run the ship, and I can't do that if you antagonise someone like Bob. This isn't the first time, either.'

'I can't help it if he doesn't like me. And I don't think anyone in that meeting thought I spoke out of turn.'

'You're wrong about that. If you put Bob in a mood, the whole office suffers.' He looked at her for any sign of remorse. The pause lengthened; then he said, in a changed voice, 'May I give you some advice? In life, you may find that rampant individualism isn't always the best way of getting what you want. People respond more readily to the idea of collective endeavour, to being part of a team. You begin to learn how important it is on a newspaper or a magazine, that sense of togetherness.'

Freya said, somewhat concedingly, 'I've never been one for team games.'

'It shows,' said Jocelyn.

'But I pull my weight. I don't miss deadlines, I don't object to working late, and I don't ask for special treatment – unlike certain people.'

'No one would doubt the quality of your work. But in some ways you don't really help at all – you're tactless with other people, and you're dismissive of their feelings. The swearing doesn't go down well, either, not from a lady.' He looked at her, waiting for a reaction. 'Is any of this getting through?'

Freya nodded. 'I'll apologise to Bob, if you want me to.'

'You don't sound very sorry.'

'I'm not!' she said with a half-laugh. 'I'd only do it to help you.'

'Well, that's –'

'But I still think you should let me write about Jerry Dicks. Joss, really, he's a one-off – and it would make a smashing piece.'

Jocelyn's look was wry, as though some point of his own had been proven. 'No doubt. But I can tell you right now, the editor won't like it. He'll say: if this fellow's so wonderful, why isn't he taking pictures for us?'

'From what I've heard about him it's probably a good thing he doesn't work for us – losing expensive equipment, falling down drunk. He's a liability. But he's a genius with a camera.'

'I'll have a talk with Brian and come back to you,' said Jocelyn, who shifted in his chair and angled a look at her. 'I saw that large bouquet on your desk. Lilies. Who were they from?'

'I've no idea,' she said almost drowsily.

Jocelyn gave his mouth a disbelieving tweak. 'Really?'

'They were just plonked on my desk – the note was unsigned.'

He nodded, watchful. 'Nice to have admirers.'

'Lovely,' she agreed, matching his airiness, and got up to leave. He came from behind his desk to head her off at the door.

'Are we still on for tonight?' he asked in a low, confiding tone.

'I don't know. Are we?'

'What does that mean?'

'Well, I wouldn't like to put you to any trouble – speaking as a "rampant individualist".'

He laughed, and took her hand lightly in his. 'No trouble. I'll be at your place around eight.' She tilted her head in acquiescence, and went out.

They had been seeing one another for just over a year. Jocelyn Philbrick, born to privilege, had once been the coming man in journalism: during the war he had shown his mettle reporting in battle zones around Malta and Italy. The scorching pace he had set in his career as a war correspondent had slowed down somewhat on entering his thirties. *Frame* had poached him from a national newspaper just after the war, and he found the perks it afforded much to his liking. He was often to be seen hobnobbing at parties and clubs in the West End, and at some point had chosen to rest on his affability rather than stretch his talent. He became attached to his position of deputy editor as to a ball and chain: he seemed stuck with it.

Freya had known little about him when she'd started at *Frame* two years before. He'd treated her in the lightly impersonal manner he extended to all the staff. This changed one evening. A group of them had gone to the private view of a painter, Ossian Blackler. Tall, tousle-haired and saturnine, Blackler was on his way to becoming a name: affiliation with the Soho demi-monde had imbued his work with a sheen of outlaw glamour. Freya recalled it as a warm night, for the crowd had spilled over from the gallery rooms on Lexington Street into the narrow walled courtyard behind. Beer and cigarette smoke perfumed the air. She had found herself in a cluster of people paying court to the painter, who was batting away their blandishments with a disdain that verged on rudeness.

'I hear the BBC want to talk to you, Ossie. What will you tell 'em?'

'To fuck off, probably,' he replied in his flat, nasal voice. Laughter greeted this blunt retort.

'You must be pleased with the prices your new stuff is fetching.'

He gave an irritated little snort. 'If people are rich enough, or stupid enough, to pay 'em, I'm not complaining.'

One of his more earnest admirers then made the mistake of asking him to which school of painting he thought he belonged. Blackler turned the full glare of his scorn upon the question, mocking both the idea of *schools* (he drew out the syllable to sarcastic length) and the imbecility of the man for raising the subject at all. He made quite a meal of it. The laughter had gone from fawning to embarrassed by the time he had thoroughly squashed his victim, but Blackler didn't seem to care. As he looked around the company for fresh disputation his eye alighted on Freya, who he had perhaps noticed wasn't laughing, and was merely watching him.

'What about you?' he said, the sneer still in his voice. 'What *school* would you put me in?'

Freya considered for a moment, then said evenly, 'Charm school.'

There was a split second of horrified silence before Blackler sniggered, almost childishly, and everyone joined in. His dangerous mood dissolved; the combative set of his mouth unstiffened, and he started talking to Freya in a spirit of near-friendliness. Soon another gaggle of cronies arrived to colonise the space around Blackler, and Freya melted back into the anonymous crowd. She was lining up another drink at the bar when Jocelyn appeared at her side. He had evidently been witness to the encounter in the back garden.

'You took a chance there, kid.'

She gave a little shrug. 'It was better than having to listen to any more of his bullying.'

His look became appraising. 'Interesting. Those men out there were so eager to impress, but you talked to him as though he was just another feller.'

'He *is* just another feller,' she replied. 'He happens to have some talent, though not half as much as he thinks.'

So she thought he was overrated? Freya sensed Jocelyn's expression changing as they talked on; it was as though he had never quite listened to her before. On her part, she could see he was handsome, fairly clever, but also a little complacent, pleased with himself – and he was old, too, at least ten years older than her. But something had bonded between them; a few weeks later he invited her to another private view, smarter this time, on Bruton Street, and afterwards they went for dinner. That date led to another, until one evening, when they had been canoodling at his flat, he suggested that she stay the night. She noticed him flinch with surprise when, after a moment's thought, she assented, and realised that he had expected her to say no, as most 'nice' girls would have done. She should probably have played a little harder to get, but she despised coyness. He would find out soon enough that she was no pushover.

Back at her desk the bouquet of lilies had become insufferable. She picked them up and, with only a small stab of ingratitude, tossed them in the bin. Then she thought of the letter from the *Envoy* in her bag, and wondered if they were serious about taking her on. If so, it would make for an interesting conversation with Joss.

14

The Villiers Gallery was situated on a paved court linking the Charing Cross Road with St Martin's Lane. It specialised in modern photography, though of late it had become a magnet to a gathering of artists and theatrical types who found a common purpose in drinking, bitching and moaning about money. A poster across the glass-partitioned door announced this evening's event, a private view of Jerry Dicks's recent photographs. *The Public Image* concentrated its gaze on celebrities of the arts and entertainment world, framed not in their professional habitat but on the street, in public, as if the photographer had caught them on the wing. Certain of his subjects were conscious of the lens looking up at them – Dicks used a Rolleiflex camera, held at waist level – while others seemed quite unaware of it as they walked down a street or mooched in a coffee bar. Some had the air of being suddenly, and perhaps unpleasantly, surprised, as if Dicks had crept up and snatched a shot of them when they were least prepared for it. A few looked ready to throttle him.

Freya, arriving early to beat the crowd, was beguiled by them: she loved the inkiness of the grain Dicks had achieved, and their dramatic alternation of light and dark. He had a gift, some alchemical magic, for making the most innocent face look troubled, or shifty. Most of the sitters she knew by repute; a handful of them she had met professionally; and one, in front of which she now stood, she counted as a friend. Nat Fane, alone of those portrayed, seemed unperturbed by the camera's questing eye. He had been photographed sitting at the long zinc counter of a bar, with an aproned barman unconcernedly polishing a glass behind him. Fane was holding a cigarette between his second and middle finger – a new affectation – and challenging the camera with a knowing smirk she remembered of old.

She had been trying to arrange an interview with Dicks, confident that the magazine would run it. That morning she had gone to see the editor, Brian Mowbray, to check with him, and could tell that something was up. They sat at his desk. Mowbray was a large, well-built man whose meaty, pallid face seemed to sweat even when it wasn't warm.

'Joss has been telling me about this fellow Dicks, and to be frank, I just don't like the sound of him.'

'I wouldn't expect you to,' she said. 'He's probably quite awful. But he's also a great photographer.'

Mowbray looked unimpressed. 'You think so? I'm not sure he's any better than what we get from our own chaps. And they have the advantage of not being a public nuisance.'

Freya bit back the sharp riposte that was on her tongue. 'It would still be a coup for the magazine. His photographs would make a good spread.'

For answer his mouth drooped with doubt. 'I'm sorry, Freya, it just isn't for us.'

'I see.'

'However, there *is* something I'd like to get you started on. We're planning to run a story about the wives of professional footballers . . .'

When she confronted Joss about this afterwards he laughed, and swore he'd not put Mowbray up to it.

The gallery was starting to fill. Outside the window she saw Nancy arrive, in her office clothes, hesitating as she checked she had the right address and peering inwards for confirmation. She was one of those people, Freya thought, who look more beautiful when unconscious of being observed. She waved through the glass, and the movement of her hand caught Nancy's attention; she waved back, smiling.

'How was work?' she said as they kissed one another.

'Oh, dreary,' replied Nancy. 'I've been looking forward to this all day.'

'Let's get a drink,' Freya said, leading her by the arm through a press of bodies. They were halfway to the bar when Nancy, distracted, tugged Freya's sleeve. Right in front of them, its nose at a shyly enquiring angle, was a small brindled whippet. Nancy, who had always been susceptible to dogs, bent down to pat it.

'What an *adorable* creature,' she cooed. She picked up the dog with a maternal tenderness and held her towards Freya. The dog's eyes, dark and yearning, gazed up at her. 'They're the most affectionate of all, you know, whippets,' she said, nuzzling its neck. She looked almost tearful as she spoke.

'He's very sweet,' Freya said, amused by the little pietà Nancy had made.

'Not a "he" – a "she,"' said a dark-haired young woman, gently taking the dog from Nancy. 'Her name's Rhoda. My pride and joy.'

The woman's hazel-coloured eyes and fine, shapely mouth seemed familiar from somewhere. She carried herself with a thoughtless grace; her fitted floral dress, cut deep at the neck, accentuated her bust and hips. Freya stared, admiring her, and then realised. 'That's you, isn't it?' she said, pointing at one of the framed photographs they had just passed. The woman barely glanced at her portrait: she was more interested in petting Rhoda.

221

'I've worked with Jerry for years,' she said in a voice that had a smoker's edge of hoarseness. 'That's quite a rare one – me, with clothes on.'

'It's very beautiful,' said Nancy, blushing.

'They're all right,' she replied, with a toss of her head. She looked at Freya. 'Do you know Jerry?'

'No. I'm Freya, this is Nancy. Would you mind introducing us?'

The woman's name was Hetty Cavendish, model and muse, and now their impromptu guide as she stopped to offer a casual comment on this or that portrait ('He took that while we were in Spain . . .'; 'Jerry didn't get on with *him* at all . . .'). It became clear that she and Jerry spent a great deal of their time together.

Nancy asked, tentatively, 'So do you live with, um, Jerry?'

Hetty shook her head and, belatedly twigging the implication, gave a throaty laugh. 'God, no! – it's nothing like that. Jerry's queer – didn't you know?'

They had arrived at the bar, where a short, balding man with quick eyes and a prematurely lined face was holding forth. It was difficult to tell if he was closer to forty or to sixty. Whenever someone else got a word in edgeways his black-eyed gaze glittered with hostility. Freya noticed his hand shook slightly as he raised a glass to his lips. This, as Hetty confirmed in a murmur, was Jerry Dicks. The only one present Dicks addressed with any hint of affection was Ossie Blackler, who was teasing him.

'The one of Olivier and his missus. Did you have to get a royal appointment for that, Jerry?'

Dicks favoured his friend with a leer. 'They're wounded people, actors. Needy. Whenever they're around you have to give 'em attention, cos they're so fucking insecure. I'm always specially nice to 'em – like you 'ave to be with Arabs and women.' His voice was lilting, refined, yet spiked with cockney inflections.

222

'Well, I do know you're specially nice to Arabs.'

Dicks cackled at what was plainly an in-joke. 'Yeah . . . actors. Once when I was working with Olivier he started telling me how to arrange the lighting – in me own fuckin' studio!' He shook his head in disbelief. 'I said to him, "Larry, I have a rule with actors. They don't teach me how to take photographs, and I don't teach them how to behave like a cunt." Ha ha!'

Blackler led a bellowing chorus of laughter in response. Standing out of his sightline, Hetty turned to Freya and Nancy with a look on her face that said *Are you sure you're ready for this?* Had she been on her own, Freya would have relished the challenge; but she sensed from Nancy's appalled expression that such company would not be to all tastes. She whispered to Hetty, 'Maybe not right this moment.'

Hetty nodded, understanding, and they sidled off. When they were well out of earshot Nancy said, sotto voce, 'What a *horrible* little man. Made my flesh creep just looking at him.'

'Hmm. He's what my dad would call "strong meat". But I think there might be something rather fascinating about him, too.'

Nancy pulled a face. 'Only in the way you might find one of those wax murderers at Madame Tussaud's fascinating.'

Freya laughed. 'He's not as bad as all that!'

They went for another wander around the exhibition. Freya noticed people – men – giving Nancy sidelong stares, to which she appeared quite oblivious. At twenty-seven she had grown into her looks; the gawkiness of her Oxford days had melted away, replaced by a voluptuous, long-limbed ease. Her mass of thick auburn hair, pale skin and green eyes were all the more striking for her new-found poise. But this evening she was noticeably distracted.

223

'Why do you keep checking your watch?' asked Freya.

'Sorry, I'm just – Stewart called this afternoon. He asked me to go to dinner – and I couldn't think of a reason not to.'

'What time?'

'In about ten minutes.' She added plaintively, 'Will you come?'

'Me? I don't think so. Can you imagine Stewart's face, expecting a quiet dinner for two and I breeze in?'

Nancy conceded the point, but with such a disgruntled air that Freya was moved to speak again. 'If it's that much of a chore, Nance, why don't you just finish it – hand him his coat?'

'I know, I should,' she said anxiously, 'but he's so decent and considerate – I can hardly bear to.'

'But you must. He's a grown-up. It will be the kindest thing to do in the long run.'

They said goodbye and Nancy went off to dinner. Left alone, Freya wondered if her motives were entirely selfless in advising her to give Stewart his marching orders. This evening, for instance, *she* would have liked to have dinner *à deux*, but instead had been usurped by Stewart, who really was a bit of a drip.

She made another tour of the party hubbub. Jerry Dicks was still surrounded by his clique, his complexion blazing like a Chinese dragon's and his eyes blearily unfocused. She decided it might be better to catch him when he was unfuddled with drink – if he ever were. She was edging her way towards the door when a voice checked her.

'Stay, illusion!'

She turned to find Nat Fane beaming at her. He was wearing a midnight-blue velvet suit and a white shirt open at the neck.

'Hullo, Nat. I've just been examining your portrait.'

'Ah. A bit scrawny-looking, d'you think?'

'You at least seem relaxed. Most of them have that fugitive-from-justice look.'

'He's got quite an eye, old Dicks. Quite an arm, too,' he said, mimicking the raising of a glass to his mouth. 'You notice he photographed me in a bar. We had a couple afterwards, then I left him to it. I heard he got so drunk that they had to carry him out of there feet first, like at the end of *Hamlet*.'

Freya had kept up with Nat since Oxford. He had arrived in London two years after she did, brimful of confidence from his reign as a theatrical princeling. One Sunday newspaper had announced him to the world as a 'marvellous boy' and predicted his taking of the West End by storm. Six years on that hadn't happened. Having carried all before him as a student actor, he had been found deficient in the more exacting environs of the London stage. His debut as Tybalt in *Romeo and Juliet* got a savage pasting from the critics, and inclined people to wonder if he really was the actor he'd been cracked up to be. He had a second try, as Octavian in *Antony and Cleopatra*, which met with no greater enthusiasm.

Though he had made light of it, Freya suspected that Nat was hurt by the rejection. The comet trail he had blazed in his youth had gone off in a fizzle. Having seen him in both plays she had kept quiet, finding herself in sad agreement with the critics – since university his acting had become mannered and hectoring. Or perhaps it always had been and she just hadn't noticed. Nat in person was always performing, always 'on', to such a degree that he had nothing left over when required to act in earnest. It was accepted that he would not be the next Olivier. Still, he had other irons in the fire. He had just started rehearsing his first full-length play, and a publisher had recently commissioned him to write a major history of the English stage.

'And what of you, my dear? *Frame* keeping you busy?'

'I'm rather vexed with them. My editor has just turned down a piece on Jerry there.'

'More fool them.'

'I'll do it for someone else. Perhaps I could apply to you for stories about him.'

Nat gave a slight smirk. 'Of course. I can see the head-line – "Dicks Uncovered". Let me arrange for you to meet at dinner. You can inspect the new abode while you're at it.'

'You've moved?'

'Indeed. I fancied Mayfair, Pandy insisted on Belgravia. South Kensington was the compromise.'

Pandy was Nat's wife. He had married, seemingly on impulse, at Marylebone Register Office a year after coming down from Oxford. The first time Freya had met her was at their wedding reception, though she already knew her by repute. Pandora Fairhurst-Dunnett, to give her full name, was, at twenty-one, a fixture on the West End stage. She had been playing Juliet when Nat was struggling in the Tybalt role, and the critical swooning over her performance was in stark contrast to his own treatment. Freya wondered at the time if he had married her in unconscious revenge; aside from her beauty, there was very little about the lady that she could imagine captivating restless, intellectual Nat. In the years since, Freya had never heard her say a word of the remotest interest to anyone about anything. Pandora's star had continued to rise as Nat's stalled. But tonight she could tell he was in a good mood; his attentiveness had taken on a dallying note.

'I espied Nancy earlier,' he said. 'Bowered in domestic bliss?'

'We're still living together, if that's what you mean,' she replied.

He paused, narrowing his eyes. 'They can't prise you two apart, can they? It's always Freya and Nancy, Nancy and Freya . . .'

'We both have *chaps*, you know,' she said.

'Of course you do,' he said airily. 'But I could tell them – they don't stand a chance. With either of you.'

'You're being rather mischievous, Nat. We get along well, Nancy and I, but it's not like we're the Ladies of Llangollen. We're not inseparable.'

His look was veiled, measuring. 'So you won't mind coming to dinner solo? No offence to your darling housemate, or your "chap."'

'None taken,' she replied. 'I'll come however you like.'

She walked briskly home through Covent Garden and up Kingsway. The mullion-windowed pubs were preparing last orders; a memory of winter chill lingered on the March night. She was pondering her encounter with Nat, and the strange course their friendship had taken. The bizarre night of racket-swishing that had begun their intimacy all those years ago had never been repeated. Though Nat made unembarrassed reference to the occasion, it was understood he would not try an approach again, and she had never invited one. All the same, she sensed that his sexual curiosity about her remained an itch, and that his marriage would perhaps be no obstacle to giving it a good scratch. For her part she warmed to him in every aspect but the physical; while good-looking in his foppish way, there was something feline and self-admiring in him that repulsed her. Nat would always be his own most ardent suitor.

She let herself in. She found a tin of Heinz tomato soup in the kitchen and lit the gas ring; while she stirred it she read a report in *The Times* about Soviet agents continuing to infiltrate Whitehall. The mood there was still nervous after Burgess and Maclean. She carried the soup through to the living room and ate it with some cheese crackers. Her interview at the *Envoy* was scheduled for tomorrow. In her bedroom she pulled open the wardrobe and considered the queue of dresses and skirts and blouses packed within. She had one or two smart things she could wear. She took from its wooden hanger a black woollen jacket, cut stylishly close, a gift from her stepmother, Diana. She modelled it in the cheval mirror. Her face looked searchingly back at her. The frown that had once smacked of wilfulness now came more slowly, and sadly.

With her library book she went back into the living room. She kicked off her shoes and lay on the couch, sipping her gin. From downstairs came the rattle of the latchkey, and the murmur of voices. She suppressed a fleeting quiver of disappointment that Nancy had not returned alone. Here came their footsteps on the stairs, and she snatched up her book so as to convey the impression that her evening had been one of intellectual absorption. Nancy was first through, and in the seconds before she had spotted Freya over on the couch her face betrayed a strain of preoccupation. It vanished into her smile. Stewart followed after, favouring her with a little wave.

'Evening. Nice dinner?'

Nancy nodded. 'We went to Wheeler's. I had lemon sole, Stewart had – what did you have?'

'Oh, the whitebait. And the oysters. All highly agreeable,' he said in his polite, undemonstrative voice.

'Wheeler's? Very smart. I had tinned soup and crackers.'

She saw Nancy giving her a look, as if to say *You should have joined us*, though to judge from the subdued mood they had brought in with the cold Freya felt rather glad she hadn't. She got up from the couch and fetched glasses from the kitchen. In a bright voice she said, 'Guess who I ran into after you'd gone – Nat Fane.'

'Really? How is he?'

'Unchanged. They've just moved to South Ken, apparently.'

'Fane – the fellow married to Pandora whatsit . . . ?' asked Stewart.

Nancy rolled her eyes. 'Don't ever let him hear you say that. He'd die if he thought people only knew him as the helpmeet of Pandora Fairhurst-Dunnett.'

'True,' agreed Freya. 'I don't think he had any inkling when he married her that she would become the leading partner.'

'She was terribly good in *Romeo and Juliet*,' said Stewart, adding, almost daringly, 'far better than him.'

Nancy clicked her tongue at this disloyalty. 'She's just a pretty little fawn, with feathers in her brain.'

Freya smiled at this rare instance of asperity from Nancy, and said, concedingly, 'Stewart's right, though. Nat's the cleverest man I've ever met, but he's not going to make it as an actor. Feather-brains, on the other hand, really has talent, proving –'

'Proving what?' asked Nancy, frowning.

'I don't know – that acting relies more on instinct than intelligence? Pandora's rather a blank in person, but up onstage I believed in her completely.'

'And the critics backed that up,' said Stewart, seeming to take heart from Freya's endorsement. 'They loved her, and they hated him.'

'The critics aren't always right,' said Nancy, who seemed to be taking this depreciation of Nat quite personally.

'No,' said Freya patiently, 'only they were this time. Come on, Nance, you remember watching him in *Romeo*. Nat spoke his lines as though they were in quotation marks. He didn't want to serve the play, he wanted to project himself.'

Nancy gave an irked shrug that withheld agreement, and the discussion appeared to be closed. Stewart was perched, awkwardly, at the opposite end of the couch from Freya, who now dragged herself upright from where she'd been lolling and invited him to sit down properly. He directed an uncertain look at Nancy, who, returning no more than a glance, indicated that he should not make himself comfortable. There

229

was a definite 'atmosphere' between them now, and Freya, surprised by a pang of pity for Stewart, said, 'I think we've got some beer in the kitchen, if you don't want gin.'

But Stewart didn't need to be warned twice. 'Thanks, no,' he said, rising. 'I should be pushing off – I just wanted to see Nancy home safe.'

They said goodnight to one another, and Nancy followed him downstairs. Freya couldn't help being curious to hear what was said between them as he left, but their voices at the door were muffled and indistinct. Some minutes later Nancy returned, her brow clouded and her mouth primmed up. Without saying a word she began tidying the room, picking up a discarded newspaper and a porcelain ashtray filled with crushed stubs. Freya let the silence linger for a minute or so.

'Is everything all right, Nance?'

Nancy abandoned her sweeping and stood still. She was twisting the tiny gold cross at her throat, a giveaway sign of her inner agitation. She sat down in the easy chair and addressed a point in the middle distance.

'Stewart and I shan't be seeing one another again.'

Freya stared back, trying to gauge her mood. 'I see. How did you break it to him?'

Nancy gave an unhappy half-laugh. 'I didn't. *He* broke it to *me*. Can you imagine? There I am, mouth full of lemon sole, and he jumps in with a line about "let's part as friends". It was all I could do not to look shocked.'

'But isn't that what you wanted? You said as much back at the gallery.'

'Yes, I know. But it should have been me telling him. It's humiliating. I asked him how long he'd been thinking about it – he said *two months*!'

Freya was puzzled. 'So why did he take you out to dinner?'

230

'Because he wanted to be a "gentleman" about it. And then walks me home, as though I'd be too upset to make it back alone.'

'But, Nance . . . it sounds like you *are* upset.'

She answered with a sad lift of her eyes, saying nothing. Freya got up from the couch and knelt, resting her hands like a supplicant on Nancy's knees. She raised her face to her, waiting it out, until Nancy, after some moments, returned her gaze. Something she had noticed had brought a gleam to her downcast expression.

'Why are you wearing that posh jacket?' she asked.

Freya had forgotten about it. 'Oh, I was just trying it on. I've got that interview at the *Envoy* tomorrow.'

Nancy was running her eye over it, admiringly. 'It looks very good on you. But not with that skirt?'

Freya admitted she hadn't given any thought to the skirt. In a trance of preoccupation Nancy stood up and stepped purposefully out of the room. She returned a minute or so later carrying two skirts, one in each hand.

'Green or black?'

Freya rose and took first one, then the other, to hold against her. Nancy watched with the appraising eye of a master couturier.

'Perhaps the black is too much with your jacket – more for a funeral.'

Freya nodded. 'And I prefer this green one anyway.' Quickly discarding her own skirt she stepped into it, then walked through to her bedroom to consult the mirror. Nancy followed behind.

'Oh, Nance, it's so . . . *chic*! How clever of you.'

She smiled over her shoulder. 'Remember the morning after VE Day?'

'How could I forget? – you darting off like a frightened deer when Stephen walked in. You were such a modest girl.'

231

'Well, I *had* just woken up half naked on his couch. I think I blushed the whole length of my body.'

Freya laughed at that. 'I got together a few things for you to wear, d'you remember, and you really surprised me by choosing those slacks. I'll always have that image of you crossing Wardour Street, with the ice creams in your hands.'

Her voice had become fond and faraway as she talked on, angling her body this way and that in the mirror. By the time she turned round Nancy had gone quiet again, her expression lost in melancholy.

'Nance?'

Jolted from her reverie, Nancy said, after a pause, 'It just set me thinking – that was nearly ten years ago. And what have I got to show for it? A badly paid job in publishing, a handful of rejected novels, and – as of this evening – single.'

Freya realised that this unhappy reckoning would feel the more acute in contrast to her own progress. But she would not let her brood. 'You forgot to mention two significant pluses. You have a first-class degree from Oxford, which is something most of us will never get near.' She stared at her until Nancy was compelled to acknowledge it, with a reluctant smile.

'And the other?'

'Why, you've got me for a housemate!'

And now there was nothing reluctant about her smile. Freya leaned in to give her a hug, and squeezed her until Nancy started to laugh.

15

A few weeks later Nancy was in the kitchen at Great James Street prodding a casserole. Freya was pouring gin fizzes for their guests in the living room. They were throwing a dinner in celebration of Freya's new job at the *Envoy*. As she went round with the cocktail jug she wondered at the slightly odd mix of people she had invited. One of them, her brother Rowan, had not been anticipated; he had arrived early that afternoon from Cambridge, unannounced, and she didn't have the heart to send him off to stay at Tite Street. Joss, of course, was there, so too Elspeth, her friend – and now former colleague – at *Frame*; Ginny Gordon, whom she had kept up with from Somerville days; Fosh – Arthur Fosh – a photographer she had got to know through work. And one more who hadn't yet arrived.

'If he doesn't show up in the next five minutes we'll have to start without him,' Nancy said, 'else it'll be ruined.' Her face was flushed from the heat of the pan.

'Righto,' said Freya, sloshing the gin fizz into Nancy's glass.

The latecomer was the only guest about whom she felt a mild apprehension. She had last seen him on the day of her interview at the *Envoy*. Simon Standish, the editor, had been decent about not keeping her in suspense: the paper was eager to have her on board. Her remit on the 'About Town' page, he said, would encompass everything from film premieres and Fabian Society meetings to ballroom-dancing contests and WI bunfights. 'We'd be looking for a light touch,' said Standish. 'Nothing to frighten the horses – or the housewives!'

'I shall keep both readerships in mind,' replied Freya, deciding not to react to his old-fashioned condescension.

'Splendid, splendid,' he cried. 'Well, that should conclude business for now – unless you have any questions of your own?'

'Just one,' she said. 'On the day I received your letter inviting me here I also got a bouquet of flowers – from this office. I was wondering whether you had sent them.'

Standish was frowning his puzzlement. 'I'm not sure I know anything about – are you certain they came from here?'

She nodded. 'The note was unsigned, but the letterhead was unmistakable.'

'None of my doing, I'm afraid,' he said, then added, grinning, 'though it seems to have done the job as a recruiting tool!'

They briefly discussed the notice Freya would have to give to *Frame* – a month, maybe six weeks – and then shook hands. She was on her way to the office lifts when a voice called her name from across the room. Turning, she saw a face that took her a couple of seconds to identify: Robert Cosway, grinning from ear to ear.

'Freya Wyley, as I live and breathe,' he said, laughing, coming from around his desk towards her. He registered the surprise in her face. 'God, have I changed that much?'

'It must be the beard,' she said, starting to smile, though he *had* changed, noticeably, in the five years since they had last seen one another. He was swarthier, and had put on some weight, though he carried it with a kind of swagger. The raw-boned youth she had known was gone. Robert was another who had got married straight after university and had moved – she had heard – to the South Coast. 'I didn't know you worked here – I didn't even know you were in London.'

He held open his palms in an expressive way. 'Started here a couple of months ago. Been working at the *Hove Courier* down in Brighton for a few years.' The homely Mancunian accent had also disappeared, she noted; he could have passed for a southerner.

'So you've moved up with – sorry, I can't remember your wife's name . . .'

'Elaine. And it's ex-wife. I'm back on my own.'

'Oh,' said Freya, measuringly, waiting for him to explain further. Instead he turned the focus back on her.

'So all's well with Standish,' he said, eyes glancing at the office from which she'd just emerged. 'I know he's very pleased to have poached you.'

Freya heard something rather arch in his tone. Robert was smiling at her, and she began to wonder. 'Would I be mistaken in thinking you sent me a bouquet of flowers a couple of weeks ago?'

His laughter indicated she had guessed right. 'I wanted to be the first to offer my congratulations.'

'But I don't understand,' she pursued, 'why would you send them before I'd even got the job?'

'Sorry, I couldn't help myself, it was naughty of me,' he conceded. 'But I know Standish. He always gets his man. Or his woman.'

So they would be colleagues, she and Robert. She had heard news of him, now and then, in the years since Oxford, and it surprised her to learn he was a journalist; with his degree in PPE and his vociferous opinions on social class he had seemed to her more likely to enter politics. When she asked him what he did at the *Envoy* he said that he had 'a roving commission' (not the only roving thing about him, was her unkind thought) though he had his sights fixed on the post of political correspondent; he knew a few MPs and liked the gossipy atmosphere at Westminster.

She had invited him to dinner to mark their fresh start, and also because she thought he might be lonely following his separation. Nancy had just served up the casserole when the doorbell went, and since she was on her feet she went down to answer it. She returned with the latecomer, who looked sheepish as he was introduced to the assembled; only Ginny, aside from the hosts, had met him before.

'Sorry to have kept you,' said Robert, seeing that everyone had started. 'The office was just *bedlam* tonight.'

'Bedlam, eh? Must be looking forward to that, Freya?' said Joss, still a little piqued by her defection from the magazine.

'I can't imagine it will be any madder than it was at the *Chronicle*,' she said, 'and at least I won't have to make the tea.'

'Golly, this gin fizz is strong,' said Elspeth, widening her eyes as she sipped her drink. 'I can feel myself getting tipsy.'

'There's wine instead, if you like,' said Freya, hurrying out to the kitchen and returning with the two bottles of claret that Joss had brought.

'So, Robert,' said Joss, working the corkscrew into the bottle, 'you've known Freya since Oxford?'

'Yes – and Nancy,' he said, with a respectful glance to his left. 'I dare say Freya has told you about the first time we met?'

'I don't think she has. Do go on,' said Joss over Freya's protests. Robert, not requiring much prompting, began to relate the story of his first morning at Balliol and the surprising encounter outside his staircase bathroom.

'So there I am, stark naked, I look up to find this girl just staring at me, quite unembarrassed.' Giggles had started up around the table.

'You make me sound like a peeping Tom,' Freya protested. 'I was only there because it was my dad's old staircase. The last thing I expected was some youth bursting through the door with his privates on parade.'

'I made rather a fuss, didn't I?' said Robert, grinning.

'Yes – and over *such* a little thing,' she replied with a sly look.

'You didn't even blush!' Robert said, shaking his head.

'I've never seen Freya blush,' said Rowan, 'not even when we were little. But she was good at making other people do so.'

'She's toned the language down a bit,' said Elspeth, continuing this third-person appraisal as though Freya herself were not there, 'though I always laugh to recall the first time someone got on the wrong side of her. These production managers came in, and one of them saw Freya and said, "Coffee for the three of us, love." Freya just said, "The kettle's over there. And I'm not your fucking love" – the whole room went into shock.'

Joss laughed and, having filled everyone's glass, said in a heightened formal way, 'Well, now we're all here, let's have a toast and wish all the best to Freya in her new job.'

As the toast was echoed around the table Freya caught Joss's eye and raised her glass, touched by a show of support that had been rather slow in coming. When she had first told him about the job offer from the *Envoy* he had looked incredulous. He asked her if she was unhappy at *Frame*. From his expression she could see he didn't understand, not really, given what the magazine had done for her. Thinking about it later, she realised she could never be absolutely truthful with Joss about her reasons for leaving. For one thing, she sensed that the magazine's decline was terminal, and that if television didn't finish it off then indecision and faint-heartedness 'from upstairs' surely would. Her estimation of Brian Mowbray's editorial capability was low, and the Jerry Dicks business had only confirmed it.

But there was another, deeper impulse behind her decision. She was more driven than Joss suspected. Joss himself was content in a position where she, at his age, probably would not have been; he had settled for deputy instead of pressing for the editorship, or else moving on. Freya wanted her journalism to be read, she wanted her name to be reckoned with. She knew this would always be difficult as a woman, and that it would be doubly difficult if she stayed at *Frame*.

Across the table Elspeth and Joss were chatting away to Rowan, whose nine years at Cambridge had set hard a shell of personal eccentricity first fired in the kiln of his schooldays at Tipton. A junior fellow in mathematics, at twenty-six he had somehow absorbed the manner of a seventy-year-old archbishop. It was mysterious to her that he was academically accomplished, and in maths of all things, a subject about which nobody else in the family had the smallest clue. It was entirely like him to have arrived out of the blue, and to be sporting, for no discernible reason, a black reefer jacket and a pair of tartan trews. She and Nancy had been preparing dinner while he mooched around.

'Are you going to do the Gay Gordons later?' said Freya, nodding at his attire.

Rowan gave her a blank look. 'Oh, I thought it was just dinner – there'll be dancing too?'

She looked at Nancy, who laughed and said, kindly, 'No, nothing like that. We were just admiring those trousers of yours.'

'Thank you,' he said, taking the compliment at face value. 'Got them in a second-hand clothes shop. My landlady did the alterations on her sewing machine.'

Freya's attention was now diverted by something Fosh was telling Ginny. He had been at Bow Street Magistrates' Court that morning to photograph Vere Summerhill, an actor and West End star presently on trial for committing 'indecent acts' with two naval ratings. Freya had been following the trial.

'I felt that sorry for the chap,' said Fosh (no one called him Arthur). 'He looks like he's aged about ten years in two weeks.'

'D'you think anything can save him?' asked Ginny.

Fosh pulled a dubious expression. 'A miracle? There seems to be a bit of a witch-hunt against queers at the moment. You heard what the Home Secretary called them – "a danger to others, especially the young."'

'The charge is "acts of gross indecency,"' said Joss. 'Apparently the phrase hasn't come up in a court since the trials of poor old Oscar.'

'From what I've heard,' said Freya, 'the prosecution's case is a sham. Summerhill picked up the two sailors at a pub and took them home. The next day, after the men left his house, they got into a fight with two others in a club. Beat them up. One of the victims turned out to be a policeman. When the sailors were arrested and the story came out about their night with Summerhill, the police did a deal. In return for dropping the assault charges the men would testify against Summerhill, claim they were "surprised" by his advances and tried to resist. Can you imagine – two strapping brutes like that being "overpowered" by a fifty-year-old actor?'

'Where did you hear all this?' asked Elspeth.

'From Nat Fane. He's standing bail for Vere.'

Robert spluttered out a laugh. 'If that doesn't condemn him in the eyes of the jury, nothing will.'

'I hope I'd have such a friend in the circumstances,' said Freya with a sharp note of reproof.

Robert said, half chastened, 'Yes, quite so. All you can really damn Vere Summerhill for is being an *actor* of gross indecency.'

'Robert,' said Nancy, marking his flippancy with a shake of her head.

'My apologies,' he said, grasping her hand in supplication. 'I take it back. Though I can't help thinking the fellow should have been more careful. Everyone knows that the best thing to do if you're queer is keep a low profile.'

'But why should he have to?' asked Freya. 'The very idea of punishing someone for what he does in the privacy of his bedroom – it's shameful.'

'I'm afraid not everyone's so tolerant,' said Joss. 'As long as the government insists on criminalising homosexual acts and treating the likes of Summerhill as outlaws, privacy can go hang.'

'The press must take a share of the blame, though, don't you think?' said Nancy. 'They so enjoy stirring up people's outrage with talk of "unnatural vices" and "lurking evil". And as Fosh says, they always invoke the young as if they're some defenceless species, ready to be exploited. Those sailors that Summerhill picked up were twenty-one and twenty-two. That's young, isn't it? Yet they both knew what they were doing when they went back home with him.'

'Of course they did. And when they were given a chance to save their skins they, well, jumped on the lifeboat.'

'Like rats from . . . ?' suggested Robert.

Freya stood up. 'Right. While you're belabouring the metaphor may I help anyone to more of Nancy's casserole?'

The plight of Vere Summerhill continued to occupy the table. While Freya was serving seconds in the kitchen Robert wandered in and offered to help. They talked a little about the *Envoy*, and what date had been set for her to start there.

Robert, gazing around in a noticing way, suddenly said, 'So, you and Nancy. How long have you been here together?'

'Nearly three years now.'

He nodded distractedly, and said, 'What she was saying about the press just then – is it a bit awkward for you that she's anti-newspapers?'

'But she's not. She's just against their prurient moralising. On that subject I'm in perfect agreement with her.'

'She's changed quite a lot since the old days. Not afraid to speak up. And something about her looks – she's become more, I don't know, *womanly*.'

Freya stopped spooning out the casserole to look round at him. 'Yes, and she can cook, too. All a man's heart could desire.'

Robert heard the challenging insinuation, and laughed. 'No, no, I didn't mean – I've got an ex-wife and a lawyer's bill to think about.'

His words were resigned, and yet in his tentative tone Freya could detect a quickening of interest. Whatever responsibilities lay on him, Robert was not the type to settle into solitariness. He had never liked being on his own.

'Is she angry, your ex-wife?'

'I should say so. We married too young –' he looked contrite as he said it – 'but I could have made it easier for her. I didn't, and I'm damned sorry for it.' Freya was sorry, too. An impulse of devilry had prompted her question, and she had accidentally pressed a tender spot. In apology she offered him a comradely smile.

'Here,' she said, presenting plates to carry, 'this one's Elspeth's, the other's for Ginny.'

He took them from her, and returned to the living room. As she opened another bottle of wine at the sink she considered Robert in the light of his marital disaster. He did seem to have been humbled by the experience; he was more thoughtful, less abrasive than the youth she had known. He had always had a roguish formality in company, but he had also learned manners from somewhere. His wife? That he was back on the market was certain, and she sensed there would be no shortage of women throwing their hats into the ring.

By the time she rejoined them Robert was entertaining the table with a little vaudevillian routine, pulling his face into contortions that shaded towards the grotesque. He had just demonstrated his 'shot-in-the-back face' and was now testing his 'Martian-invader face'. Ginny and Nancy were both helpless with laughter. The men were more loftily amused. Freya watched him for a few moments, and realised what was afoot.

'Can you do a "sex-life-in-ancient-Rome face"?' she asked him.

Robert blinked his surprise. 'How did you – ?'

'*Lucky Jim*, I believe?'

He threw his hands up and said, 'At last – someone else who's read it! Will you please tell them what a bloody marvellous book it is?'

'It's very funny, in parts. Nance, you remember me in stitches a few weeks ago reading that library book?'

Nancy's frown cleared into recognition. 'Oh, so that was it? Gosh, I wish I'd borrowed it from you now.'

'I'll lend you mine,' said Robert eagerly. He looked around the table. 'It isn't just a comedy, though. It's a sort of blast against all that's stuffy and pompous and narrow-minded about this country. "Merrie England"! It feels like –' he seemed to be searching for the momentous phrase – 'like the book I've been waiting to read all my life.'

'Good Lord,' said Joss mildly.

Robert, seizing on his ally, said to Freya, 'Didn't you think it was something written just for people like us?'

Freya allowed a pause before she answered. 'It *is* terribly funny. You can't fault it for entertainment. But I wasn't so enamoured of Dixon. He seems to me – well, a selfish sod, actually.'

'What d'you mean?' asked Robert, frowning.

242

Freya, aware that nobody else at the table knew the book, decided to keep it brief. 'He's an assistant lecturer who wants to get on but despises academia and the people in it. He hates his boss and his awful son – which you can understand – but he also hates the woman he's involved with, Margaret, who's a bit of a pill, it's true, but hardly the loathsome witch he makes her out to be. There's something self-congratulatory there, and an underlying nastiness about women – like he's settling a score.'

Robert gave her a blank look. 'Are you joking? What about Christine?'

'Well, he fancies her, and wants to get her into bed. But that doesn't mean he particularly likes her.'

'I think you've misread him,' said Robert, shaking his head. 'Dixon exaggerates his resentments for comic effect. He's bored and frustrated by the people above him, by the situation he's in – but not by women. He's just fed up with the woman he's with.'

'Possibly,' said Freya, in a voice that implied very little possibility at all.

'Oh, Freya! I wish someone else had – Nancy, I'm going to insist that you read this and tell me I'm right.'

Nancy gave a tolerant lift of her chin. 'After this I feel I must.'

Ginny, still giggling, said, 'But, Robert, you didn't answer Freya's original question – can you do, what is it, a "sex-life-in-ancient-Rome face"?'

Robert smirked, and composed himself before narrowing his eyes and protruding his lower lip in a mime of gormless lechery. This time they fell about laughing, even the men, and Robert obliged them, without much persuasion, by performing an encore.

Freya, recovering herself, said, 'Very good, though as I recall it doesn't seem very different from your "sex-life-in-Oxford-University face".'

'– and that wasn't even an act,' added Nancy, at which Robert roared in a nervous show of mirth.

Over pudding – Freya had made a chocolate mousse – Elspeth told them about a news item her mother had sent her from their local paper in Lancashire. The town had recently been presented with a pair of statues, the work of a renowned sculptor, who unveiled them with great to-do at the town hall. Elspeth's mother had enclosed a photograph of the statues with the news story.

'What I hadn't realised, of course,' said Elspeth, 'was that the figures were male and female *nudes*. Now no one here would bat an eyelid at them, but up in the provinces . . . The newspaper recorded the mayor's comments on inspecting the statues. He said, and I quote, "Art is art, and nothing can be done to prevent it. But there is the mayoress's decency to be considered."'

'Quite right, too,' said Fosh, laughing. 'I only hope they didn't offend the eyes of your sainted mama, Elspeth.'

'Funny, isn't it? She just wrote, "They did look awfully nice together," as if they were off on honeymoon or something.'

'Oh, bless your mother!' said Nancy. 'My father would have been shoulder to shoulder with the mayor, I'm afraid.'

'My God, this country,' said Robert, eyes half closed in disbelief. 'Has there ever been a place for such puritanical, curtain-twitching killjoys? I beg your pardon, Nancy, I don't mean your father any disrespect –'

'None taken,' Nancy smiled. 'He's Catholic, in any case, not puritan. He'd be horrified even to hear such things discussed.'

'It does seem we've talked about nothing but sex this evening,' said Freya.

'Yes, as the oldest person here I must say I'm shocked by your modern ways,' said Joss.

'How old *are* you, by the way?' asked Rowan, out of nowhere.

Joss angled his head to the question. 'I'm – how old d'you think I am?'

'Dunno,' said Rowan. 'About fifty?'

Freya burst out laughing. 'He's thirty-nine! Sorry, darling,' she said to Joss, who looked slightly stunned. 'Rowan, I think as penance you should go and make the coffee. There's a pot on the shelf above the sink.'

Rowan obediently rose from the table and headed off to the kitchen. Elspeth widened her eyes comically. 'Glad he didn't try to guess my age.'

Joss looked across to Freya. 'Isn't he meant to be good with numbers, your brother?'

'I don't think maths at Cambridge helps in this instance,' said Freya, who dropped her voice. 'Rowan's not very worldly, as you can probably tell. I have the feeling that most conversation passes him by.'

'He's very sweet, though,' said Nancy. 'He regards Freya like some kind of deity.'

'Not an assumption Freya would necessarily discourage,' said Joss drily.

'He certainly jumped to it when you told him to go and make the coffee,' observed Ginny.

The talk had moved on to other things by the time Rowan returned from the kitchen bearing a tray with cups and a twin-handled clay vessel. Freya looked at it for a moment: whisps of steam were rising from its narrow neck.

'Rowan, why have you brought that old thing in?'

'You said there was a pot above the sink, so I made the coffee in it.'

'That's actually an amphora. Mum brought it back from Corfu. It's not –' She looked at Rowan, his face a perfect blank of incomprehension. 'Oh, never mind. Greek coffee, anyone?'

*   *   *

Elspeth, Ginny and Fosh left around midnight. Robert stayed on for another nightcap, gossiping about life at the *Envoy* and the state of office politics there – 'like the Balkans,' he said. Only when Nancy yawned behind her hand did Robert twig it was time for him to leave. After clearing the dinner table Joss helped Freya make up the divan for Rowan, who stripped down to his shorts to perform a bizarre series of exercises before settling down. Sometimes she hardly knew what to say to him.

Joss was already in bed by the time she had finished tidying up in the kitchen. The bedside lamp cast a feeble glow. Outside she could hear the occasional hiss of car tyres along the street; it had been raining. She put a record on the turntable and placed the needle on its revolving edge. It was Thelonious Monk's 'Well, You Needn't', whose tune she couldn't get out of her head.

Joss watched her as she got undressed. 'Won't you keep him awake with that?'

'He's probably asleep.'

He said, after a pause, 'My God, do I really look fifty?'

Freya chuckled at his half-wondering, half-pleading tone. 'Nothing like. I think your grey hair confused him. Pay no mind – Rowan hardly knows his *own* age.'

He didn't reply; she could tell from his silence that he was mulling on it. An idea sparked in her head. She went to her stack of records and picked out an old Dinah Shore album. She replaced the Monk with it, having checked the song she wanted, and dropped the needle again.

'Here, this one's for you,' she said, as the lyric wafted across the music's stately swing.

I may be wrong, but – I think you're wonderful!
I may be wrong, but – I think you're swell!
I like your style, say – I think it's marvellous.
I'm always wrong, so how can I tell?

Still in her slip she did a little shimmy around the bed. By the end she had laughed him out of his drooping mood. She accepted his 'bravo' with a bow, and climbed into bed.

'Rather fun, wasn't it, this evening?' he said.

'What did you think of Robert?'

'Oh . . . seemed a smart young fellow. Quite amusing. Quite pleased with himself. I imagine he would have enjoyed that little performance of yours just then.'

'I don't think so,' she said with a half-laugh.

'But weren't you two – ?'

'God, years ago! He was a virgin when we first met.'

'You mean to say you deflowered him? No wonder he was making those calf-eyes at you.'

Freya shook her head. 'Flattered as I am, I can assure you it wasn't me he was after. It was Nancy – couldn't you tell?'

She could sense him making up his mind. 'Maybe it was both of you,' he said, leaning over to switch off the bedside lamp. For some moments they lay in silence, listening to the occasional sounds of the street – footsteps, a door closing. A car slid by the house, its headlamps casting a wobbly pattern of lights across the bedroom ceiling.

She thought again about Robert. She had wondered before this evening if their long separation might have had an estranging effect, but they had settled into their old friendship without any awkwardness. The years between them had just fallen away. She was not mistaken, though, about his particular attentiveness towards Nancy; he had never been good at dissembling. Had Nancy noticed it, too? Much as she liked him, Freya could not regard Robert as dependable – too selfish, too easily bored. The danger was that both of them were on the rebound, Nancy from Stewart, Robert from his marriage. They would have stories to swap, she supposed. Her mind drifted on, turning up scenes, conversations, from their past together. An involuntary laugh escaped her.

In the dark she felt Joss turn to face her. 'What's funny?'

'Oh, nothing,' she said, but he was curious, and pressed her. 'I was just remembering. Talking about Robert set me off – his "deflowering", as you charmingly put it.'

'Ah. Dreaming about the old flame . . .'

'No, nothing like that. Don't get cross about this, but after the first time we had, *you know* – Robert rolled off me and said something –' she began to laugh properly as the words resurfaced – 'he said, "You're not just a woman, you're a right good chap, too." I'm sorry –' The laughter seemed to seize hold and shake her – she couldn't help it.

Next to her, Joss harrumphed with a kind of scornful amusement and waited for her fit to exhaust itself. When at last she was calm she put a placatory hand on his shoulder.

'Sorry. It seemed funny at the time.' There came no reply from him, and she wondered if she had said too much: men didn't tend to like it when you recounted episodes from your sexual history, even in jest. Perhaps especially in jest – one day they might end up the butt of the joke. Into the silence she said, 'Oh dear. Now you must be thinking me some awful virgin-despoiling slut.'

She waited for a reaction, half wishing she hadn't been so unguarded. 'Not really,' he said, putting his hand to hers. 'I think you're a right good chap.'

16

Robert proved himself a friend during her first few weeks at the *Envoy*. Though he had not been there long, he had quickly commended himself to the staff. He seemed at home as he introduced Freya around the place, and she was quietly impressed that some of the older hacks would hail him on sight. Most of them called him 'Robert', and sometimes 'Bob', a diminutive she knew he hated but never made a point of correcting. He got on with people, flattering them like an agent with his clients. The volatile, combative youth of Oxford days had mastered his moods, and had come to learn discretion. Once, as Freya was relaying some gossip about a mutual acquaintance to a circle of staffers, Robert had smoothly interrupted her and steered the conversation elsewhere. When she mentioned this to him later, he explained that the man Freya had been discussing was a close friend of a senior staffer: it might not reflect well on her to be seen passing on tittle-tattle, however innocently she had come by it. But he often gossiped about people, she objected. 'Yes. Behind *everyone's* back,' he replied. Robert had done it as a favour, but she realised he meant it as a lesson.

She started to notice the subtle ways in which he would play one person off against another and yet stay friendly with both. Whenever she happened to attend an editorial conference she was fascinated by the impression of *plausibility* he created around himself: he never raised his voice, yet he always had his say. If discussions became heated, or tempers threatened to boil over, Robert would step in to cushion egos and dilute the tension. Where once he thrived on contrariness and discord now he was the office peacemaker – the *Envoy*'s very own Francis of Assisi.

But she soon discovered that Robert hadn't lost his old acerbity; he had simply learned to hide it, like an assassin his dagger. Whenever Freya got him on his own, at lunch or over a drink after work, it came almost as a relief to hear him skewering this or that colleague. 'That cockchafer,' he said, a favourite new word of his. The irreverent cheek of *Lucky Jim* continued to obsess him, and as well as quoting lines and pulling faces he would rail, in Jim-like fashion, against the stifling conspiracies of deference and superiority that kept young chaps like himself 'in their place'. Freya heard hypocrisy in this, and pointed out to him his own tendency to flatter those in charge. But Robert shook his head and claimed it was purely strategic on his part; if he was to get where he intended then 'sucking up' to the bigwigs was part of the deal. So where *did* he intend to be? she asked. Robert replied with a look she would never forget: it was a droll sort of frown that seemed on the one hand to question her need to ask, and on the other implied that, since she *had* asked, well, wherever he damn well pleased.

Their renewed friendship naturally enfolded Nancy in its compass. Because Robert was lodging in a grim Mile End bedsitter – his divorce had reduced him to a 'pauper' – they tended to socialise at Great James Street. If they were cobbling together a supper in the kitchen he would often be included. She found herself observing Nancy and Robert together, but couldn't detect any romantic current crackling between them. He flirted, on reflex, with almost every woman he knew, and Nancy, still brooding on the end of her affair with Stewart, seemed content with being friendly. The past infused the air around them like pollen. They talked about Oxford and the friends they had made there, and only one subject, the short-lived passion between Robert and Freya, remained taboo.

One of the first things she did at the *Envoy* was to set about nailing down an interview with Jerry Dicks. It wasn't easily done. When she rang his flat in Soho the same young man would answer and claim no knowledge of his whereabouts. On telephoning his studio an assistant said he was 'on the Continent', but couldn't be more specific. Eventually the gallery let her know that Jerry was back in town and would meet her at the Café Royal at one o'clock the following day; she arrived ten minutes early and waited for over an hour. He didn't show.

Later that week she was informed that Jerry had 'forgotten' their appointment (no apology) and would meet her at his club on Dean Street. This turned out to be a narrow uncarpeted room on the second floor above a grocer's shop. Behind the bar stood a woman, perhaps fifty, her face a clown's mask of make-up touched with a glitter of malignity; upon seeing Freya enter she fairly screeched, 'Members only!' The clientele sat in attitudes of vacancy, shoulders slumped over their drinks. Freya told the woman she was there to meet Jerry Dicks, to which she replied, sourly, that he was barred. "Asn't paid a fuckin' bill here for three years.' At the end of the bar a head lifted; a man mumbled something about finding Jerry in 'the Dutch', round the corner.

Back on Dean Street she endured a little pang as she passed Gennaro's, where she hadn't set foot in years, not since her nightmare performance at lunch after VE Day. She sometimes reminisced about it with Nancy, who said that it was the only occasion she had ever seen her look 'inconsolable'. She walked on to Old Compton Street and into

Soho's lunchtime foot traffic of draymen and grocers and shopboys. A newsagent was twirling a pole to draw down the striped awning on his window. The late-spring sky, tinged with blue, held a promise of warmth to come. She had never been in the Dutchman's Cape, a retiring little pub on Romilly Street. Outside, an aproned barman was sluicing the pavement with a bucket of soapy water. Seeing nobody she recognised in the front bar she tried the room upstairs; athwart the landing lay a brindled whippet, whose mournful brown gaze seemed familiar to her.

She passed through into the room, where huge gilt French mirrors played a trick of perspective by seeming to double the size of it. There, reclining on a horsehair couch in the corner, was the whippet's owner, Hetty, whom she had last seen at the Villiers in March. When Freya called her name there was no recognition in her look, though curiosity induced her to rise from the sofa and approach, her hip-swaying model's walk only a little unsteady.

'I'm looking for your friend Jerry. He's rather elusive.'

'That's the way he likes it,' she said with a sloppy smile.

Glancing at her watch Hetty said she'd just make a tele-phone call if Freya wanted to wait. Her right eye, she now noticed, had the tiniest cast in it, the flaw that rendered her face more human, and therefore more beautiful. While she was gone Freya looked around the room, the blinds drawn to shield the little huddles of twos and threes, drinking, murmuring; it was a sanctum for the sort of people who regarded daylight as an unsatisfactory hiatus between nights, when the real fun happened. Soho was honeycombed with such bolt-holes, hideaways, dens; you could never know how many there were.

'He's there now,' said Hetty, returning. 'I'll take you.'

With Rhoda the whippet trotting at their side they moseyed deeper into Soho. In a quiet flagged court Hetty stopped and rang the bell at an unassuming doorway. Some moments later a gangly youth she addressed as Kenny admitted them. They followed him up a staircase whose precarious wooden banisters hadn't seen paint in years. The flat, on the second floor, was seedy even by the standards of its fly-by-night neighbours; grimy net curtains muffled the daylight, and hairline cracks zigzagged along the lumpy plastered walls. It hardly seemed fit habitation for a renowned photographer. But then Jerry Dicks himself hardly answered to the type. They found him in the living room, sitting cross-legged in an exhausted armchair, the air almost blue from cigarette smoke. He was wearing a collarless shirt and grey trousers with thin braces pooling about his waist like the dropped strings of a marionette. He stared from unsmiling eyes at Freya and made no movement other than to drag deeply on his Turkish cigarette.

Hetty performed the introduction. Dicks nodded, and scraped the glowing tip of his cigarette against the ashtray. His small head was accentuated by his outsize ears, which protruded like the handles of a prize cup.

'The *Envoy*. That's the lefty one, isn't it?' he said.

Freya tipped her head. 'It has liberal sympathies. I'm sorry we didn't manage to meet the other day – at the Café Royal.'

'Oh. Were we meant to? Kenny –' Dicks nodded at his assistant – 'takes down all the phone messages. Can't read his bleedin' handwriting most of the time.' Kenny murmured an apology and disappeared somewhere. A silence fell, so Freya began to explain the profile of him she had planned, how it would require a couple of afternoons just talking, with perhaps a look through his archive to pick out a few of his favourite portraits – she felt sure he had some stories to tell . . .

Dicks stared off, a blank. He couldn't have been less interested. Then, without warning, his face broke into a wide grin that revealed his irregular discoloured teeth. Freya was disarmed for a split second until she saw what had occasioned this remarkable change: Rhoda, the whippet, had just slunk into the room, and Dicks, leaning forward, picked her up with avuncular fondness.

'Ahhh . . . me pal!' he cried, stroking the dog's narrow head. His smile was entranced.

Hetty, watching this reunion, said with a laugh, 'You look a bit like her, you know.' And Freya too now saw a certain kinship in the dark eyes and pointy features of dog and man.

Jerry, after some more petting of Rhoda, addressed the business in hand. 'So, an interview . . . How much?' His eyes were back on Freya.

'What d'you mean?'

'I mean, how much do I get paid for it?'

'Well – nothing,' she said. 'We don't pay anyone to be interviewed.'

Dicks gave her a disbelieving look. 'What? You're expecting me to give up my time for *nowt*?'

'It doesn't work like that, darling,' said Hetty. 'It'd be like a sitter asking you to pay them for taking their picture.'

'I pay *you*!' he said accusingly.

'Not much. And *you* don't pay me in any case, it's the agency.'

But Dicks grumbled on; he couldn't understand why he should put himself out for nothing. He had a living to make, didn't he? Hetty, in a patient voice, reasoned with him, explaining the deal: the newspaper got the interview, the photographer got the publicity, and both of them got the benefit in sales and reputation. He still looked unimpressed, and Freya realised that she would have to win him round personally. As far as he was concerned she was just a face he didn't know, from a newspaper he never read – a pest, in short.

'By the way,' she began, 'I called in at your club earlier. Vera was asking after you.'

Dicks paused, momentarily thrown that she knew either his club or its proprietor. 'Haven't been in there for a while. Vera – *la vieille dame sans merci*! Did she really ask after me?'

Freya caught his eye, and gave a little comic grimace. 'To be honest, no. What she said was, "Tell the cunt he owes me money."'

Dicks, not expecting this verbal slap, tucked in his chin: she had flashed him the merest glimpse of personality, but it was enough. He threw back his head and cackled mightily. Hetty, she saw, was giving her a knowing look. There was something expansive and forgiving in Jerry's tone as he told her about Vera. They'd known each other from way back, of course – Vera had been running the Dean Street club for years, 'with all the charm of a Soviet border guard'.

'Yeah,' he reflected, 'she's a hero to thousands, that woman, and not a fuckin' friend in the world, ha ha!' His laugh, initially vigorous, had turned wheezing.

'So, Jerry,' said Hetty, perhaps sensing the moment, 'I'm sure you can see your way to chatting for an hour or two with Freya here. Your picture in the paper – what d'you say?'

Dicks shook out another cigarette and lit it. He gulped down the smoke. 'Dare say I can. I'll even put on a shirt and collar for yer,' he added with a giggle. 'But you'll need to gimme some notice. Twiggez-vous?'

'What sort of notice?' asked Freya.

'Oh, a few weeks. I've got a shoot to do in Paris next week, then it's on to Zurich, Genoa, Milan. I tell you, I'll need a fuckin' rest cure by the time I get back.'

Freya asked him if they might arrange a meeting before he went on his travels, but Jerry wouldn't hear of it. Hetty had a try too, but it was really like arguing with a spoilt child. Eventually the door knocker sounded from below to break the impasse, and Kenny came up escorting a couple of men, both hard-faced and businesslike in suits. They offered neither a greeting nor a smile, not even for Rhoda the whippet. Hetty, without exchanging a word with the newcomers, signalled to Freya that it was time to leave. Jerry waggled his hand in a half-hearted goodbye.

'Stubborn old bugger, isn't he?' said Hetty as she accompanied Freya down the stairs.

'I'll winkle him out somehow. We have a friend in common – Nat Fane –'

'Yeah, I saw you talking to him at the Villiers that night. Nat's rather fascinated by Jerry. Maybe a bit envious of him, too.'

'Envious? Why?'

Hetty's smile was enigmatic. 'Well – Jerry lives on his own terms. He does what he likes, because he doesn't care what people think of him. Nat, though, he *really* cares what people think.'

They were at the door when Freya said, 'Those two men who just came in – who were they?'

'Oh, Jerry knows all sorts of villains,' she said. 'He's always up to something – I think those two buy up his dirty pictures to sell in the clubs round here.'

'Really?'

'Nothing very serious. Boys with big cocks, stuff like that. It's quite a nice earner for him.'

'Does he need to? I mean, with *Vogue*, and the gallery –'

'Jerry's terrible with money – he runs through it. Why d'you think he was so keen to charge for an interview?'

They stood talking for a few minutes more outside the flat. Freya was about to leave when Hetty, almost as an after-thought, put out a restraining hand. 'I was forgetting you work for a paper. What I mentioned about Jerry and his pictures – can you keep mum?'

Freya nodded, of course she would. Hetty held her gaze for a moment, and smiled. 'I only told you that cos I like you.'

256

The verdict in the trial of Vere Summerhill was out. The defendant was found guilty of committing acts of gross indecency with two young naval ratings and sentenced to six months' imprisonment. At the *Envoy* that afternoon Robert and Freya were summoned to the editor's office: Standish was planning to run a series of articles about the case.

'I want the repercussions of it examined from every angle – talk to the judge, to the Director of Public Prosecutions, to the police. We should also get an interview with the Lord Chamberlain's Office about homosexuality on the stage – we have to find out whether Summerhill will ever be allowed to work in theatre again.'

'There's also the medical point of view to consider,' said Robert. 'Some doctors believe that queers can be, well, cured by treatment – electric shock therapy, female sex hormones and what have you.'

Standish looked doubtful. 'Yes, but we can't make it too explicit. Our readers don't like that stuff forced down their throat – as it were.'

Robert glanced at Freya, who said, 'With respect, we should treat our readers as grown-ups. The real danger is ignorance – if people still think homosexuality is a "disease" then of course they're going to fear it. We should definitely talk to the British Medical Association about how effective this treatment is. For all we know the whole idea of medical intervention might be a mistake.'

'But what's the alternative?' asked Robert. 'Do you really think people are going to put up with a lot of sodomites doing as they please?'

Standish made a grimace. 'I think "inverts" is the word here, Robert. "Sodomite" is rather, um – distasteful.'

Freya felt a sudden bleakness of spirit descend on her. If the *Envoy* was supposed to be the liberal end of the newspaper market . . . But no, the battles had to be chosen carefully. 'I don't think we should lose sight of Summerhill in all this. He's the victim, after all.'

'Not in the eyes of the law,' said Robert with a shrug.

'That's exactly what we're debating,' she replied levelly. 'The law may well be at fault. Anyway, I could do a piece on Vere, gather tributes from people in the business.'

'I don't think we should turn him into a martyr,' said Robert. 'Summerhill knew the risks, consorting with those lowlifes – he just made the mistake of getting caught.'

'We've been through this before,' said Freya, nettled. 'To say he shouldn't have got caught presupposes he was doing something wrong. The counterargument is that the state has no right to intervene in what goes on in private between consenting adults.'

'Quite so,' said Standish. 'Robert, if you concentrate on the legal and judicial side, Freya can take care of the medical and moral questions. And I like the idea of personal tributes – we could use that picture of Nat Fane outside the court.'

Robert groaned theatrically. 'As if *he* needs any more publicity.'

The next day, while Freya was writing her weekly column, Robert sidled over to her desk. 'Doing anything for lunch?'

'I'm insanely busy,' she said without looking up.

'Not even a quick sandwich at the Marquis?'

There was a pleading note in his voice. When she said she could spare him three-quarters of an hour he looked grateful. The Marquis was a musty old-fashioned pub situated in the warren of courts off Fleet Street. Sawdust carpeted the floor. She arrived to find Robert at a corner table with a pale ale on the go.

'Let me fetch you a libation,' he said, getting up.

When she asked for a ginger beer he sniggered, and went off to the bar. It took her a few moments to work out what

258

had amused him. Settled at the table Robert began talking about their meeting with Standish; he was pleased that they had been entrusted with a 'big story', he continued, given they were relative juniors in the office. This could be a significant step-up for both of them.

Absorbing this, Freya said, 'I didn't want to say anything in front of Standish, Robert, but – do you really *want* to do this story?'

He looked at her. 'What d'you mean? Of course I do.'

'It's just that, I don't think you much care for Summerhill or for what he's been put through. You don't like queers and never have. "Ginger beers"! If I didn't know you better I'd say you regard prison as exactly what they deserve.'

Robert's face froze for a moment; he looked stunned with disbelief. 'Why would you say that? I've got nothing against Summerhill or his kind –'

'But you have. Yesterday you said that if they got caught they only have themselves to blame. It alarms me to think of you reporting on this when your starting point is that Vere Summerhill and "his kind" are basically criminal.'

Robert was shaking his head. 'I've never said that. And I don't think prison sentences for homosexuality are justified. All I was proposing was the need for discretion. I don't think it's monstrous of me to say I'd rather they kept themselves to themselves.'

'– because you're revolted by them. Which is why I'm wondering how you can possibly write about this in an unprejudiced way.'

'For God's sake, I'm a *journalist*, that's the job – you learn how to evaluate the information, not get bloody emotional about the arguments. I could ask the same about your impartiality. How do you know your sympathy for Summerhill won't affect what you write?'

'None of us is absolutely impartial, I agree. All you can try to do is give someone a fair hearing. And in the case of a homosexual it strikes me that a woman would be naturally more disposed to understand, because she knows what it's like to be feared and despised by society.'

'What the hell are you talking about?' said Robert, his face puckered in disgust.

'Well, look at recent history. Forty-odd years ago our government imprisoned women because they had the temerity to demand the vote – to demand the *basic rights* of a citizen. Whether the suffragists back then felt much affinity for the likes of Oscar Wilde, also languishing in jail, I couldn't say. But times have changed, and women who've grown up on stories of their mothers and grandmothers being persecuted for their beliefs perhaps look on this outlawed minority and feel, I don't know, a recurring sense of injustice.'

'The two aren't comparable,' he said. 'Suffrage was a political question. Homosexuality is a moral one.'

'Robert, you sound horribly like a politician. Do you really think morality and politics are somehow independent of one another? One of the reasons Asquith's government refused to countenance female suffrage was their fear it would undermine the *moral* fabric of the family – that a woman who was allowed to vote would neglect the duties of "hearth and home".'

'Your analogy's rot in any event. Whatever their political inclinations, most women don't feel the slightest sympathy for men who hang around public lavatories for their thrills.'

'That's just what I'd expect a man to say.'

He was glaring at her now. 'You're so bloody self-righteous, you know.'

She paused for a moment. 'And I thought you'd changed, too.' She said it with a half-laugh and got up to leave. Robert, with an anguished groan, rose to stop her.

'Freya, please – don't. Don't go.'

'Why not? Everything I say seems to annoy you.'

Robert hung his head, and took a deep breath. 'I didn't even mean to talk about this, I wanted to –' He looked in forlorn appeal to her. 'Please stay, just for a few minutes.'

She sighed, and took her seat again. He watched her as she took out her papers and tobacco and rolled a slender cigarette – roll-ups were her new thing; she liked their home-made feel. As she smoked he began a tale of woe. The divorce proceedings had hit the buffers; Elaine had had a change of heart and wanted to give the marriage another try.

Freya was nonplussed. 'Wait – I thought you already *were* divorced. You said she was your "ex-wife".'

'Well, she is, in all but name. We decided months ago on a separation. Now it seems that she took the arrangement to be – more temporary.'

'You have a lawyer, though – you told me.'

'Yes, I hired one down in Brighton and just assumed he'd get on with it. But nothing's happened. She's told her lawyer she expects me to come back.'

They were silent for a few moments. Around them the pub's lunch-hour activity was sluggish; there was hardly a stir beyond the clink of glasses, the scrape of a bar stool against the wooden floor. Freya wasn't sure what Robert expected her to say.

'Have you talked to her about it?'

'Not much. Letters, phone calls.'

'Wouldn't it be better to sit down and have it out with her? Letters always leave room for ambiguity. With a face-to-face conversation at least you know where you stand.'

Robert looked away, brooding. When he spoke he seemed to be dragging the words out of himself. 'Face-to-face with her . . . is the last thing in the world I want. I know I've behaved badly, why make it more difficult than it is? I don't love her, and that's the end of it.'

261

'She may need to hear that from you,' said Freya, expelling a plume of smoke, 'if you're determined to go through with a divorce.'

He closed his eyes again, as if to blank some inward pain. 'I don't want to go through a divorce. I just want to *be divorced*, gone, out of her life.'

There was something about his refusal to take responsibility she thought pretty abject – strange, too. In the office Robert was always on hand to negotiate or conciliate, to soothe the disgruntled feelings of a colleague. And he certainly wasn't shy about putting himself forward in editorial meetings. His professional and personal lives simply didn't fit together. In private he let things drift, probably in the hope that they would resolve themselves. Some mixture of frankness and affection suddenly emboldened her.

'Do you remember back in Oxford – that night I saw you at the Union with your new girl, what was her name?'

Robert looked sheepish. 'Cressida.'

'That's her,' she smiled. 'God, I was furious with you! It wasn't just that you'd thrown me over. It was realising that, if we hadn't run into one another, you'd just have gone on with your life, and left me to find out for myself. It was cruel and yet passive at the same time.'

Embarrassed, he had started to knead the middle of his forehead with his fingers. 'You're right,' he said quietly. 'I can't bear confrontation – I'll do anything to avoid it.' At last, he dared to catch her eye. 'Only please say *you've* forgiven me.'

'Well, of course I have,' she said, rolling her eyes, 'but that's not the point. I'm trying to prevent you making the same mistake. Don't just let it lie! Be responsible. Arrange a meeting in Brighton, or wherever, and tell her the truth –'

'I can't.'

'*You can* – and you must. Delaying will only make it worse. And more expensive. You can't afford to have a lawyer on the meter.'

Robert nodded ruefully. 'Funny, isn't it, how over the years you've acquired such good sense, while I'm still –'

'The same old sodding cockchafer,' she supplied. Robert looked stung for an instant on hearing this, and she realised his mood was too fragile to stand even a little teasing. She quickly added, 'It's why we love you, Robert.'

The words had an emollient effect. He smiled again. She realised that she had been learning something from him these past weeks, something she had never much appreciated before: that tact sometimes worked better than truth-telling.

17

Unforgiving Eye:
Portrait of a Soho Jester
by Freya Wyley

In the teeming urban jungle of Soho Jerry Dicks is
everywhere and nowhere. He is its very own Mr Kurtz.
For weeks I tracked his vanishing presence all over,
but picked up only rumours of his whereabouts. In the
pubs and cafes where he's known to be a regular they
shrugged at my enquiries. 'Jerry was in a while ago,
but . . .'; 'He's been in Paris, I think . . .' He is a man
always on his way through somewhere. He has a flat near
Berwick Street and a studio off Kensington High Street.
I first wrote to him at the former, and some weeks later
the Post Office returned my letter with 'Not known at
this address' scrawled across it. I later discovered that
the handwriting was his own. Nor is there any use in
trying the telephone. A friend of his said that in twenty
years he has never known him to answer one.

This elusiveness would not be remarkable but for
the fact that Jerry Dicks is an internationally renowned
photographer. His work has been exhibited in London,

Dublin and Paris. His portraits of the great and good have adorned the pages of *Vogue*. I had glimpsed him once, from a distance, at a private view of his recent work at the Villiers Gallery, off St Martin's Lane. He was surrounded by admirers and well-wishers whom he kept in a roar with tall stories and ribald jokes. It did not seem an appropriate moment to interrupt him, though afterwards I wished I had. It would be another three months before I managed to clap eyes on him again.

His friend and sometime model Hetty Cavendish said that when in the right mood Dicks can be 'the most entertaining company in London'. He has been adopted as court portraitist and jester to that exclusive clique of writers, artists and drinkers who have made Soho their personal fiefdom. The painter Ossian Blackler is his closest friend and a notable collaborator: it is his custom, whenever painting a portrait, to use Dicks's photographs of his subject as an aide-memoire. The two men often holiday together in Spain and Morocco, where they are sometimes accompanied by Hetty Cavendish, presumably in the Dorothy Lamour role. Not everyone is so enamoured of him. At *Vogue* and other magazines Dicks is known as a troublemaker, mislaying expensive equipment, provoking people, arriving late at shoots or failing to show up at all. A colossal spendthrift, he has been through lean times, giving rise to rumours of his association with loan sharks, pimps, racketeers and other characters of low repute.

When I asked him about his acquaintanceship with Soho's underlife he laughed, or rather, he unleashed a savage bronchial cackle. 'People are always claiming to know me,' he said. 'I've not the foggiest who they are.' But in his time has he not encountered some shifty characters? 'Oh, yeah. I met this very sinister cove once, quietly spoken, tight suit – tried to put the bite on me for some money.' He stopped, and gazed off. So who was he? I asked. 'Turned out to be my bank manager. Never saw him again.'

One day in mid-June I finally ran Jerry Dicks to ground, and we went to a small Italian restaurant on Brewer Street, close to his flat. Though it was a lunchtime he ate nothing; his one concession to 'victuals' (his word) is breakfast, when he has either scrambled eggs or a kipper. He made up for this austere regimen by drinking and smoking a great deal. When the waiter was about to pour the bottle of Soave, Dicks indicated his glass and said, mildly, 'Just up to the brim, thanks.' By the time I finished my spaghetti vongole the bottle was empty and he had ordered another. In person he can be viciously rude or impossibly charming. I caught him on a good day; his mouth, sullen in repose, frequently split into a wide grin. With ears that protrude either side of his small head he suddenly resembled Mickey Mouse.

About his past he is comically unreliable. When he said he was born on the pier at Skegness 'and sold off to a touring mime troupe' he didn't seem concerned whether I believed him or not. As far as the record goes he was actually born in Chester around 1912. In his early twenties he nursed ambitions to be a draughtsman and worked for some years at a cartographer's in Covent Garden. Tiring of that, he quit and loafed around Paris, where he used to earn his keep as a street artist and sign-painter. He still speaks good French, throwing in the odd Anglo-inflected phrase such as 'Twiggez-vous?' (You understand?) He came by his trade through the war. Having learned to work film cameras he was assigned to the Army Film and Photography Unit and saw action in Malta, Tripoli and Normandy. He said that he acquired his first Leica by wresting it from the hands of a dead German. As the Allies advanced through northern France he photographed scenes of atrocious carnage. 'You never forget the smell of a burning corpse.'

In post-war London he found his work much in demand, and earned enough to allow him to open a studio. While many admire Dicks's photographs of urban ruin and desolation, it is his eye for the landscape of the human face that most intrigues. A short man, he holds his Rolleiflex camera at waist level, obliging his subjects to adopt an awkward stoop; their faces in consequence look quizzical, vulnerable, possibly guilty. Certain actors playing up to the camera suddenly take on the disturbing aspect of asylum inmates. Writers don't come off much better. Nathaniel Fane, clad in pinstripes, looks like a half-starved spiv. The theatre critic James Erskine, bulbous-eyed, wears the fearful aspect of an offender preparing for a night in the cells. Even his old friend Ossian Blackler seems to shrink before the unforgiving lens, his thwarted gaze like a fox that's been chased out of the henhouse.

How much these portraits owe to chance and how much to design is difficult to tell. Dicks spends long hours in his darkroom punching up the grain and contrast of his monochrome prints, but their atmosphere seems to be shaped by an unheard dialogue going on between the photographer and his sitter – or 'victims' as he prefers to call them. Some of them are clearly in deep discomfort. The photographs he has exhibited in *The Public Image* cock a snook at the measured, classical approach to portraiture of his contemporaries. He slyly referred to Norman Parkinson and Cecil Beaton as 'my so-called rivals'. Where they flatter and coddle, Dicks interrogates his subjects, pursuing the 'truth' of a face to the point of cruelty. There is something of the devil in this recording angel. The wonder of it is that so many are willing to present themselves to his dark-adapted eye. 'I've no interest in making people look good,' he said. 'I want to put their soul on view. And if they haven't got a soul, then I'll make do with their conscience.'

'Very good,' said Joss, looking up from the newspaper rather sternly. 'Very . . . lively.'

Freya knew his tone too well to miss a faint withholding in his praise. They were in the living room at Great James Street, as early-morning sunlight bulged across the floor. Seated crosswise on the easy chair, she waited for a moment, and said, '"Very lively." That's your code for "lacking in subtlety" – am I right?'

Joss's reluctant laugh indicated he would not be drawn into a fight. 'I thoroughly enjoyed it as a piece of writing,' he said carefully.

'How else would you enjoy it?' she asked. 'As a piece of cake?'

'Don't be provoking. I was very entertained, and I'm sure readers of the *Envoy* will be, too.'

'Right. But for argument's sake, had you been editing it what improvements would you have made?'

He rolled his eyes heavenwards, a habit, she noted, he had picked up from her.

Holding up his palms in surrender he said, 'Please note, this is a comment, not a criticism – I was quite amused by the way you shielded him from any imputations of unpleasantness. I mean, you'd hardly know from this that he's a drunk who sponges off his friends, consorts with known criminals and happens to be as queer as a nine-bob note.'

She bristled at that. 'I think some of it's implied. And I'm not likely to mention his being queer, am I?'

Joss looked to Nancy, who had just entered the room with her breakfast tea, still in her dressing gown and dozy from sleep. 'Nancy, be my witness. Didn't you tell me you thought Jerry Dicks a revolting specimen?'

Nancy blinked at the question, seeming to find it a little demanding at this time of the morning. 'Well, I couldn't say for certain. I didn't meet him, whereas Freya actually did. Super article, by the way.'

'*Thank you*, my darling,' smiled Freya. 'Some felt it rather pulled its punches about his character.'

'I thought it was very fair,' said Nancy. 'You mention his reputation for troublemaking, unprofessional behaviour and so on, but you offer that against a proper reckoning of his talent, which does seem . . . unusual.'

Freya turned a pointedly triumphant look to Joss, who glanced at his watch and rose from the table. 'Couldn't have put it better myself,' he said, effectively concluding his defence. 'I'm off. See you tonight.'

He picked up his battered old briefcase and approached Freya. She held out her cheek for him to kiss, imitating a prim maiden aunt's gesture she knew he didn't like, then laughed heartily at his exasperation.

When he had gone she made them a fresh pot of tea and flicked through the paper with brisk unconcern. Whatever Joss might think, hers was easily the best piece in today's paper. She wondered whether Jerry Dicks might read it, and decided that he probably wouldn't. She heard Nancy chuckling under her breath and looked over to where she was reading on the couch. It was the same library copy of *Lucky Jim*.

'Have you got to the hangover scene yet?'

Nancy nodded, eyes closed in smiling bliss. After some moments she became aware of Freya steadily regarding her. 'It just feels so *different* from everything. The way Jim picks apart things, motives, prejudices. The self-mockery. You know Robert can quote whole reams of it by heart?'

'Yes . . .' said Freya, though she wasn't sure she did know that. They tended to knock around as a trio, so whatever Nancy had heard him say she would have heard too. Robert liked to quote from the book, of course, but she had not heard him recite 'whole reams' of it. Unless – she felt a sudden tweak of panic. She didn't want to ask Nancy whether she had seen Robert on his own, first because to put the question would sound like prying, and second, she would feel excluded if it turned out they had. And after all, she and Robert saw one another at the office nearly every day; they'd often have a cup of tea and a chat. Did she tell Nancy every time that happened? There might be nothing in it.

Still turning it over in her head Freya said, 'Has Robert ever talked to you about his divorce?'

Nancy, who had returned to the book, looked up in confusion. 'Erm – no. I only know what you've told me. Why d'you ask?'

'Oh, just wondering,' she replied, sensing she could have been more subtle.

'I have the impression that he'd rather not.'

Freya felt almost light-headed with relief. Her suspicion that they were confidants was mistaken. She rolled a cigarette and said, 'By the way, you know I mentioned that villa in Italy my stepmother goes to? Well, she's invited me to stay.'

'How lovely. Whereabouts exactly?'

'In Fiesole. Just outside Florence.' She paused for a moment before continuing. 'I was wondering whether you'd like to come too.'

Nancy's eyes widened in astonishment. Did she mean it? Of course, she replied. Diana would be there for a month – it belonged to her aunt or someone – and was always inviting her to go. They could stay for a week, or ten days, if they could get the time off. Stephen said it was one of the loveliest places he'd ever been to. They would go to Florence and visit the galleries and churches and the rest of it, or they would lounge by the pool drinking and reading all day.

'Oh, it sounds *heaven*,' cried Nancy.

270

'We'll have to pay for the tickets to Rome, and then a train, but the place won't cost anything.'

She still looked uncertain. 'Is Joss coming too?'

'No. I mean – I haven't asked him.'

'Won't he expect you to?'

Freya shrugged. 'I suppose he might. But I don't really want him there the whole time.'

They laughed, and when their gazes met Freya sensed, with the intuition born of long friendship, that Nancy had someone else in mind she hoped might get the nod, someone they'd been recently discussing. But neither of them gave voice to the thought, and they talked on excitedly of what day they should go, and what food they would have, and how much Italian they could speak. *Poco* . . .

As the summer crept on, the air became still and sultry, modulating to a violet shade by the early evening. Seeking refuge from the parched streets, from the buses and the grimy pigeons, Freya had discovered a small pocket of secret London. Halfway down Chancery Lane towards Fleet Street an open gate offered pedestrian access to Lincoln's Inn and a quiet square with its own gardens. Bomb damage still obtruded here and there, as if some giant had taken a calamitous misstep; but most of its stateliness had been spared. One of the buildings, a later Victorian addition in mauve brick, reminded her of Balliol, and she would occupy one of the benches adjacent to it while eating her lunchtime sandwiches.

One morning when the sun was playing a long game of hide-and-seek with a dreary cortège of clouds she took a coffee break from the office and sat in the square, intending to read a letter she had just got from her mother. Instead she drifted into a daydream, from which she was only roused by a shadow falling across her vision. The shadow had spoken her name, and she looked up, hand shielding her brow. It took a few moments for her to absorb the contours of his face, and once she had time to focus it caused her to jump.

'Alex?' she said, sounding almost fearful.

'I thought it was you!'

'That's so odd – I'd only been thinking of Oxford a few minutes ago.'

Alex McAndrew: just to hear his voice again made her heart beat faster. He was still handsome, though his lean face and greying hair no longer seemed youthful. Judging by his dark suit and tie she supposed he was something in the law, as most people around this neighbourhood were. But no, he worked in a Defence department at Whitehall, he said, having spent some years abroad. Freya recalled how close he was to his mother, and Alex seemed touched when she asked after her; she was still up in Edinburgh, though in poor health.

He had sat down on the bench next to her, and as they faced one another he shook his head in a sort of smiling disbelief.

'Freya. You know, you haven't changed – not one bit.'

She would have dismissed this as blandishment from anyone else, but she found herself laughing, almost skittishly. 'I'm not sure about that. I'm going to be thirty next month.'

'I see your name in the papers, of course. I've often wondered how you were.'

You only had to look for me, she thought. But then she hadn't kept up with him, either. She could remember the last time they had met, it must have been early in 1947, when she was visiting Nancy in Oxford. It had been a freezing cold day – that bitter winter! – and they'd taken shelter in a pub off the high street. They were muffled up, stamping the cold out of their feet, when she had spotted him sitting at a table with a woman and a man she didn't

272

know. From the embarrassed way Alex had greeted her the encounter was not a delightful surprise for him; he had introduced his two friends (the man had a foreign name, she thought) but did not invite her and Nancy to join them. She recalled feeling hurt by this, though she could understand his awkwardness: that was probably his girl, the one he had given her the brush-off for.

She wanted to ask him if he was married – he wore no ring – but she didn't. Instead, she said, 'Actually, it's you I have to thank for where I am now. No, I mean it – if you hadn't asked me to write for *Cherwell* I don't think I'd have got started at all.'

He inclined his head to the compliment. 'Then I'm very pleased and honoured to have been a handmaid to your talent.'

How lovely it was to hear that old-fashioned graciousness again. They talked on, reminiscing about Oxford and catching up with the present whereabouts of this or that one of their peers. Freya was not surprised to find that Alex had lost touch with them all; even she, who had been only a year at the university, had made more of an effort to keep up. There was something of the loner about him; there always had been. Yet despite his apparent indifference to the ties of youth she sensed his pleasure in encountering her, and he seemed delighted to hear that she and Nancy were sharing a flat. She hesitated before mentioning Robert, but Alex responded to the name with a smile of acknowledgement. They hadn't been friends at Balliol, he said – 'I don't think he was much interested in me.' Freya didn't correct this impression.

When she saw him glance at his watch she felt a surge of melancholy, for she knew that any agreement to stay in touch would be wasted on Alex. He had gone his own way for this long: it was unlikely that he would seek any renewal of acquaintance with people he had let drop. So she was secretly astonished when he almost *implored* her to come to his place for dinner one evening soon. They could celebrate the end of rationing while they were at it.

'We'll have steak, and a really good bottle of wine. What d'you say?'

'Smashing,' she said, still half wondering if this was just the fond pretence of people who didn't intend to see one another again. Yet before he went off he asked for her telephone number, and carefully took it down in a notebook.

She walked back to the office lost in thought. Alex – after all these years! It struck her that he'd not pried very deeply into her life. He hadn't asked her whether there was a man on the scene, for instance, and she hadn't volunteered anything. Would Joss object to her swanning off to dinner with someone she used to be crazy about at Oxford? Would she bother to tell him in any case? There had been a bit of coolness of late between them. Despite his protestations to the contrary, she suspected Joss still resented her jumping ship at *Frame*, where sales were falling every week. He had supported her during her time at the magazine, and perhaps thought she owed him – and it – more loyalty.

Something else, more personal, had rocked the boat. Her thirtieth birthday in August had come up a few times in conversation, and as often as she insisted she didn't want any fuss made Joss kept harping on the idea of a party. She didn't feel up to it, and anyway the flat was too small. That wasn't a problem, he said, they could use his house in Hampstead, or else hire rooms somewhere. Curious, she eventually said, 'Why are you so keen for me to have a party?'

Joss looked confused. 'Because . . . you might enjoy it. You told me you never had a twenty-first, and there's not been any other big event since.'

'What d'you mean, "big event"?'

'Well, big like a wedding, or giving birth, or – I don't know . . .'

She looked at him very steadily. 'I see. You want to throw a party because you feel sorry for me. Poor old Freya, unmarried and childless at thirty!'

'That's not what I meant. I just thought it was a milestone in your life, and given there hasn't been one before –'

'Ah yes, you can also include not getting a degree. Another big one missed.'

'Why are you being so touchy?'

'Maybe because you're being so fucking patronising. Did it ever occur to you that I might have different priorities? What about getting my first salaried job, or my first cover story on the magazine – aren't they *milestones*?'

Joss looked cowed by this sudden vehemence. 'Of course they are. For God's sake, Freya, I was only trying to be nice. Sorry! You're turning thirty, and I wanted to help you mark the occasion.'

She stood up, and with as much queenly disdain as she could muster, said, 'Well, you needn't.'

But even as she stalked out of the room she was beginning to feel she had overreacted. Joss *was* only trying to be nice, it was in his nature, but he had given himself away by making more of the event – the 'milestone' – than he needed to. It seemed he really did think of a woman in conventional terms: marriage and family for him trumped career and achievement. It wasn't as though she had ruled herself out as a wife, or even a mother; rather that she wasn't ready for it, not at the moment, not when she was halfway up the ladder. She had promised herself never to take a backward step, and so far she hadn't. But if she ever did find herself hankering for a husband and kids and took a rest from the shinnying, she knew there would be no getting back on it. 'Funny business, a woman's career . . .' – she was remembering the Bette Davis speech from *All About Eve*, she had quoted it once in a piece – 'the things you drop on your way up the ladder so you can move faster. You forget you'll need them again when you get back to being a woman.'

A couple of hours later when she had calmed down she found him again, and apologised. She had protested too much, she said with a laugh, and was an ungrateful bitch.

Joss, warily putting his head outside the doghouse, said, 'Look, I don't want to force you to do anything –'

'I know. I was just being – what did you call me that time? – "a rampant individualist". My fault – slapped wrists.'

'I won't mention it again.'

'No, no, you were right – I should have a party. We can put up a banner to greet the guests: "Thirty – A Milestone At Last"!'

'Freya –'

'I'm *joking*. I'd like to have a party, really – it's sweet of you to think of it.'

She meant it, though she also felt a sympathetic fuse between them had blown; they didn't know one another quite as well as they thought. Not long after this she decided to invite Nancy on the Italian holiday.

It was the two photographs that had done it, she thought, as she made a weary turn into Great James Street. She had just heard a church bell ring one in the morning; the house was deathly quiet as she let herself in. Alex, true to his word, had telephoned and asked her to dinner at his flat in Bayswater; he'd even cooked them steak, as promised, and they'd drunk a bottle of old claret. Her unsteadiness on the staircase attested to the quantity of whisky they'd had afterwards. Without turning on a light she stepped into the kitchen and gulped down a long glass of water. In the living room she flopped onto the couch, reclining her head so her eyes met the ceiling. What an evening . . . A few moments later she heard a door open and Nancy, in pyjamas, appeared in the room.

276

'What are you sitting in the dark for?' she asked.

'I didn't mean to wake you,' said Freya.

'I was awake anyway,' she replied, switching on the table lamp. She peered at Freya, whose rag-doll posture on the couch prompted her to ask, 'Are you drunk?'

'I was. It's worn off. I walked half of the way home.'

Nancy seemed to hear the flatness of her tone. 'What happened? How was Alex?'

Freya paused, not sure which to answer first. 'D'you mind if I have a cigarette before . . . ?' Once it was rolled and lit, she started on the story of her evening. Alex had been talking about his job at the Ministry of Defence, which she had been slow to realise was quite a senior position. How had he managed to rise through the ranks so quickly? Alex had given her an odd look then, and said that he oughtn't really to tell her this – it was technically breaking the law – but during the war he had worked for a 'hush-hush outfit' in Military Intelligence. Suffice it to say by the end he came under a severe amount of stress; on his superior's advice he had decided to take up his place at Balliol, deferred since 1941.

'Good heavens,' said Nancy, wide-eyed. '*Alex* . . . we always did wonder about what he'd done. Remember that argument you had with Robert about men going in for safe office jobs?'

Freya nodded, and took a long drag on her cigarette. 'In any case, there was more to come. You know the photographs?'

There were two, dating from Freya's last weeks at Oxford. One of them was of Alex that Freya had taken: he was standing outside the lodge at Balliol, his head cocked to one side, his face seeming to express a gentle plea for leniency, for mitigation of some sort – she had always found it unaccountably touching. The other was of a group of them lounging by the river which showed Freya with her eyes fixed, somewhat adoringly, on Alex. Nancy, who had taken the picture, had teased her about it. She hadn't looked at either photograph much in the intervening years, but she had considered them just the thing to kindle a nostalgic mood. They had finished eating, and Alex had poured the last of the wine when, like a children's conjuror, she produced the pictures, slightly creased at the edges, more silvery than black and white. She told him how she had dug them out of an old box of college memorabilia, and remembered his words the other day about her not having changed a bit! Well, here was evidence to the contrary –

All this time Alex had kept his head bent in examination of the pictures. When at last he looked up his eyes were filmy with tears, and not ones of tender remembrance, she thought, but drawn from some private well of misery. She stared at him, perplexed, and asked him what was the matter. Her voice seemed only to hurry on his collapse; he turned his face away, and his shoulders quivered from silent wretched sobs. What is it? she asked again. 'You, in that photo,' he panted out. 'The way you're . . . looking at me . . .' She reached across the table to take his hand. 'I was in love with you, Alex – you knew that.' She said it gently, as though it was water under the bridge, but he still looked stricken by some grievous apprehension. He wished – he wished that things could have been different between them. Then Freya recalled the last time they had encountered one another, the pub in Oxford, she had been with Nancy, and he had been with two friends, a man and a woman. 'You seemed embarrassed, and I supposed that the girl was your . . .'

Alex straightened his gaze, and said, in a quiet voice, 'Not the girl. The man. His name was Jan.'

So there it was. All that time, and no one had the smallest suspicion that Alex was queer. He'd met Jan in London during the war; he was a Czech navigator attached to the RAF. He'd come up every so often to stay in Oxford, though of course nobody knew, and Alex never dared introduce him. They were together for nearly eight years, before Jan went back to Czechoslovakia – and disappeared. Freya, stunned, was trying to fathom how Alex had kept it secret for so long, from her, from everyone. How could she not have known? He said: 'You forget that I worked in Intelligence, where everything was encoded, hidden. Secrecy became second nature to me. The invert learns to deceive from an early age – society has forced him to play the double agent in his own life.' He admitted, though, that he was as close to telling Freya as he'd ever been. She saw that he meant this as a compliment, but she still felt a bit of a fool.

As for Jan, Alex had been trying to track him down for two years. He had gone to ground, whether by choice or by compulsion he didn't know.

Nancy, her legs folded underneath her on the couch, had kept the silence of sympathy during this narrative. At length she spoke. 'I know you must feel hurt by this, but imagine how awful it must have been for him. All those years, not being able to tell anyone.'

Freya tilted her head minutely. 'I wish he'd trusted me. His mother has no idea, of course, still thinks he'll bring some bonny bride up to Edinburgh one day . . .'

'Oh *God*,' said Nancy feelingly.

Freya thought again of Alex's face, surprised by tears as he gazed on the photo of their vanished youth. Perhaps it was knowing how much she felt for him that had doubled his determination not to let his secret slip – he couldn't bear the idea of her recoiling from him once she found out.

'I wonder –' Nancy began. 'I wonder why he told you this *now*?'

Freya held her gaze for a moment. 'I wondered about that, too.'

18

She didn't have to wait long to find out. Her intuition that Alex had more to tell proved correct, though its exact nature was more serious than she could have guessed. In the ordinary run of things she would have told Nancy straight away, but circumstances and her own temperament militated against it. It so happened that the next time she saw Alex was the day before they set off for Florence, and she didn't want to sabotage the holiday spirit before they'd even got off the plane. She could almost persuade herself that her withholding was a matter of tact, the virtue she had adopted in a spirit of 'better late than never'. But in fact she had kept quiet out of what she vexingly knew to be her own wounded pride, and a lingering sense that she may have been duped.

He had telephoned her at the *Envoy* one morning, less than a week after they'd had dinner. His alacrity rather surprised her, though in the wake of that night she realised that nothing ought to surprise her any more.

'I'm just calling to say sorry for the other night,' Alex began meekly. 'I ought not to have burdened you with it.'

'There's no need to apologise. I'm over the initial shock, but I may need a few weeks for a full recovery.'

There was a silence at the end of the line, and she wondered if her light-hearted tone had offended him. But no, he was only considering his next words. 'The truth is, Freya, there's one other thing I need to talk to you about, and I can't do it over the telephone. It relates to –' It was a discreet invitation to fill in the gap.

'Oh. When were you thinking?'

'Today, if you possibly can.'

'Um, I'm not really –'

'Please. It's important.'

She glanced at the wall clock. 'Where are you now?'

'In a telephone box about two streets from your building.'

Now she felt a flutter of alarm. This was not the steady, self-contained Alex she knew – or thought she knew – it sounded more like some needy stranger impersonating him. But she could hardly refuse. She asked him to give her half an hour. Where should they meet?

'The same place as last time,' he said and hung up.

He was sitting on the bench, her favourite one in New Square. The look he directed at her from beneath his brow was watchful. His outward appearance had changed since last week. He might almost have slept in his clothes, they were so crumpled; his shirt didn't look quite clean, and the bluish stubble lent a furtive touch. When she sat down he tried a smile that seemed suddenly pitiable.

'Sorry to drag you out. I called in sick at work.'

'It's fine,' she said, keeping her tone bright.

Alex seemed to gather himself to begin, and then shook his head; a dispirited sigh escaped him. He began, haltingly, 'If I asked you to – to help me out of a jam – would you do it, no questions asked?'

She stared at him, but he wouldn't meet her eye. 'If I was able to, yes – of course I would.'

He nodded, barely. 'Even if it meant lending me some money?'

'Yes. I mean . . . how much?'

281

'A lot. A lot.' He blew out his cheeks. 'Three hundred quid.'

Freya gasped out a laugh. 'Are you joking?'

'No,' he said, 'far from it. You earn a pretty good screw, I would have thought.'

'Nothing like that! Alex, I'd gladly lend you three hundred if I had it –'

'Well, how much *do* you have?'

She shrugged: this wasn't the sort of question a friend asked. But his evident desperation demanded an answer. 'Not even a hundred. In my bank account, maybe twenty. And about forty in savings.'

He winced, distractedly, then looked to her in renewed appeal. 'D'you know anyone you might – I mean – touch for a loan?'

'Alex, I want to help. *Please* tell me what this is about.'

He leaned forward, his head lowered. For a while he didn't say anything, and she didn't push him. In the gardens office workers and the occasional begowned lawyer sauntered by, oblivious to their tense mood. A little breeze hurried through the square. At length Alex said, 'What I told you the other night – you know what it'd mean if it came out, at the ministry.'

'Nobody there knows, surely?'

He shook his head, no; or at least, not yet. He had been careful, always, when he was with Jan. In recent years he had had to seek out company – *of my sort*, he said drily – but even then he had been circumspect, about names, places you could go, people you could trust. As he said, the double life had become second nature. It was a stroke of bloody awful luck that had done for him. It went back to his days in Military Intelligence, when for purposes of information they sometimes resorted to narks, black marketeers, other lowlifes. He had not for a moment imagined encountering them again. My mistake, he said, with a bitter laugh. He had been drinking in some dive one night when he thought he saw someone, a snitch he had used during the war. He cleared out of there pretty quickly, hoping he hadn't been spotted.

Some weeks later he was approached by the same man – name of Sewell – who had 'taken an interest' in his old wartime associate. He'd heard (this came with a smirk) that Mr McAndrew was now a person of influence in Whitehall ... Alex, caught unawares, brushed the man off, but he sensed trouble in the offing. Two days later he received a package at his flat; it contained a sheaf of photographs of himself in the company of certain young men. 'Trade,' Alex supplied, in a quiet, unillusioned tone. There was no note, only a telephone number. Sewell, answering his call, explained the terms, with all the nonchalance that Alex recalled from ten years before. He could hear in Sewell's voice the relished irony of getting the upper hand on his former employer. His dilemma was stark: either pay for the photographs, or face a call from Scotland Yard.

'When did this happen?' asked Freya.

'A few months ago,' said Alex. 'The first mistake I made was getting caught. The second was to pay up immediately. That was when Sewell knew he could play me. There was more to follow. There's always more.'

Freya, who had listened to this in a mood of sympathetic indignation, now felt prodded by a little dagger-point of doubt. 'And you last heard from him – when?'

Alex paused to think. 'About ten days ago.'

'I see,' she said, scrutinising him. 'So that was a few days before you invited me to dinner –' and killed the fatted calf for me, she thought.

'Yes, I suppose it was . . .'

'– and gave me the lowdown on what you were up to at Oxford – all that guilt and secrecy. Now I see why you told me.'

'Well . . . I told you because you're a friend.'

283

'Yes, a friend you could immediately put the bite on. All those years of silence, then you invite me to dinner. I'm surprised you didn't ask me for the money there and then – why wait another five days?'

Alex's face had passed through confusion into shock. 'You've got it wrong. This was never a plan. I am mortified – *mortified* – to ask you for money. Can you not tell?'

She was regarding him narrowly. 'Maybe you didn't want to, but clearly you overcame your scruples.'

Alex slowly sank his head into the cage he had made of his hands. 'God almighty, this is worse than – Freya, please, I'm appealing to you as one of the few people in the world I've *ever told* this stuff to. I'm sorry the timing looks off, but there was nothing I could do about that. Someone is extorting money from me, and with great reluctance I'm asking for your help.'

Her pride had been piqued. She'd thought Alex had wanted to renew their friendship because he'd missed her – perhaps even loved her. He had certainly given that impression over dinner last week. How could she have allowed herself to be fooled? To him she was merely someone to be tapped for a loan. She wondered if his dishevelled appearance was part of the ploy, too.

'I don't have that sort of money, Alex. And I don't know anyone who does.' There was a cold note in her voice she didn't much like, yet couldn't disguise.

Alex heard it, for certain; he nodded sadly, and said, 'I'm sorry to have asked you. I made a mistake.' They had both got to their feet. It was obvious that she had embarrassed him. 'I hope you won't refuse to shake my hand.'

The grave humility of his gesture pierced her. She couldn't tell if she was punishing him or punishing herself. Was it both? Unsmiling, she merely shook his hand, and watched him as he walked away.

*   *   *

284

'And you're sure Joss doesn't mind?' asked Nancy as they lugged their suitcases towards the bus station in Florence.

'Of course not.'

But in fact he did mind, as she knew he would. She had fobbed him off with a story about Nancy being exhausted and in need of a break, and her stepmother insisting that Freya bring her to the house for rest and recuperation. (She didn't tell Nancy about this subterfuge.) Joss's crestfallen look on hearing that he was surplus to requirements caused a pang, enough for her to plead with him to come out for the last weekend. His huffy agreement to this almost provoked her to tell him the truth, namely that she preferred Nancy as a holiday companion.

The bus stuttered through the outskirts before beginning its wheezy ascent of the hills. The heat and dust of the streets mingled with the close smell of tobacco, exhaust fumes and sweat. Gazing out of the window Nancy remarked on the meagreness of everything, and it was true, the stalls and shops seemed hardly equipped to serve its people, little old ladies with stolid, wrinkled faces sitting in doorways and swarms of tanned thickset men in white vests or short-sleeved shirts. Carts and taxis and buzzing Vespas jammed the narrow ways, and their bus kept beeping and halting in its effort to get clear. Huge billboards advertising aperitifs loomed towards them, then fell behind.

As the winding road climbed, the houses became fewer and farther between. When they reached the main piazza of Fiesole, Freya presented the note she had made of the address in the hope that the driver might direct them onwards. He seemed to recognise the name, and the volley of demonstrative Italian he shot at them was met by her with much nodding and *si-si*-ing.

'What did he say?' asked Nancy, as the bus pulled away in a gritty cloud of fumes.

'I have *no* idea,' she replied. It seemed respectful just to appear to understand. 'Wait, I've got Diana's map somewhere.'

The directions to Villa Colombini were quite straightforward, though the final half-mile up a rutted cart track, the early-afternoon sun ablaze, caused a torment of sweating and swearing. Their stiff, exhausted smiles at the gardener (*'Buongiorno, signorine!'*) softened once they emerged onto a terrace, its walls overrun with dark green creepers. Freya whistled softly. A commanding panorama over the basin of Florence, with somnolent wooded hills at the rim, had stopped them in their tracks.

'Golly,' murmured Nancy.

The gardener, or perhaps he was the major-domo, took charge of their slick-handled suitcases, and, before disappearing into the house, nodded them towards a trellised stairway around which roses straggled. It dropped down to a forecourt that led in turn to a swimming pool of brilliant blue. Nobody was about, and all that could be heard within the tranquil enclosure was the distant sawing of cicadas. The water's perfect glittering surface seemed to call Freya forward.

'Hold this a sec, will you?' she said, taking off her wristwatch and handing it to Nancy. She kicked off her sandals and pulled off her sweat-soaked dress over her head. She thought about taking off her slip, too, but decorum checked her.

'Erm, Freya . . . ?' said Nancy, alarmed.

Freya rocked back a step, and then sprinted for the edge. Her dive broke the surface with a sharp crack. The shock of the water, colder than it looked, nearly tore the breath from her, and as she came up for air she gave a protesting shriek.

'You madwoman,' shouted Nancy with a laugh.

She had just hauled herself gasping out of the pool when an elderly lady in a green sundress and a wide-brimmed straw hat appeared from the shadows of the house. She gave a little whinny of surprise.

'Hullo! You're *very* keen,' she said, frankly appraising Freya in her soaked underclothes. 'Now which one of you is Freya?'

The lady introduced herself as Kay, Diana's aunt, and the owner of the house. She was firm-bodied, strong-jawed, with a penetrating ice-blue gaze. She spoke in the formidable clipped accent of her generation. But her manner was warmer than her appearance, and as they talked she became genial and confiding. She asked them about their journey, and grimaced at the account Freya gave of the pensione in Rome they had stopped in overnight.

'Ye-e-e-ers, I can imagine the fleas. And then that footslog to get here – no wonder you wanted to cool orf!' She was staring again at Freya, who realised she was showing a lot of herself through the clingy dampness of her slip.

'It's a wonderful place you have,' said Nancy, hand shading her eyes from the sun.

'Thenk you. Been in the family for years. Perhaps you'd like to see around?'

They fell into step as Kay conducted them through the cool, shuttered rooms, some with the unstirred air of disuse, others festooned with the clutter of long acquaintance – a piano room, with piles of sheet music spilling out of the padded stool, and on the wide mantel a domestic shrine of silver-framed family photographs; a library, and a desk with a typewriter where Kay worked; upstairs led to a huge living room with a card table and plump old sofas swathed in blankets and paisley shawls. In a basket by the fireplace lay a careless pile of old magazines. She spotted a *Frame* among them. Then they filed down a corridor lined with prints and crossed another, smaller, living room to the kitchen. Here a short Italian woman was conversing with the major-domo, who smiled as if at old friends. Kay briskly introduced them as Tomas and Marina ('she's our housekeeper') before getting down to business in rapid Italian. It seemed that lunch was to be prepared for them. Diana and Stephen were due back any moment from their trip into town.

'I'll show you the bedrooms,' Kay was saying over her shoulder as they followed up another flight of stairs. On the landing she paused outside a bedroom, and looked at them with a sudden candid vigilance. 'Do you wish to share a room?'

Freya and Nancy looked at one another, momentarily thrown. It seemed unlikely that space was at a premium. 'We can share, if it's more convenient –'

'Oh, no, we've heaps of rooms, it's no trouble . . .' Her bright manner seemed for a moment to suggest that sharing might be more 'fun', but then thought better of it and allocated them rooms next door to one another. 'Right, you get settled in – the bathroom is down the corridor. Lunch at half past one.'

She left them admiring the view out of the first bedroom. Nancy turned with a knitted brow of puzzlement to Freya and said, sotto voce, 'Does she think we're . . . ?'

'I'm not quite sure,' whispered Freya.

'Why would she presume . . . ?'

'Who knows?' said Freya, which concluded the matter. She pulled aside the mosquito net to open the window. 'My God, Nance, is this the most –'

'– beautiful place ever? Yes. We've only been here ten minutes and I'm dreading the moment we have to leave.'

Freya was up at eight the following morning to plough up and down the pool. Kay was already on her deckchair doing the *Times* crossword in the shade, occasionally peering over the paper to check the swimmer's progress. When Freya emerged dripping from the water, hair dark and sleek against her black swimming costume, she stretched herself out on the lounger, her chest still heaving from the exercise. Kay looked over at her.

'My dear, you look like a marvellous *otter*. Shall I pour you some tea?'

They talked about the house. It had been left to Kay's grandmother by her first husband, whose family had made their money in a Midlands brewery; they had been part of an expat community in Florence and were friends with the Trollope family (there were signed first editions by Anthony in the library). Kay, the oldest of three sisters, used to holiday here in childhood, 'when the place was very cut orf – no motor bus then'. Once their parents became too infirm to travel Kay, unmarried and footloose, decided to take over the maintenance herself. She had improved it a little at a time, installing electricity and paving the courtyard entrance. Then she had the swimming pool put in, tamed the garden ('an awful mess') and planted the lemon trees in front of the terrace. She made her own oil from the olive grove below. Of course she depended on Tomas and his boys for the upkeep, fixing the roof, replacing the old tiles and what have you. There was always something that needed doing.

'So you're on your own here?' asked Freya.

'Well, there's Marina looking after the kitchen and the laundry – and I have a few neighbours hereabouts –'

'You don't get lonely?'

Kay's good cheer was unyielding. 'Do you know, I never have! Perhaps it's – well, I suppose I've never met anyone I could live with.' She paused, holding the thought. 'Or, more accurately, I never met anyone I couldn't live without.'

She said it lightly, as she said almost everything, but Freya took it to heart. To have lived so long – how old was Kay? Sixty? Sixty-five? – without someone to bounce off, to share that knowledge of your time hurrying on . . . It was brave, but it was sad, too. She recognised something of that proud cussedness in herself, and it disquieted her. What if she ended up alone?

'Good morning,' called Diana, strolling down from the terrace, a peach in her hand. 'I saw you from upstairs – you seemed to be having a *very* grave discussion.'

'Oh, I don't think it was so grave, do you?' Kay said. 'Freya was just asking me if I minded awfully being on my own.'

Diana wore an emerald-coloured swimsuit that showed off her perky breasts and slim waist. She bit into the peach and said to Freya, 'Aunt Kay's one of the most gregarious people I know. We used to go to her parties during the war, when she lived off Hyde Park Gardens. Drinking like there was no tomorrow! It was very fast set.'

Kay laughed. 'I've slowed down a little since then. But I still like company – we'll have a full house next weekend.'

'Really?' said Freya, trying to conceal her dismay. It seemed quite perfect just the way it was. 'Who's coming?'

'Oh, some friends of ours,' said Diana. 'And an art-critic friend of Kay's – an American chap.'

'Lambert Delavoy. Very eminent – in his field,' said Kay, with an ironic hint that he was unlikely to be eminent anywhere else. 'I look forward to Stephen jousting with him.'

Her remark was prompted by the appearance of the latter, carrying a breakfast tray of coffee and fruit. Freya considered her father through narrowed eyes. He was still tall and lean, and the toffee-coloured hair he was vain about hadn't noticeably thinned. The creases around his eyes and mouth suited a face that in younger years was somewhat bland in its regularity. The only other suggestion of his entry into middle age was a stoop, the occupational hazard of a painter, forever craning forward to the canvas.

'Who am I to joust with?' he asked pleasantly.

290

'Delavoy. He and his wife are coming here for dinner on Friday,' replied Diana, who then explained to Freya, 'He's written some frightful things about Stephen's work.'

'The swine,' said Freya, feeling indignation on her father's behalf, since he rarely deigned to show it on his own.

Stephen shrugged. 'Hardly surprising. I don't think he's really liked anything much since Poussin. Coffee?'

Freya secretly admired this nonchalance in her father, and wished she could master it herself. It was so different from her own defensiveness before criticism, even the well-intentioned sort; she thought of her recent prickliness with Joss. At the *Envoy* she was making an effort to be more accommodating, because she was still relatively new and accepted that her editors might know better. It was just that, by and large, they *didn't* know better, and the 'improvements' they made on her copy only weakened it.

She had another swim before going off in search of Nancy. She found her lying across her bed writing her diary, her face and shoulders pink from the bath she had just had. Her long hair was turbaned in a white towel.

'Here's some coffee,' she said, setting down a cup. 'Sleep well?'

'Yes, apart from a moment early this morning when I woke up and wondered where on earth I was. D'you have that?'

She nodded. 'Strange-bed syndrome.'

Nancy capped her pen and closed the diary. Rising from the bed she peeked through the shuttered window.

'It looks tremendously hot out there.' Her fair skin burnt quickly in the sun.

'You might wear a hat. But we can keep to the shade.'

'How should we get into town?'

Freya widened her eyes knowingly. 'I've found just the thing.'

A quarter of an hour later they were whizzing down the hill road astride a Vespa, screaming with laughter at the speed and Freya's erratic steering. Riding pillion, Nancy had her arms wrapped tight around her waist. Having wheeled the vehicle (a fetching mint green) into the courtyard Tomas had offered them a quick driving lesson, which stretched their meagre Italian. The first time Freya tried it the bike shot out of her grasp and went careering into a flower bed. Tomas eventually climbed onto the thing himself and puttered twice around the courtyard. '*Ecco, e facile*,' he said, hopping off.

'This beats the bus,' shouted Freya over the motorcycle's insistent wasp-drone. As the road levelled out the traffic began to thicken, and they were soon halting at junctions while workaday Florence hurried crosswise in dust clouds and bleating horns. Only once did they have a scare, when Freya momentarily confused the accelerator with the brake; she couldn't understand why they were speeding up at a crossroads when she was frantically trying to slow down. Nancy's shriek of surprise tore past her ear just as she swerved sideways over the cobbles and onto the pavement, juddering to a stop before a huddle of startled pensioners. '*Scusi, scusi*,' she gasped, her armpits on fire with sweating panic.

Her legs felt jellyish when she stepped off the bike and propped it against a shaded wall near the Piazza del Duomo. Nancy's auburn hair had blown up like candyfloss under the force of their rapid descent down the hill. On catching herself in the reflection of a shop window she groaned with dismay, and wouldn't take another step until she had hidden the damage under a headscarf. The city sweltered and cowered under the late-morning sun; the poster-caked streets and the dark entrances of churches were secretive, huddled around their own charged history, while the locals stood about and watched, faces worn to indifference. At the

Uffizi the July tourists swarmed as thickly as ants, and with one look at each other they fled without entering. There was a refuge in the musty sequestered air of the Duomo, into whose candlelit gloom they seemed to slide like water. Something of Nancy's unselfconscious devotion had rubbed off on Freya over the years, and she wandered down the echoing nave in a trance. It wasn't that she believed in any of it – for her it was a mostly benign conspiracy – but she couldn't help swooning before the church's vast vaulted spaces, and the solemn endeavour of an age when building and carving and glazing constituted more than mere feats of design.

Doubling back down a side aisle she spied Nancy, head slightly bowed, at a shrine to the Virgin. From a distance she seemed to be examining the pocket of her dress, but was in fact searching for a coin; she dropped it into a slot in the wall. Then she fixed a slim white candle in the tiered brass tray, ghoulish with wax, and lit it with a taper. She stood still in contemplation for some moments, before taking a step away and crossing herself. Freya held back until Nancy had completed her devotions, and timed her approach to make it seem a natural coming-together. They ducked out of a side door as another gaggle of tourists were flooding through.

Outside again the heat assaulted them. They started to look for the restaurant that Kay had recommended, but somehow kept making wrong turns. The streets they took alternated glare and gloom; they tried to hug the shadows but the sun quickly found them out. Nancy, drained from the effort of breathing, lingered in a doorway. Then Freya spotted a trattoria directly opposite, and decided they should eat there.

'My body seems to be undergoing its very own heatwave,' said Nancy, fanning herself with a menu while a waiter smoothed out their paper tablecloth.

'You do look a bit flushed,' admitted Freya. '*D'acqua, per favore.*' She mused for a moment. 'I rather love Kay, don't you? She's like someone out of Forster. You know what she said to me this morning? – "My dear, I would like to influence you unduly." I couldn't help laughing.'

'I think she rather likes *you*,' said Nancy, weighing her words.

'You think she might be – well, yes – it would explain a few things.'

It hadn't occurred to her when they talked this morning about living on her own. Now she thought of it, Kay had said she'd never met anyone she could live with – not *any man*, as most women would have said, but *anyone*, the ambiguous pronoun. Perhaps Kay really was reconciled to a solitary life, but it seemed unfair that someone so gregarious should be alone just because society wouldn't –

It was no use. The subject was too tender to bear in silence. She had to get it out or it would poison her.

'Nance, there's something I've got to tell you, and I need you to be honest with me. It's quite important.'

Nancy stared over the table at her. 'What is it?'

She took a deep breath. 'You remember the night I got back from dinner with Alex, and you wondered why he was telling me all that stuff about himself now – why he'd waited so long? Well, I found out.' She recounted the story of his being tracked by his old wartime snitch, the photos, the blackmailing. That sort of thing happened quite a lot, it seemed; there were criminal syndicates that made big money out of extorting queers, especially those in public office. It could go on for years.

'Of course I felt terribly for him – how could I not? Then he asked me if I could lend him cash.'

Nancy gasped in disbelief on hearing how much. 'Three hundred?! Is he mad?'

'No. Just desperate. Of course I told him I didn't have that sort of money . . .'

Nancy shook her head. 'Poor Alex. To be caught like that, with no recourse to the police, to the law – to anything.' She brooded for a moment, before looking to Freya. 'So what did you do?'

Freya turned away, feeling an unpleasant warmth. 'That's just it. I did nothing – actually something worse than nothing. I basically accused him of opportunism. The timing of it felt too deliberate – he'd waited less than a week to telephone, and next thing I know he's asking me to bale him out.'

Puzzlement chased over Nancy's features. 'But you said yourself – he's desperate. And even if it does look suspicious, he surely wouldn't have asked you unless it were a last resort.'

It was what Freya had been afraid of hearing: the truth, more or less. Pride had tricked her. She had been so touched by Alex's confessional spirit at dinner that the bombshell of his blackmail story had made a chaos of her reasoning. The abruptness of his request for a loan would have surprised anyone, but she had been far too quick to judgement. Could she not have grasped that Alex was genuinely pleased by their reunion *and then* decided to ask her for help? She shrank to recall the way she had spoken to him – *I don't have that sort of money*. It was true, but she couldn't forget the ice in her tone.

She pressed her joined hands against her lips. Nancy was watching her, and not for the first time she felt grateful that her friend refused to make accusations against her, however deserved they might be.

'I wish I knew a way to help him,' she said presently. 'In my wilder moments I thought of asking my dad. He's the only person I know who'd have three hundred pounds to lend.'

295

'But you can't think of paying,' said Nancy. 'You can't get involved.'

'If I thought it might save him I would.'

They ate some lunch, though the heat had taken away their appetite. As she sipped black coffee Freya returned to the subject, probing it like a sore tooth.

'Of course I can't tell anyone about it. And you mustn't either, Nance – promise.'

'Who on earth would I tell?'

'I don't know. You might let it slip in front of someone – like Robert.'

She had said his name with a dissembling airiness, thinking she might catch her out if anything was going on between them. But Nancy returned only a frown. 'I wouldn't dream of telling him, or anyone,' she said, looking Freya in the eye.

She thought back to the argument she'd had with Robert about the Vere Summerhill case. They had both written about the wider implications of his sentencing and the diminishing hope of leniency towards other homosexuals. Even if the public attitude to Summerhill had softened – he had put on a noble front in the dock – the law wasn't going to budge. And now the irony of Alex's story dropping right in her lap. Any other journalist would have hotfooted it straight to the editor and stopped the presses. The scandal of a queer in the heart of Whitehall was something you could make your name on. Alex must have known that, and yet he trusted her as a friend to keep his secret. *Oh God* – the more she turned it over the more callous she felt.

Walking back to the spot where they'd left the Vespa they passed the Duomo again, its majesty dwarfing all around it. Freya watched nuns file out of a side entrance. She turned to Nancy, busy wafting herself with a fan she had just bought at a market stall.

'I noticed you lighting a candle in there before we left. You looked a picture of devotion.'

Nancy smiled. 'It's odd, I hardly ever think of doing that in London. It must be the Italian influence.'

'So what did you pray for?'

'Oh . . .'

'Go on. You must have asked for something.'

After a pause Nancy said, 'Actually, I didn't ask for anything. I was – giving thanks.' A quick deprecating laugh escaped her. 'That sounds awfully pious; I don't mean to. It's just, I often pray for things, then feel rather selfish about it. He isn't there just to petition. So I try to remember to thank Him as well, you know –'

'For what?' asked Freya, curious.

'For everything! For my being here, in this beautiful place. For my good fortune.' She laughed again, and said, 'For being spared a violent death with my driver on the road this morning.'

'Really?' said Freya, not sure how lightly this was meant to be taken. It remained an unfathomable part of Nancy that she could believe in this communion with the unknown. It was as though she were able to draw upon a vast company of friends and intimates whom she would refer to openly yet never introduce; St Francis de Sales had been the first, back in Oxford. Unfathomable, and in some obscure way, enviable, for there were times (like now) when she would have welcomed help from this ethereal assembly.

They had reached the parked motorcycle by the time she decided to say it. 'Nance, do me a favour? Next time you're back there, light one for Alex, will you?'

The drowning heat discouraged any further trips into town. For the next few days they kept to the villa, reading, dozing, swimming, lolling on deckchairs in the shade. With Stephen usually off painting somewhere, the four women

297

formed their own little society around the pool. Diana and Nancy made lunch and talked about books, while Freya obliged Kay, a card fiend, by playing a lot of canasta and whist. Kay also mixed the drinks, her favourite being an extra-strong negroni that made them all a bit woozy by teatime.

On the Thursday the sun, without disappearing, eased off the glare a notch, and the air was touched with a liquid softness. The pool's electric blue-green had cooled to a glimmer. All morning squadrons of tiny swifts had dive-bombed the water's surface for a sip. Nancy, who after the first day had shunned the sunlight, was at last persuaded by Freya to take a dip. The paleness of her skin dazzled against the peacock blue of her swimsuit and the thick russet rope she made of her hair.

'It's freezing!' she yelped, lowering herself gingerly into the water.

'Just get in, you ninny,' laughed Freya, already immersed. Anyone observing them both would perhaps have been tempted to extrapolate character from their very different styles. Nancy favoured a slow, stately breaststroke, legs kicking softly behind her like a frog. Freya in contrast sharked through the lengths with her stern front crawl. She had always been a good swimmer, and loved the propulsive thrust her long legs gave her; she remembered Nat Fane once describing her movement through the water as 'phocine', which she later discovered meant 'seal-like'. A compliment?

Having taken a deep breath she was plunging below to explore the soundless angular world of the pool, its smooth white walls and sloping tessellated floor. Turning, she was surprised to see Nancy approach, waving in slow motion; her hair had come unloosed from its braid and she thought, not for the first time, of Millais's Ophelia. Freya put a kiss to her palm and blew it towards her. A slender thread of bubbles escaped Nancy's lips as she smiled – or was she laughing? – and began gravitating upwards. Freya caught up alongside, and they broke the surface together with an exhilarated gasp.

They were still idling there when Freya saw from the corner of her eye Marina, the housekeeper, descending the trellised stairway towards them. She was waving a piece of paper in her hand. '*Telegramma per Mizz Nancy*,' she called, and Freya felt her heartbeat start to thicken. A telegram always meant doom – unless it was a birth. She would remember this scene, she thought, the sway of the water, suddenly cold again, the rasping of the cicadas somewhere beyond, the quick way Nancy heaved herself out of the pool to meet her messenger. Freya looked around to where Diana and Kay were sitting, and they must have caught the mood of crisis, too, for they were abruptly silent, leaning forward, braced against this ill wind just blown in. With mechanical urgency she climbed out of the pool, dripping, and held back a few yards from where Nancy stood, opening the little envelope now and reading.

Oh Jesus, thought Freya, as Nancy's hand flew to her mouth. Dead. Someone is dead. They would be going home, packing tonight. Misery would accompany them, like a chaperone. Nancy was looking around, her face a mask of shock. She seemed quite unable to speak.

'Nance. Is it bad news?'

Nancy stared at her, almost in fright, but she was shaking her head. She swallowed hard before she found her voice, which was small. 'No, it isn't bad, it's – my book. They're going to publish my book.'

Freya took the note from her hand and read: DOUBLE PERSONAL SOLD TO S&G STOP NEXT SPRING PUB STOP CONGRATS.

And then they were suddenly in each other's arms, crying, and laughing, and whirling each other round. Marina, smiling in confusion, was also embraced, and kissed, and then dispatched by Kay to bring down a bottle of champagne. Freya found herself giddy, giddy with the sense of having escaped an atrocious fate and somehow emerged the other side into euphoria. With nothing at stake in the news but relishing its unforeseen arrival Kay and Diana had taken charge of the moment, offering one toast after another, whereas Nancy, for so long invested in the cycle of raised and frustrated hopes, looked slightly dazed by it all. Freya, drinking more quickly than any of them, detected a tiny quiver of dismay stirring below her own mood. It came of an awareness that this moment would mark the first step in Nancy's eventual detachment from her – from her influence. Success did that, even to the closest friends. It fortified self-esteem, it offered new chances to experiment, to explore, to determine the person you wanted to be. Hitherto Nancy had lived – both of them knew it – in Freya's shadow. It was her apprenticeship. Nancy colluded in it because she regarded Freya not just as her best friend but as a guide. The moment was coming, not yet, but soon, when the apprentice would leave behind the tutor entirely.

The sun had dropped down behind the hills by the time Stephen got back, his face and hands madly splotched with paint.

'What's all this?' he said, catching the dizzied air of elation.

'We're celebrating, dear,' said Kay. 'This brilliant girl has just got her novel accepted. She's to be an *author*!'

'Oh, Nancy,' he said, hugging her lightly. 'That's marvellous. You must be – What's the matter?'

'I'm sorry, I'm sorry,' gasped Nancy, her eyes silvery with tears. 'It's just that everyone's been so lovely to me –'

Diana laughed, and draped her arm around Stephen. 'They've been like this all afternoon. I haven't seen such tears since we were at the Coronet for *Brief Encounter*.'

'Answered prayers,' said Freya.

'What?'

'"There are more tears shed over answered prayers than unanswered prayers." St Teresa of Avila. Nance told me that.'

The remark met with bemused looks, because she had quoted the line so wistfully. Kay, searching for a link, said, 'I always loved that Tennyson poem – do you know it? *Tears, idle tears, I know not what they mean* . . . But this is all rather morbid. One more round of drinks, then dinner, I think.'

Another surprise awaited Freya before the evening was over. They had returned to the terrace after dinner, by which time a decided nip in the air and the afternoon's booze were making her shiver. She hadn't packed any warm clothes, but Nancy had, and told her to borrow a cardigan which she'd left in her room.

So Freya had gone up, as directed, and switched on the light. Nancy's suitcase lay half open, clothes foaming out beneath the lid. A book of Maugham short stories lay on the bedside table next to a hairgrip, a pair of earrings, her purse and some loose change. She picked up the grey cardigan that was hung on the back of the chair.

On the bed was her diary, closed, but with something protruding invitingly from its edge. It was a letter, with a British stamp. She had only once peeked at Nancy's diary, years ago, by accident; her short-sightedness had mistaken it for the novel she was writing. She could still remember the lines she had glimpsed: *Her great appeal is in the bold way of saying exactly what she is thinking – sometimes before she has even properly thought.* Freya had quickly clapped it shut, not bothering to check who Nancy was writing about: it couldn't have been anyone else. Now, without intending to snoop, she flipped back the diary's cover just to satisfy her curiosity about the letter – whose correspondence was so important that she'd brought it with her on holiday?

She knew the handwriting instantly, untidy and babyish, with letters slanting one way and then the other. Robert's. Robert had been writing to her, and Nancy had not let on. Freya felt a hollowing in her stomach. It wasn't a betrayal, she couldn't call it that, for there was nothing that should prevent them writing to one another. And yet it felt underhand; she had been excluded, just as she and Robert had once excluded Nancy back in Oxford. There could be only one reason why he would have written to her, instead of using the telephone. He was in love with her. And she with him? Her mind was racing now as she recovered the most recent occasions on which they'd talked about him. Well, then; start with the lunch on Monday when she'd asked her not to tell Robert about Alex being blackmailed. There hadn't been a flicker, not a blush that might have given her away. It shocked her to realise how adept Nancy had become in dissembling.

She heard footsteps coming up the stairs. The letter, clutched in her hand like Desdemona's handkerchief, she hurriedly replaced inside the diary. She had half feared Nancy catching her red-handed, but it was only Diana, who went past without even noticing her. Freya felt annoyed with herself for skirting around the question of Robert; she ought to have had it out with Nancy straight away, instead of tangling herself in these tendrils of doubt and secrecy and suspicion. Impossible to ask her about him now; it would not take Nancy a moment to realise she had been snooping in her room and found Robert's letter. She put on the cardigan and went downstairs.

The remainder of the evening was a trial to her. The bubble of jollity that Nancy's news had floated among the others was not to be popped any time soon. Kay had hauled them into the music room where Nancy accompanied everyone on the piano. Diana sang something from *The Boy Friend* that Freya didn't know, and then Stephen did a version of 'And Her Mother Came Too' that made them hoot. He gurned charmingly in response. Freya, trying to keep a smile pasted to her face, knew that a request was coming, and she declined as graciously as she could when it did.

'Oh, but Freya, you must,' said Kay, brightly resistant to anything that might poop the party. When she refused again Stephen and Diana took over trying to wheedle a song out of her.

It was Nancy, as always, who perceived that she was out of sorts. Leaning round the piano she called to her, gently, 'Darling, you should go to bed – you look done in. But before you go, we could perhaps try this –' She played the first faltering notes of a song Freya took a moment to recognise. When she did, she languidly picked herself up from the chair and sat down beside her, thigh against thigh. At first she offered only a few notes high up the scale, colouring to the main chords. They played it right through, neither of them singing the lyric; then Nancy started it again, more intensely this time, really using the pedal, and when she saw that Freya wasn't going to sing, she began it alone, quietly.

Are the stars out tonight?
I don't know if it's cloudy or bright,
'Cause I only have eyes for you, dear . . .

Freya watched her from the corner of her eye, touched by the feeling in her voice and the unselfconscious play of emotion across her face. Oh! If they could only stay like this, the two of them together, instead of Nancy outgrowing her. She had thought it would be a gradual parting of ways, a good few years before they had to give up their domestic idyll. But now its end would be hastened by Robert, the boyfriend, the one who'd almost estranged them years before. The song was gathering for its last go-round, and with a little squeeze on her heart she finally gave her voice to it.

You are here, so am I,
Maybe millions of people go by,
But they all disappear from view
And I only have eyes for you.

She took the applause, and then took herself off to bed, feeling her eyes start to brim again. But it wasn't to a restful night she went. The strains of the piano downstairs lingered on past midnight, past one, when she at last heard Nancy's footsteps on the landing. She listened to her getting ready for bed, the creak of a window opening, the susurration of feet on bare boards. And still she found no peace. Nancy would not breathe a word about Alex, she trusted her absolutely on that. But what if Robert, with his persistence – ? No, she mustn't go over it again.

The night air was thick as pudding. Her bed was a torture rack. No single part of it was cool to the touch; the sheets twisted sweatily about her legs. She had flipped her pillow over half a dozen times and still it blazed against her skin. The illuminated dial on her wristwatch read twenty to three: hours to go before I sleep. Without really thinking about it she got up, and tiptoed out of her room into Nancy's. She mustn't give her a fright. Was there even room in this bed?

'Freya?' came Nancy's sleep-blurred voice. She was wearing one of her long virginal nightdresses: the habits of the convent school died hard.

'Can I get in with you?' Freya whispered.

304

There came a grunt of affirmation; Freya lowered herself onto the bed's furthest edge so as not to disturb her. It was better, if not by much. Nancy's even breathing lulled her, and she felt her mind winding down to a still spot.

As she listened to the birds tuning up outside, she remembered something: Joss was arriving tomorrow.

19

'Good holiday?' said Robert, setting their drinks on the table. They were in the Marquis, on a lunch hour.

Freya nodded. 'Pretty good. Beautiful house, amazing weather – apart from one gigantic thunderstorm on the last night. Which I suppose was rather amazing too.'

'I enjoy a storm,' he said vaguely. She studied his face, waiting for him to enquire about Nancy, but all he said was, 'Nice tan, by the way.'

She glanced at her bare arms, the dark skin already beginning to flake. 'When Joss saw me he said I looked like a street Arab.'

'He was out there, too?'

'Just the final weekend. We argued for most of it.'

Robert made a clicking sound of regret. 'That doesn't sound like love's young dream.'

'It's not. We've always argued, but the fun has gone out of it. Now we just snipe at each other.'

'Ah. I fear you may have reached the end of the third phase.'

'What's that?' she asked.

'A theory of attraction I've been working on. The first phase begins in the groin – the seat of carnal desire. The second moves upwards to the heart, where feelings of tenderness and sympathy are incubated. In the third and final phase it moves up again, to the brain, the HQ, where you finally decide whether you're going to do any better or not. Probably the sex has gone off but at least she keeps a clean house, knows the drill about dinner on the table, and so on. That's the intellectual perception, and it always outlives the other two.'

Freya considered this. 'Does the sex go off?'

'Of course,' he replied with nonchalant authority.

'But surely you look for the one where all three work in concert. You have the physical and the romantic phase in a kind of equilibrium, and the brain informs you that this is a good thing.'

'Doesn't happen, though. Not in my experience. You may get the first two in tandem, at the beginning, when you're so intoxicated by the object of your desire you don't even think about what it means. But once you find yourself in the third phase – the analytical phase – you're already calculating the odds, whether it's better to stay or to cut and run.'

'That's too glib. You're reducing something quite mysterious and complex to a set of responses. Cynical, too – you don't allow for the way people change.'

Robert shrugged, unconcerned. 'It's a theory, as I said. But so far it's been upheld by observation.'

'Do I take it you've successfully concluded your divorce?'

He looked at her with a knowing smirk. 'Now who's being cynical? Yes, it's done. She has answered to the whip, and I take leave to consider myself her ex-husband. Not before time.'

'A free man. Congratulations.'

He inclined his head in acceptance. 'Talking of congratulations, I shall be calling at Great James Street to offer my own to Nancy. She must be delighted.'

'She's cock-a-hoop. I can't think of anyone who deserves it more.'

Robert was nodding. 'Nancy Holdaway. It always *sounded* to me like an author's name . . .'

He's free to go after her now, she thought. Try as she might, Freya couldn't quell her misgivings about him. Robert would want to play the field; he was cavalier about romance in a way that Nancy most definitely wasn't. And she could hardly feel sanguine about a man who talked of a woman 'answering to the whip', even if she was his ex-wife. She watched him as he absently fed peanuts into his mouth.

'Robert. You remember back in Oxford when you went off with that girl –'

'Cressida. Funny how you can never recall her name.' His expression had turned wary.

'Well, much as it irked me at the time, I was arrogant enough to think it was your loss. Call it the resilience of youth –'

'Right,' said Robert quickly.

'But some people aren't so robust. They're more sensitive about – matters of the heart.'

His eyes had become hooded, like a bird of prey. And yet she detected a puzzlement there, too; she would have to spell it out.

'What I mean is – please don't hurt Nancy.'

He gave an irritated shake of his head and began to bluster. He wouldn't dream of hurting her, and in any case what did she think –

'Don't say it's none of my business,' she cut him short, 'because it *is*. If you're serious about her, then fine. Nancy's loyal and kind and clever and she will look good on your arm. But she mustn't be toyed with.'

'You don't have to tell me this,' he said sulkily. 'Freya, I've changed a lot since Oxford. I know I was a bloody fool back then. But give me a little credit. All the things you love about Nancy I love too. She's a great girl. Why would I do anything to hurt her?'

She held his gaze for a long moment. She had always spoken frankly with Robert, and now she had put in her proprietorial twopenn'orth there was nothing more she could do. And perhaps Nancy was more worldly than she seemed. No one who read her novel would think her a soft touch. Robert was giving her a level look across the table. Maybe divorce had chastened him, forced him to grow up. You could only hope.

They had another drink before they returned to the office. Robert had become excited about a piece of gossip that had recently chanced his way.

'You remember that conversation we had with Standish, months ago, when he asked us to follow up the Summerhill trial? Well, I've heard something pretty extraordinary from my chap in the ministry –' He stopped himself, and narrowed his gaze at her. 'Actually, I'm not sure I should even be telling you. You might try to pinch it for yourself.'

'Robert, the day I need to rely on you for a scoop –'

'All right, all right. Just keep it under your hat for now.' He gave a glance over his shoulder before lowering his voice. 'You know how jumpy they all are since the Burgess and Maclean business – the whole atmosphere in Whitehall has got very cloak-and-dagger. According to my fellow there's a rumour that someone pretty high up in the MoD is passing secrets.'

Freya felt her whole body go cold. 'Passing them – to whom?' She realised that this was not the question she really wanted to ask.

'Not confirmed – it's all encrypted.'

She swallowed before she could find her voice. 'Does your man know who it is?'

Robert shook his head. 'Of course it may turn out to be a load of cobblers. Wouldn't be the first time a rumour got out of hand, especially in a government office. But this chap of mine – he's not often wrong.' He looked at her. 'Are you OK?'

She forced a smile. 'Yeah, I'm fine. I just need a bit of air. I'll see you back at the office.'

Her hands were shaking as she picked up the telephone and dialled Alex's work number. She didn't know how she ought to start: with an apology for her unfeeling behaviour at their last meeting, or with a warning about the rumour? In the event she could offer neither. The prim voice at the MoD switchboard informed her that Mr McAndrew was absent on leave for a few days, but if she would care to leave a message – ? Freya thanked her and hung up. She then tried his home telephone, which rang without response.

She wondered if Alex had already gone to ground. Perhaps someone had tipped him off about being investigated. But surely it hadn't got that far yet? Her heart turned over to think of him under such stress, caught between the Scylla of the legal system and the Charybdis of an underworld sting. She would help him in any way she could – and God help *her* if she had left it too late. As for Robert, she faced a dilemma. She could tell him about Alex and swear him to silence, something in which she had no great faith. Or else she must keep it in the vault and hope that his investigation would draw a blank. The danger that lay in this second option was of her own making. She thought back to the afternoon in Florence when she had confided to Nancy about Alex being blackmailed, so the vault door was already ajar. That was the way with a secret; the more people who knew the more vulnerable it became. With romance in the offing did Nancy have it in her to resist telling Robert?

Somehow she had to get hold of Alex – a challenge in itself. Time had driven a wedge between them. She knew none of his work colleagues, or his friends, if indeed he had any. By temperament he was not one to whom intimacy came easily; at Oxford she remembered how reluctant he was to trust others (and now she knew the reason). The only person he had ever been close to – apart from the mysterious Jan – was his mother, back home in Edinburgh. Freya had asked him about her when they met that day, and Alex had returned a look of gratitude that she had remembered her. In the library of the *Envoy* she found a telephone directory for Edinburgh and spent a couple of hours ringing every McAndrew in the book – to no avail.

Joss, hands in pockets, leaning at her bedroom door, wanted to know why he hadn't been asked to dinner at Nat Fane's.

'I really don't know,' replied Freya, doing her make-up before the dressing-table mirror. It was the truth, though she was secretly relieved the invitation was only for her; relations were still very brittle.

'Bad manners, I'd say. It's not like we'd invite him to dinner without his wife.'

Freya considered this. 'I imagine Nat would rather like that. And Pandora won't be there anyway this evening.'

'What, has she left him?'

'Not yet. Just the country. She's doing a film in New York.'

Joss gave a mirthless laugh. 'I see. He's clearing the field so he can make a play for you.'

Freya didn't flinch from the mirror. 'I think not. We established our non-attraction to one another long ago, back in Oxford.'

'Pretty rum, all the same. Maybe he's got someone lined up for you – one of his attractive young friends from the theatre.' He was still skittish about turning forty, and no assurances from her could help him.

'I don't think pimping's his style either. Would it surprise you if Nat had just invited me for the pleasure of my company?'

311

Joss pulled a face. 'Not really. Lucky him! The pleasure of your company seems to be at a premium these days.' He caught the reflection of her face in the mirror for a moment; their eyes spoke to one another, and he slouched out of view.

She took the Tube from Holborn to South Kensington, and walked the five minutes to Nat's place. She was wearing a black velvet cocktail dress that showed off her legs, and a rope of tiny pearls gleamed at her throat. Nat had come up in the world. An inheritance from a late aunt had enabled him and his wife (also from money) to buy a large flat on two floors in Onslow Square, its stuccoed pillars and black-and-white marbled entrance announcing their affluence. But she hadn't expected the new plum-coloured Rolls-Royce parked in front.

'Darling Freya,' purred Nat, answering the door with his best alligator smile. His all-white suit was offset by an aquamarine silk shirt.

'I see you've been shopping,' she said, accepting his kiss and thumbing at the Roller.

He sniggered. 'A little pricey even for me, dear. It's Ossie's.'

He led her down the hall into a long dining room where the guests were already at table. Two or three looked up expectantly at her. 'Sorry, am I late?' she said to Nat.

'No, no. Jerry's not here yet. It's a point of honour that he must be the last to arrive – like the Queen.'

'Yeah. He's probably out photographing some guardsman's cock,' said Ossie Blackler, puffing on a black cheroot. His tone was flat, and charmless.

Nat, pulling a *what-can-you-do-with-him?* face at Freya, said, 'Very well, let me perform some introductions . . .'

As well as Ossie she already knew Hetty Cavendish, who greeted her warmly. Seated next to her was a young actor, Roger Tarrant, whose chiselled features and almond-shaped eyes were almost cartoonishly beautiful. He was one of the leads in Nat's new play, and wore the affable air of a man who expected nothing of his fellow diners but their unqualified admiration. Opposite them was a solemn, pale-faced girl named Gwen, the latest in Ossie's rolling harem of playthings, and along the table a livelier girl named Martine, who Freya suspected was Nat's plaything for the night. She also appeared to be doing most of the serving, in concert with the hired cook. There were two older people at the table, Felix Croker, the theatre impresario, and Edie Greenlaw, an actress with the languid magnificence of an ageing Cleopatra. Freya liked her expressive, heavy-lidded eyes and the queenly way she sipped at her cigarette, clamped in an ivory holder.

'I fancy by your colour you've been abroad,' said Nat, pouring her a glass of straw-coloured wine. 'A touch of the Provençal sun, perhaps?'

'Fiesole,' she replied. 'As a matter of fact I met someone at our hostess's who was asking about you. Lambert Delavoy.'

'Ah, Delavoy! I suppose his fat wife was there too?'

'She's not as fat as he is,' said Freya, offering accuracy where gallantry was impossible – she had disliked both of them.

'I dare say,' Nat conceded. 'Let us call her the lesser of two ovals.'

'Is that a line from your play?' asked Hetty with a smirk.

'Not at all. I save all the best stuff for my guests – just like the wine.'

'Delavoy is a fuck-pig,' said Ossie, unable to compete with his host for wit and so twanging the air with an obscenity instead.

'Ladies, Ossian, ladies,' said Nat with weary tolerance.

'Nothing they haven't heard before,' said Ossie, glaring around the table.

'Who *is* this Delavoy person?' asked Edie, from the other end.

'A critic and journalist, dear,' said Nat. 'And an American, I'm afraid.'

Roger Tarrant said, with a sniff, 'Wouldn't you like to put 'em all up against a wall and shoot 'em?'

'What, Americans?'

'I mean journalists – smug bunch of –'

'Errr, Roger,' Nat interposed, 'you're evidently unaware that an esteemed member of the profession is sitting *right next* to you.'

'Oh, I beg your pardon,' said Roger, smiling at Freya. 'It's just that I'm rather fed up with journos, sniping away. At least as actors we give something of ourselves.'

Freya stared at him. 'Do you? I thought you just recited other people's lines. Anyway, if all actors were stood against the wall and shot, that would be the end of acting. If all journalists were shot, that would be the end of democracy.'

'Touché,' Nat crowed, then said, in an effort at peace-keeping, 'But of course you're all creative in your different ways, be it modelling, or acting, or writing, or painting – we all make something –'

'Apart from Felix,' sneered Ossie.

'I make money,' protested Felix Croker, 'and happen to keep half the West End theatres going at the same time. Or doesn't that count?'

Edie, evidently pairing up each guest with a profession, turned to the hitherto silent Gwen. 'And what line are you in, darling?'

The girl blinked and blushed. 'Oh, I'm with Ossie,' she mumbled.

'Yes, I see that, but what do you *do*?'

Before she could reply Ossie said in his unillusioned tone, 'Homework. She does homework.'

Freya had a sense of the whole table aghast, but Edie didn't miss a beat. 'Thank goodness it's not a school night, then.'

Perceiving the need for a change of subject Nat said to Freya, 'Your father's got a show coming up, I see. I spotted him at the Café Royal a few months ago and kept my profile tilted *just so* in case he looked up and felt an overmastering urge to immortalise me in oil. I'm sorry to say he didn't even *glance* in my direction.'

Freya said, 'I could ask him for you.'

'Oh, I couldn't possibly afford his prices myself,' Nat replied. 'I just thought he might one day conceive an interest in my phiz and decide to paint me, you know, for the nation.'

Freya couldn't help laughing. 'You should listen to yourself . . .'

'But I do!' he said. 'Martine here was kind enough to read out a whole newspaper article about me the other day. It ended: "If Fane's ego were not tethered with strong ropes it would rise and float away over the horizon."'

'He has the piece pinned above his bed,' said Martine, adding hurriedly, '– so he tells me.'

But the mistake was out, and Nat, covering for it, said, 'Martine's not a bad artist herself. That little sketch you did of me –'

'Oh, I'm just a student,' she said to Freya. 'Your father's stuff is wonderful – those London park paintings . . .'

'I'll tell him,' smiled Freya. 'He's very proud of those.'

Nat said, with decision, 'I prefer the portraits, but then I'm no nature lover. Countryside bores me. I see a hill as no more than an obstacle to be got round, and a stream as something that disgorges a trout for supper. As for a beach, what is one supposed to do with it?'

'Comb it?' said Freya.

Roger piped up, 'Really, Nat, how can you of all people despise nature – it's there in all that poetry and painting you love.'

'*Ça va sans dire*. Art has been nature's great beneficiary. By all means let Wordsworth have his daffs and Keats his mists and mellow fruitfulness. Constable must attend to his clouds and Turner to his storms. But the actuality of nature means little to me, and I do wonder if it meant much to Wordsworth beyond something to write poetry about.'

'You should spend more time out of doors, darling.'

'I don't see the need,' Nat shrugged. 'I've never skimped on visual experience, it's just that I prefer it in a gallery, or a theatre, or a cinema. The fluid movement of dancers on a stage seems to me more beautiful and mysterious than anything you might encounter in the Lake District. The only nature that moves my soul is human nature, and human form. The sweet curve of a woman's mouth, the graceful slope of her neck, the twin domes of her –'

'– arse,' supplied Ossie, defiantly unlyrical.

'I was thinking of higher things,' said Nat, shaping an hourglass with his hands.

A distant knocking had sounded from the hall.

'That'll be Jerry,' said Nat. 'He'll have a few things to say about the beauty of the human form.'

Freya had half expected Jerry Dicks to be plastered, but on being led into the dining room by Nat he seemed merely cheerful. His suit and tie were unrumpled, and a grin lit up his debauched clown's face. A skinny roll-up poked from his fingers. He took the vacant seat between Edie and Freya. Asked to explain where he had been, Jerry blew out his cheeks and said, 'I've been dashin' about like a fart in a bubble bath.' No more detail was forthcoming.

'Have you two met?' said Edie.

'I interviewed him for the *Envoy* a few months ago,' replied Freya.

'Oh yes, I read that. Did you enjoy being in the newspaper, Jerry?'

Jerry picked a flake of tobacco from his teeth. 'Couldn't say. I didn't see it.'

'But *surely* you did,' Edie pursued, 'if only out of curiosity?'

Freya jumped in. 'No, I can believe it. It was hard enough just getting him to agree to an interview in the first place.'

'Unlike some people,' said Martine, glancing at Nat.

'I don't like the papers,' said Jerry. 'They give me the wiffle-woffles.'

Edie and Freya exchanged looks of incomprehension. It was the sort of old phrase Jerry liked to trot out, as if he had just come from Collins's music hall. Perhaps he had.

'What on earth are you smoking, by the way?' Edie asked, sniffing the air. 'Smells like . . . *old rope.*'

'No, that's just Felix's latest production.'

Jerry stared at his roll-up for a moment. 'Kif. Cannabis resin. I smoked a lot of it when I was in Morocco.'

'He gets it from his bumboys – among other things,' said Ossie, leaning across the table to pluck the frail-looking cigarette from Jerry's fingers. He took a long drag of it and held the smoke in his mouth before exhaling.

Hetty called down the table: 'Would you like some poached salmon, Jerry?'

Jerry smiled and waggled his hand in refusal. He smoked and he drank – he didn't eat.

'What's it like?' asked Freya. In answer Ossie held it out for her to take.

'You have to suck it right down to feel the benefit,' he said.

'Oo-er!' giggled Felix. 'Ossie's off again.'

Hetty, watching intently, said to Freya, 'Be careful. I had a few drags and went half mad on it.'

' 'Strue,' said Ossie. 'She tried to take her drawers off over her head. It's – what-d'you-call-it – an hallucinogen.'

317

Freya drew on the limp stub and felt the bitter rubbery taste of the resin engulf her nose and mouth. She was determined not to cough, and didn't until she felt the smoke billow hot and sour in her lungs. 'Fuck,' she gasped, which provoked Ossie's humourless machine-gun laugh: *ha ha ha ha ha ha*. He pronounced each *ha* individually, without inflection.

'I hadn't envisaged my dining room being used as a drug den,' said Nat archly. 'The Sobranies I was going to offer now seem a little *déclassé*.'

Jerry had taken out his pouch and papers to roll another one. When Ossie whispered something to him it triggered one of his tubercular cackles. For a few minutes they talked in low voices to one another, ignoring the other guests. Freya got up to help Martine clear the plates. Nat's hireling had made a summer pudding, which was carried off to the table, while the host lingered in the kitchen to consider a bottle of amber-coloured wine. Freya leaned over to take a look.

'Château Filhot. A Sauternes, from 1904,' said Nat, sniffing the cork. 'You see the stuff I pour down their throats,' he added wistfully.

'I'm sure they'll appreciate it,' said Freya.

'D'you think so? Jerry will swig it down like bootleg hooch. Ossie and that sweet cretin Roger will do the same. Felix will pretend to know but hasn't a clue. That leaves the ladies: Edie I can't tell, though at least like Felix her birth pre-dates the wine. Martine – no. Hetty drinks gin and Nescafé. And the schoolgirl drinks – milk? Which leaves us.'

He poured them each a glass, and took a sip, his eyes closed as if in prayer. He whistled softly: 'Fifty years old and yet fresh as a breeze. I think it can be safely said that no one else in the world is drinking this wine at this moment.'

Freya had taken a sip, too, and felt embarrassed. 'I'm sorry, Nat – it's delicious, but I'm no connoisseur, either.'

318

If Nat was disapppointed he hid it well. 'Christ, it's only a bottle of wine,' he said, his tune abruptly changed. 'Here's how.'

They drank again, and she sensed him watching her over his glass. He was in an odd mood tonight, preoccupied, though his hosting could not be faulted. Did he perhaps miss Pandora? That was, she thought, unlikely. He lit a cigarette, picked up the bottle and guided her back into the dining room, where Jerry was entertaining them with another of his tall stories. The kif had made a bluish fog over the table, and Freya took a couple of long drags when her turn came round. Time seemed to thicken and slow. She found herself giggling at Jerry's vaudevillian patter; egged on by Ossie and Hetty, he strung together a magical routine of jokes, impersonations, surreal flights of fancy, before topping them with a tale about being drunk and ill in a hotel bedroom where the wallpaper frightened him 'horribly'. It was Poe, as narrated by Max Wall. Somehow he used his spindly body to act out the sinister whorls and curlicues of the wallpaper's pattern while simultaneously describing his own befuddled self cowering beneath the blankets – by which point the whole company were crying tears of laughter.

Bottles kept arriving at the table, and emptying without notice. As the clock struck half past midnight a slow exodus began. Roger and Felix were the first to go, taking Martine with them. Ossie was slumped in his chair, eyes glazed like a doll's. Gwen, with urgent whispers, got him to his feet.

'How are you getting home?' Edie asked them.

'Motor's outside,' he mumbled, his dark hair stuck sweatily to his forehead.

Gwen looked in appeal to the others. 'Could you help me out with him?'

Freya and Jerry, each with an arm around the shoulder, slow-walked Ossie out onto the pavement, Edie following behind. The Roller gleamed imperious under the street lamp. Gwen had optimistically opened the driver's door, but Jerry, trying a few slaps across Ossie's face, couldn't rouse him. He said, 'This one's too pissed to go in the *back* seat.'

'But how will we get home?' wailed Gwen.

Edie, surprising them all, announced that *she* would drive them. She didn't live far from Ossie in Notting Hill, it turned out; she'd got merry without being paralytic, and she had at least stayed off the kif.

'Are you sure about this?' asked Freya.

'I've been driving since I was twenty-one, darling,' said Edie, briskly pulling on her gloves and climbing behind the wheel. They managed to shovel the near-insensible Ossie into the back with Gwen, who had turned in panic to Freya and said, 'He'll hit the roof if there's a scratch on it.' But Edie, warming to the role of chauffeur, had already started the engine and cried, 'All set?'

The car pulled out, like a boat heaving massively into water, then – with an insolent toot of the horn – surged off into the blue-black night. Freya went back into the house with Jerry. She realised, on returning to the dining room, that some perceptual mischief was at work. The detritus of smeared glasses and loaded ashtrays and discarded plates were sprawled on the table like a still life gone wrong. Indeed the stillness of the room seemed quite arbitrary; some objects had detached themselves from their background and floated into her field of vision. She was very far from sober. As though in a dream she reached with both hands for a coffee pot, still warm, and keeping a close eye on it succeeded in tipping the vessel over an empty cup. From its spout poured something black and aromatic – why, she'd made herself a coffee! She asked Jerry, seated opposite, if he cared for a cup, and was rather glad when he declined. She didn't trust herself to repeat the manoeuvre.

Jerry had just decanted half of a bottle of claret into two glasses, of which the first he quaffed down in one. He placed the second daintily in a waiting position while he got out his cigarettes and offered one to her. She smoked, happy to listen to Jerry running on about his time in Tangier and his first encounter with cannabis when he and Ossie were on holiday. He talked fondly, almost fraternally, about Ossie, and Freya, disinhibited by booze and kif, asked him whether there'd ever been anything more than friendship between them. Jerry was unruffled by the question and said that when they first knew one another he'd been physically attracted to Ossie and wondered for a while if the feeling might be reciprocated. The reality soon dawned that Ossie was the most ravenously heterosexual man he'd ever met ('only two things he cares about – painting and fucking') and also the least trustworthy; it wasn't that he made a point of cheating on women, merely that he saw himself under no obligation to be faithful to them.

They had been talking for half an hour or so when Freya noticed they were the only ones left at the table. When she pointed this out, Jerry shrugged and said he'd last seen Nat and Hetty smoking in the kitchen. The cook had gone off hours ago. Then something else occurred to her.

'Why did Martine leave when she did? I thought she and Nat might be –'

Jerry made a pursed comic face. 'Nat's another one who likes to change the bowling. Twiggez-vous?'

She could feel the coffee begin to steady her; the furniture had stopped playing games of perspective with her eyes. Jerry was now talking about the races, another passion he shared with Ossie. Both of them had their own bookie and would drop hundreds of pounds on a single bet. Ossie, he said, had got into serious trouble recently with some shady blokes he'd borrowed money from; they'd threatened to break all his fingers and then his arms if he didn't cough up. 'Inconvenient for a painter, that,' Jerry sniggered. In the end he had to leave town while one of his 'patrons' sorted out the debt.

Prompted by his evident intimacy with the low life, Freya suddenly said, 'Do you know a man called Sewell?'

Jerry paused on a frown. 'Vernon Sewell, you mean?'

'I'm not sure. I gather he was an informer for the MoD in the war.'

'That's Vern. He's also a fuckin' thief. I'd be sorry to hear you had any business with him.'

She told him the story of Alex, of his counter-espionage work during the war and the unfortunate re-emergence of Sewell in his life; the compromising photographs of him, the blackmail and now the threat of public exposure. Jerry's olive-black eyes were watchful as he listened, flicking ash off his cigarette and knocking back great draughts of wine.

At the end of it he scratched his ear, and said, without emotion, 'Sounds like he's for it, your friend.' He asked her if she knew where the photographs had been taken. She recalled the name of a club – the Myrmidon – that Alex had mentioned, though she had no clue of its whereabouts.

'I know it. For queers with expensive tastes. Oh dear.'

Freya thought she may as well come to the point. 'Can you help me get him out of it? Maybe introduce me to this –'

Jerry snorted in sardonic dismissal. 'I don't think you'd like to meet Vern – *not quite your class, dear.*'

'I've met plenty of lowlifes in my time. I work for a newspaper, don't forget.'

'You've no idea. Vern's a proper slag – the sort who'd sell his own grandmother and then ask for a receipt. You think he'll just *give* you these photos?'

'No,' said Freya, 'but he might give them to you.'

Jerry turned away, shaking his head; he wasn't interested. Freya, aware of his nest-feathering instincts, said, 'I'm sure we could negotiate a quid pro quo.'

He laughed in scoffing disdain, and squinted at his watch. 'Sorry, love, but you haven't got the quids to tempt me.'

He rose from the table, announcing it was time for him to push off. On his return from scouting the kitchen he said, 'Dunno where our host has got to. Tell 'im Jerry said goodnight.' He winked at Freya and patted down his pockets to check he had his keys and his snout. And then he was gone; she didn't even hear the front door shut behind him. He had taken his leave in the silent, slinking way of a cat, vanishing into the night as it pleased him. The cat that walked alone.

Freya, surveying the empty room, had a sudden sense of exclusion, as if the other guests had moved on to something more interesting and not bothered to ask her along. It seemed very odd of Nat to have disappeared without so much as a goodnight. Fully alert again, she got up and wandered about the rooms, half expecting to find him lounging on a sofa with a book, or listening to a record. There was no one about. She was back in the hallway when she heard voices from somewhere below; they rose and fell, their hum strangely secretive. Then there was a noise she couldn't identify, followed by a kind of laughing cry of protest. She followed the sound down the stairs to the basement. A fancy gas lamp, turned low, was the only illumination in the corridor. From what she presumed was a bedroom at the end came the sound, more distinct now, of two or perhaps three people talking.

As her footsteps clacked on the parquet flooring, the voices behind the door fell silent. They had heard her approach too late. She hesitated, wondering for a moment whether she ought to enter, since they were plainly quite reluctant to be disturbed. But to turn back would be demeaning – would make her look like a skulker, a creeper. She put her hand to the doorknob, expecting it to be locked. It wasn't. The sight that greeted her had the air of a staged tableau: Nat, fully clothed and masked, a riding crop in his hand, and, bent over the arm of a plump velvet sofa, Hetty, naked but for her black knickers, pulled down just below the crimsoning globes of her buttocks. Freya's first thought was *Not again*. That the door was unlocked now struck her as deliberate, for neither one of them moved.

Nat, in his 'stage' voice, snarled at Hetty, 'You little fool, with your mewling. We are discovered!'

Hetty, also adopting a faux-actorly tone, began trading recriminations with Nat, calling him a 'blackguard' and accusing him of plotting her dismissal from the house. Then she turned in appeal to Freya and said, 'My Lady, please forgive.' They had evidently been working on this vignette of erotic intrigue – and its sudden exposure – for some time.

Freya realised she would have felt less embarrassed if she'd simply interrupted them having sex; there was at least a sincerity about being caught in flagrante. What she couldn't stand was this play-acting, the coyness of their pretending to be domestic underlings and her own unwitting role as the 'mistress' who discovered them. Conniving at another's sexual humiliation could not arouse her. And yet . . . and yet there was something about Hetty's veiled expression and beautiful pale limbs disported on the couch that she couldn't tear her gaze from. She could feel her mouth had gone dry.

Hetty seemed to catch this furtive current of feeling, because when she spoke again she used her own voice, not the stage one.

'So are you coming in, or are you just going to stand there?'

20

August was ticking off the days to her thirtieth birthday party, and there wasn't a damned thing she could do about it. Joss had taken the whole business in hand; he had organised the catering, hired a jazz band, arranged for a small marquee to be set up in his garden. He had got the invitations printed and posted them himself, rightly suspecting that Freya would find any excuse not to. Even her mother was going to make the trip to London for it.

Freya tried to show herself grateful. Joss had gone to such trouble, even when she'd been offish with him these last weeks – months – and had at times contrived to avoid him. It pained her to see him devotedly planning the 'big day' (as he called it) for she sensed in it his effort to patch up the listing hull of their relationship. Both of them knew, could not help being aware, that something was amiss between them. But she couldn't bring herself to join in the repair work.

To conceal the upshot of her evening at Nat's she had taken the precaution of wearing pyjamas when Joss was staying overnight. There could be no innocent way of explaining the angry red weals across her backside. He didn't ask her much about that night, though she could tell he had his suspicions. In the days following she winced each time she sat down. She hadn't even told Nancy about what had happened, partly out of embarrassment, and partly out of caution. Nancy and Robert were spending a lot of time together, and she could no longer feel certain about entrusting confidences. This thought was more depressing to her than any of the awkwardness with Joss.

Meanwhile there had been not a peep from Alex. Telephone calls to his home rang on, drearily. His office met her with polite stonewalling; he was absent on leave, they insisted. In the end she had written him a note and hand-delivered it through the letter box of his flat in Bayswater.

11 Great James St, WC
9 August 1954

Dear Alex,

I've been trying to get hold of you for weeks. Where are you? I have been through a perfect hell of shame and self-accusation over what I said to you that day in Lincoln's Inn. You asked for my help, with great humility, and I refused it, with unconscionable boorishness. Perhaps you wondered what could have possessed me to behave in such a way; I can hardly explain it to myself. I suppose your story knocked me sideways. We'd only just been reunited and the next thing you were asking me to lend you £300. I mistook this for opportunism and felt it as an insult to my pride. Wrong, wrong, wrong! I now realise how hard it must have been for you to ask, and feel ashamed of myself for the cold and brusque way I turned you down. I most humbly beg you to forgive me.

Of course if I *had* that sort of money I would give it you, gladly. Alas, I don't. And I don't know if it would get you out of your jam in any case. But you must believe I desperately want to help you. If there is a way, please let me know what I should do. I can't bear the thought

of you going through this on your own. Please *please* tell me that you're all right, and that you still consider me
　Your dear friend,
　Freya

The quiet of Stephen's flat should have helped, but for some reason it sounded to her like the quiet of disapproval. She had been hunched over the piano keys nagging at a piece by Thelonious Monk. Maybe she was going too heavy on the left hand. She had transcribed the head of the tune quite easily, its dancing notes as playful as a nursery rhyme. But the soloing passages that followed were much trickier. Of course, she could always revert to the safety of the old ones – Gershwin, Cole Porter, Ivor Novello. Crowd-pleasers.

Outside, the grey afternoon sky was nervous with rumbling. Little spits of rain flecked the windows. She decided to play something merry to lift her mood, and was halfway through 'Ain't Misbehavin'' when she heard the door opening.

Stephen appeared in the doorway.

'Hullo there. Not at work?' he said.

'I took the afternoon off.'

'I was going to make some tea –' He went off to the kitchen, while she refocused her attention on the vexing Monk. Each time she thought she'd got the hang of it she stalled. The thing just wouldn't come. The rain was in earnest now, forming little rivulets that plaited their way down the panes. On his return with the teapot and cups Stephen sat back on the sofa for a minute, listening to her play. When she halted again, he looked up.

'I like that.'

Freya half turned on the piano stool. 'It's something I'm trying to get up for next week.'

Stephen gazed out at the rain. 'Looks like I just missed a soaking,' he said softly.

327

'Dad,' said Freya, 'how can you tell when something is . . . finished?'

'You mean, like a painting?'

'No, no. Finished as in "over". For instance, with you and Mum. When – *how* did you know it wasn't going to work any more?'

'Ah.' Stephen ran through a few facial expressions before settling on one that approximated to resignation. He wasn't sure, he said; it all seemed so long ago. Things hadn't been good between them for a while; once war came and Cora decided to move to the country they began to drift apart. It was more of a mutual decision, really –

'I'm pretty sure Mum didn't think of it like that . . .' Freya interjected, then raised her hands to forestall Stephen's groan of protest. 'I'm not trying to have an argument about it. I'm asking about a general state of mind. How do you – how does *one* – know when a relationship is . . . kaput?'

Stephen had gone from looking puzzled to pained. After some throat-clearing noises, he said, 'I suppose . . . you come to a point when you realise that those strong feelings of love are no longer –'

'Yes, but what *is* that point?' she asked impatiently.

'I'm trying to explain it!' he said, matching her exasperation. 'It's the point when – you look someone in the face and cease to feel, um, protective of them. You may still find them attractive, or amusing, or whatever, but there's no longer that tug at your heart, that reflex which once made you desperate to protect them, to keep them from harm. Because they've become like . . . anyone else.'

She nodded. 'You know Robert, my old friend? He has a theory that love proceeds in three distinct phases, working upwards – first the physical attraction, then the sentimental or romantic phase, and finally the cerebral, which governs the others. We argued about it – to me it sounded too schematic. I think your idea of protectiveness is better.'

'Or maybe just . . . kinder.' He squinted at her. 'What's brought this on? Are you and Joss – ?'

She turned away, back to the piano. She flexed her fingers thoughtfully, and had another go at the Monk. The phrase structure was repetitive, yet lopsided. The basic challenge of the piece was to make it fluid without seeming trite. She faltered, stopped, and swore loudly.

'I've been trying to get this straight for *hours*.'

'It's Thelonious, isn't it?'

'Uh-huh. You know Joss has organised the party for me. I want to play this as my sort of thank-you to him.'

Stephen gave a small uncertain laugh. 'Really?'

'What's wrong with that?'

'Well, am I much mistaken, or is this one called "Well, You Needn't"? Doesn't sound very grateful!'

She stared at him for a moment. The title – she'd been so distracted it hadn't even occurred to her. 'Oh *God* . . .' She lowered her head into her hands.

'It'll be fine! No one will know it,' Stephen said quickly.

'*I'll* know it,' she said, not lifting her gaze. 'Those words will be in my head the whole time I'm playing.'

'Can't you do something else?'

'Like what?'

Stephen shrugged a little. 'How about the thing you and Nancy were playing that night at Kay's house? *I only have eyes for you-ou-ou-ou*.'

Freya felt suddenly very close to tears. 'I can't. Not that.'

'Why not?'

'It's what we played on VE night, at this piano. In this very room. It's – *our* song.'

'Right, right,' said Stephen, trying to reverse away from his suggestion.

'I can't just pretend it's for him,' she said, a catch in her throat. That title: how had it escaped her? She looked again at the notes above the piano, but they were blurring before her, swimming. What a waste of time. A tune she couldn't play at a party she didn't want for a man she – After all he'd done for her, and she couldn't even manage a proper thank-you.

The next morning she was at her desk when the telephone rang. It was, astonishingly, Jerry Dicks on the line.

'I thought you never used the telephone,' she said.

'True. This is an exception – so don't make me regret it.' He wanted her to come to his studio. 'Conversation we had at Fane's the other night. You asked me about a certain – party.'

'Mm. And *you* said I didn't have "the quids" to tempt you.'

Jerry's laugh acknowledged the line. 'Also true. But a mutual friend has put the bite on me – asked me to do you a favour.'

Freya was momentarily stunned into silence. It had to be Hetty. She was the only other person apart from Nancy she'd told about Alex being blackmailed – and possibly the only human being other than Ossie that Jerry Dicks would put himself out for. At the other end he made an impatient noise. '*So* . . . Are you comin' here or not?'

She took down his address. When she rang off she looked up to find Robert eyeing her over his typewriter. He was still sniffing around the story his 'chap' in Whitehall had put his way; there was a tenacity about Robert that put her on guard.

'Who was that?' he asked.

'A contact,' she replied, and heard her own caginess. 'Jerry Dicks.'

Robert gave her a speculative look. 'What, already? Are you two best pals now or something?'

'We have things to talk about,' she said, putting her cigarettes in her bag.

'I find that hard to believe. You told me the old queen hated newspapers – what was his great phrase – ?'

'They give him the wiffle-woffles. I think it's more a distrust of the people who work for them.' Standing, she narrowed her eyes at him. 'Sometimes I know what he means.'

He shrugged off the slight, and returned to his two-fingered typing.

On the Central Line from Chancery Lane to Notting Hill Gate she became lost in a reverie. The strange thing was, she had recounted the story of Alex to Hetty that night without mentioning that Jerry had declined to help her out. It seemed she had interceded with him entirely off her own bat. A 'mutual friend' indeed . . . Freya had a sudden image of Hetty's face looming close to hers, her mouth darkly swollen, so close she could smell her hair. The kif and the booze had done their bit. And yet she wasn't that far gone; in fact, she'd found herself quite willing once she'd shucked off her clothes.

Jerry's studio was in a Victorian mansion block on Hornton Street in Kensington. An assistant greeted her at the door. In contrast to the Soho flat it was light and large, with high-corniced ceilings, cream-coloured walls and a distinct air of prosperity. In the main room another assistant was fiddling with a camera on a tripod; an old armchair stood before a wide hessian backcloth where the photographer liked to position his 'victims'. Jerry himself was next door in the print room, shirtsleeves rolled up and striped braces criss-crossing his narrow back. He was standing at his work table examining contact sheets, their multiple silvery squares glistening in his hands. The assistant hesitantly cleared her throat.

'Jerry, Miss Wyley's here –'

He glanced briefly over his shoulder and grunted something, which the assistant took to be a dismissal; she gave

Freya an apologetic smile and started backing out of the room.

'Shut the door behind yer,' Jerry called. Still with his back to Freya he said, 'Have a gander at these.'

She came over to the long table and stood beside him. He handed her his magnifying loupe and pointed at the contact sheet that had been absorbing him. She placed the loupe over the strip, bending her head to look – and was startled to see a black-and-white portrait of Hetty sprawled naked on an unmade bed. The coincidence of what she'd just been remembering on the Tube was almost sinister. Was Jerry already wise to what had happened at Nat's? But when she stole a glance at his face she read nothing sly or knowing in his expression; it really was a coincidence.

'These are recent?' she said, to cover her confusion.

'A week ago. Tip-top, ain't they?'

Freya murmured her agreement, her eye moving along the strip of multiple Hettys, standing or reclining, hardly seeming aware of the camera's lens. She could just make out the dark cleft between her legs.

'She's never coy, is she – with the camera?'

Jerry nodded. 'Like it's no odds to her whether she's wearin' clothes or not.' The pictures were intended for Ossie, he added, who sometimes preferred to paint her from photographs.

He carefully slid the contact sheets into a frosted-paper sleeve, and paused, as though something had just occurred to him.

'She must hold you in *very* high esteem – Het's never asked me for a favour like this.'

He took out a small key, which he used to unlock one of the table's built-in drawers. He extracted two buff-coloured envelopes, and tipped a sheaf of photographs from each onto the worktop.

332

'I do hope these won't shock you,' he said with a snigger. He arranged the photographs side by side, with the watchful air of a street seller displaying his wares to a customer. There were about thirty of them, ten by eights in black and white. Jerry explained that they had one thing in common: all were taken at the Myrmidon Club.

'So, your friend – what's-his-name – he may be in there.'

A few were of men formally posed in drag, gaudy with make-up; others were hurried snapshots of men in company, drinking, kissing, fondling. Some were more explicit. She had leafed through them all once, and was about to say that he wasn't in any of them when a face sprang out at her. The heavy mascara and rouge might almost have been a disguise; but she knew those eyes for certain. Alex was standing arm in arm with another man, similarly made up. Both wore stockings and suspenders.

'That's him,' she said quietly.

Jerry peered at the shot. 'Ain't she pretty?' he laughed.

'You took this?' she said.

He returned an incredulous face. 'You must be kidding. That's some tuppenny smudger's.' His pride had been piqued.

'So why have you got it?' she pursued, baffled.

Jerry sniffed. 'I've got a darkroom. Sewell pays me for the developin'. It's not like he can take this stuff to Boots the chemist.'

She looked at the photograph again, and her heart turned over to think of Alex, so discreet about his private life even his close friends had never suspected. Now the life had been breached.

Trying to keep her voice steady, she said, 'You won't know this, but he worked for MI5 during the war – my friend there.'

Jerry shrugged. 'So he did his bit. Won't help him if these come out.'

333

She felt a lurch of indignation at his callous tone, and stifled it. He was trying to help her, after all. She asked him what would happen next, and Jerry said, in the same illusionless way, that he'd be 'in touch' with Vernon Sewell – though he couldn't make any promises.

'I want to come with you – when you meet,' she said to him.

Jerry gave her a sceptical look. 'I don't think so. Vern's not nice, I told yer. He doesn't like women – doesn't like anyone much.'

'I don't care. I want to come. Besides, I'm the only one who can identify Alex in these – pictures.'

Again he shrugged, as though to say *Your funeral*. He stared at her for a moment, a sardonic twitch at his mouth. 'Fond of stickin' your fork in other people's dinners, aren't yer?'

She heard the provocation, but only said, 'So you'll ring me when . . .'

He gave a little lift of his chin, and waggled his hand, indicating that she should let herself out.

Getting home that evening she heard laughter echoing from the top floor. She entered to find Robert and Nancy in the kitchen, the remains of a chicken supper strewn over their plates. She noticed how relaxed they seemed in one another's company.

'Would you like a beer?' Nancy asked, holding up a bottle. 'Sorry, I would have saved you some dinner if I'd known –'

'It's fine, I'm not hungry,' she said, making an effort at brightness. 'I heard great peals of laughter as I was coming up the stairs . . .'

Robert, trading a conspiratorial look with Nancy, said, 'We were just recalling a few choice extracts from an old diary. At one point she described me as "a bumptious Mancunian braggart" – one of her nicer remarks, as it turned out.'

The diary was there on the table. Freya stared at it as though she couldn't believe her eyes, or her ears. 'You read Nancy's diary?' Her voice sounded almost horror-struck.

'No, no, *she* read a few things out – most of them from Oxford days.'

Nancy looked a little sheepish at her surrendering this privacy. 'He pestered me, and I gave in.'

'True. I've always been madly fascinated to know what she writes in there.'

Freya smiled, despite her feeling of exclusion. Why had Nancy never favoured her with a recital from the diary? 'Anything about me there?'

'Loads – so I gather,' said Robert. 'But she won't read those bits out.'

An uneasy pause followed. Nobody seemed to have anything to say for a moment. Freya took down a bottle of gin from the cupboard and poured herself a couple of fingers. 'Anyone else?'

Nancy began to clear the table while Robert leaned back and sipped his beer. Freya took a chair and began rolling a cigarette: it wasn't the first time recently she felt she had interrupted a scene of domestic contentment. The lovebirds. There was no hint that she was unwelcome – it was her flat, really; she had found it and asked Nancy to move in – but the dynamic had changed.

Standing at the sink, Nancy looked over. 'Joss rang, by the way – something about the party he wanted to ask you.'

Robert widened his eyes humorously. 'Ah, Gerty at thirty! Are you all set?'

Freya shook her head. 'The party's all Joss's idea. I don't know why he's so keen to have one.'

'Oh, Freya,' said Nancy, protesting, 'you *do* know. It's because he loves you.'

No, she thought; it's because he's afraid to lose me, which isn't the same thing. She took a swallow of gin to drown the unworthy thought, and it burned all the way down her throat.

'So who's coming?'

'Every-bloody-one,' sighed Freya. 'All my family, including two grandparents; a load of journos, people from *Frame* like Elspeth and Fosh, and a few Oxford people – Ginny, Alex maybe –'

Robert sat up. 'Alex? Alex McAndrew? I didn't know you were still in touch.'

'We weren't, for years,' said Freya. Nancy had her back turned, but she must have been listening. 'I ran into him by accident a while ago.'

'Christ. McAndrew . . . what's he up to now?'

Freya hesitated a moment. 'Civil Service,' she said vaguely. From beneath her brow she watched Robert digest this news. Before he could ask anything else she came up with an emergency diversion. 'Nat Fane's coming, of course.'

That did the trick: Robert wrinkled his nose as though a week-old herring had been wafted in front of him. 'Oh, I might have known. Will he be wearing his cape and kid gloves?'

'Not sure. I can ask him for you, if you like,' replied Freya.

'Ha ha,' he deadpanned. 'Well, despite that, I'm looking forward to it. You must introduce me to your mother. I'm good with people's parents, you know.'

'That's true, actually,' said Nancy over her shoulder.

'In that case, perhaps you could do us all a favour and keep her away from my stepmother. The last thing I need is them butting heads.'

'Consider it done,' said Robert, who was now giving Freya an odd look. 'Are you all right, by the way? You look awfully uncomfortable on that chair.'

'I've just got a sore back,' she said. Back*side* would have been more accurate, where she felt bands of pain fiercely aglow; but she preferred not to mention this for dignity's

336

sake. She also feared that Nancy might make an inspired connection between a bruised derrière and her attendance at Nat's dinner last weekend.

The dishes done, Nancy dried her hands and asked Robert if he would like another beer. My God, thought Freya, what next – fetching his slippers? They had begun to talk about what sort of day they'd had, Nancy at her publisher's, Robert at the paper. It was strange, listening to them, how comfortably domesticated they had become. It had never been like that with her and Joss. Perhaps, she thought, that was the problem.

The meeting had been arranged in an Italian cafe on Earlham Street, off Shaftesbury Avenue. Freya had never set foot in the place, though she had walked past it dozens of times before. They sat on a tan-coloured vinyl banquette; each Formica-topped table was supplied with an ashtray and two plastic bottles of sauce, one red, one yellow. It was an hour after the lunch rush, the air still fusty with the smell of fried food. Jerry Dicks had taken a sidelong look at what they were eating at the next table.

'The stuff people put in their gobs,' he muttered. 'Make yer sick.'

The waitress set down a pot of tea between them. Jerry, regarding it indifferently, lit a Senior Service and exhaled through his nostrils. He had already given Freya his instructions. She was not to reveal that she worked for a newspaper. She was not to reveal any personal connection to Alex. If Sewell was to ask her anything she was to reply as briefly as possible. On no account was she to engage him in any conversation relating to his work. From Jerry's warning tone it had become hard to imagine Sewell as anything other than a monster in human form.

When a man of nondescript appearance with a bulbous nose and inch-thick spectacles seated himself on the bench next to Jerry she assumed that Sewell had sent a minion, an errand-runner from the underworld. He was of an age with Jerry but without his puckish demeanour. His face, though pitted and pouchy, hadn't anything rebarbative or sinister or even mildly unpleasant in it. There were no handshakes offered. The two of them instantly fell into a low mumbling sort of talk, from which she nonetheless gathered that the man in front of her was Vernon Sewell himself. The expectation had been of a gorgon; the reality was a Pooterish nonentity in an ill-fitting suit. After repeated glances across the table he gave a little sideways nod at her.

'Who's this?' he asked. His voice was tidied-up cockney.

Jerry, refusing to rouse himself to an introduction, said, 'An associate. No one you need bother with.'

'An associate. So what does she do?' He still wasn't looking at her.

'What does she *do*? Ah. Matter of fact she's a rat-catcher. Useful to have around the place.'

Sewell curled his lip in disdain. 'Always the joker.' He did look at her now. 'Who are you again?'

Freya said, in her politest voice, 'As Jerry said: I deal with rats. And other vermin.'

At that he held her gaze, and then laughed. Not receiving a straight answer was part and parcel of his world: what did it matter to him who she was? The laugh had exposed his pale receding gums. Jerry, reverting to business, asked him if he'd brought the 'stuff', as discussed. Sewell leaned down to his briefcase and withdrew from it a bulky envelope; he pushed it across the table to Jerry, who opened it and, without removing the photographs, flicked through them like a teller counting out banknotes. As his examination continued, Sewell waited; after a while, perhaps unnerved by Jerry's silent auditing, he began drumming his fingers on the edge of the table.

'I'm sorry to let this lot go,' he said. 'The mark was playin' along quietly enough, hundred at a time.'

Without looking up Jerry said, 'Last I heard you had him up to *three* hundred.'

'Well . . . I charge in instalments, like. Some of 'em have bunce put aside for a rainy day. I know when they're shammin'. This one, though, told me he couldn't pay – and I'm startin' to think he was –'

Jerry was hardly listening. Unable to hold her tongue Freya said, 'Do you know why?'

Sewell gave a little start at the interruption. 'What?'

'Do you know why he couldn't pay – your *mark*? Because he gave most of what he earned to his mother, who's a widow. There wasn't any left over to pay off a slag like you.'

Jerry was staring at her. This was not part of the plan. Sewell, incredulous, was also staring at her. 'Jerry. What's goin' on? Your rat-catcher has got some front talkin' to me like that –'

Jerry may have been angry with her, but he had also scented mischief. 'I dunno, Vern. A widowed mother – have to say, shame on you.'

Realising he would get no change out of Jerry, Sewell turned to her. 'What's your game? You this poof's intended or summink?'

'Vern, Vern,' murmured Jerry.

But Freya's blood was up now. 'No, nothing like that. I'm just someone interested to know what a thieving, crawling, blackmailing *fucker* has got on my friend.'

Sewell made a sound like air escaping from a balloon. 'Now you're hurtin' me feelings. Jerry, I'm disappointed in you –' He rose, gathering about him his shredded dignity, but Jerry grabbed his sleeve.

'Vern, before you go, the negs. *The negs.*'

Sewell shook him off angrily. 'You can fuckin' whistle for 'em! I'm not dealin' with you – or your tart.'

339

He was gone. The door of the cafe slammed in his wake. Jerry was shaking his head.

'That's torn it. I tell you to keep yer trap shut and instead you start givin' him lip.'

'I couldn't help it, sorry –'

'It's your friend who's gonna be sorry. Before it was touch and go. Now it's odds-on Vern'll shop him just for the hell of it.'

Freya stared at the leaves floating at the bottom of her teacup. So much for the acquisition of tact. If Jerry was right, she had just signed Alex's arrest warrant. And yet they had come so close to yanking him out of the fire . . . She looked at Jerry smoking, cigarette held inside his palm, old-lag style. An instinct prompted her to ask, 'Have you ever been in prison?'

Jerry squinted at her. 'Not that I recall. Why?'

She shrugged. 'Do you ever think that Vern might black-mail you? I mean, he knows that you're –'

'One of them,' supplied Jerry, with a snort. 'Vern's the type to sniff out a weakness. But with me he wouldn't dare. He knows I've got enough to put *him* away. 'Slike we got a pistol at each other's head.'

The clank and hum of the cafe intervened for a moment.

'He wasn't what I was expecting,' she said presently.

Jerry frowned. 'Vern? What – thought he'd have horns an' a curly tail?'

'Just not someone so . . . insignificant. You'd pass him in the street without looking. I remember at Nuremberg, the Nazis in the courtroom, how ordinary they looked –'

'Hold on a minute. Vern's a wrong'un, but he ain't a fuckin' war criminal.'

Freya considered. 'All I mean is, it's disconcerting. Impossible to, you know, "find the mind's construction in the face".' When Jerry returned a puzzled look, she said, '*Macbeth*.'

340

'Oh. Shakespeare,' said Jerry, his tone indicating a weary disdain. His gods were from the music hall, not from drama.

'If he goes to prison – Alex – it'll be the end of him.'

Jerry twisted his features into an expression of cool nonchalance. What else did she expect? 'As long as Vern's got the negatives, your friend is never gonna be safe. Either he keeps payin' or it's off to Pentonville.'

Freya looked past Jerry's shoulder through the window, at the street and its bunched traffic rumbling on unanswerably. It was the sound of London, oblivious to her failure, oblivious to everything but its own hurry.

21

Sitting at an open window high above the street Freya gazed on the buses and cabs honking, growling, along the Strand. Pedestrians and window-gazers were reduced to toy figures toddling along the pavement. The sky was a careless blue expanse on which flossy clouds were lazing. Outside on the ledge a pigeon strutted in Napoleonic style, chest out, its tiny piercing eyes scanning this way and that.

On the single bed her mother's suitcase yawned open. An evening dress had already been taken out and hung on the back of the door. A moment later Freya heard footsteps approach the door and Cora entered, drying her hands on a towel.

'Well, the bathroom is reasonably clean,' she reported.

'You could have had one en suite at the Savoy,' said Freya.

Cora laughed. 'I'm not made of money, darling. This place will do perfectly.'

Freya felt the crêpe de Chine of the dress between her fingers. She was unaccountably touched by the effort her mother had made in coming up to town for the night, party outfit in tow. They decided to have tea down in the residents' lounge. Reclining on one of the scallop-backed plush sofas Cora watched her daughter roll a cigarette.

'I recall certain painter friends of Stephen's who rolled their own – usually the very poorest.'

342

'Would you like me to make you one?'

Cora shook her head in refusal, but continued to watch mesmerised as Freya filled and rolled the paper, then sealed the edges with the tip of her tongue.

'Now while I remember –' She took a card from her handbag and passed it across the table; inside it was a cheque for a sum that made Freya blink in astonishment. 'I couldn't *imagine* what you might want, so . . .'

'Mum, really, this is – I thought you just said you weren't made of money?'

'Well, I'm hardly a pauper!'

Freya leaned over to kiss her, and mumbled her thanks.

'– and anyway you'll need a bit extra for when you settle down,' her mother continued, eyeing her over the teacup.

'Who said anything about settling down?'

Cora gave her a level stare. 'You know, when I was thirty, I'd been married seven years and had had two children. It doesn't seem to me wildly out of the question that one day Joss is going to – well –'

'Please don't get your hopes up.'

Her mother tilted her head in an appraising way. 'May I ask you something, darling? Do you and Joss ever, you know –' she lowered her voice – '*share a bed*?'

Freya rolled her eyes. 'Oh God, Mum, *of course* we do. That doesn't mean you've got to plunge into marriage.'

Cora's reply began with an exclamatory noise that somehow mixed objection and acceptance. 'I don't see how it can last indefinitely. Sooner or later you've got to decide. In my day they called it "living in sin".'

'They still call it that,' said Freya. If her mother had known how things really stood between her and Joss she might have kept her own counsel. But of course she did not, and so felt free to enlarge on the matter.

'The truth is, it's different for men. They know they can just string you along and take their time about settling down.

343

A woman doesn't have that luxury. If she doesn't seize her moment, well, there's a chance it may not come again. I dare say Joss thinks the world of you, but nothing is certain until you've got him wrapped up tight.'

'What – like a python? Joss is ten years older than me. Have you considered that there might be more urgency on *his* side?'

She found her mother's sad little shake of the head rather maddening. 'Doesn't work like that. Where marriage is concerned men need to be prompted, at gunpoint if necessary.'

Freya gave a tight smile, and said, 'You remember my friend Robert, from Oxford? He's just had his divorce papers through – and he couldn't be happier.'

This succeeded in bringing a halt to her mother's musing on the different priorities of men and women. Their conversation turned to the party and who among the guests her mother might know.

'Oh, isn't it wonderful about Nancy?' said Cora. 'When I got your postcard about her book I felt a little tear in my eye.'

Freya smiled. 'What a day that was. We were both in the swimming pool when the telegram arrived. To be honest, Nance's face when she read it, well – she looked so shocked I thought it had to be somebody ailing, or dying. Or *dead*. So the actual news was even better, because it felt like a reprieve, too.'

Cora nodded, a distance lighting in her eyes. 'I remember her talking about her writing when we met for lunch that time in Oxford. No one like her for blushing! Tell me, does she have a young man?'

'As a matter of fact she does. The man I just mentioned – Robert.'

'Really? But weren't you and he – ?'

'Briefly.'

344

Cora gave a little pout of surprise. 'Gosh. Very Bloomsbury. So do you think they're going to last?'

'Who knows. Maybe you should ask her tonight.' She looked at her mother, who seemed to be pondering the idea. 'I'm joking, by the way. Please *don't* ask her. They've only recently got together, so it's very lovey-dovey. In fact you can hardly separate them.'

'Darling, you sound a little envious.'

Freya shook her head. 'Not at all. Believe me, Robert's about the last man in the world I'd pick for a mate.'

She had a curious sense of something wrong with this reply, but couldn't put a finger on what it was. In any case there wasn't time to mope. She had to get back to the flat to let Rowan in; he was coming down from Cambridge and had reserved the divan for the evening. She kissed her mother goodbye: they'd see one another at the party a few hours hence.

She was no sooner through the door at Great James Street than Nancy came hurrying out of her bedroom, wearing the expression of one with urgent news.

'You'll never guess who rang for you – *Alex*.'

Freya gave a little start at the name. 'When?'

'A couple of hours ago. At first he asked for you without saying who it was – shyness, I suppose – but I recognised his voice, so we talked for a few moments. He said he'd been out of town for a while and had only just picked up your party invitation. He wasn't sure he could make it tonight but said he'd try, and, well – that was it.'

She was stunned. He had practically dropped off the face of the earth these last weeks and now, out of the blue, he was back. She supposed he must have read her remorseful letter as well. Without another word she reached for the telephone and rang his number. Nancy watched her as she held the receiver to her ear. Freya returned a little shake of her head: no reply.

'How did he sound to you?'

'Not very keen to talk. But not desperate.'

Infuriating to have missed him. Still, it seemed he was back in London if he'd just picked up her invitation.

'All well with your mum?'

Freya nodded. 'She's staying at the Strand Palace. We had a pleasant little chat about my prospects at thirty. She thinks it's high time I stopped living in sin and got Joss to lead me to the altar.'

Nancy grimaced in sympathy. 'Oh dear. What did you say?'

'I think I pretty much squashed her illusions.'

'But what if Joss did want to, um, lead you to the altar?'

Freya allowed herself a disbelieving chuckle. 'Nance. They'd have to *drag* me.'

Her brother arrived from Cambridge in the late afternoon, bearing a sponge cake his landlady had made. The HAPPY BIRTHDAY FREYA she had inscribed with fondant icing had been smudged to near-illegibility by the time they lifted it from its tin. Freya cut them each a slice.

'This is awfully good,' she said through a mouthful of cake. 'Compliments to the landlady.'

Rowan, in a striped tie, V-neck sweater and dark trousers, looked ever more like a lanky schoolboy. 'I've got something else for you,' he said, and went to rummage in his suitcase. He returned with a thin, squarish package wrapped in brown paper; she opened it to find a long-playing record, *Songs in an Intimate Style* by Peggy Lee. Freya held it up for Nancy to inspect.

'You love her, don't you?'

'I do! You dear boy, how clever of you to choose this.'

Rowan nodded ruminatively. 'Actually, it was Margery's idea. I told her it was your birthday and you liked that sort

346

of "cocktail" music, so she suggested I order this for you. It arrived just in time.'

Nancy said, 'Who's Margery?'

'Oh, my landlady. She's very good with things like that.'

A look passed between Nancy and Freya, who said musingly, 'You seem rather friendly with this landlady of yours. Now I recall, the last time you were here she'd done some running repairs on your trousers.'

'Yes. She does all my cooking and washing, too,' Rowan said, with no hint of humour in his voice. 'It's as good as having a wife, really.'

Freya narrowed her eyes a moment. 'How old is this *Margery*, by the way?'

He protruded his bottom lip, frowning. 'Not sure. Possibly about thirty-seven. Or thirty-nine? Why do you ask?'

Freya looked her brother in the face, and read not the smallest trace of knowingness on it. He was impossible to tease, because he had no feeling for irony or incongruity. 'No reason. Just wondering.'

'It's nice to get on with your landlady,' said Nancy, probing a little herself, 'given how much time you spend under the same roof . . .'

Rowan took the comment, characteristically, at face value. 'I quite agree,' he said. When he had gone off to the bathroom, Freya shot Nancy another significant look.

'You see, my mother would gain more satisfaction as a counsellor if she concentrated on Rowan and his landlady.'

'Do you think there's a spark between them?' asked Nancy.

Freya laughed. 'I think "spark" would be asking rather a lot of Rowan. I'd guess it's more Darby and Joan than Troilus and Cressida.'

'I hope this woman isn't taking advantage of him.'

'With all the washing and sewing and baking it could be that *he's* taking advantage of *her*.'

She glanced at her watch, and gave a little gasp of panic. Two hours to the party and she hadn't even had a bath yet. She had just turned the taps on when Nancy edged in behind her, holding a little box with a ribbon tied around it.

'I've been worrying about giving you this. I'm not sure you'll –'

But Freya had already removed the ribbon and pulled open the box. On the velvet lining lay a tiny gold cross and chain.

'Nance! It's beautiful.'

She picked it up, as fine as silk thread and so fragile-seeming it might break at a touch. Pulling her hair away from her neck she fixed the catch and felt its lightness trickling against her skin. She stepped in front of the bathroom mirror, which presented their paired reflection. The cross glinted at the hollow of her throat. Behind her Nancy's hopeful expression sought her approval. Freya joined her hands in pious expression, and they both laughed.

'Darling,' she said, turning from the glass to throw her arms about Nancy.

While she was soaking in the bath the telephone rang and she sat up very abruptly, ears pricked. She thought for a moment it might be Alex again, but the steadiness of Nancy's voice soon indicated the call was for her. Though she couldn't make out the words, she could hear something dismayed, then displeased, in Nancy's tone. She was arguing with someone.

Freya had forgotten all about it by the time she was out of the bath and getting dressed. With twenty minutes to spare before they set off for Hampstead she went into the kitchen to make them drinks. Nancy, sitting alone at the table, looked up, her face clouded.

'Robert telephoned,' she said. 'He's very sorry but he can't come to the party.'

'What?'

'He said he's working on a story that will take him all night. I told him nothing could be that important, but he just kept apologising and saying it was impossible for him to get away.'

'But he's not meant to be on the late shift.'

Nancy shook her head. 'I made it pretty clear I was furious.'

Freya couldn't understand it. For all his strenuous ambition Robert was not one to miss a party for the sake of work – and *such* a party. Perhaps Standish had got hold of a story that needed immediate attention.

'Churchill hasn't died, has he?'

Nancy made a face. 'Even that wouldn't have stopped Robert coming. I'm so sorry, Freya.'

At that moment Rowan wandered in wearing a double-breasted blazer and trews that might have suited a cashiered major on a golfing holiday. 'Something the matter?' he said.

'That blazer, for starters,' said Freya, eyes widening. 'Don't tell me – the landlady picked it out for you.'

Rowan returned a look of artless surprise. 'She did, as a matter of fact.'

She saw Nancy's shoulders jerk in silent laughter. 'Right, a sharpener before we go? I've got Kay's recipe for her special negronis here.'

Joss's house was on Downshire Hill. Guests were already milling about as they walked through the living room into the back garden. A jazz quartet was spiking the soft evening air with reedy trills and squeaks. The 'special' nature of Kay's negronis, Freya had discovered, was their flooringly strong alcohol content. The slight swoon she'd had on stepping out of the taxi confirmed it. At her side Nancy looked steady, and she entwined an arm self-protectively through hers.

Across the lawn Stephen was gently escorting his father towards her, making sure the old boy got in a word before the party became too noisy. Grandpa Wyley, of a distant Victorian vintage, was looking frailer these days and grasped a walking stick in his bony, liver-spotted hand. But he was socially game and enduringly dapper in his dress; a silk handkerchief peeked from the breast pocket of his cream-coloured jacket. The tips of his shoes gleamed like spoons.

'Ah, the birthday girl,' said Mr Wyley in his friendly, quavering voice. She leaned in to kiss him on his cheek and listened, chortling, with a mixture of affection and duty, while he revisited a favourite story of her truanting from school as a girl. She seemed to have made a habit of running away from things.

'Dad, this is Freya's great friend Nancy,' said Stephen, folding her into the family circle.

Freya loved the way Stephen had always called his father 'Dad', where others of that generation would have called their male parent 'Father' or 'Pa' or even 'Pater'. As she half listened to Nancy recounting the history of their friendship to the old man, Freya said quietly to Stephen, 'Have you talked to Mum yet?'

He nodded. 'She seems in very good fettle. I introduced her to Diana.'

'Oh *God* . . . how did that go?'

'Very respectful on both sides. Like two prizefighters touching gloves.' He turned to face the white marquee where the band had just struck up. 'Joss has pushed the boat out for you, I must say.'

'I know. Sorry about the other day, all that nonsense at the flat. I felt rather guilty . . .'

'Well, you needn't,' said Stephen with a wry little chuckle. 'Anyway, it sounds like the music has been taken care of. Perhaps you could put me on your dance card for later.'

'You bet!' she smiled.

350

Amid the guests crowding the lawn she spotted the host, and left her father talking to some of her old colleagues from *Frame*. Nodding this way and that as people waved and grinned at her, she felt like someone who'd just won a prize without being able to ascertain for what.

Joss, breaking off from a conversation, studied her. 'I've always loved you in that thing,' he said rather sadly, and kissed her on the mouth.

'That's why I wore it,' she said. It was a long sleeveless dress, oyster-coloured, silk. She had worn it on their first dinner date, and very seldom since. They had drawn away slightly from the throng; it was clear from his troubled frown that he was about to deliver a Big Speech. She felt a sharp jab of self-rebuke as he began, stumblingly, a pained account of how things stood: he realised something had been 'off' between them for a while, he wasn't sure why, perhaps he hadn't been very supportive of her in the new job, or else he'd been prickly over some change in her behaviour. Whatever the reason, he was damned sorry for it, and he wanted more than anything to get back to the way they had once been, because –

'Joss, please, *I* should be the one apologising,' she cut in. 'I've been so preoccupied with one thing and another it's almost like I've forgotten how to behave. Instead of being the nice girl you thought I was I've been a moody cow, and I'm sorry. This –' she gestured around at the clusters of people – 'is wonderful and lovely and much more than I deserve.'

'I never thought you were a nice girl,' he said, a smile twitching his mouth, 'and it is *exactly* what you deserve – to be surrounded by all the people who love you and cherish you.'

The kindliness of these last words made her eyes moisten. She felt her mood turning dangerously confessional. 'Joss, there's something I –'

Whatever she had been preparing to say was interrupted by Nancy, urgent at her shoulder and pointing at the French windows where an inconceivable figure had just emerged, uncertainly looking about for a face he might recognise. She hurriedly excused herself from Joss and slalomed through the press of people towards him, her own uncertainty going like tom-toms in her chest.

She called his name, and turning to her Alex smiled, a smile that had always contained in it (she saw now) a plea for understanding, for mitigation.

'Nancy told me you'd rung, but I couldn't quite believe you'd turn up.'

'How could I miss this? My dear, dear Freya –' he seized her in an embrace so fierce it almost winded her – 'what a friend you've been to me.'

She was confused. The last time they had met she had rebuffed him when he'd asked to borrow money. 'Alex, you got my letter, didn't you?'

'Of course. And I feel ashamed that I should have put you in such a position. But that's all finished with.'

'What d'you mean?'

He gave her a fondly sceptical look. 'I heard what you did, Freya. A man called Jerry Dicks telephoned me – he said, "The genie is back in the bottle," and that the negatives were in his safe keeping.'

'But how – how did he do that? Did he pay him off?'

'I don't know. Maybe. What I do know is that your intervention saved me. I took three weeks' leave of absence and disappeared. There was no way I could keep paying, so I took off north, to Scotland, expecting Sewell to blow the gaff at any moment. I was quite prepared to – to make a permanent exit.' Alex held up his hands to forestall her expression of concern. 'When he went quiet I began to wonder what had happened – then a couple of days after I returned to London an anonymous telephone call came through. I was to wait in my flat until Jerry Dicks called. He told me you were the one who'd sparked the whole thing off. Honestly, it's like being granted a pardon . . .'

She had searched his face as he spoke. In spite of his relief a vitality had gone out of him; his complexion had a grey, shrunken look, and a haunted distance had settled in his eyes. The years had ambushed him. And to think he owed his deliverance to a man like Jerry Dicks. There was a warning there.

'God, Alex, you came close . . .'

'I know. That's why I'm getting out of here, the MoD, London, this bloody country. It's never going to be a place for people like me. It never was.'

'Where will you go?'

He sighed. 'Eastern Europe, maybe. I haven't given up on finding Jan. I hear from people that he's still alive.'

They talked a little while longer, until the pressure of attention from other friends began to drag her away. But before they parted she made him promise that they would meet again: she had become too wary of his disappearing act. He kissed his joined middle and index fingers and waved them to her in goodbye.

The late-August sky had darkened to indigo, and time had started playing its weird trick of leaping ahead in hours rather than minutes. The lawn felt velvety beneath the thin soles of her shoes. In the marquee the jazz quartet had just launched into their second set, a flighty uptempo number that was pulling guests onto the dance floor. The drummer's sizzling hi-hat was making her blood tingle, and she decided it must be time for a dance. But whenever she took a step nearer to the music more well-wishers interposed themselves. The party was now at full gabble. Joss had cast the net wide in his invitations, so wide it seemed impossible she should know this many people, let alone consider them her friends. She kept glimpsing unlikely pairings in company, unlikely in the way a dream shuffled a deck of faces that had no connection to one another outside of her own acquaintance with them. How else to explain the incongruous spectacle of Elspeth chatting away to her grandfather as if they were pals of long-standing?

She had just managed to gain the entrance to the tent when she felt a hand snaking close around her hip. Nat Fane, wearing a purple velvet jacket and a rather girlish scent, leaned in to drawl, 'I am dying, Egypt, dying.'

'Oh. May I ask the cause?'

'Neglect, darling. I've been at this party an *eternity* and yet you've vouchsafed me not a word, not a *glance.*'

'I've had quite a full evening,' she smiled.

He returned an archly reproving look. 'You've had fuller ones more recently, I think.'

'Nat, best to release me at this point,' she said, gently unhanding herself from his embrace. 'Your wife's nearby. She might start to get jealous.'

'You don't know Pandy,' he said in a brittle voice. 'She came back from New York full of her conquests, none of them professional.'

'Ah. I trust you weren't so indiscreet –'

'Speak low, if you speak love.'

He held her by the wrist, scrutinising her, and she realised that he might actually be serious. They had not spoken since the night she had stayed at his flat. She knew there would be a follow-up, a reckoning between them; she had not for a moment envisaged a confrontation here. She sensed one or two guests glancing their way, polite but puzzled, and she said quietly, with a public smile, 'Nat, I don't think this is the time or place –'

'The place is immaterial. The time, I should say, is *long* overdue.' The teasing drollery had gone from his voice. He was serious, after all. She felt herself to be moments away from a 'scene', and looked about for a diversion. But there was no one in their proximity to whom she could appeal. Nat's grip was tight, almost painful, on her wrist.

The quartet had just struck up, at a jaunty lick, 'I've Got My Love to Keep Me Warm', and an instinct told her what she must do. Fixing him with a square look she said, 'You might ask a girl to dance.'

Nat, disarmed for a moment, seemed to remember where he was, and with a little dip of his head invited her to the floor. Holding one another they began to move to the music. It occurred to her that she had never danced with Nat before, and now she understood why. The fluency that had made him famous as a writer and talker eluded his command as a dancer. His tall frame seemed of a sudden all knees and elbows, and though he took the lead he was unable to steer her around with any confidence. Their bodies clashed on the offbeat, then continued awkwardly together, striving but failing to catch the music's lilt. Nat's hands were sweaty, and his feet kept treading on hers. She had never danced with anyone so clumsy before, and as the song reached its end she felt herself nearly swoon with relief. But it wasn't over: Nat held her until the next song began, and off they went, almost jostling one another as the trumpet blared in their ears. This time she tried to lead, but he soon put a stop to that. Other couples moved around them, oblivious to her plight. She shifted her eyes briefly to his face and saw on it only a glazed determination. The song seemed to go on for hours.

'May I cut in?' asked Nancy, humorously taking Freya around the waist and guiding her away from Nat.

As they swayed together she rested her head against Nancy's shoulder and muttered, 'Oh God, *thank you* . . .'

'Darling, you're pouring with sweat!'

'I know. The result of what Nat would call a *mauvais quart d'heure*.'

'Oh dear. What happened?'

'He seems to have gone mad – he thinks he's in love with me.'

Nancy gave a start. 'What? Did he tell you that?'

'No, I headed him off and we danced instead. Which was almost as bad. Fred Astaire can rest easy.'

It was strange, she thought, how dancing with Nancy was simpler than with anyone else, the way they fell into step without really having to try. It had been like that since the first night they met. She supposed it would be a shock to everyone here if they knew who was truly the heart and soul of her life. Her eyes flicked to her, and then away. Nancy had never made any secret of her own devotion; she was proud of the passionate friendship between them. But could that survive if she and Robert made a go of things? What if she decided to move out of the flat? The thought of it made Freya feel sick. But that surely didn't mean she was *in love* with Nancy?

The dance floor was now a forest of swaying bodies. Nancy was so close she could smell the scent behind her ears, the cream she used on her face. She had only to lean in and ask, *Do you know how I feel about you?* But she felt, for once in her life, afraid – afraid of pressing the eggshell fineness of feeling between them and cracking it. The music changed, and Nancy beamed back, unsuspecting; and Freya knew the moment was gone.

By half past midnight the party was winding down. She was seated, cross-legged, on a sofa in the living room, rolling a cigarette and half listening to Fosh and two old *Frame* colleagues shoot the breeze. A diet of champagne and gin had smothered her in a fog of tipsiness. She was thinking of tomorrow morning, when it was all over, and they would begin the post-mortem on the occasion, picking through the memorable moments. From the garden she could hear the trumpet purring quietly, almost tearfully, through 'It Never

Entered My Mind'. Elspeth wandered in and plumped down next to her.

'Maaah-vellous party, darling. Have you enjoyed it?'

'I couldn't have liked it more,' said Freya with a giggle.

There had been another birthday cake, made by her mother and carried into the marquee with a mingled look of shyness and pride. As she cut the first slice and the cameras flashed she felt like a bride – a bluffing bride. The band had struck up 'Happy Birthday' at a jazzy stroll, and Stephen gave a short toast that made an amusingly laboured play on Freya's enthusiasm for a 'scoop', first as a girl with Gennaro's ice cream, later on Fleet Street as a roving reporter. Whoops and cheers were raised. She had wondered if Joss might say something, too, but he had hung back.

Where *was* Joss, as a matter of fact? After their little heart-to-heart earlier in the evening they had barely spoken to one another, and for the last hour he had disappeared altogether. Elspeth hadn't seen him either. Freya got up and began scouting the rooms, offering quick smiles to avoid being detained. Not there, or there. Having tried the slowly emptying marquee she returned to the house and went upstairs. He wasn't in any of the bedrooms, or the bathroom. At the top of the house was a dusty attic room used for storage, its shelves crammed with box files and back issues of magazines. She rarely came up here, but seeing a blade of light under the door she climbed the stairs.

'Joss?' she said, and on a reflex knocked before entering. She had a sudden wild suspicion that he might not be alone – but he was. He stood at the open window, and turned on hearing her enter. 'What are you doing up here?'

He stared at her, and held up his cigarette by way of explanation. There was something blank in his expression, as though he had already asked her something and was impatient for a reply. But he still hadn't spoken.

'Sorry,' she said lightly, 'have I neglected you?'

He gave a dismissive snort. 'Do you mean this evening, or in general?'

There was nothing very friendly in that, so she pushed past it and began talking about the party, thanking him again for his generosity – they'd had a smashing time. Joss nodded, though his face didn't soften as he listened. When she mentioned the dancing he interrupted her.

'I saw you, by the way. With him.'

'Him?'

'Nat Fane. In the marquee. Quite a spectacle.'

'Yes, we were dancing – badly! I didn't know until now he had two left feet.'

'Didn't appear to stop you,' he said, then shrugged. 'I always thought there was something of the snake about him.'

Freya, keeping it civil, said, 'He can be wonderful company when he's in the mood.'

'Oh, I'm sure there are compensations.' Sarcasm rang off every word.

'Joss, what's the matter? Tell me, honestly –'

'Honestly?!' he said, with another snort. 'Dangerous word to use. I didn't want to believe it until I saw you together this evening. Do you suppose it was pleasant for me to watch him with his paws all over you?'

'I couldn't really help it. He grabbed hold and wouldn't let go.'

'I wonder how much of a struggle you put up the other night. Those whip marks on your arse must have hurt. What, you think I hadn't noticed?'

She had underestimated him. She thought she might have got away with it. Either she could try to limit the damage or else pour the whole thing out, which would only be calamitous. The night in question was vivid to her; it was not, however, fathomable, or explicable. Joss had just asked her something, and her attention came back into focus.

'No. He didn't force me. I let him . . . Nine or ten strokes, I suppose.'

Joss shook his head, baffled. 'Why? Why did you let him?'

She took a deep breath. 'I don't know. It excited him.'

'But not you?'

'Not that part of it, no.' Candour was luring her to the edge of the cliff.

'Oh. So you let him fuck you as well?'

She shook her head.

Joss narrowed his eyes. 'I don't believe you.'

Freya knew that, with any luck, she would get through the rest of her life. But she wasn't sure how she might get through the next five minutes. 'I didn't. We didn't. He's not my type. Never has been.'

'But you don't mind dropping your drawers and letting him beat you with a cane.'

She said quietly, 'A riding crop. Not a cane.'

For some reason this caused Joss to lose his last vestige of restraint. He grabbed her arms hard and thrust his face close to hers. 'If that's what you wanted then you could have *asked me* – I could fucking thrash you to your heart's content!' And so saying he turned her roughly about, like a teacher with a disobedient pupil, and landed a smack on her backside.

'Get off me,' she said, pushing him away. The colour was high in his face, his eyes ablaze.

'What, you don't like that?' He had grabbed for her arm again, and they struggled for some moments. She was having a fight with Joss. It seemed comical, except that it wasn't remotely funny. How had this happened? His grip was tigerish. 'I could go a bit harder,' he said tauntingly, and smacked her once, twice, a third time. He wasn't letting up.

'Joss – fuck! – *all right*, I'll tell you, just –'

He stopped, breathing hard, his eyes daggered at her. 'Go on, then.'

She shook off his hand, and caught her breath. It was possible he might not even believe what she had to tell him. 'There was someone else in the room with us – with me and Nat. A girl.'

Joss blinked his confusion. 'What?' His voice had leapt on the syllable; there was almost a squeak of laughter in it.

'Hetty. You don't know her. She's a friend of Nat's who shares his – habit. She was the reason I stayed. She wanted to watch me being "spanked", and I let her.'

Joss, dumbfounded, was struggling to speak. He clamped his eyes shut, his fingers pinching the bridge of his nose. This had passed beyond his comprehension. Eventually he looked up. 'So – he's smacking you, you're taking it, she's watching. Is that it?'

His voice to this point had been touched with pain and puzzlement – but now all she heard in it was his contempt.

'That was the start. When Nat was done I got onto the bed with Hetty and she finger-fucked me, till I came. Then I did the same to her. And he watched. So we all got something out of it.'

A vein at Joss's temple was throbbing steadily, like some internal alarm. She may have imagined his body tensing in readiness to strike her, his expression curdling from disbelief into disgust. But she had no trouble remembering the low-voiced revulsion as he muttered, 'You sick fucking deviant bitch. You filthy slut – get out. Get out of this fucking house before I throw you out.'

She returned a cool, appraising look at him. 'I'll take that as a goodbye,' she said, and stepped out of the room.

22

Freya was twelve years old when she first realised that her father was having an affair. Her discovery of it was purely accidental. Bunking off school one morning she had come up to London and made straight for the flat in Tite Street. Stephen was of course surprised to find her at the door, but he didn't tell her off or send her packing as her mother would have done. (Cora was away visiting friends in the country.) While she was mooching about the studio someone else called, a woman of striking looks named Nina. Both she and Stephen seemed flustered by one another, though they quickly made an effort to appear otherwise. The three of them went out for lunch at the Corner House in Coventry Street. She had liked Nina, a stage actress, but she had asked impudent questions and tried to unsettle her. Stephen eventually gave her half a crown to go and buy him a newspaper.

She was returning from this errand when she paused at the cafe's glass-fronted door to observe her father and Nina together. That was the moment she knew. It wasn't that they were kissing or holding hands or even touching one another; it was something in their faces as they talked, the slight angle at which Nina leaned towards him, the nervy movement of Stephen's hands. Beyond the initial sting of outrage and betrayal Freya was troubled by complicated feelings of fascination, and of envy. It was envy of the adult world, a place where you might be so consumed with love for another person that you would risk everything for it. Her father, whom she had thought immune to temptation, had proved himself quite other. He, too, had a private life, driven by its own compulsions and desires. It became a matter of profound interest to her that you could choose to live on your own terms. *To thine own self be true* was the watchword, with the unspoken corollary *and stuff everyone else*. You just needed to be brave enough, or selfish enough.

Only after living in the adult world herself did she begin to see the drawbacks of that uncompromising philosophy. It became apparent to her that the truth was not necessarily a way to set yourself free; that in fact it might poison friendships and rupture bonds of trust beyond all hope of healing. The greater wisdom, perhaps, was to be selective in telling the truth and thus spare your friend (your victim) its scouring force: to keep silent, even in the face of provocation. Freya saw this, and knew it to be true kindness; but a gulf still lay unbridged between what wisdom dictated and what her instinct demanded.

She woke, chasteningly alone. Grey light was leaking through the uncurtained gap of her bedroom window. *Get out of this fucking house*. She had taken Joss at his word, and left without a goodnight to anyone. She had managed to find a cab at the foot of Haverstock Hill that took her home. There would be no way back. She couldn't imagine him even wanting to hear an apology; he would sicken at the sight of her. It touched her painfully to recall how his face had passed from confusion, to humiliation – to cold-voiced fury. *You deviant bitch*.

She got up and put her head round the door of the living room: Rowan had already gone, leaving his bedclothes in a neat pile. In the bathroom mirror her eyes looked bruised and puffy. Dressing quickly, she walked out to the shop on Theobald's Road to buy the newspaper. The unpeopled

Sunday street looked the other way. The newsagent took her fourpence for the *Envoy*. She was halfway back to the flat when she saw the headline, just below the fold. WHITE-HALL OFFICIAL EXPOSED AS DEVIANT. Her heart took a jolting leap. She ran a disbelieving eye rapidly down the column, drinking in the newsprint like poison. 'Alex McAndrew, 33, a senior civil servant with a distinguished war record', was being investigated on charges of gross indecency at a London nightclub, the Myrmidon. An inquiry had already begun as to how he had been granted security clearance to such a high level. But the extra twist of horror was in the story's byline: by Robert Cosway.

So that was why he had missed her party. He wouldn't have dared let it slip he was about to blow the whistle on Alex, her friend. She could feel bile rising in her throat. Of all the ruthless things he could have done . . . She raced up the stairs and grabbed the telephone. On the third ring it was picked up, and an unfamiliar voice answered.

'Alex?'

No, not Alex, but his lawyer, who asked her to identify herself before muffling the receiver. Alex came on the line, his voice eerily calm. Reporters had turned up at his flat this morning just after seven; now a whole mob of them stood waiting on his doorstep. The lawyer had arrived half an hour ago. There was a pause before he asked, 'How on earth did Robert Cosway get hold of this – not from you?'

'Of course it wasn't from me,' she gasped out. 'Alex, why would I have gone to Sewell about those – ?'

'Don't say anything else – this line's probably tapped. I know you did all you could, Freya. But I can't understand how he knew so much.'

Nor could she. There were three people she'd told about Alex being blackmailed. Apart from Nancy, whose silence on the matter she absolutely trusted, there was Hetty – likewise – and Jerry Dicks, who'd gone out of his way, untypically, to outflank the threat of Sewell and his photographs. Her efforts had come to nothing.

'Alex, what are you going to do?'

'God knows,' he said, resigned. 'Mr Patterson here recommended I make for the hills, but I fear it's too late for that –' He broke off for a moment to mumble with the lawyer, and then came back. 'Excellent timing. The police are outside.'

'Tell your lawyer to let me know where they're taking you. Alex –'

'Freya, I have to go –' There was further muffled, indistinct talk, and the receiver was hung up.

Her heartbeat was going at a dangerous lick. Nancy was out. She rang Robert's number, but the telephone was one shared by the house, and the person who eventually answered had no idea where Robert was, or even *who* he was. She paced around the room, thinking. Where would he be at this hour? She looked at her watch.

Five minutes later she was walking, half running, down Chancery Lane towards Fleet Street. Her brain was overheating with theories about Alex's exposure. Who was behind it? She wondered if Sewell had welshed on whatever deal he had made with Jerry Dicks and had kept back some of the photos to sell on the sly. But Jerry would have been wise to such tricks; he'd have made sure Sewell had given up the lot – or else. Hadn't he said he had enough on the blackmailer to put him away for years? Jerry had stopped up the danger from that end. It had to be down to something – someone – else.

Entering the lobby of the *Envoy*, deserted but for the man at the desk who waved her on, she took the lift to the newsroom. The door to Standish's office stood open. She made a beeline for it.

Standish, unshaven and tieless, had his feet up on the desk. He didn't look very surprised to see her.

'Why wasn't I told about the Alex McAndrew story?' she said.

He pushed his chair back and swung his legs to the floor. 'Please, come in.'

She ignored his sardonic pleasantry. 'Well?'

'We knew that you had a personal connection to McAndrew and that you'd probably try to block it –'

'Too fucking right I would have done.'

'Calm down. It's a story, a queer in the MoD. A huge story. It's not like we could ignore it.'

'You could if you had a conscience. How d'you dare call this a liberal paper, really – hunting down a man for what he does in his private life?'

'I don't make the laws. And in any case, it's not just his being queer that's got him in trouble. They reckon he's been communicating with certain gentlemen in Eastern Europe.'

'That's balls – Alex isn't a spy. He's been looking for a friend of his from the Czech air force. They met during the war.'

'I'm sure his lawyer will argue the same. Look, if it hadn't been us it would have been someone else. Try to see it from a professional point of view. It's a story in the public interest.'

'That's what they always say when some poor fool's been hung out to dry –'

She saw Standish's eyes flick to a point over her shoulder. She turned, just in time to catch a glimpse through the glass partition of a figure disappearing. She darted out of the office and was on his heels as he hurried down the corridor, pretending he hadn't seen her.

'Robert,' she called out. He stopped, and turned round to face her, his jaw jutting defiance. She narrowed her eyes. 'How could you? How could you, knowing what you knew?'

'It's my job, Freya. I work for a newspaper that pays me to report things. This one's bigger than anything I've ever had. What, you expected me to hold off just because I knew him at Oxford?'

'No. Because you knew *I* was Alex's *friend* – that's why. You really must have hated him to rat him out like that.'

Robert protruded his lip and shook his head. 'I've no particular feeling about him one way or the other. I just got the story.'

'Yes, and I wonder *how* you got it. Did Sewell make you a deal?'

'Who's he? I made no deal with anyone.'

She paused. So if he didn't have the photographs – 'How then? Who tipped you off?'

'I told you, I've got a fellow at the ministry who keeps me apprised.'

'Who – what's his name?'

He shot her a sceptical look. 'Come on. I protect my sources, like you would. I just put two and two together.'

She stared hard at him. 'I don't believe you. You're not clever enough to have worked it out yourself. I hope to God you didn't get it from Nancy.'

A twitch of resentment creased his face – a face she was feeling a violent urge to slap. He said, dropping his voice, '"Not clever enough" – ha. This story's going to be all over the papers, for weeks. It'll be on television. And I'm the one who broke it. Standish has already said he's giving me Home Affairs, my own office, whatever I want. I'll probably get a car. So you tell me which one of us has been clever.'

'A car! I hope you fucking crash in it, you unspeakable cunt –'

Robert laughed, shaking his head. 'Your language – it's priceless. I'll recommend they switch you to the crossword.'

'Fuck you. You ruin someone's life for a car and a promotion. Don't you have any shame?'

'You don't change, do you? Always the self-righteous cow. What the hell are you doing working for a newspaper if you can't stand people printing the truth?'

'Nearly the right question,' she said, her rage suddenly tearing away a veil. 'It's what I'm doing working for *this* newspaper. You know, I'd rather poison myself and get it over with – cos that's what would happen anyway if I stayed in the same fucking room as *you*.'

He frowned at her, puzzling at the implication. 'You're not going to resign?'

'Watch me,' she almost snarled. 'And don't try showing your face at the flat again – ever.'

At the Strand Palace, over a bacon-and-tomato sandwich, Freya listened as her mother talked about the party; but the event now seemed so remote to her it might have happened in another lifetime. Cora hurried on about her old friends, the excellence of the catering, her disappointment at Diana being so 'pleasant', her annoyance at Stephen's unwithered agelessness. When she paused a moment to squint at her daughter and ask if anything was the matter, Freya only smiled and said she was still hung-over from the night before. It seemed to satisfy her.

In silent relief she eventually handed her mother into a carriage at Charing Cross. Cora had made her promise that she and Nancy would come for a weekend at Finden very soon – she had *so* enjoyed seeing Nancy again.

She walked back to Great James Street, head and heart burdened with the drama of the last twelve hours. She had decided to spare her mother any rehearsal of it, partly because she knew she wouldn't understand, and partly because she feared to choke in the telling. The empty Sunday stillness of the flat depressed her, though she felt in no mood for company. Nancy's bedroom door stood open, her party dress from last night crumpled on the bed. She must have heard by now about Robert's treachery: the newspaper lay open on the kitchen table, its headline the writing on the wall. Freya was turning away when her eye snagged on the tantalising sight of Nancy's diary, expectant on her bedside table.

And all at once it fell into place. She knew, suddenly and absolutely *knew*, how Robert had got his story. In a trice she snatched up the black-boarded volume with its marbled endpapers and began riffling through its recent entries. It must be somewhere in the last ten days of July, she thought, when they were in Florence. She felt certain that a clue, *the* clue, would be yielded up to her –

F.'s odd mood these last days is finally explained. We had stopped at a little trattoria & she told me that Alex McAndrew had called at her office a few days ago asking her to lend him money – hot on the heels of his queer revelation it turned out a blackmailer had him in his pocket over some photographs taken in a nightclub. He needed £300! F. of course didn't have that kind of money, or anything like, but she was beside herself with remorse – & believes she has let him down. I told her it wasn't her fault, but still she fretted, & begged me not to tell anyone, especially <u>Robert</u>. Felt rather offended that she thought I might betray her confidence, but I didn't say anything. We walked back via the Duomo to where we'd left the scooter . . .

She sat on the bed and read it again, aghast that her secret should have been entrusted to so frail a receptacle. Nancy didn't even bother hiding the diary away; it was always lolling on her desk or her bed, inviting temptation. Which wasn't something Robert would have resisted overmuch: she could imagine him, pricked by curiosity, casually flipping its pages in search of references to himself – only to stumble upon *this* dynamite. *Alex McAndrew*, right there in Nancy's steady, even cursive. Oh, the ghastly mischance of it! Alex, undone by the few strokes of a pen. A tear rolled off her eye and ploshed onto the open page. She dabbed at it with the edge of her blouse, smudging a few words. She closed the diary, and half lay, face down on the bed. She didn't know if they were tears of rage, or sorrow, or loss; or all of them at once.

For a long time she lay there, until the scrape of the latchkey from below and footsteps on the stairs roused her. She stood up and moved to the bedroom doorway as Nancy reached the landing. Their eyes met, and Freya knew a moment of truth, another one, was coming.

'Oh, darling,' Nancy said, her brow creased with pity.

'When did you know they were going to run the story? Did Robert tell you?'

She shook her head. 'I only found out this morning, when I saw the paper.' She came forward and clasped Freya's forearms in sympathy.

'But you know how he got hold of it?'

Now she nodded. 'He told me – one of his contacts at the Ministry of Defence had tipped him off. They knew there was someone in the building who was using an encrypted code to communicate with his handler. I never would have dreamed Alex could be a double agent –'

'Oh, but he isn't! He was trying to trace Jan – his old lover. That's why he was using a code. They've got him because he's *queer*, not because he's been passing secrets. And it's not from anyone in the MoD Robert found out.'

Nancy frowned. 'But how else could he – ?'

'He got it from *you* – from your diary! It's the only way he could have.'

Nancy's hands dropped, releasing her. Her expression had clouded. 'How would you know that?'

For answer Freya stepped back into her bedroom and snatched up the book. She held it out as though Nancy hadn't seen it before. 'Because it's here, written down, everything I told you about Alex when we were in Florence.'

Nancy held herself very still. 'You read my diary?'

'Yes, I did – and so did Robert. I just had to make sure it was in there.'

There was an unsteady pause between them. Then Nancy stepped forward and took the diary from Freya's hands. 'You shouldn't have done that,' she said quietly. 'Of all people I'd never have thought you'd do that.'

'And I wouldn't have, but – but I knew that *he'd* read it, and I needed to prove a point.' She had been wrong-footed, and now she heard the weakness in her excuse. 'Nance, I'm sorry, I wouldn't have done if it hadn't been absolutely neccessary.'

'Really. So you *knew* that Robert had read it, and because of that you had to read it too. Please, you'll have to explain – how do you know? Why shouldn't Robert have got the story from somewhere else?'

She heard a cold, sceptical edge in Nancy's voice, and shrank from it. 'I just know, because I know Robert. I saw him at the office this morning and had it out with him. He was almost hugging himself with delight – the editor's promised him the Home Affairs desk. God, I knew he was ambitious, but I never imagined he'd stoop to this –'

'He was surely only doing what the editor told him to – find the story – and you resent him for succeeding. A promotion? He deserves it.'

Freya couldn't believe her ears. 'How can you be taken in like this? Nancy, listen to me, two weeks ago Robert as good as admitted he thought the idea of a mole in the MoD was cobblers – his word. Next thing, he's got Alex cold. *The only way* he could have done was by opening that book and finding Alex's name there.'

'So you say.'

'Why d'you not believe me? Leave aside the fact I've resigned over this – yes, I've quit! – this all comes down to trust. You're too nice to believe that Robert could be this underhand, this unscrupulous. But I *know him*. And he wouldn't think twice about violating someone's privacy if he thought it might give him an advantage.'

Nancy stared at her, almost pityingly. 'You've never really forgiven him, have you, for throwing you over back then. You resent him, and you resent other people for liking him.'

'God – give me strength! You want the truth? I considered Robert a friend, I enjoyed his company and found him charming. Yes, he once dropped me, and I thank my lucky stars he did. It was easy to forgive him, we were so young. What I'll *never* forgive is his betraying Alex for a fucking news story.'

Nancy, eyes cast down, shook her head. 'Please don't say anything else. I mean it – please.'

A cold premonition of disaster had gripped Freya within. But she kept going. 'I only wish you could see through him as I did. I can't stand the idea of you not knowing –'

'Freya, *stop it*! Not another word. I wasn't going to tell you this yet, because I didn't want it to come between us. Robert's found rooms to rent, and he's asked me to share them.'

It took her a moment to find her voice, lost somewhere near the bottom of her throat. 'But . . . you're not going to, are you? I mean, why would you do that?'

Nancy gave an incredulous gasp. 'Because we want to,' she said, and added, in a quieter voice, 'I want to.'

Freya felt that something had dislodged in her head, because she couldn't order her thoughts into a coherent sentence. Distracted, her voice came out in an odd croak. 'Where?' It wasn't the question she wanted to ask; her mind was playing an involuntary trick.

371

'Near here,' Nancy replied. 'We could still, if you were willing –'

'I see,' she said, and paused. 'So given the choice between him and me . . .'

Nancy said nothing, which was tantamount to an admission. The shock of it made her regroup. She could beg Nancy to forgive her over the diary, say it had been a mistake; she'd apologise to Robert and set things right between them. Anything but let her go. Anything but that.

Apologise to Robert?

'Why would you let him ruin your life? He'll never change.'

Nancy stiffly looked away. 'It's already done. I'm going to move in. You can choose to see us or not – I hope you will.'

Freya wasn't sure how long it was before she answered. She was staring past Nancy at the rooftops and chimneys framed in the long window. She had always liked their solid last-century steadiness: they had survived bombs. She would miss looking at them. In time she would be able to imagine herself living somewhere else, with other views and staircases and bedrooms not known to her. Her present life was breaking up and scattering the wreckage in front of her.

She managed to smile, and, in a moment that could have broken her heart, Nancy smiled back, mistaking a farewell for a truce.

III

That Girl

23

It was all going up, fast. Freya kept craning her neck as she drove through the north London streets, trying to adjust her eyes in the shadow of another high-rise. When had this happened? She had left behind a more or less horizontal city and returned to find a vertical one. It was as though an invisible alien race had descended on the town and immediately set about throwing up their space-age cabins. 'Streets in the sky' she'd heard them called. Flats stacked high, one on top of another. And the best thing about these cellular habitations, apart from the view, was that they had 'all mod cons' – even their own bathrooms. She stopped at a traffic light and looked up through the windscreen at a looming tower. She grinned, and shuddered.

Strange to be back after all this time. She used to be wary of taking a backward step, but this felt different, it was a place at once familiar and transformed. More traffic, more shops, more noise, more adverts, more colour, more hustle and bustle. And more people, inevitably, streaming across the junction as she waited for the green light. Rome, where she'd mostly been living for the last eight years, had seen change, too, but it wasn't something you noticed as much when you stayed put. And in any case it was still in the dark ages compared with thrusting modern London. The two capitals seemed to be moving at different speeds, one at the pace of a horse and cart, the other of an express train.

She had joined the traffic heading west along the Euston Road when something made her double-take. It was the gigantic arch fronting Euston Station, shrouded in scaffolding. A repair job. But no, wait; looking closer she saw that huge chunks of it were missing. Not everything was going skywards after all; they were taking this old giant down. How had she forgotten that? She had read about its proposed demolition months ago, there had been an outcry and a late campaign to save it – up in smoke, by the look of things. Amazing that something she thought so immovable, so much a part of 'her' London, could be made to disappear. An old song came to her, and she hummed a few bars.

In time the Rockies may tumble
The Arch it may crumble
They're only made of clay . . .

That stuff looked to her more like granite. But it was going all the same.

She turned down Gower Street, dodging around the buses, and took a right into Shaftesbury Avenue. Dusty blossom shimmered on the trees, and the air, following a recent shower, had a sharp, rinsed smell. She parked on Greek Street, just round the corner from the restaurant. Kettner's patina of *fin-de-siècle* grandeur had been chipped away down the years, but within Soho it retained a certain faded respectability, like the madame of a brothel down on its luck. On the way in she glanced sideways at the long mirror and saw a stranger: herself, only like a boy.

She had taken the plunge that morning at a salon on Upper Street. The hairdresser, Bernard – or *Buh-naaard*, as the ladies addressed him – had looked startled when she asked for 'the lot off'. He gave her a quizzical look, and she explained: she wanted it short and gamine, like Jean Seberg in *Breathless*. Bernard hadn't heard of her. He took her hair in the palm of his hand, as if weighing it, and said, 'Are you sure?' His expression made her think she was consenting to an invasive and possibly dangerous operation, but she nodded anyway. As hanks of dark hair dropped silkily to the floor under the busy threshing of Bernard's scissors she began to quail at her boldness. Minute by minute she had the impression of being sheared, like one of those wretched Frenchwomen being punished for collaboration in the war. Her ears seemed to stick out, and her face looked suddenly bare and defenceless. She was on the verge of tears when Bernard, oblivious to her dismay, stared at his handiwork in unfeigned wonderment. 'You've got the look for this,' he said, and called over one of his minions. She cooed the standard flattery. Bernard now held the mirror at different angles for Freya to check the back of her head. It was awful; it was exciting.

The dining room was at a steady roar with Friday lunchers, packing in early for the weekend. Stephen and Diana, looking nervous with excitement, rose to greet her at the table. It was a delayed reunion; they had been on holiday in Scotland when she got back a fortnight ago. She embraced them both.

'What on earth have you done to your lovely hair?' cried Stephen, running a hand over Freya's boyish crop.

'I like it,' said Diana, with quick diplomacy. 'Very Continental – *ooh la la*!'

The delight in their gaze was mingled with an unabashed curiosity. Her return to the country had been as abrupt and unexpected as her disappearance into exile. Apart from the occasional Christmas, she had hardly been back in the eight years since; once, when her mother was ill in hospital with pneumonia, she had stayed for a week, no more. It had been almost a point of honour with her.

377

In the weeks following her thirtieth birthday she had decided to up sticks. She gave the landlord at Great James Street his month's notice and moved into Stephen's flat in Chelsea while she readied herself for departure. She would go to Fiesole. Kay was more than happy to have her as a house guest at the Villa Colombini. An international newspaper, based in Rome, offered her a reporter's job, and for a year she commuted from Florence. She and Kay became good friends, and remained so even when she left Fiesole and got an apartment in Trastevere, near to the paper's offices. At first she had thought of her Italian adventure as lasting no more than a few months, a sojourn that would allow her to take stock before she moved back to London. But the more she thought about it the less appeal her old life held. She wasn't one to pine for absent friends. She had always known when to leave – a city, a job, a man, a country. Or so she told herself.

'Why Islington, though?' Diana was asking.

'The rent's cheap,' replied Freya, 'and Canonbury Square's nice, in a shabby sort of way. I like places where you see a bit of life. In Trastevere they live in the open – they even hang their washing out on the street.'

'Heavens! At least we've got launderettes.'

'We're jolly glad to have you back, anyway,' said Stephen. 'I imagine your mother is, too.'

Freya nodded. 'I went down to Finden last weekend. There appears to be a new man on the scene – *Gerald*.'

'That so?' he said, leaning forward. 'Did she introduce you?'

'We had lunch at the Cow. Very sporty, wears a cravat. He's been teaching her to play golf.'

'Good Lord, she must be keen. The times I used to beg Cora to play tennis.'

They had just started on their food when a ripple of interest disturbed the atmosphere. She looked round, inquisitive like

378

the rest, and watched a young woman in a short sweater dress tottering across the room towards a crowded corner table. She was a brunette, no more than twenty-one, full-lipped and doe-eyed, with a large high bust almost comically disproportionate to her delicate frame; one false step would perhaps topple her over. The girl's dark fringed hair made Freya mournful for the recent surrender of her own.

'Who's the popsy?'

Diana stared at her. 'Chrissie Effingham. You know, the girl in that bread advert. The new face of Revlon?'

Freya's expression remained a blank, and Diana stifled a laugh.

'Gosh, you really *have* been away. She's everywhere!'

Stephen was still squinting across the room. 'The lady certainly carries all before her.'

Diana rolled her eyes heavenwards. 'You can stop staring now, darling. Anyway, they all want to be her friend, as you see. She was a waitress when they discovered her. What was the line – ?'

' "The face that launched a thousand tips," ' Stephen supplied.

'Hmm. Supposedly has all sorts of boyfriends. She's going out with that actor, Roger Tarrant, or maybe he's the previous –'

'I remember him,' said Freya. 'We met once at Nat Fane's house. Very good-looking, and very stupid.'

Stephen gave her a scrutinising look. 'Do you keep up with him – Nat, I mean?' The rumour around her parting from Joss was that she and Nat had been having a long affair.

'I've had a few letters from him – funny ones – over the years. We haven't seen much of one another, though he's been nice to me since I came back. He's lent me a car.'

Diana, seizing an opportunity to fish, said, 'And what of the chap you were seeing in Rome – Dani? Wasn't he – ?'

'Italian?' she said, deliberately obtuse. 'Yes. We had a thing for a while. But it never got very serious.' She had put it off long enough, and did a little fishing of her own. 'I wonder what Nancy's up to these days . . .'

Stephen's expression was doubtful. 'I imagine, being an MP's wife, she's bored to sobs.'

'Yes, but she has her own career, too,' said Freya, loyal in spite of her own objections. 'She's not *just* a wife.'

Diana nodded. 'Quite, darling. She's got a new one out, I think. The last one I read of hers I couldn't make head nor tail of.' There was a little pause before she added, 'Will you be seeing her?'

'I shouldn't think so,' she replied in a casual tone. 'I don't even know if she's still in London. I imagine them to be living somewhere like . . . Berkshire.'

Stephen was shaking his head. 'It amazes me you've never bothered to find out. Honestly, why don't the two of you just – ?'

'Stephen,' said Diana, warning him off the tender subject.

She couldn't blame him. Even now it seemed unreal that she and Nancy hadn't spoken to each other in all this time. In their last days at Great James Street they had kept up a front of pursed politeness as boxes were being piled in the hallway and removal vans idled outside. They hadn't argued again, by tacit agreement. The farewell scene Freya was envisaging – the fit culmination to their friendship – had dissolved on returning late from work one night to find the hall empty and Nancy gone. She had left a note with her new address and telephone number, which Freya took to be an apology rather than an invitation to stay in touch. The abruptness of it winded her. Her first instinct was to damn the note as cowardly. Later – years later – she considered it in a more forgiving light: Nancy had left like that because it was too painful any other way.

Five years ago a letter had arrived at her apartment, forwarded by her mother. It had enclosed an invitation from Mr and Mrs Joseph Holdaway to the wedding of their daughter Nancy . . . She had agonised for a few days as to whether she should go, and finally decided against it. The ghost at the feast. She hadn't sent a formal reply but, in lieu of a wedding present, she had bought a porcelain statue of St Francis de Sales and dispatched it care of Nancy's publisher. She had never heard back.

They were on to pudding, and the sight of Stephen patiently breaking off a dark wedge of treacle tart with his fork reminded her of something.

'I was driving alone the Euston Road on my way here – d'you know, I'd quite forgotten they were pulling down the Arch.'

Diana made a grimace. 'Don't start him on that. He spends more time at protests with the Victorian Society than he does at the studio.'

Stephen shook his head sadly. 'I can't bear even to pass by the place. We tried to stop them, God knows. I thought Betjeman might have a nervous breakdown. I suppose it looks – awful?'

Freya nodded in silent sympathy.

'He used some very blunt language of Macmillan the other day,' said Diana, trying to lighten the mood. 'I told him – that's worthy of Freya.'

'He's beyond contempt,' muttered Stephen. 'If we can't get a Tory prime minister to defend a beautiful old thing like that there's no hope for us.' He said the Coal Exchange in the City would be the next to go.

The model and her entourage had risen from their table in the corner and were ambling, with much self-consciousness, through the room. As they came by, Freya looked up and happened to catch the eye of the girl, Chrissie, whose smile at her seemed at once to offer friendliness and a shy hope for its return. Disarmed, Freya was halfway towards smiling back, but the girl was already being hustled out of the place by her handlers, lest another speck of her stardust be squandered on a roomful of nobodies. The air seemed to decompress on their exit, and the curtain of conversation descended once more.

'My God,' Freya said, 'she looks like she's still in sixth form.'

'Young people are all the rage nowadays,' remarked Diana. 'No one else gets noticed – not if you're over thirty.'

Freya snorted a laugh. 'That's cheering.'

'Don't worry – with that hair you could pass for twenty-eight, easy.'

Oh God, the haircut. She had forgotten about it, and picked up a spoon to examine her reflection. Her face ballooned in its convexity, bulbous and idiotic; she laid it down with a wince. Nobody ever looked smart in the back of a spoon.

Outside the early-spring afternoon was nudging on, the air tainted with the mingled aroma of frying onions, petrol and drains. They walked up to where she'd parked the car. Stephen whistled on seeing it.

'Good grief. You didn't say it was a Morgan.' He caressed the green coachwork tenderly, as if it were a racehorse. 'What's his *other* car?'

'Dunno. I think he has a few.'

'Don't get a prang, for heaven's sake. This thing's worth a fortune.'

Diana, who'd gone round the front, had found a slip of paper jammed under the windscreen wiper. With a dubious look she unfolded it.

'Oh dear. Parking ticket.'

'What's that?' said Freya, taking it.

'It's a fine, darling, from a traffic warden. You're not allowed to park here, didn't you know?'

Freya stared at the small print. 'Two pounds?! That's ridiculous. And what's a traffic warden?'

Stephen laughed. 'Welcome home. There he is – that chap in the uniform up the road. They're all over the place now.'

I really am out of step, thought Freya; tower blocks, parking restrictions, 'personalities' the age of school-leavers. Returning from exile would require a period of adjustment. At least no one had stopped to laugh or point in horror at her haircut.

'Next time,' said Stephen, nodding at the Morgan, 'walk a witch's circle around it once you've parked.'

'What on earth's that?' she asked.

'Just a spell. My friend Terry told me about it – you walk a circle and create a sort of force field, warding off evil spirits. And parking tickets.'

Freya looked to Diana, who shrugged her incomprehension. 'He's getting very superstitious in his old age.'

But Stephen only tapped his nose, as if he'd just dropped a word to the wise.

Once they had said goodbye Freya decided to walk up to Heal's to get a few things for the flat. Buses growled in convoy up Tottenham Court Road, and unfamiliar shopfronts glittered, pleading for attention. Ever since she'd got back to London she found herself glancing at the faces of passers-by, wondering if the next one would be Nancy, however unlikely the odds. She had claimed at lunch not to know whether Nancy was still in London. In fact she'd read a profile in a newspaper that mentioned a house somewhere near Regent's Park. She imagined what would happen if they encountered one another right now, on this pavement.

But perhaps Nancy wouldn't recognise her, with her new short hair, and the hooped sweater and Capri pants she was wearing. What if she walked right past her? The possibility dismayed her, and put an edge on her own vigilance: one of them had to be on the lookout. In Heal's she wandered through a bright daydream of domesticity, dazzled by the huge table lamps and gleaming clocks and jazzy rugs. She had the impression people were more prosperous. Instead of old ladies in frumpy hats and coats, young couples strolled about as if they had all the money and leisure in the world. 'May I help you, madam?' a salesgirl asked her, and Freya realised she must have looked lost. She quickly bought some wine glasses and left.

Walking back down Charing Cross Road she stopped at Foyles. She had got out of the habit of buying new books while in Rome; she would borrow from Kay, whose library was a trove of eighteenth-and nineteenth-century literature, much of it cased in forgotten old editions. Their pages were thin as onion-skin and mottled with age. Freya had gorged on Eliot, the Brontës and Henry James, the occasional Trollope, and latterly a good deal of Somerset Maugham, who was about as modern as Kay's taste allowed. In Foyles she raked her gaze along the new fiction hardbacks, their titles and authors unknown to her. Another world that had moved on. But at last her eye snagged on one she did recognise, and she took it down from the shelf: *The Hours and Times*, by Nancy Holdaway. It sported a sash over a plain dust jacket, announcing it as one of the season's recommended reads. Her fourth novel, according to the flyleaf, anatomised 'with great delicacy and authority a quartet of friends as they come to terms with grief, temptation and mortality'. She was disappointed to find no author photograph on the back flap.

It was late afternoon by the time she got back to Canonbury Square. She ascended the stone steps to the raised pavement and let herself in, inhaling the hall's smell of camphor, nicotine and worn carpets. Her flat occupied the top two floors, with a view onto the little railed garden dividing the square. Cars made sluggish circuits around the perimeter. She had looked at a nicer place on Guilford Street in Bloomsbury, her old stamping ground, but it seemed too close to Great James Street. She couldn't go back, however much she'd have liked to.

The flat didn't feel properly her own yet. None of her pictures on the wall, no rugs or quilts to lend a bit of homeliness. Boxes, still sealed, crouched in the back bedroom. The kitchen, with an oven and wall clock that had served the previous tenants, had the mannered look of a stage set. In the hall she had propped up her tall cheval mirror, its glass spattered with black spots. It had been a present from Joss, and gone everywhere with her, silent witness to so much. She remembered once, towards the end with Joss, he had caught her staring distractedly at herself and said, 'Are you all right?' It felt like the hundredth time he had uttered the words, and she snapped. *Stop asking me that – it's like a question you torment me with – if I wasn't all right I'd say so.* Joss had reared back, startled. She knew what he was really asking her: *Am I all right?* He wanted her reassurance, the vital thing you crave from the person you love. She couldn't give him any.

After the night of the party they hadn't seen one another, though they had spoken on the telephone to arrange the return of various things – clothes, books – she had left at his house. A friend of his brought them to Great James Street; they fitted into a single box. Two years after moving to Rome she'd heard from someone that Joss had got married. *Frame*, faced with mounting debts and a dwindling readership, had closed in 1958. She didn't know where Joss had gone, and she didn't ask.

She made herself some tea and rolled a cigarette. She was starting at the *Journal* on Monday, and knew she ought to use the remaining time to put the flat in order. Balls to that.

Instead, balancing an ashtray on the sofa arm, she took the book out of its Foyles bag and flopped down on her back. She read the blurb again and turned to the title page. *The Hours and Times*, A Novel. Her earlier perusal had missed the dedication on the next page.

For F.W.

She sat up, prodded by an intimate shock. Of all the unlikely things . . . Or did Nancy have in mind someone else with the same initials? Perhaps; but no. Freya felt sure she was F.W. That Nancy should have done so, without a word of warning, rather spooked her. It might have been a peace offering, except that she, the dedicatee, had known nothing of it. No one had taken the trouble to send her a copy.

She began the first paragraph, but the words danced out of reach in her head. She kept turning back to that extraordinary page and the initials. She got up from the sofa, intending to break this little circuit of obsessiveness. On the kitchen table was a recent note from Nat Fane; he still wrote in the hand of a flamboyant actress, though no longer in mauve ink.

Dearest F,

Welcome back to Blighty! The car is at 15a Wimpole Mews – you have Thos's number already, I think.

Once you have your own telephone installed please call and arrange a time to drop by. The 'bachelor rooms' here will amuse you.

SO MUCH to catch up with – a lifetime may not be enough.

Love, Nat xxx

Back on the sofa she picked up the telephone, mentally girding herself. She had Nat's number in front of her, could

almost hear his voice purring down the line, *My dear . . .*
She yawned, and replaced the receiver. She felt too tired.

She took up *The Hours and Times* once more, still running
phantom candidates for the honour through her head. It
would be a grave disappointment should F.W. turn out to
be someone else. But she was trying to trick herself. She
knew it could be no one else.

24

The offices of the *Journal* were on the ninth floor of a brutal glass-fronted block. From her desk Freya could see the sluggish grey-green ribbon of the Thames and a higgledy-piggledy assortment of warehouses on the opposite bank. They looked vulnerable to development, as most things made of brick were nowadays. She had just come from her first staff meeting, where the editor, Ivan Brock, had introduced her around the table. A handful of them she knew already, jobbing hacks who had ridden the Fleet Street merry-go-round for years; they exchanged nods ranging from friendly to the merely courteous. The only one whose eye she refused to meet was her old boss Simon Standish, who had upped sticks from the *Envoy* a few years back.

The tea lady had just delivered 'the cup that cheers' when Freya heard a familiar voice hail her across the room. It was her old friend Arthur Fosh.

'Bloody hell! Freya – is it really you?'

Fosh was bulging a little under his corduroy suit, and his beard was flecked with silver, but otherwise he seemed in fine fettle. A certain incredulity tweaked the edge of his grin.

'It's been a while,' she grinned.

'Has it ever. My God, you just . . . vanished!'

'Only to Italy. Eight years in Rome.'

'Ah. Did you get that haircut on the Via del Corso?'

'No. Upper Street – last week. Still snapping away?'

'Busier than ever. The paper's stepping up its pagination, which'll mean more room for photographs.'

They bandied names of friends between them, trading reminiscences of old times. Fosh seemed in no hurry to move on, and grew expansive about 'the game'. As they talked she felt his gaze become more appraising and speculative.

'I suppose you had some hotshot Romeo out there?'

She laughed. 'You know what those Italians are like.'

Fosh lifted his chin, acknowledging both the sentiment and her evasiveness. 'I ran into Joss, you know, just after your birthday do . . . He was pretty sore.'

'I can imagine.'

'He said you'd been seeing Nat Fane behind his back.'

Freya sighed. 'That's not exactly how it was' – as Joss well knew, she thought. Fosh's expression had brightened with curiosity, but she was too aware of the earwigging opportunities around them. 'I'll tell you about it sometime,' she offered in concession, and Fosh returned a knowing look.

'By the way, d'you know much about Chrissie Effingham?'

'Only what I read,' said Fosh with a shrug. 'Party girl. Hangs about the Corsair a lot.'

'What's that?'

'Club in Mayfair. Quite a scene – actors, TV people, politicians. The odd pop star. Crawling with girls, you know.' He gave her a wink as he turned to go. 'You'd fit right in.'

He walked off, his arm raised in silent farewell.

Berwick Street had always been the tattiest thoroughfare, even by Soho's low standards. But she liked its fruit and vegetable market, and finding herself nearby one afternoon she wandered over. The market had survived, only now it cowered in the shadow of a tower block that had wiped out

389

the south-west end of the street. She was pretty certain that Hetty used to rent a flat in the row of old terraces, though she'd not visited her there, and now never could. She walked round the corner to the paved court where Jerry Dicks lived. Was that his door? She knocked on it, with no idea of what she would say if he answered. She lifted her gaze to the clouded sashes, wondering. There was no reply.

She walked back to the car. Only half doubting her father's mumbo-jumbo, she had taken to walking a witch's circle each time she left it, and hadn't had a parking ticket since. She drove out of Soho's bustling grid and, on a whim, crossed Regent Street into Mayfair. She had reversed into a space on Savile Row and was climbing out of the car when she felt a weird sluggishness in her movement. Her slender frame suddenly required more of an effort to manoeuvre. It was inconceivable to her that she was putting on weight; even in Italy, where the temptations to eat were stronger, she had never had difficulty staying thin. Clothes she had worn ten years ago still fitted her. It must have been a trick of the mind – the new job had been tiring her.

Inside the hushed vestibule of Albany the hatted porter took her name and put the phone to his ear. Yes, Mr Fane was in residence. She had often gazed at the princely graciousness of the facade and wondered how it looked within. The porter conducted her along the covered rope-walk into a white-walled court, surrounded on all sides by manicured window boxes on grand Georgian sills. Red and white tulips leaned their heads forward, eavesdropping. A collegiate calm reigned; even their footsteps sounded muffled on the wide flagstones. Nat was waiting for her at the far end of the colonnade, the door to his ground-floor apartment ajar. She nodded her thanks to the porter, who tipped his hat and withdrew.

'Well, it's about time,' said Nat, grinning. 'I seem to recall your promise to visit three weeks ago – or was it four? I would have gone to look you up in Islington, had I known how to *find* the place.'

Having kissed her with the slow solemnity of a cardinal, he waved his arm in extravagant invitation, and she crossed the threshold. The living room was shaded and cool; through folded double doors she could see a second one, its mirror image, with another large fireplace in its marble surround. 'They don't call them flats,' he continued, as though correcting her. 'They're known as sets.' His walls displayed an eclectic array of artwork, landscapes jostling for attention with satirical prints and modish abstracts, while gleaming black-and-white photographs boasted of his wide-ranging theatrical acquaintance; pride of place, inevitably, went to an imposing portrait of himself, cross-legged and steeple-fingered in a director's chair, staring right into the camera's eye. They had reproduced this one a good deal when stories began to appear about *The Hot Number*, Nat's first screenplay.

They sat at opposite ends of a red damask sofa and drank milkless Earl Grey. Nat had retained his youthful air of nonchalance. He still dressed like someone who expected a photographer from *Vogue* to stop by at any moment. Today it was an expensive narrow-trousered suit of fine dogtooth check with a knitted navy tie. Freya had wondered if he'd be awkward with her after their odd coming-together (she couldn't find a better word for it) that summer, but he treated her with the same feline mixture of affection and distance as always. She liked that about him. They were discussing his divorce from Pandora.

'She's an improbable creature, and so am I. It was success that did for us in the end – or at least the timing of it. When she was the cynosure of New York eight years ago I was still failing to write my first play. I resented her, I admit it. Once *The Hot Number* took off, Pandy soon sickened of the acclaim I got. My brilliance had quite alienated her! And being no longer the star *du jour*, well . . .'

'I heard her on some radio drama the other night.'

Nat arched an eyebrow. 'The case rests.'

'Quite a nice place to be a gentleman bachelor,' she mused, looking around the room. 'Didn't Byron live here?'

'Among others. I do rather enjoy it. I have the whole town on my doorstep, and yet work in splendid isolation. Whenever I'm in the throes of composition that dear old porter guards me against pests from Porlock. It probably encourages selfishness, but then, why pretend? – I *am* selfish.'

Freya said, 'I see now my good fortune in being admitted.'

'Don't be absurd! You are one of very few I should welcome at any hour. How's the car running?'

'Like a dream. I offered a chap in management a lift somewhere the other week. His eyes almost popped out when he saw it was a Morgan. He was probably wondering how I could afford it – and I decided to keep him guessing.'

'That's the spirit.' Nat cocked his head, and continued, in a changed tone. 'By the way, I was talking about you to an old friend the other day. Hetty.' There was a glint of a challenge as he said the name, but she met his gaze without fluster.

'Funny you should say. I was just on Berwick Street, and noticed her old flat had gone. How is she?'

'Living down in Brighton, with a couple of dogs she rescued from the pound. Still does a bit of modelling. She has a –' he hesitated, with a wicked smirk – 'boyfriend.'

Freya nodded, still holding his eye. 'I also tried Jerry Dicks's place round the corner. Is he still there?'

Nat shook his head. 'Old Jerry's fallen on evil days. He's in and out of the sanatorium with his lungs. And there's nothing to be done about his drinking.'

'That's very sad,' she murmured, rising from the sofa and moving to the window, whose view beyond the military-trimmed privet hedge showed a vaulting parapet: his neighbour, the Royal Academy. 'There are picture jobs I was hoping to get him for at the *Journal*.'

'Afraid not. Jerry's over as a photographer. The only glass he looks through now is a shot glass – darkly.'

Genius always paid for the gift; Freya remembered the Henry James line. She would have to rely on Fosh instead, a good sort and a genial companion; but he would never be half the photographer that Jerry Dicks was. She left the window and wandered the room, pausing at this or that picture. One, of a *corrida*, she had last seen on his wall at college. She felt Nat watching her, and presently she turned to him.

'D'you happen to know a place called the Corsair?'

'I was there with my agent last Friday. Why?'

'Oh . . . I'm minded to write something about this new infatuation with youth – all of a sudden people seem to regard it as the most magical thing that's ever happened. I gather Chrissie Effingham and her friends go there.'

Nat smiled knowingly. 'Miss Effingham and I are acquainted. She's going to feature on a slot I'm doing for *Parade*.'

'What's that?'

'Late-night arts programme. On the BBC . . . ?' He squinted at her in lordly suspicion. 'Do you even *own* a television?'

She made a comical grimace. 'I have a Dansette.'

'My dear, you're positively antediluvian. "Telly" has to be your first port of call if you're to write about youth. And of course there's the extra attraction of it allowing you to gaze upon my lovely features.'

'That does sound irresistible.'

'Hmm. The boys have all gone mad about Chrissie Effingham. Quite the little sex-doll.'

'Really? The girl I saw looked barely out of knee socks.'

Nat's expression was wry. 'She's legal, by all accounts.'

'Diana said she was seeing Roger Tarrant.'

Nat wrinkled his nose. 'Long gone. I felt for the poor girl having to suffer Roger's company. It's one thing for a man to suppose that the world revolves around him –' he made a modest pause – 'but Roger believes the cosmos does too, and history, and the workings of destiny. I mean, he's an *actor*, for pity's sake.'

Freya laughed. 'You were an actor once, Nat.'

'"The greatest of faults is to be conscious of none,"' he shrugged, lighting one of his plump Turkish cigarettes.

'Chrissie, anyway . . .' Freya said, getting back on track.

'Yes, indeed. Why don't you come to the studio and watch the recording? I can introduce you.'

Nat got up and poured out more tea. He padded over to a console table where a tall pile of new books stood. He had just popped out to Hatchard's this morning, he explained, and bought in bulk. After a quick glance over his shoulder at her he plucked one from the stack and wandered back to the sofa.

'Seen this?' He was holding up a copy of Nancy's new novel.

She nodded coolly. She had finished it a week ago and was still puzzling over it to herself. Nat had paused, waiting for a reaction. When none came he lay back against the cushions and began leafing through it provocatively. After some moments he made a little show of noticing something and looked up.

'*For F.W.* I wonder who that could be?' He even scratched his chin.

Freya gave him a level stare. 'Mysterious.'

Dropping the pretence, he gave a little chuckle. 'Come, my dear. I'm only curious. Have you seen her at all?'

Freya shook her head. 'Not once. But I've read all her books – including that one.'

'I thought you would have,' he said. '*The Hours and Times*. Interesting title. Does the story explain it?'

'Not that I recall. Why?'

Nat looked rather pleased she didn't know. 'From the Sonnets. *Being your slave, what should I do but tend / Upon the hours and times of your desire.* Would that have a bearing upon its . . . themes?'

'You'll have to read it yourself.'

'I intend to. Perhaps they'll ask me to adapt it into another award-winning film.'

'Congratulations on that, by the way. I forgot to say.'

'Oh – you mean the small matter of my being the youngest writer in the Academy's history to win Best Screenplay? Don't mention it.'

He seized this moment to take her on a proud tour of his set and a peek at the award, glimmering on the chimneypiece in his study. Freya showed willing, but it was their previous conversation about *The Hours and Times* that occupied her thoughts – notably its protagonist, Stella, whose resistance to the stifling dreariness of life in a Thames Valley commuter town leads her first into indiscretion and thence into calamity. A thirtyish single woman, Stella presented a notably unappealing character for most of the narrative: wilful, abrasive, spoilt, demanding, extravagant, she nearly becomes the unwitting engine in a family's doom. No reader could have liked her and yet, by the same token, none would ever forget her, so thrumming with life was the portrayal. Freya, bewitched and repelled by Stella's awfulness, had pegged her as one of Nancy's greatest creations when, towards the end of the book, she came across a line of dialogue: 'Stella has at least one attraction, you know – that bold way of saying exactly what she's thinking. Sometimes before she has even properly thought.' The words hit Freya with the force of a slap. She knew that line; she had read it years before, almost word for word, in Nancy's diary. Only then it was a comment about *her*, Freya, her best friend. She was stricken. That Stella, this odd, vexing, emotionally incontinent creature, could have sprung from somewhere other than Nancy's imagination hadn't occurred to her. But now the appalling suspicion took root that the woman was actually a version of herself. And the dedication, 'For F.W.', seemed to bear it out.

'Am I boring you?' said Nat with cool bemusement.

He had been lecturing about a portrait of someone or other. Freya looked up.

'Miles away, sorry. You were saying – ?'

'No matter. Perhaps you were still thinking of your erstwhile friend – or her latest book?'

Nat was shrewd, as ever, but she didn't quite fancy taking him into her confidence on this. It would make her look vulnerable – and potentially a bit of a fool if it proved she was mistaken. Instead she said, deflectingly, 'Have you ever had a book dedicated to you?'

His expression turned martyred. 'It grieves me to say I haven't. I've dropped hints, which thus far my writer friends have chosen to ignore. But it's a delicate business. Wilde, when he was in prison, learned that Alfred Douglas had dedicated a volume of poems to him, and was *furious* – said that Douglas ought first to have asked his permission. There's gratitude. Mind you, knowing Bosie's poems, Oscar was well within his rights to complain.'

'For once I feel on Bosie's side. A dedication is a kind of gift, isn't it? You don't seek permission, you just . . . bestow it.'

'Or withhold it, in my case.' There was a plaintive note beneath the drollery.

'Nat, if ever I write a book, it's yours.'

He stared at her. 'Do you swear it?'

She laughed, which he seemed to regard as good as an oath. They continued with their inspection of his various memorabilia and *objets d'art*. The only moment of awkwardness arose when they came to his bedroom; she was aware of remembering what had happened the last time she had been in a bedroom of Nat's, and from his look of amused complicity so was he. But the spectacle of the room itself provided a helpful diversion; its swagged velvet curtains, gilt mirrors, cream carpet and four-poster bed with scrolled headboard reduced her once more to fits of laughter.

'It looks like something out of Versailles . . .'

'My decorator's bill suggested that may have been his previous job.'

The large mirror threw back their reflections. She saw again the faint violet crescents beneath her eyes: the barometer of fatigue. She needed to get some sleep.

They talked on for a little while. As she finally got up to leave she noticed a card on Nat's mantelpiece, and a name she hadn't encountered in years. *A dinner in honour of James Erskine*. She held it up for his attention.

'Ah, yes. It's the old boy's eightieth birthday – or no, his eighty-fifth.'

'Gosh. Remember that night he came to Oxford? I pestered him to help me place a piece about Jessica Vaux for the *Chronicle*.'

Nat raised an eyebrow. 'Ambitious little cuss, weren't you? I recall the evening principally for the taxi ride from the station. Jimmy, whom I'd known for all of ten minutes, put his hand on my knee and asked me if I was homosexual.'

Freya smiled. 'I remember you telling me. Wasn't it – "Dear boy, are you a votary of Greek love?"'

Nat yelped with laughter. 'Bravo, you're quite right! I must preserve that one. Jimmy . . . first lion of the theatre I ever interviewed.'

'Not still writing, is he?'

'Writing? – I think not. Last time I saw him at the Garrick he was hardly *walking*. A mangy old lion now, I'm afraid.'

He accompanied her out via the building's back entrance on Vigo Street, where they performed a little minuet of parting. They would meet again, he said, once the TV people had set up his interview with Chrissie Effingham. As they kissed one another goodbye he was still laughing about 'Greek love'.

Progress at the *Journal* was making her impatient. When she accepted the job of feature writer she had laid down a marker about introducing a women's page. The editor had agreed to raise the idea among the management, but since her arrival there had been no mention of it. She also couldn't help noticing that the best stories were automatically handed to men; women staffers, outnumbered on the paper five to one, were confined to lighter features on society weddings, household questions and the latest beauty products – none of which she cared a rap for.

Having bided her time she arranged a meeting with Ivan Brock, an editor of the old school who had worked his way up from provincial newspapers. He had spent most of his life among men – public school, university, army – though in person he was less chauvinist than some of his contemporaries. On arriving at his office she found him ensconced with his deputy, Frank Mogg, and Simon Standish, whom she had so far managed to ignore. She assumed that these two would clear off so that she and Brock could talk in private, but as she took a seat neither of them showed any sign of budging. It occurred to her that Brock felt safer with them in the room.

'Now I hope this isn't a meeting to negotiate money,' the editor quipped, 'because you're already making a sight more than the others out there.'

Freya happened to know this wasn't true, but she had decided to choose her battles. She shook her head and smiled like a good sport.

'I was wondering if you'd come to a decision about the women's page. You know a couple of our rivals have already got one.'

'Yes, indeed, we have discussed this at management meetings, and the competition has been noted –' He halted, as though he had already made an important concession. He rested his chin on his fist, and looked around the room.

'What sort of things do you propose to discuss on a "women's page"?' asked Frank Mogg, pronouncing the last two words as if they might be an exotic fruit.

Freya realised she'd save time by spelling it out. 'Well, we'd address a range of matters that concern women today. For instance, working mothers – the difficulty of keeping a house and doing a job. Also, unmarried mothers, or women who have to deal with violent men, or mothers trapped at home with small children while their husbands are out at work –'

'Aren't there weekly magazines for that sort of thing?' he asked. 'I mean, we're the *Journal*, not *Woman's Journal*.'

Freya stared at him. 'Those magazines take a very old-fashioned line on a woman's place in the world. They're just coffee-morning supplements with recipes and gossip about the royal family. But there really are women who want more out of life than tips on how to keep a husband happy or the best way to clean an oven.'

Standish cleared his throat. 'Sounds like useful stuff to me. I wish my missus would read pieces about how to keep her husband happy.'

There was some knowing laughter. Freya gave no indication of having heard him; she didn't even look in his direction.

Brock shook his head, saying, 'Problem is, Freya, we've only got so many pages at our disposal. News has to be the priority. Then there's the editorial, the letters page, advertising, sport, TV and radio – there's not much room left for housewives' choice –'

'I heard they were about to increase the number of pages.'

'Don't know where you got that from.'

'Anyway, this isn't just about housewives. I want a page for women who have jobs, women who are out in the world, like men –'

'Career girls,' Mogg supplied.

'Whatever you want to call them. You must understand – there are women who'd like to be judged on something other than how to run a house. And would prefer not to be beholden to men.'

'Have you got something against men?'

'No. Only the bastards who've wronged me.'

Standish, stifling a laugh, said, 'Freya's always been a bit of a spitfire. We've had our little differences, haven't we?'

She glanced at him now. His attempt at chumminess was detestable, but she kept her tone cool. 'If you're referring to the last time we spoke, I'd say it was more than a "little difference".'

He turned to address Mogg and Brock. 'When I was editor at the *Envoy* Freya took me to task for a scoop we ran on that fellow McAndrew at the MoD –'

'– who was subsequently proven innocent of the charge but went to prison anyway for being queer. It was a disgraceful story that destroyed a man's life. I resigned, because I was ashamed to work for such a paper.'

'What she fails to mention is the fact she knew McAndrew personally and tried to withhold information about his activities. Robert Cosway got hold of it anyway and we broke it the next day. Eight years – long time to bear a grudge.'

'Easier than you think where a fucking arsehole's concerned –'

'Whoa, that's enough of that,' said Brock, rising from his chair. 'Keep it for the public bar. Gents, would you mind stepping outside a moment?' He was staring at Freya with

400

pained disapproval. Standish and Mogg slouched out of the room.

Brock composed himself for a moment. 'I'm a fairly broad-minded sort, but I do draw the line at certain things – a woman swearing is one of them. It sounds common. There's no excuse for it.'

She could hardly believe her ears. 'What about men swearing?'

'I don't much care for that, either, but they can be excused their rough language – it's a product of the parade ground and the sports field. Many are of a generation that came through the war –'

'I came through the war, too. I was in the Wrens.'

He blinked in surprise; it was apparent he had underestimated her.

'I have to ask you something, Freya – are you unhappy here?'

'No. Why d'you ask?'

'Well, I sense that you're frustrated by the people, and by the work being offered to you. I'm sorry that we can't yet accommodate a ladies' – a women's page, but that shouldn't be a cause for despair.'

'It's not just that,' said Freya. 'I keep suggesting ideas that either get shelved or get nabbed. For instance, a few weeks ago I asked if I could write about high-rise buildings and their effect on people who've been moved there. Mogg said no, then I see that very piece in the paper – by a man. I told the literary editor about the new Doris Lessing novel; he hadn't heard of it but said he'd make enquiries. A bit later I find out that he'd just commissioned a review – by a man. There's a pattern here. Anything juicy or interesting gets assigned to the blokes. Why? I'm at least as good as they are, and in quite a few instances *better*.'

Brock looked half hypnotised by this show of self-belief, and Freya wondered if he might be thinking he'd made a

401

mistake in hiring her: a woman who fought her corner was possibly a headache he didn't need.

'What are you working on at present?' he asked, after a pause.

'Oh, a piece about the new cult craze for youth. I'm chasing a possible interview with Chrissie Effingham. The model?'

'Yes, I know who she is. That would be a good story. I'll make sure nobody takes it off you.'

Freya realised he was trying to be conciliatory, and forced herself to say 'Thank you'. But she didn't feel grateful, she felt indignant about being undervalued.

She was on her way out of his office when Brock said, casually, 'So you worked with Robert Cosway?'

She nodded. 'Briefly. We knew one another from university.'

'I met him the other night for the first time. Very bright fellow. My wife and I were introduced and found him charming . . .' He continued in this vein for a while, expressing his admiration of Cosway's stance on immigration and his timely attack upon the racialist right. When Freya said nothing he looked at her searchingly. 'Do you, um, have a view on him?'

Freya considered for a moment. 'I do, as a matter of fact. But given what you think of women who swear you'd probably rather I kept it to myself.'

She gave him a cursory nod and left the room without another word.

25

She crossed Canonbury Square in a mid-morning lull, the pavement damp from the night's rain. From somewhere not very distant came the echoing clank and grind of building work. The doctor's surgery on St Paul's Road was an early-Victorian terrace of shabby grey stucco. She was fed up with feeling tired for no reason and had telephoned for an appointment. She had told herself there was no reason; yet her heart was beating thickly, as if her body were trying to communicate some urgent message that her mind continued to block.

In the waiting room the air was solid with some cloying, tarry medication. A couple of old men, blank-faced and flat-capped, sat in stoical silence. They looked scraped dry of hope, and even of expectation. A young mother in the corner dandled a child whose burbling monologue poured out indecipherably. While she waited Freya leafed through a copy of *Punch* and marvelled at its consistently feeble cartoons. She supposed they put the magazine in doctors' waiting rooms to make whatever happened when you were in the next room comparatively amusing. When her name was called by the receptionist she felt embarrassed for a moment that she had got the nod ahead of the two old boys. But if they thought her a queue-jumper they gave no sign of resentment.

The GP was a fiftyish bespectacled man with an aquiline nose, large bony hands and an unsmiling demeanour. He wore a dark three-piece suit and a raffish paisley tie which she imagined had been bought for him by his wife. He was writing on a pad with a fountain pen and didn't look up as he invited her to take a seat. He continued scratching away for a minute or more, until she was almost moved to lean over and peek at whatever was occupying him.

Finally he faced her and introduced himself as Dr Maybury. He took down her details in an uninterested manner and then leaned back in his chair.

'And what seems to be the problem?'

She started to explain her tiredness, glancing at him now and then, though his impassive expression didn't change.

'How are you sleeping?' he asked after a pause.

'Not well. Some mornings I lie in bed wondering if I've actually been asleep at all. By late afternoon I'm yawning.'

'Might it be to do with your change of circumstances?'

'Possibly. From my bedroom I can hear the traffic on Upper Street; it sometimes keeps me awake. But then my apartment in Rome was quite noisy, too . . .'

'Do you eat properly? You look somewhat underweight.'

'I've always been quite skinny – it runs in the family. I just eat when I'm hungry, like most people.'

'That isn't a tenable generalisation,' he said, deadpan. 'Do you drink? Smoke?'

'Both.'

He nodded. 'Have you noticed any discomfort of late? Stomach pains, constipation, feelings of nausea?'

She considered for a moment. 'I've had slight stomach cramps now and then. Nothing very painful.'

He asked her to lie on the raised couch. 'May I . . . ?' He felt her stomach, and then examined her eyes, pulling down the lower lids. 'I wonder if you're anaemic. That can often

404

cause tiredness.' He glanced at his notes. 'You're . . . thirty-seven. Do you have regular periods?'

Sitting up on the couch, she shook her head. 'Fairly irregular. It's always been that way. I suppose my last was . . . two or three months ago.'

'Do you have –' he began, and seemed to reverse from the question he intended to ask. 'Have you considered the possibility that you may be pregnant?'

She gave a half-laugh. 'I did – for a couple of seconds. But I'm absolutely certain that I'm not.'

'I see. So you've not had sexual relations in some time?'

She frowned at him humorously. 'I didn't say that. I had a relationship, off and on, for a few months. It ended last year. But we had sex quite regularly.'

She waited for an answering note of disapproval, but Maybury's voice remained level, unhurried. He wanted to know if she had taken 'precautions', and she nodded. In her head she was making some quick calculations as to timing; she had never kept a diary, so she couldn't be accurate beyond a doubt.

It seemed that he had been calculating, too. 'So . . . as best you can remember, you've menstruated since the last time you had . . .'

'Yes. Which is why it's impossible that I should be pregnant.'

He stared at her briefly, his expression ambiguous, unsettling. She got down off the couch. He held out her coat, meaning to help her into it, but she took it instead and folded it across her arm.

'I'm going to send you for a blood test. You may have a touch of anaemia. I'd also like to check for pregnancy –'

'What?'

'The chances are negligible, but one has to make sure. You understand. My secretary will arrange an appointment for you at the hospital – it's just up the Holloway Road.'

She felt a prickle of irritation. 'Is that really necessary? Couldn't you just give me a prescription for sleeping pills?'

'Miss Wyley, I hope you're not presuming to tell me my job.'

'No, but let me tell you about mine. It involves long demanding hours –'

'I'm sure you're very busy. In the meantime, try to get some proper rest, and eat healthily. I know you journalists all like to booze, but you might think about cutting down. That would be one way of improving your chances of a good night's sleep.'

Freya lifted her chin in seeming compliance, while privately dismissing his advice as a waste of time. She had lived through a war, through rationing: proof enough of her hardiness. She was nearly out of the door when he handed her a small plastic bottle.

'What's this?'

'For a urine sample – they'll need one at the hospital.'

'Like they haven't got enough piss there already,' she almost said, but didn't.

She took her visitor's pass from the man at the gate and parked the car. It was her first sight of Television Centre, its gigantic cellular crescent of brick and glass part spacecraft docking station, part Soviet mental hospital. In the foyer she was directed upwards to the recording studio and wafted along an interminable curving corridor. She spotted a couple of bright young dolly birds heading somewhere and on an instinct followed them. Blatting through swing doors they led her into the stuffy, cavernous semi-hush of the studio, its floor a sea of tangled cords and leads, its ceiling clogged with a gantry of dazzling spotlights. She picked her way past camera operators and technicians towards the wings, where a seated figure, pale and languid, was watching her.

'Darling!' called Nat, his neck encircled by a white ruff of tissue paper while a girl attended to his make-up. She hadn't seen him wearing so much slap since Oxford. He sent the girl off with a nod, and invited Freya to take a high stool opposite his own perch. 'Welcome to the pleasure dome,' he said drily. 'What do you think of this place?'

She made a comic grimace. 'It's rather . . . Orwellish, isn't it?'

Nat sniggered. 'Yes, we'll be serving Victory gin after the show. In the meantime let's have some tea.' He sang out his request to a passing minion, whose obedient 'Straight away, Mr Fane' made Freya smile. She raked her gaze around the place.

'Isn't there an audience?'

'Not for this. Though there's the court of Effingham – wherever Chrissie goes, they go.' Her eyes followed his to a little knot of gabbling youths, the girls in tight miniskirts and thigh boots, their hair teased into tottering beehives, and a couple of older, floppy-fringed men in suits and ties. She was wondering where their queen was when a fawn-like figure emerged from the shadows. Chrissie, freshly primped from make-up, had the self-conscious, pigeon-toed gait of a tutored novice. With the exception of her chest, she was vanishingly slight, her bony frame accentuated by the long-sleeved Mary Quant dress that finished just above her knee. It was a look Freya had been noticing since her return, the waif whose legacy of malnutrition during the ration-book years was skinny limbs and plaintive saucer eyes. She quietly remarked on it to Nat.

'Then it was worth starving for,' he replied. 'That look's making her a fortune.' His face became abruptly animated as the subject of their whispers approached.

'Hullo, Nat,' she said. Nat took her extended hand and planted a reverential kiss on it.

'Chrissie, you ravishing creature! Ready for your close-up? Let me introduce you to one of my dearest friends, Freya Wyley.'

'Hullo, Freya,' she said with reflexive politeness and the shy smile Freya remembered from the restaurant. 'I do love your hair.'

'Thanks,' she said.

'I've thought of having mine short, actually.' She brushed her dark fringe from her eyes. The girl's voice hadn't been trained as rigorously as her walk; her south London roots poked from under the thin crust of RP.

'Not likely, sweetheart,' interposed one of the suited men, stroking her long hair with proprietary entitlement. He was staring now at Nat and Freya. 'Bruce Haddon. I'm Chrissie's manager.'

They shook hands, and Haddon began to reel off his 'ideas' about the way he wanted the interview to proceed. He was cocksure, fussy, emphatic, and not half as clever as he imagined. He was still talking when Nat, who had listened with the half-amused, half-mystified smile of someone watching a monkey juggling golf balls, cut him short.

'*Thank you*, Bruce,' he said, hopping off his stool. 'I shall bear most, if not all, of that in mind. Now let's have Miss Effingham in the chair, and we'll pop a microphone on to catch that silvery voice of hers.'

Nat placed his hand lightly at Freya's back, steering her towards the TV monitor at the side.

'You might prefer to watch my performance – or rather *our* performance – on this,' he said, and with a quick backward glance he lowered his voice. 'Remarkable, isn't it, that such an imbecile gets to run the girl's life? And those others – the moustachioed griffin is her accountant; that tubby lady, with the smaller moustache, is the agent; the woman next to *her* a legal assistant. All battening on young Christine in the hope they'll ride her coat-tails to payday.'

408

Across the floor one of the clipboarders was signalling for him. He turned to Freya with a lazy grin. 'Showtime!'

The recording was a prickly affair. Chrissie, bemused and sometimes baffled by Nat's line of questioning, kept shifting her large brown eyes sideways as if to appeal for help from 'offstage'. The director of the programme would step forward to remind her to keep her eyeline on the interviewer, and a minute later she would forget. Then Bruce Haddon decided to wade in, complaining that the questions were too windy. ('Do we need all the long words – who the hell knows what "cynosure" means?'). When Haddon interrupted a third time, Nat lost his temper and rounded on him: 'D'you know the meaning of "cretin", or is that word too long for you as well?' The director was eventually forced to separate them, though not before Nat had laid down instructions regarding Haddon and the rest of the court: 'If they move, *kill* them.'

Watching from the sidelines Freya thoroughly enjoyed the contretemps, though she felt for Chrissie, tongue-tied and blinking under the lights. There followed more argument about who was to stay while they did audio pickups for the broadcast. Nat insisted that they all cleared off and left Chrissie in his charge; the court finally made their exit, but Haddon refused to budge. He watched morosely as Nat and Chrissie re-recorded a few exchanges, both of them more at ease without the distraction of an audience.

By the time they were finished it was nearly eight o'clock. An arrangement had been made to meet up at the Corsair. Nat said that he would join them later, and with a surreptitious wink suggested that Freya drove Chrissie to Mayfair. Haddon, still impersonating a limpet, escorted them to the BBC car park. Upon seeing the Morgan he was momentarily dumbfounded.

'What a smashin' motor!' said Chrissie, wide-eyed.

'Oh. A two-seater –' said Haddon.

'Sorry about that,' shrugged Freya, realising Nat's craftiness.

'I'll call a taxi for us, Chrissie,' he said.

Freya said, 'I can drive her.' Haddon started to object, but Chrissie decided to put her foot down.

'Bruce, I want to go with Freya. You get a taxi and we'll see you there.'

Haddon looked put out, and Freya, relishing the moment, said, 'Don't worry, I'll look after her.'

He stared at them for a moment. 'Ask for my name at the door,' he said and stalked off.

It was a fine spring evening, the retreating light still pearly. Freya said, 'Shall I put the hood down?' Chrissie smiled and clapped her hands like a child off to a birthday party. The late rays of the sun bounced off the glossy amber walnut of the car's dashboard.

They had just nosed into the traffic flowing out of Shepherd's Bush when Chrissie began rummaging in the soft leather bag she had in the passenger footwell. After a moment she produced a ball of yarn spiked with knitting needles, and the front of a scarlet woollen jersey. She set to work. Freya couldn't have been more surprised if she'd pulled out a French horn and started playing it.

Chrissie saw her looking at it. 'You don't mind – while we talk?'

Freya shook her head and said it was fine.

'It's a birthday present for me nephew,' she explained, the needles ticking along. 'I love knitting. Helps me to relax.'

'D'you find it hard to relax otherwise?'

'Well, I get ever so nervous with interviews an' that. I mean, Nat's lovely, but half the time what he's sayin' just flies over my head.'

'That's not uncommon.'

'Oh, so you find that too?'

410

'I think Nat would be very upset if you claimed to under-stand everything he said.'

The girl absorbed this with a serious expression. Freya by degrees coaxed her into talking about her life. She was the youngest of three sisters, had grown up in a council house in Bromley. Her mum was a dinner lady, dad had a job at a local printworks. School had been a secondary modern – 'It was a bit rough,' she said – and at weekends she had waitressed at a cafe on the high street. That was where the scout from the model agency had spotted her, two years ago.

'So you went straight from school into modelling?'

'Yeah. Dad was a bit worried. He thought I should wait and get some qualifications, but I couldn't see the point. And once the work started comin' in it didn't really matter.' She looked sheepishly from under her fringe. 'It's silly, you know . . . I can earn more in two weeks than he does all year. A grown man!'

'I'm sure he's very pleased for you.'

'Oh yeah, yeah,' she said hurriedly. 'I'm gonna buy a house for them.'

She probably earned more this week than *I* do in a year, thought Freya.

Chrissie bent her head back to her knitting, click-clack, click-clack, chatting while she concentrated. They had just reached Notting Hill Gate when a car burst out of a side road right in front of them, causing her to brake suddenly.

'What the bloody hell –' Freya cried, slamming on the horn in fury. Craning her neck upwards at the windscreen she shouted after the offender, 'Mind where you're going, you *fucking arsehole*!'

The traffic droned on, unconcerned. She glanced sideways at Chrissie, who'd fallen silent, her knitting limp in her hands.

'Sorry about that,' she said with a half-laugh. Freya had hardly ever apologised for her language before, but the girl's open-mouthed astonishment had tripped her up. Chrissie gave a sudden giggle.

'I never heard a lady swear like that before.'

I am setting a terrible example, thought Freya. 'Well, I'm no lady, as you can tell.'

'My mum'd hit the roof if she heard me talk like that.'

Freya shrugged. 'An old habit I got stuck with. I went to a "progressive" school, before the war, where they allowed us to do pretty much as we liked. Swearing was just another thing, and I took to it.'

'Say something else,' said Chrissie, staring at her.

'What?'

'Go on. Please. It's funny! It's like hearin' your teacher swear.'

'Christ, I'm not that fucking old!'

Chrissie spluttered out a laugh, which made her laugh in turn. Piqued by the unwelcome reminder of her age, Freya gunned the accelerator. The engine snarled into life, its feral, clattering howl echoing up through the trees. The car almost leapt along the Bayswater Road, the ground hurtling away beneath them. Next to her Chrissie gave a little shriek of frightened laughter.

The Corsair was on three floors of a Regency house on Charles Street. They had parked round the corner and were approaching when Freya's mouth unfolded into a helpless yawn. Chrissie looked enquiringly at her.

'Haven't been sleeping well,' Freya explained.

'Oh, me too! Terrible insomnia.'

'My doctor told me I might be anaemic.'

Chrissie came to a halt on the street and opened the leather bag into which the knitting had been stowed. 'Why don't you try these?' She handed her a brown glass bottle of pills. 'They'll knock you out good an' proper.'

412

Freya frowned at the label. They were Tuinal. 'Aren't these a bit strong?'

'I've got some Seconal, if you'd rather.' Chrissie's eyes narrowed with maternal anxiety. 'Honestly, you have to look after yourself. I'm good for nothin' if I haven't popped one of these.'

Freya handed the bottle back to her. 'I'll wait until the tests come through. Thanks all the same.'

The low-lit corridor and staircases of the club were faced with smoked mirrors that seemed to throw back Freya's image questioningly. Once the black-tied manager realised that she was with 'Miss Effingham' the welcome became expansive, and he personally ushered them to a shadowed circular booth as if they were royal travellers, exhausted from a long trip. On their table the foiled heads of champagne magnums peeked over the lip of a silver bucket. Chrissie's party from the recording studio were already helping themselves.

Chrissie waggled her hand at them, and leaned over to Freya. 'There's someone I want you to meet,' she said, steering her to the bar where a few more of the court were loitering. One of them, legs scissored on a stool, was a thin black girl in an orange minidress. Chrissie threw her arms about her.

'Freya, this is Ava, my pal!' It was artlessly said, though it implied that the retinue around her didn't merit the designation.

Ava's smile was a slightly reluctant tweak of the mouth. The interest was all in her eyes. Her black curled hair was as short as Freya's own.

'You weren't at the studio,' said Freya.

She shook her head. 'Been workin'. How d'you know Chrissie?'

'We've only just met, over at the BBC.'

The girl stared at her, sipping her drink through a straw. Freya was mesmerised by her face, angular like a carving, and impassive as a sphinx. Chrissie explained that they had met at school; Ava, a couple of years older, had been her sister's friend first. As if to demonstrate their closeness she leaned over Ava's drink and sucked on the straw.

'*Ugh!* I thought it was water!' she said, wrinkling her nose.

'Vodka, isnit?' Ava said softly, adding for Freya's benefit, 'She doesn't drink.'

Just then Bruce Haddon reappeared, darting a quick daggered glance at Freya. He asked Chrissie if she had 'everything' she wanted, to which she replied with a quick impatient nod, possibly in the hope that he might now leave her alone.

'You must have shifted some,' he said.

'Yeah. Freya drove like greased lightnin'.'

This didn't go down well, either. His expression seemed to say he'd already pegged her as a bad influence. Pointedly ignoring Ava and Freya, he said to Chrissie, 'We've got some VIPs in tonight. Come over to the table when they arrive, OK?'

Chrissie seemed to sense his rudeness. When he said 'OK?' again she lifted her chin in acquiescence, and he went off.

'Who are these "VIPs"?' said Freya, raising her eyebrows in mock excitement.

'No one,' replied Chrissie, offhandedly. It was the first time her front of good humour seemed to droop. 'Just people Bruce wants me to be nice to, you know.'

Her mood was soon restored when the club's maître d' invited them to take a side booth for themselves and brought over some food. It was only chicken sandwiches and chips, but Chrissie and Ava pounced on it as though they hadn't eaten all day – which was in fact the case. As she ate Chrissie politely asked Freya about her job, though her range of reference was limited. It turned out she didn't read the

414

papers much; she preferred watching the news on telly. She was also keen on *Coronation Street*, and looked amazed on discovering that Freya didn't own a TV.

'So what d'you do when you're at home?'

'Oh, I read . . . I listen to stuff like this,' Freya said, nodding at the stage where a tuxedoed jazz band had just kicked off, their backdrop a shivery curtain of gold lamé. Chrissie, still munching on a sandwich, bopped unselfconsciously to the syncopated beat. Ava, more reserved, steered a watchful gaze around the room. When it landed back on Freya it had sharpened a little.

'I've been trying to think who you remind me of,' she said. 'It's that actress, isnit? – the one with the short hair. *Roman Holiday*.'

Freya gasped out a laugh. 'I think you're flattering me.' She stared at the girl again. 'Actually, you're the beautiful one. People must have told you.'

Ava considered. 'No, not often. Hardly at all.'

'So you're not a model – ?'

She shook her head. 'They don't really have girls my colour – you've probably noticed . . .'

Freya, whose seat faced the doorway, spotted him first. He had arrived with some other men, dressed in suits and ties, and something inside her tightened at the sight of his face. He was talking in a familiar nodding way with the manager. She lowered her head and muttered an oath, prompting Chrissie to lean forward and ask her what was up.

'I've just seen someone . . .'

'Who?'

'The spectre at the feast.'

The girls both turned in his direction before she could warn them not to. Chrissie looked back at her and said, almost in apology, 'They're Bruce's crowd – the "VIPs". Do you know Robert Cosway?'

415

Freya lifted her eyes again and saw, to her horror, that Robert was not only making a diagonal across the floor to their table but waving hullo at Chrissie and Ava. She supposed she had about five seconds' advantage on him – five seconds before he realised who their other guest was. The smile on Robert's face as he saw her suffered a fleeting death-wobble that perhaps only Freya could detect. His head had jolted back in surprise – disbelief – and yet, like a boxer on the ropes, he kept his guard high.

'Freya?'

'Hullo,' she heard herself say.

He was shaking his head, as if he might sieve this awful waking dream out of it. Chrissie was looking from one to the other.

'You know each other?'

Robert was still holding his smile in place. 'Oh, Freya and I go a long way back. Great friends . . .'

She saw him swallow at that risky presumption. He hadn't lost his looks. The puppyish softness of a face that had once threatened corpulence had instead merely rounded; the beard had gone, but a bluish tinge shadowed his cheeks. Robert had come up in the world. He had abandoned journalism to stand as Labour candidate for a marginal seat in the Midlands, and won it by a comfortable majority. His rise thereafter had been rapid. Welcomed into the Shadow Cabinet, he was being sharpened as a spearhead for the party's general election campaign two years hence. Perhaps it was the politician's confidence, she thought, that helped him to carry off this awkwardness.

With a bumptious air of familiarity Robert eased himself into their booth. 'And how do you know these young ladies?'

Freya stared straight ahead, not trusting herself to speak. Chrissie jumped into the silence.

416

'I've just been doing an interview at the BBC. Freya gave me a lift here.' She seemed to be figuring out a problem in her head. 'So *how far* do you go back?'

'We met at university,' she said, staring at Chrissie. 'Later we worked on the same newspaper. We haven't seen one another in – seven or eight years?'

Ava said uncertainly, 'You must have a lot to talk about . . .'

Calmly, Freya said, 'On the contrary. We have nothing to say to each other at all.'

The air at the table seemed to freeze. Robert's tittering laugh in reply was conciliatory, though on looking up she saw a flare of panic in his eyes. The last thing in the world he wants is a scene, she thought. Lowering his voice he asked the girls if they wouldn't mind leaving him and Freya alone for a moment. Freya's immediate instinct was to get up and leave with them, but something – a tiny pricking of revolted curiosity – kept her in her seat. Ava and Chrissie, edging out of the booth, were silent, like children being sent upstairs while their parents had it out.

When they'd gone Robert leaned forward, elbows on the table. 'Does it have to be like this?' His voice had turned husky, confidential.

'Like what?'

'You being hostile, and hateful. Looking like you wished I was dead.'

'That's pretty much how I feel.'

'Even now, after all these years?'

'It's not that long. What, you think I should be over it? I should forgive you for destroying my friend's life?'

'He went to prison. I didn't murder him, for God's sake.' When Freya didn't say anything more Robert heaved a sigh and continued. 'D'you ever hear from him? McAndrew, I mean.'

417

She shook her head. She had visited Alex when he was in Pentonville. He had been stripped of his freedom, his career, his reputation: there was nothing left to say. He served eight months of his sentence, during which time his mother died. He left London shortly after they released him, and nobody seemed to know where he might have gone: Canada, or Czechoslovakia, it was said. Freya had not heard from him again.

'I don't know how you have the nerve to ask. Or even to mention his name.'

Robert sat back, enduring the silence that followed, occasionally looking up to offer a tight smile at a well-wisher. She wondered why he was even bothering with her. His life had moved on; he was a rising star. She was preparing to get up and leave when he said, 'Nancy still talks about you.'

It was the one thing he could have said to make her stay. At last she lifted her eyes to him. 'How is she?'

He seemed relieved to have found a conversational outlet. 'She's well. Hard at work. I wonder if you've seen her latest, it's called *The Hours and* –'

'I've read it,' was all she said. Another pause intervened.

'She was hopeful you might come to the wedding. It hurt her that you weren't . . .'

As much as it hurt me? she wondered. 'How does she like being a politician's wife?' she said.

The question seemed to startle him. He gave a nervous laugh. 'She's – she's, er, very supportive. Takes an interest, you know. She was surprised when they gave me Shadow Home Secretary. I think most people were!' He had always had a knack for self-deprecation, she reflected. It was one of the few things she could still like about him.

'I read somewhere that you're going to be campaigning at that by-election – in the Midlands.'

Robert nodded. 'Netherwick. We've got a hell of a fight on our hands. The Tory councillor there, Lobbett, he's been

418

stirring up a lot of anti-immigration feeling. You've heard their slogan? "If you want a nigger for a neighbour, vote Labour." They've put it on leaflets! That's what we're up against.'

'But you're fighting the good fight.'

He heard the irony in her voice. 'Makes me look quite human, doesn't it?'

She stared at him. 'Almost.'

'Freya . . .' He shook his head, at a loss. 'I remember the last time we spoke, in the office that day – I'd never *seen* anyone that furious. D'you remember what you called me?'

'Perfectly,' she replied. Her voice didn't waver. There was no wryness or regret in it. Robert had tried to buy her off with charm, his preferred currency, and he could tell it hadn't been accepted.

'I don't suppose you'll have me for a friend again, will you?' The words had a kind of yearning in them.

The shake of her head was slight but unmistakable. She stood up, and smoothed down her skirt. 'Good luck in Netherwick,' she said, by way of farewell. She was moving off when he called her back.

'Is there anything you want me to say to Nancy – any message?'

At that moment she almost pitied him. 'Just tell her . . . I said hullo.'

She could feel his gaze following her as she headed for the door. In the opposite corner she saw Chrissie at Bruce's table, hemmed in by a press of people eagerly grabbing their fill of her. She decided it wasn't worth fighting her way through them just to say goodnight.

She was double-stepping up the corridor of mirrors when she met Nat handing in his coat at the cloakroom. He tipped his head enquiringly.

'Going so soon? I thought we might make an evening of it.'

419

'Sorry, not tonight. I'm beat, for one thing. For another, I've just had a *mauvais quart d'heure* with Robert Cosway.'

'Ah.' Nat widened his eyes, interested. 'Did you swat his face with your gauntlet?'

'I spared him that. I think he wanted us to make up.'

'That's rather optimistic of him.'

'I find his reflexive grin so odd – like it's stuck to his face. The only time it faltered was when he first caught sight of me. He also seems to be friends with Chrissie.'

Nat smirked. 'Always had an eye for a pretty girl – you of all people should know. What did you think of Miss Effingham?'

'She's a sweet girl – adorable, really. That's why I'm not going to write about her. She's just too . . .'

'Young?' he suggested.

'No, no, the opposite! I kept looking for the madness of youth and instead I found this child-woman with her knitting and her not swearing and her mumsy advice about a good night's sleep. Honestly, I felt more like her kid. A badly behaved kid at that.'

He shook his head. 'What's the world coming to when we can't rely on the young for some old-fashioned delinquency?'

Freya patted his sleeve fondly. 'Thanks, anyway. For introducing us. Somebody should look after that girl.'

'Ha, she has a whole praetorian guard looking after her, in case you hadn't noticed. Haddon is all over her like a cheap cologne.'

'I don't mean like that. They're just hangers-on. I mean a proper friend, somebody to keep her from harm. She's an innocent, Nat.'

'Now who's the one sounding maternal! I fancy she's tougher than you think – and she's certainly not short of friends.' Nat had dispensed with his coat and was straightening his tie in preparation for the crush of the Corsair's lounge. He bent forwards to plant a kiss on her cheek. '*Ave atque vale*, dearest. Or "hi and bye", as the young people say.'

She waved to him before taking the stairs and exiting into the lamplit dark of Mayfair. She felt another yawn coming on as she walked to the car.

26

The following Friday she was back at the surgery at the behest of Dr Maybury: they had received the results of her tests from the Royal Northern. Freya had asked if she could have them over the telephone to save herself the bother of coming in, but the secretary said it was policy for the GP to inform her in person. So she fidgeted through another twenty minutes in the waiting room, another straight-faced riffle through *Punch*, before her name was called and once again she found herself in the chair adjacent to the doctor's. He was wearing the same suit with a different tie.

His manner seemed a notch warmer on the social thermostat, she thought.

'Miss Wyley,' he began, 'I have your blood and urine tests from the hospital, as my secretary informed you.' He had tweaked his mouth into a slight apology of a smile, and she felt a tingling of relief that she wasn't seriously ill – this had been her worry when they had asked her to attend in person.

'A touch of anaemia?' she ventured.

'You are indeed somewhat anaemic,' he agreed. 'You are also pregnant.'

The word was so bald and preposterous that she actually laughed. 'What? That's impossible.'

'Not so. You are four months pregnant, in fact . . .' He proceeded to explain how she might have missed the symptoms, it wasn't uncommon for a woman of her age to over-look certain telltale signs –

'Wait, wait. This is a mistake. You must have my results mixed up with someone else's.'

Maybury looked at her in the manner of one who had looked at many such patients protesting their diagnosis, someone who had heard all kinds of blustering talk about mistakes being made and tests fouled up. In the little contest of bluff he had the winning hand, always, and his opponent could only, in that pulpy phrase, read 'em and weep.

She had one ace left to play. 'But I've had a period in the last three months – I swear it.'

'You don't have to swear it, Miss Wyley; I believe you. A woman may conceive and yet still have a light period in the weeks following. She may not know it, but she's still pregnant. In your case it explains why you have been feeling tired, the stomach cramps –'

'Oh, for fucking hell's sake *please* tell me this is a mistake.' She would beg him: she would get down on her knees and beg him, if only he could tell her . . . The doctor talked on, but nothing he said could she take in. It was just a voice. She noticed instead his club tie and wondered which one it was – the RAC, perhaps, or the Nines. In the top pocket of his jacket was clipped a metal biro. But on his desk blotter lay an expensive-looking fountain pen. So how did he decide which one to use? Biro for the prescriptions, and maybe the Parker for the correspondence. Head stuck ostrich-like inside this reverie, she was abruptly recalled to the matter in hand by Maybury's raised voice.

'Sorry, I didn't – ?'

'I said, have you considered what you wish to do?'

Freya looked away. How could she possibly have decided? He'd only just *told* her, for Christ's sake. 'No, I haven't – I mean, apart from knowing that I don't want the thing at all.'

Maybury's gaze was fixed on her. 'There are certainly risks in childbearing for a woman of your age,' he said, adding drily, 'aside from the personal inconvenience to yourself.'

She couldn't keep the pleading note from her voice. 'What – what can I do?'

He paused, and dropped his voice to an undertone. 'Unofficially, I could put you in touch with a consultant, outside of this area. He would be prepared to . . . make an arrangement. I'm sure you know what I'm talking about.'

She nodded her understanding, and Maybury returned a grave nod of his own. He picked up his fountain pen. (So that's what it was for.)

'Give me your telephone number,' he said, and seeing her puzzled look he shook his head. 'What you decide to do does not concern this practice. I will pass on your number, and you'll receive a telephone call in due course. There must be no communication with me on this matter at all. Do you understand?'

He wrote down her number and capped his pen. Perceiving her benumbed air he said, in a gentler voice, 'I'm sorry that this news isn't . . . what you wished to hear. I suggest that in future you take more care protecting yourself.'

She knew she'd been spared a lecture, but she winced all the same, feeling the injustice of it.

Outside, on the surgery steps, she felt dazed. The sun had come out to loll on a high divan of off-white clouds, its faint warmth mocking her plight. A 19 bus heaved past, faces steady and incurious at the windows. She crossed the road, a monosyllable droning around her head: How? How? She thought of Dani – Daniele Clerici – the last man who had shared her bed. They had been together, off and on, since the summer of last year. He was a couple of years younger, a carefree type, boyishly handsome with a wispy dark beard and a pouty lower lip she rather liked. He was their newspaper's advertising manager, and had pursued her for months before she gave in and agreed to a date. They started going out, in a desultory fashion. At weekends they smoked a lot of dope, listened to Chet Baker on her Dansette and ate at restaurants in Trastevere. Both of them liked cinema, though they often argued about what they saw. He chaffed her whenever she became remotely cerebral about a film, claiming that she overcomplicated things. Dani revered Brando, and she would laugh at him trying moody imitations in the mirror: 'A one-way ticket to Palookaville . . .' he would mutter in his accented English. He thought *Vertigo* was boring, and she began to think he might not be all that bright. Most of the time they rubbed along happily, or at least contentedly, but if he went off on his motorbike to visit friends or his family in Lazio, she didn't miss him.

But still, she wouldn't have been so stupid –

She was halfway up Compton Road when it blindsided her, in a rush, slamming like a door in her face. They had broken up without much ado at the beginning of December, when she already knew she was going back to London. Then, in the dead slump between Christmas and the new year she had gone to a party, thinking he was still with his folks in Rieti. Instead, he was there too, and stunned by dope and the wistful holiday mood they collapsed into bed. A last dance, as it were, before they said *arrivederci*. Mother of God, *that was it*, the reckless moment – and now a tiny sliver of him lay curled up inside her. She stopped and grasped hold of a railing, her gorge lifting helplessly towards her throat. She steadied herself, gasping, holding on. To vomit on the street, in broad daylight, was a humiliation not to be borne.

She got back to the flat, her stomach still on the waltzers, and hid herself under a blanket on the sofa. She was moaning and shivering piteously. The worst of it was that she didn't have anyone to call, anyone she could make a fool of herself in front of. She had been slow to re-establish any of the old friendships she had abandoned eight years ago. Nat, probably her closest pal, could never be a confessor to her. He'd listen well enough, but he didn't brim with compassion, and likely as not you'd end up in one of his plays. The one person she would have told in bygone days was no longer available to her. There was always her parents, of course, whose love had been unstinting. And yet she could hardly bear to explain to either of them how badly she had fucked things up. They'd want to know about the father, and what kind of support she could expect – as if she had any intention of telling Dani.

What made it more painful was knowing that Stephen and Cora would be thrilled at the prospect of being grandparents. Rowan, her brother, had not produced on that front. Phlegmatic and insular, he was still a bachelor fellow at Cambridge, where (as far as she knew) he was simultaneously involved with three different women, all older. Each one knew about the other, it seemed, and their mutual complaisance was likely to preserve the arrangement.

She was making a consolatory pot of tea when the doorbell rang. Traipsing down the stairs she began to wonder how long it would take Maybury's consultant to telephone. The thought of a secret sharer in her belly had become more dismaying by the minute. A surprise awaited her on the doorstep. It took a couple of seconds to realise that the gawky schoolgirl with dark hair pulled back from her pale face was in fact Chrissie Effingham.

'Hullo,' she said, peering hopefully over Freya's shoulder into the hall. 'I just called on the off chance. Nat gave me your address.'

'Oh. D'you want to come in?'

If there was any hint of uncertainty in her invitation Chrissie's eager little nod overrode it. She was dressed in an 'off-duty' ensemble of baggy Fair Isle sweater and ski pants, with a contractual minimum of make-up. She followed at a respectful distance up the stairs. In the kitchen Freya poured the girl a cup of tea and pointed her through to the living room.

'I haven't got round to decorating yet,' said Freya, as Chrissie's inquisitive gaze took in the high ceiling and the mismatched furniture shipped back from Rome. She folded herself into the corner of the sofa where she'd been maundering. Chrissie, facing the windows onto the square, said she'd never been in Islington before.

'It's all right. I like the old squares. Evelyn Waugh used to live here.'

'Who's that?' said Chrissie.

Freya smiled. 'Just a writer. So . . . your day off?'

She nodded. 'You too?'

'Not exactly. Usually I'd be at work, but I had a doctor's appointment this morning.'

'Oh yeah, you thought you might have anaemia. What did he say?'

'He said that I'm . . . yes, anaemic.'

She got up from the sofa and picked a record to put on the player. The needle dropped on a loose-limbed, mid-tempo number with a skip in its step; a creamy tenor saxophone floated over the top. It was meant to lift her mood. Chrissie nodded along to the beat, and examined the record's sleeve in wide-eyed curiosity.

'Dexter Gordon. *Doin' Allright*. He looks happy! You listen to jazz a lot?'

'A fair bit. What d'you like?'

'Oh, different stuff. Petula Clark – she's good.' She stared at Freya for a moment. 'Nat says you're quite – what was the word he used? – bohemian.'

'Is that so?' She laughed. 'I've been called worse.'

Chrissie smiled at her. 'Your face is so different when you laugh.'

'Isn't everybody's?'

'Not like yours. When you answered the door just then, you looked so . . . sad. Like you had the cares of the world.'

Freya dropped her gaze, saying nothing. Chrissie continued her inspection of the room. She stopped at the painting on the mantelpiece. 'That's you, isn't it? – with long hair. When's that from?'

'My dad gave it to me for my twenty-first.'

She looked round at Freya. '*Aww*, I bet he's really proud of you, isn't he?'

Her agonising about her parents and the calamitous news was too raw even for this innocent remark. A hot surge sprang so abruptly behind her eyes that she had no time to stopper it. She felt stupid to be crying in front of this girl, a stranger, but it was beyond help.

Chrissie's own eyes had widened in appalled sympathy. 'Oh! Oh, Freya! What's the matter, darling?' She came to sit next to her, but her tentative hand on hers, far from staunching the flow, only quickened it. Even if she'd wanted to, Freya's throat was too choked to speak.

When she at last caught her breath she raised her salt-stung eyes to Chrissie. 'Sorry!' she muttered, in a gluey voice.

'Don't be silly,' she chided gently. 'What is it? Please tell me.'

Having put the girl through that unseemly display she could find no reason to keep dissembling. With her knuckles she blotted her eyes. Looking heavenwards she said, in a voice as steady as she could manage, 'The doctor said that – as well as being anaemic – I'm pregnant.'

Chrissie's congratulatory 'Oh!' wavered in the face of Freya's evident misery. In a coaxing voice she said, 'Is it really that awful?'

428

Freya nodded slowly.

'Because you're not married?'

She met that with a worldly chuckle. 'No, not because of that. It's just – I don't want a child. I have nothing to do with the –'

Chrissie clamped a hand over her sudden intake of breath. 'Oh no! It's him, isn't it? *That's* why he asked us to leave the table the other night so he could talk to you.'

'Who?'

'Robert. Robert Cosway's the father, isn't he?'

She stared at her for a moment, and laughed again. 'No, he's not. I could curse him for a lot else, but not that.' She saw the doubt in Chrissie's face. 'How could it be? That was literally the first time we'd seen one another in eight years.'

'So it's . . . ?'

'Not someone you'd know. He's barely someone I know. It doesn't matter. I wouldn't want a child even if I were madly in love.'

'Oh . . .' said Chrissie, looking away. 'That *is* a shame.'

Freya heard a faint disapproval in the girl's voice. Dexter Gordon's saxophone bleated on pleasantly for a few bars, before she said, 'Oh well, at least I know now why I've been so tired.'

Chrissie was gazing at her. 'Of course. You're gonna have to look after yourself – lots of sleep, eating prop'ly . . . Have you had breakfast?'

She shook her head, and Chrissie, jumping off the sofa, was suddenly bright with purpose.

'Eggs and bacon, do you the world of good! Shall I go and make some?'

'It's nice of you to offer, but the cupboard's bare, I'm afraid. No fridge.'

Chrissie, mock stern, put her hands on her hips. 'What are we gonna do with you? No telly, no fridge . . . Let's go out, then.'

Freya groaned, and drew up her legs on the sofa. She wasn't hungry, nor ready to interrupt her sorrowful mood of self-pity. But Chrissie wouldn't be put off, and took to pleading. She had to eat! By degrees her resistance waned and, with a sigh, she surrendered. She couldn't help feeling a little flattered that the girl should be so insistent on looking after her.

They emerged onto Canonbury Square, where Chrissie made a beeline for the black Daimler parked opposite. Her driver had been waiting there the whole time. A man in a dark suit got out on seeing her and held open the rear door.

'This is Ken, my driver,' she said over her shoulder. He nodded at Freya. 'Where should we go?'

The car purred down Canonbury Road. In the back seat Chrissie's hands were busy with her knitting needles while they talked.

Freya chose a place at the Islington Green end of Essex Road, an Italian-run cafe with Formica tables, white-tiled walls and windows half steamed with condensation from the coffee machine that squealed in the background. They could see Ken in profile through the car window, stolidly absorbed in the *Mirror*. The clientele were builders, market people, locals; their entry caused one or two to glance up, but no one appeared to recognise the famous face. The waitress brought them tea the colour of brick. Freya rolled herself a cigarette and watched while Chrissie chowed down bacon and eggs, black pudding, fried bread. She had a trencherman's appetite for one so slender.

'So how do you know Robert Cosway?' said Freya.

'Oh, we met him through Bruce, at the Corsair. Always lovely to us, you know. Actually Ava thinks Robert's a bit of a hero – not many politicians would stick their neck out for coloured people like he does.'

Freya blew out a thin jet of smoke. Her silence was sufficiently pointed for Chrissie to return a searching look.

430

'What happened with you two? He said you used to be great friends.'

'We were. Once upon a time we were in love. I was about your age.' Opposite her Chrissie was saucer-eyed, waiting. 'He betrayed a friend of mine which I . . . couldn't forgive.'

'What?'

She shook her head sadly. 'Let's not go into it. He may have changed, for all I know. The worst of it was that he married Nancy – my best friend. I haven't seen her in eight years.'

Chrissie looked aghast. 'Eight years? I don't know how you do that – I couldn't stay mad that long. I just couldn't.'

'Well, you're a nicer person than I am. I keep my wounds open. I can't help it.'

'But how could you do without your best friend?'

'I don't know. I used to think I didn't need . . . people. I never really troubled about friends, at school, or in the Wrens. It's not that I didn't have any, it's just – they didn't seem that important to me. I suppose that makes me sound rather cold, doesn't it?'

'You don't seem cold to me,' said Chrissie, considering. 'Tell me about her – your friend.'

'Nancy? Oh . . . We met one another on VE Day, just by chance. She was quite shy, gawky. Very beautiful. We went back to my dad's flat that night and danced and played the piano till all hours – drank a lot of gin. I think we even smoked cigars, in honour of Churchill. Horrible! From then on we were fast friends. When she left Oxford we lived together in Bloomsbury, like a couple of students – or like an old married couple. We had some wonderful times.' Hearing herself become expansive, Freya stopped. 'Sorry. I don't know why I'm burdening you with my personal history.'

Chrissie replied simply, 'Cos I asked you.'

'What about *your* pals? Ava seemed nice.'

431

'Yeah. She still lives in Bromley, like most of my friends.'

'But you don't?'

'Oh no, I moved to town about a year ago. My agent found me a flat on Curzon Street – it's quite small. Just room for me and Alfie.'

'Alfie?'

'My dog. He's a Jack Russell. I'd be lost without him.'

'You don't have a boyfriend, then?'

She shook her head. 'Not since Roger. And he wasn't really . . .'

'What d'you mean?'

Chrissie winced. 'I shouldn't say . . . Bruce'd go up the wall if he knew I was talking to a *journalist*.'

Freya made a *pfff* sound. 'Trust me, this is all "off the record".'

'Yeah. Just two girls natterin' together,' said Chrissie, relieved. 'Anyway, Roger and me weren't stepping out. The agency just made it look that way, for the papers. He's queer, you see.'

'Ah,' said Freya, imagining the frenzy in newspaper offices on being thrown that titbit.

'You can't believe half of what they say – stuff about "sex parties" and me havin' it away with all sorts of different men. I don't think I've been to a sex party in me life!'

Freya smiled at her. 'Me neither – though I long to be asked.'

It took Chrissie a moment to realise she was joking; she giggled nervously. Just then a harassed-looking woman pushed a baby in a pram past the window where they were sitting. Freya looked away, and continued rolling another cigarette.

Chrissie watched her light it and said quietly, 'They say that smoking's not very good for expectant mothers . . .'

Freya let the remark hang for a moment. 'That's to assume that I'm going to be a mother.'

432

'Aren't you? Really?'

Freya squinted through the smoke, and gave her head an almost imperceptible shake. She could see how disappointed the girl was. 'I'm sorry if that bothers you.'

Chrissie shrugged. 'I think you'd be a good mum.'

'Oh, *please* don't say that. And don't look at me like that, either.'

'But why are you so set against it?'

Freya kneaded her brow with her hand. 'You're too young to understand. I've worked my whole life to get where I am now. I had to fight for it, too, because if you're a woman you're never given the same chances. The rows I've had . . .'

Chrissie looked at her slyly. 'Did you swear a lot?'

'Of course. The point is, I never took a backward step. I knew I was good, it was just a matter of seeing the opportunity and taking it. A man wouldn't have to think twice, he'd take it and ask for more, but a woman – well, ambition doesn't look so attractive on her.'

'Yes, but what's this got to do with – ?'

'Being pregnant? Because if you take the time off to have a child you opt out from the game, and you may never get back in. All that striving, up in smoke. You're nice to think I'd be a good mother, but I'm not sure I would. Quite apart from wondering what the hell I'd say to it, I'd probably resent the child for holding me back. That's not very maternal, is it?'

Chrissie stared off into the distance. She thinks I'm irresponsible, thought Freya – and hard-hearted. They began to talk about other things, what Chrissie was going to do next: a new billboard campaign, a possible film role, a job in New York. There was a lot going on for her. As she listened it occurred to Freya that she was actually old enough to be *her* mother. And would that have been so awful? She was a nice girl, cheery, well mannered, respectful, certainly more agreeable than *she* had been at twenty. Maybe they'd have

433

had fun together, been the sort of mother and daughter who borrowed each other's clothes. You didn't have to be a stick in the mud just because you were past thirty.

But these were idle imaginings. Easy to be a mother once the daughter was grown up. Rather less so when she was an infant, with the mewling and puking, and you trying to get some sleep and hold down a job. Not to mention instilling the child with a moral code! She would have to stop swearing, for a start – which was highly fucking likely. Well, if she couldn't set a good example she might at least guard against setting a bad one. Was motherhood so outlandish a possibility?

She thought back to this morning's appointment with the GP and felt the abrupt return of her panic. No, she couldn't do it. No part of her *wanted* to do it.

The waitress had just put down the bill on their table, and Chrissie was staring at it in embarrassed silence.

'What's the matter?' said Freya.

'The breakfast . . . Three and six. An' I haven't got a penny on me.'

Freya laughed. 'And there I was thinking you were the highest paid model in London.'

'It's just – these things don't have pockets, and Bruce takes care of the money.'

'Oh dear,' said Freya, pulling a grimace. 'What shall we do?'

The girl bit her lip. 'I could go and ask Ken if he's got some. Else we could –'

'Offer to do the dishes?' she suggested, producing her purse at the same time. 'Don't worry, it's on me.' Chrissie put her hand to her chest in relief.

'Oh! Thank goodness. How awful of me – asking you out to breakfast and not a bean on me. I am sorry . . .'

'You can pay for the next one.'

Chrissie, nodding earnestly, said that she would, for sure. She'd like that.

A few days later there was another ring at the door. Outside was parked a large van blazoned with Harrods livery. A man in a cap stood on the step.

'Wyley?' he said, reading off a dispatch notice. 'Miss Eff Wyley?'

He had a delivery for her.

'I haven't ordered anything.'

The man shrugged, and recited her name and address. 'Been sent on someone's account, it looks like.' He called to his mate in the van, who got out and unlocked the rear. Moments later he was wheeling onto the pavement an enormous cardboard box on a metal trolley. It would be a two-man job to lift.

The flat cap said, 'Don't tell me, you're on the top floor.'

She nodded, and he slumped his shoulders with a groan. It took them twenty minutes of huffing to manoeuvre it up the narrow Regency staircase and into her flat. As she signed for delivery she noticed the account name on the document: C. Effingham. When they'd gone she started cutting open the box, still in the dark as to what it contained. From its squarish shape she guessed it would be a Harrods hamper, stuffed with all the food Chrissie believed she ought to be eating. She dug out layers of protective grey padding until she reached something hard-edged and wooden, wrapped in a plastic shroud. It was a few moments before she realised, with a curious sense of being both excited and offended, what it was.

Chrissie hadn't sent food. There, sleek in its walnut finish and reflecting her face in the convex black screen, crouched a brand-new television set.

27

She knew the handwriting on the envelope the moment she saw it, as distinctive as a voice. Because it had been sent care of the newspaper, she had marked it PERSONAL in the corner. Nancy's mature, unflappable cursive hadn't changed down the years, though the NW postmark was new. Freya felt a pouncing jolt of curiosity as she tapped the letter on her desk, delaying the moment.

She was obliged to delay it a little longer when the editor appeared and called her into his office. Brock was minded to run something about Jimmy Erskine on his eighty-fifth birthday, and having heard that it was the old boy who'd given Freya her first break when she was at Oxford, well, she was the 'obvious candidate' for the job. It seemed that Jimmy had written a book, too (Nat had got that wrong), a follow-up to the first volume of his memoirs.

'I've got a copy of it somewhere,' said Brock, rummaging through his stacked in-tray. He found the book and passed it across his desk to Freya.

'*Ecce Homo*,' she read. 'Bit of a risky title, I would have thought.'

'What? Oh, I see – "homo". Ha ha.'

Jimmy had agreed to be interviewed at his flat, Brock continued, though in a letter to his publishers he had appar-

436

ently stipulated that his interviewer must not be 'a twelve-year-old', 'an unpublished writer', or 'a woman'.

Freya chuckled. 'I could take offence at that.'

'We'll give him notice that you're coming. You can turn on the charm.' She was on her way out the door when he said, 'How's the Rise of Youth piece, by the way? Get anything out of Chrissie Effingham?'

'I'm working on it,' she said. 'But I'd better press on with this if it's his birthday coming up.'

Brock nodded. 'Yeah. Age before beauty.'

Back at her desk she picked up a knife and slit open the letter. The text was closely written, in fountain-pen ink, with no crossings-out.

12 Regent's Park Terrace, NW
May '62

Dear Freya,

It seems such an age since I wrote that name, though it has been often on my mind in the years since I saw you last. I had no idea you were back from Italy until Robert came home the other night with the astonishing news that he'd run into you by chance at a members' club. He said that you'd had a 'good long chat' together, though I wasn't at all convinced of this, either from his tone or from what I know – knew – of your feelings towards him. He became very cagey when I pressed him for details, which inclined me to think the 'chat' was neither good nor long, and that you have not forgiven him for what he did.

Perhaps you have not forgiven me, either? I have had a long time to ponder what happened with Alex and your absolute implacable bitterness towards Robert and the rest of them at the *Envoy*. It was dreadful – truly, one of the worst experiences of my life – to be caught between the two people I most cared for in the world and be help-less to reconcile them. I remember the look on your face when I told you that Robert and I were going to share rooms: it felt like I'd just stabbed you through the heart. In the years since, believe me, I've thought of that moment many times, and wonder what I might have done differ-ently. The atmosphere between us in the weeks before we vacated Great James St was nearly the most horrible part of all.

Robert did tell me something, however, which I would like to believe was true: that you asked after me. (Pardon me if this was not the case – Robert's enthusiasm for what he perceives to be true is sometimes at variance with what is actually so.) He also said that you had read my books. If so – and again, I take nothing for granted – you will have noted the dedication included in *The Hours and Times*. Without quite acknowledging it to myself I hoped that some day, somewhere, you would come across it and know that, whatever else had happened, you were still in my thoughts. You have never left them.

I realise that I should have written this letter years ago. But you were so proud and angry and unyielding in the wake of what happened that my courage failed. And once you had left the country I felt that I had been absolved of the responsibility for making peace between us. That was a mistake: the repair work on our friendship ought to have been my priority. Being busy, being in love, were my excuses – inadequate ones, I admit, and I am sorry for them.

Even now I'm nervous of seeking a rapprochement. After I sent you an invitation to our wedding I was torn between hoping and dreading that you would come. When you didn't reply I was hurt, but in some small part I was relieved, too. That's how formidable an influence you have been, Freya. But I shall stop being a 'ninny' and

438

come out with it. We are having a little gathering here at the house on Thursday week, just a few close friends and some colleagues of Robert's from the party. (We entertain quite a lot since his promotion.) I would be so pleased if you could come. Let me assure you I don't expect any great scene of reconciliation between us. But I would dearly love to see you again.

Yours,

Nancy

PS You have our address. It's 7.30 for 8 p.m.

She sat at her desk, motionless. She felt rather stunned by the tone of the letter, the way it delicately balanced the qualities of contrition and kindness. It brought back Nancy's voice to her keenly. How could she turn down an olive branch proffered with such humility, with such rueful wisdom? Nancy could tell that the 'good long chat' she and Robert were supposed to have had at the Corsair was nothing of the sort. She had Robert's measure as a spinner of yarns, but she covered for it without offending Freya or belittling him. She reread it; again she felt the open-hearted character of her old friend, and her gentle reaching out to the possibility of reunion.

On a third reading she felt her critical instincts tauten, like a string on a bow. The letter was not an entirely blameless effort: two phrases in it caused her lip to curl. Nancy's reference to 'being in love', albeit cited as an excuse for her distraction, was a shaming reminder of her foolishness over Robert. In the face of Freya's warnings she had fallen for him, then compounded the error by marrying him. How deluded did she want to show herself?

The other phrase that displeased her was more difficult to cavil at, though she would have a go nonetheless. *We entertain quite a lot since his promotion*, she had written towards the end. Nancy had never been one to swank, which made the note of smug satisfaction all the more surprising. *We entertain*, do we? And there was surely no need *at all* to refer to his promotion, as if she didn't know that Robert was Labour's coming man. That she had put the line in parentheses was practically an admission of its irrelevance.

It occurred to her that she might be nitpicking. Perhaps her objections said more about her than they did about Nancy. She didn't want to hear Robert being puffed up, he was conceited enough as it was, but perhaps Nancy couldn't really be accused of anything other than stating a fact: they were a sociable couple. In any event, Freya could not deny her pleasure in receiving the letter, which in its quiet way conceded that the fault had been wholly on their side. It was tantamount to an apology. Would it not be the right thing to match Nancy's graciousness with her own and accept it?

She had picked up Fosh at his flat en route and was now scanning Bedford Avenue for a parking meter. Lolling in the passenger seat, Fosh had looked about the Morgan and drily pronounced it to be 'very *groovy*'. She shrugged, not wanting to admit that she'd miss the thing once Nat asked for it back.

After the cold spring there was at last a mellowing in the air. Sun glinted through the latticed branches of the solemn beech trees. Across the sky an aeroplane's languid vapour trail was disappearing. There happened to be a space directly opposite the red-brick mansion block where Jimmy Erskine lived, and she swung the car into it. Fosh got out his heavy old Rolleiflex from the boot and they headed up the steps.

Inside, as they waited for the lift he mused brightly, 'James Erskine. D'you know, I honestly thought he was dead.'

'Might be best to keep that to yourself. There's a whole chapter in the memoir about his fear of dying.'

440

'Oh, so he's got a book out, too?'

'Published by a small press and reviewed hardly anywhere. *Ecce Homo*, it's called.'

They were admitted to the flat by a cheery fellow in a striped apron named George, who seemed to be the old boy's manservant. He led them through a hallway hung with a lot of dusty paintings and photographic portraits of theatrical bygones; thence into a stuffy living room. The two-bar fire was on, despite the mildness of the day, and the windows overlooking the street were shut firm. A sour smell of Brasso and mothballs permeated the place. The furniture was all pre-war; certain things, like the gramophone, possibly pre-Great War. There was no television, but by the armchair hunkered a huge old wireless, the sort that once would have crackled with the voices of the Crazy Gang. George, bending his ear to a closed door, gave it a respectful knock.

'Jim? Your visitors are here.'

From the other side of the door came an indecipherable muttering. George offered them a smile that seemed to plead for patience. He joined them in the middle of the room and, dropping his voice, said, 'He's just had a new set of teeth put in. They're giving him some grief.'

He asked them if they'd like tea, and disappeared off to the kitchen. Fosh, staring in bemusement around the room, silently picked up an ancient pair of lorgnettes from a side table and gawped at Freya through them. He replaced them quickly on hearing the far door open: Jimmy Erskine's bald head poked out like a venerable tortoise from its shell, followed slowly by the rest of him. He had shrunk to gnome-like proportions in the years since Freya had last clapped eyes on him, though the sartorial style was largely unaltered: a checked three-piece suit, dicky bow, and cream-coloured spats over his shoes. A monocle glazed his left eye.

He shuffled towards them on his cane, wheezing piteously, and stopped. Everything about him looked tired –

441

everything but his eyes, which blazed fiercely in the ruined mosaic of his face.

'What's this – it requires two of you to conduct an interview? One holds the page, the other reads the questions off it, I presume.'

Freya gave a polite laugh. 'No, he's the photographer. I'm doing the interview.'

Jimmy shook his head, and muttered, 'The monstrous regiment advances.'

She ignored that. 'Actually we've met before, quite a few years ago. Freya Wyley.'

Jimmy frowned and shook his head. 'I think not.'

'Spring of 1946,' she continued. 'We were introduced at the Oxford Union.'

The old man paused, staring ahead. 'Then possibly at the Oxford Union I may know you again.'

George returned at this moment carrying a tea tray and invited them to sit down, since Jimmy hadn't. Fosh asked Jimmy how he would like to be photographed.

'Oh, *clothed*, I think,' said Jimmy, running his eye up and down Fosh.

'No, I mean, would you prefer to be standing or . . . ?'

Jimmy waved away the suggestion and lowered himself into an armchair. 'I'm not standing for anything. Snap away as you wish.'

George, having poured them all tea, was backing out of the room when Jimmy looked around and asked him where the biscuits had got to. They didn't have any in, the manservant replied.

'Then would you kindly go and purchase some. Those sponge ones with the orange and chocolate on top.'

'Jaffa Cakes.'

'No, no, I don't want cakes. These are biscuits.'

'Yes, I know the ones. They're called Jaffa Cakes,' George explained.

442

Jimmy looked unimpressed. 'Well, whatever the blazes they're called, I should like a plate of 'em.'

George hurried off, and Jimmy leaned back to gaze in a bored way at his guests. Fosh, checking the focus on his camera, said, 'Congratulations on the book. A triumph!'

Jimmy nodded. 'It has its moments. But it's a mere distillation of the diaries that I've been keeping since 1931. They're now close to half a million words. I'd have liked to put the lot out. My publisher thought otherwise.'

'Oh, shame,' said Fosh, raising the camera to his eye. 'Personally I don't think you can have too much of a good thing.'

He's laying it on a bit thick, Freya thought; the old boy's going to slap him down. But Jimmy, far from suspecting flattery, accepted Fosh's compliment as his due. 'I'm not alone in thinking the diaries the best of my *omnia opera*. A hundred years hence I'd like them to be considered alongside Pepys and Evelyn. In some respects I'm a better diarist than either. They had the Plague and the Fire to help 'em, after all.'

'You had the war,' Freya pointed out.

Jimmy shook his head. 'But I hardly used it. World events, politics, these are less important to the true diarist than who said what at lunch, and whether X really did cut Y in the street that day. Anyone can write history. But it takes an artist to render gossip and opinion interesting.'

He took a sip of his tea, and continued. He was one of those talkers who saw no reason to share out the conversation, since he regarded his own portion as more entertaining and instructive than anyone else's. But his was not a generous form of sociability; he didn't inspire others to say brilliant things. If he could not dominate a room, he would sooner be out of it.

Fosh, having shot a reel of film, announced that he'd got enough. As he was readying himself to leave he said to

443

Jimmy, 'Best of luck with *Echoes of Homer*. I look forward to reading it!'

He winked at Freya on his way out. The door closed, and Jimmy pursed his lips in the manner of someone who'd just been done by a three-card trick.

'A *very* pert fellow, I must say. When he was buttering me up a few minutes ago I assumed he'd at least read the book. In the event he couldn't even remember the title.'

'I suppose *Echoes of Homer* is a sort of accidental compliment . . .' she said consolingly.

Jimmy made a little 'huh' sound. 'Given how nervous my publishers are about *Ecce Homo*, perhaps I should use it. So . . . how old is he, your colleague?'

'Fosh? Oh, mid-thirties, I should say.'

'Hmm. I wonder what his cock's like.'

Freya stifled a snort of mirth. Jimmy, noticing the shorthand pad she was scribbling on, added, 'You can strike that last from the record, dear. Don't want to startle the innocent eyes of your readers, do we?'

'I'm not sure they'd believe their eyes if they saw it,' she said. 'As a matter of fact I've another friend you, um, admired, when we were at Oxford – Nat Fane.'

'Ah! Saw him at a dinner they gave me just the other night. Still playing the cleverest boy in the class.'

Freya looked up from her notepad. 'And yet you're full of praise for him in your book. Didn't you nominate him the best young playwright under forty?'

Jimmy lifted his chin imperiously. 'Fane's got talent, no question. One could only wish he weren't so prodigal of it. His first couple of plays were remarkable, and he seemed likely to push on to greatness. Alas –' he made an explosive motion with his hand – 'the playwright has been taken hostage by the controversialist. He appears to have got hold of the idea that he must have *something to say*, as though his audience were waiting for the Great Fane to come down

444

from the mountain and tell us about Suez or race relations or, God help us, the Bomb. Whereas what we really want is a well-made play with characters and situations that intrigue and provoke us.'

'I don't imagine he'll be bothered with the theatre now that he's writing screenplays for Hollywood.'

'Ugh,' he exclaimed, wrinkling his nose in distaste. 'I don't care how many awards it won, *The Hot Number* was a wretched thing. It combined all his very worst faults – glibness, modishness, self-advertisement. A good editor would have taken him in hand. But I fear there's no one brave enough to try.'

At this moment George returned from his errand, Jaffa Cakes in tow. He handed the packet to Jimmy, who emptied half of the biscuits onto a plate and began contentedly feeding them into his mouth; it didn't occur to him to offer Freya one. In the meantime she had spotted a painting on the wall and got up to take a closer inspection. It was a small oil of a man's face in a convex mirror, froggy in aspect yet enchanting for his amused eyes and childlike smile.

'I've seen this before,' said Freya.

Jimmy paused, and raising himself unsteadily on his cane shuffled over to join her. He stared at the portrait. 'That is my dearest friend in the world, László Balázsovits. "Was", I should say. He died four years ago this month. This he bequeathed to me in his will. He had little else . . .'

Moments passed. He was lost in contemplation, his breathing stertorous. Glancing sideways she saw that tears bulged in his eyes.

'It's a lovely picture,' said Freya gently, and waited for him to recover his composure. 'Did you know that my father painted it?'

Jimmy wiped his eyes and replaced his monocle, the better to glare at her. 'What? Your father, you say – Stephen Wyley?'

She affirmed it with a nod.

'I see . . . László was a great admirer of his. I remember how outraged he was over that business with Gerald Carmody, back in the thirties. I'm sure you heard about it.'

Freya had heard: in the autumn of 1936, Stephen had contributed to what he believed was a theatre charity, only for the papers to expose it as a fraudulent cover for a Fascist splinter group. When the identities of the backers came to light, he found his own name among them and was dragged into the ensuing scandal. For a few months he became a pariah. László wrote a letter to *The Times* in his defence. The ironic coda to the story was Stephen's belated discovery of his Jewish ancestry.

'Yes, and then my dad discovered he was half Jewish himself. He was shocked at first and then quite pleased.'

Jimmy said, 'I believe László talked to him about it. His own family had been forced to flee some pogrom or other back in the nineteenth century. Lost nearly all their money. But I never knew a man who bore his misfortune so lightly.' He continued to stare at the painting. 'One has always felt a certain pride in this place as a haven for the émigré. And yet the garden of England is still rank with the weeds of intolerance. I never thought Mosley's idiots would amount to anything, and they didn't, but that strain of xenophobia endures. "Keep Britain White", indeed. Is *that* what we beat the Nazis for?'

'The voters of Netherwick may enlighten us on that score.'

'Hmm? Oh, the by-election . . . I was listening the other night to that young Labour MP, what's-his-name –'

'Robert Cosway.'

'Yes, him. About time someone talked sense on immigration. Met him once – had plenty of charm . . .'

'I know,' said Freya, who ever since Robert had become the immigrants' friend had felt the purity of her animus somewhat adulterated. You couldn't straightforwardly despise a champion of the oppressed. She waited for Jimmy

446

to continue his song of praise, but the old man's expression had altered. She wondered for a moment if he was going to speculate about his 'cock'.

'Don't quite trust him, though, do you?'

Here was a different music to her ears. 'No. I don't.'

'He reminds me rather of an actor. A good one, I should say, got all his lines and gestures down. Yet still one detects in him something . . . counterfeit. I imagine he'll go far.'

Good old Jimmy, she thought. He hadn't been a critic for nothing. They were on their second pot of tea when George returned with a tray loaded with squat brown bottles. 'Time for the master's medicine,' he announced, and proceeded to measure out a selection of pills from each bottle. There were a lot of them.

'I take so many damned pills I've started to rattle,' Jimmy complained.

George, with a little glance over his shoulder at Freya, said, 'Pills for his asthma, for his blood pressure, for his arthritis. Not forgetting his eyedrops . . .'

'For glaucoma,' the patient explained. 'That would be fate's cruellest trick, turning me blind. An echo of poor old Homer, indeed.'

His tone was at once self-pitying and stoical. Freya saw that some rallying was required: 'Well, even blindness doesn't stop you being a writer. Milton dictated *Paradise Lost* to his daughters. Maybe George can be your amanuensis.'

'George? No, no. Anything more than a shopping list is beyond him. I'd be spelling out every word.' George, with a tolerant chuckle, continued counting the pills. 'It isn't just the eyes. The energy is gone. Time was when I would write from nine in the morning to six or seven in the evening, clattering away at the typewriter. The words *poured* out of me. They don't any more.'

'Well, instead of writing you'll have more time for living,' said George coaxingly.

Jimmy gave a gloomy shake to his head. 'I subscribe to the theory that no writer lives absolutely, just for the joy of living. When he stops writing, life becomes practically meaningless. Would Keats have rejoiced in the song of a nightingale, or the brightness of a star, if he hadn't been able to write poetry about 'em? Perhaps he would . . . But I fear that life cannot be faced without the shield of prose to deflect all the slings and arrows. For sixty years and more I wrote to live – to earn a living – but it would be more truthful to say that I lived to write.'

George tapped the tray, now dotted with pills. 'Well, while you're still breathing, here's your medicine. Shall I do the drops for you?'

With a flutter of his hand Jimmy dismissed him. He sat there for a moment, looking disconsolate, then slowly lifted his eyes to Freya. 'And so I return to a condition that becomes, unavoidably, the spiritual home of the aged – we call it, the Dumps.'

Freya pulled a sympathetic expression. 'There are still reasons to go on.'

'Really? Name three of 'em.'

'OK. One – you're not actually blind.' At that Jimmy made a harrumphing noise which seemed to be short for *Is that the best you can do?* I'll have to throw him a bone, she thought. 'Two – you've written a wonderful memoir.'

This drew an approving grunt. 'Perhaps you could remind my publishers of that. So far they've spent all of tuppence on promoting it.'

'Three,' she continued, her eye alighting on his side table just in time, 'you still have half a packet of Jaffa Cakes left.'

On returning to the flat she gave a start on entering the living room; she still wasn't used to the sight of the television squatting there, like a shiftless and rather sinister house pet. She had written a note to Chrissie thanking her for the gift, though it didn't stop her secretly wishing that she'd sent a fridge instead.

She took her copy of *Ecce Homo* from her bag and opened it. Before leaving she had asked Jimmy to sign it, and while he looked for his spectacles and pen she had one more go at jogging his memory: could he really have forgotten that evening at the Oxford Union when he caved in to her pestering? She would write up an interview with Jessica Vaux and he promised to help her place it at the *Chronicle*. Jimmy listened, and made a shrugging face.

'What munificence. They should raise a plaque to me. But at my age I can't be expected to remember every instance.' His pen was poised over the title page of his book, and as if to confirm his imperfect recall he said, 'Your first name again?'

'Freya,' she replied, '– Wyley.'

Jimmy looked up. 'Yes, I know that. I'm not *senile*.'

The handwriting was tiny, crabbed and wavery. She had not anticipated much warmth in the inscription, but the old man had surprised her.

For Miss Freya Wyley
Who was kind, and admired this book.
James Erskine, London MCMLXII

She had left a bookmark in there, a page torn from her notepad with a telephone number scribbled on it. For a moment she couldn't remember whose it was. Then she did: it was the doctor who had rung a few days ago to arrange the disposal of the unwanted guest in her stomach. He hadn't given her his name, only an address and an appointment for the following Monday.

28

Almost until the point she needed to start getting ready she was in two minds about going. She had rehearsed the arguments in her head all day. If she did go, she would be conceding ground in an estrangement she had nurtured for years. In spite of her avowals that no 'great scene' of reconciliation was expected, Nancy would count it a victory if she entered her house. Robert, having felt the edge of her asperity that night, would presume that she had at last relented. The thought of that false smile plastered across his face was a strong incentive to stay away.

But if she didn't go it would reflect badly on her, not least because she would be snubbing Nancy's noble effort at fence-mending. And would it not also cast herself as an obsessive keeper of grudges? She would seem perhaps quite pitiable in having neither the capacity to change nor the largeness of soul to forgive. And yet might there not also be something magnificent in her implacable aloofness? Her rejection of them still had meaning; they had done her wrong. If she were to climb down now it would surely diminish that proud flexing of her will eight years ago.

And her unforeseen condition was playing havoc within her. Aside from the weariness, she found herself prey to strange moods: she was skittish, light-headed, forgetful. Before work that morning she had parked the car in an obscure little cul-de-sac and left without walking a witch's circle. She had returned to find a parking ticket and promptly burst into tears. Those fuckers! The first time she had forgotten to walk the circle, and she'd been stung . . . It took her some moments to calm down. The shadow passenger inside her was the cause of this, there could be no other explanation. She was twenty weeks, a little over. She kept checking herself in the mirror, looking for signs. Perhaps there was a slight thickening here, and here. Yet nobody else had noticed; Nat, Fosh, her dad, Diana, she had seen them all in the last couple of weeks and no one seemed to suspect. There had been no curious looks, no appraising glances.

The only person who knew, apart from the GP, was Chrissie Effingham – which struck her as the oddest thing of all. Chrissie: not a friend, barely more than a stranger, and yet Freya had found herself making a confidante of the girl over breakfast in a caff. Chrissie's big hungry eyes came back to her, accusingly. She had looked so *hurt* when she realised that Freya wasn't going to keep the child. It was the first moment she had felt her resolve wobble. The encounter with Chrissie had jolted her in an unlikely way: she had conceived a tenderness for her that was possibly romantic, and possibly maternal. Such was the disorder in her head she was at a loss to distinguish between them. For the first time in her life she felt not wholly in possession of herself: decisions that she would have made in an instant now loomed before her as perilous leaps into the unknown.

Regent's Park Terrace modestly echoed the architectural shape of Regent's Park itself. A long rectangular common garden screened the run of flat-fronted houses, linked by a necklace of wrought-iron balconies. The street was uncertainly placed in the social hierarchy. The grandeur of the park was a mere stroll south-west; the tatty streets and pubs of Kentish Town were not so far to the north. On the cooling night air came screeches of protest, or maybe desire – the monkeys were also having a party, at London Zoo. She had parked the Morgan, hood down, in a nearby crescent and walked a double circle as a protective measure against the wardens. She didn't know they knocked off at six thirty.

As she tapped the door knocker she tried to suppress her nerves – 'intensities of flutter' (she had been reading Henry James) – and wondered if either of the hosts would answer the door. To her relief they did not: a man in a dark suit and bow tie admitted her, and then handed her on to one of the waiting staff. She took a glass of wine from the tray. A few guests were chatting in the hallway, but the majority had colonised the long living room. The 'little gathering' Nancy had mentioned in her letter was a proper crowd, and presently at full gabble. She absorbed the room's decor, trying to guess whose taste had determined it, his or hers. The dark William Morris wallpaper seemed at once sociable and earnest. The paintings and prints, though few, had been thoughtfully chosen. On the mantelpiece was a photograph of Robert in statesmanlike pose at a rally. And everywhere books, racked higgledy-piggledy along the floor-to-ceiling shelves, overflowing onto chairs and the faded velvet sofa, or else stacked in tottering ziggurats against the wall. She noticed the new Doris Lessing lying on top of one, and John Braine's latest on another.

She moved about, pausing at the edge of various clusters of people, scanning faces for anyone she might know. Some she encountered were familiar to her, but only in the way you recognised them from newspaper photographs. The French windows at the far end had been opened to accommodate the overspill, and she edged her way towards them. She hadn't got far when a figure interposed himself, and there was Barry Rusk, her old editor from the *Chronicle*.

'I thought it was you,' he said, by way of greeting, 'but the hair confused me. Very Joan of Arc.' Barry wore his career hack's face with a jovial resignation; fifty-odd years of Fleet Street boozing had soaked into its contours and turned it violently florid.

'I'll take that if you mean Jean Seberg's Joan.'

'That's the one. Not hearing voices, are you?'

'Not yet.'

Barry wanted to know what she'd been up to. 'Last I heard you were engaged to Joss Philbrick, but then threw him over for Nat Fane.'

Freya laughed. 'I'm afraid your fact-checkers have let you down, Barry. I've never been engaged to anyone. And Nat's just a friend.'

'I see . . . So you're writing for the *Journal* now? Your man Brock's here, somewhere,' he said, nodding vaguely at the throng. 'Getting along there?'

'I suppose so,' she said, 'when they're not stealing stories from me.'

Barry lifted his chin knowingly. 'Ah. They should know better. "A volatile commodity", Jock Renton used to call you. Asked 'em for a rise yet?' This was a sardonic reference to the argument Freya had had with her bosses at the *Chronicle* when she got wind of a colleague's recent pay rise – one who was junior and, crucially, male – and demanded one for herself. Barry was chuckling at the memory. 'I'll never forget the look on old Jock's face when you finally lost your rag and said, *Just give me what you fucking owe me*. I thought he was gonna expire with the shock!'

'Not enough to shock him into giving me a rise, though. I've wasted a lot of energy over the years trying to get my due.'

'Yeah, but you're a fighter, and people admire that –'

'But I don't want to fight anyone. I only want to be given the same as –'

'Ah, this *is* good news! Freya Wyley doesn't want to fight anyone,' interrupted Robert, his politician's smile on full

453

beam. At his side was Ivan Brock, eyes shifting from Freya to the host, perhaps gauging the warmth of their connection.

Barry shook hands with Robert. 'Congratulations on the win – you must be delighted.' The papers, full of the Labour victory at Netherwick the day before, generally agreed that Robert's championing of their candidate had clinched it.

'Well, it was closer than we'd have liked, but –' Robert turned to embrace the room – 'the mood is buoyant, as you see.' He was at ease, rather less his usual overdefined self, she thought. A glow seemed to lift off his smooth-shaven cheeks.

'It should put the wind up Macmillan,' said Brock. 'The Tories probably thought they'd hold on, despite everything.'

'You mean, despite their running a blatantly racist campaign? Look, this isn't just about beating Bryan Lobbett and his goons – we've broken a lance against all those who think it's OK to call for repatriating "niggers". This sends out a message: we aren't that society any more. Anyway –' Robert stopped himself, and held up his hand – 'this is a party, not a party broadcast. How's everyone for a drink?'

Barry waggled his glass encouragingly. 'Nice place you've got here, Robert, right by the park.'

Robert dipped his head in acknowledgement. 'It's fine. The neighbourhood's been run down and neglected, but it's showing signs of rejuvenation. A bit like the Labour Party. Where are you living, Freya?' His beam was back on.

'Islington.'

'Oh, whereabouts?'

'Canonbury Square.'

'A good address! Orwell once lived there. And Waugh, I think? Odd that writers of such divergent politics fetched up in the same spot.'

Freya nodded, saying, 'And yet they had a purpose in common.'

454

'What would that be?' asked Robert, with an uncertain chuckle.

'I suppose – to tell the truth about the mean-minded and hypocritical age they lived in. To lament the decline of a certain fair-playing, unbiddable Englishman. And to rail against the type who had taken his place. Perhaps you've read them differently.'

The way she eyed Robert and the cool tone in which she spoke could hardly have been more pointed. She couldn't help it: she would always be his antagonist. Barry wore the silently amused smirk of a neutral. Brock, clearing his throat, decided to deflect potential strife. 'You see, that's the sort of piece you should be writing for the paper. Something to fire up the left *and* the right.'

Freya looked at him for a moment. 'I already have written it, a few years ago in the *Statesman*. I think they headed it "The Disasters of Waugh".'

'Oh yeah, I remember that,' said Barry pleasantly.

Robert was shrewdly diplomatic in his response. 'As I said, I'm very glad you don't want to fight anyone.' He held her look for a moment, then with a flash of his smile he led Brock away, to more congenial company. Barry waited until they were out of earshot.

'That was . . . interesting. Batten down the hatches, here's Freya Wyley and her very own cold front.'

Freya answered his theme with a wintry smile.

'Does this go back to that . . . ?' He had the newspaperman's memory and appetite for gossip, especially the sort relating to their own kind.

'Of course. Are you going to tell me now that he's a "great bloke"?'

Barry laughed. 'Not really. I've met worse. Cosway's a hustler. The sort who'd enter the revolving door behind you, and yet always get out in front. Weren't you two – ?'

'You know we were. At Oxford, a long time ago.' Her tone was sharp.

'Right, sorry. Blimey . . .' He shook his head. 'I hope you don't take a bite out of me. I'm not sure I'd recover.'

'It's simple, Barry. You must never, ever cross me, that's all.' She gave her sweetest smile. 'Shall we get another?'

They zigzagged through the close press of bodies towards a waiter holding a tray of drinks. Through the French windows she caught sight of her, and her heart dropped a sudden curtsy. Nancy was engaged in conversation, and Freya had a moment to observe her unawares; her hair was tied back and she wore a floral print dress that showed her long pale arms. Some withholding in her manner suggested that she was being polite rather than friendly to her inter-locutor; it pleased Freya that even at this distance she could read the nuances of her old friend's demeanour. She was going to turn away, but as if by some invisible thread Nancy's eyes lifted at that exact instant to meet hers. Freya, as if discovered spying, was momentarily at a loss, but Nancy wasn't: her eyes flashed and she raised her hand in greeting – in beckoning. So here it comes, Freya thought, trying to compose herself as she manoeuvred around the guests blocking her path. She had given nothing much away in her reply to Nancy's letter, just a couple of lines thanking her for the invitation and accepting it. Not cold, but not warm, either: the social minimum.

Now, with Nancy right in front of her, there would be no mistaking of mood or manner. They knew each other too intimately for that. Freya, with a sideways glance, gave an awkward half-smile as she held out her hand – it didn't feel right, somehow. Nancy responded with a quick dimissive laugh at this formality and leaned in, lightly placing her hands on Freya's shoulders and planting a kiss on the side of her mouth.

'I'm so glad you're here,' she said, her smile (*that smile*) taking in Freya, who felt almost weak-kneed from the bright confidence of her greeting. 'This is Freya,' she explained to the young man at her side. 'My oldest friend!'

She had been curious as to how Nancy would introduce her, and again she was disarmed by her straightforwardness – no mention of fallings-out or *froideurs* or anything at all that might have shadowed the moment. *My oldest friend* was enough. The young man was Philip Holbrook, a secretary in Robert's office, mid-twenties, hair parted down the middle, shortish but not bad-looking – though with an impatience about having his say. He was eager to revert to the conversation they'd been having about the party's triumph at Netherwick, about what the win 'meant' and its possible bearing on the '64 election; it was almost as if he, not Robert, were the Member of Parliament. While he talked Freya felt Nancy's appraising look fasten on her, and encoded within it a mutual sense of frustration that Philip and his interminable political monologue were keeping them from the vital event of their first conversation together in nearly eight years.

'Are you a voter?' he asked Freya, once he was ready to let the women have a trundle.

She shook her head. 'I've been living in Rome for a while, so I missed the last two elections.'

'I see. And before that?'

'Oh . . . Labour, as far as I remember.'

A light suddenly gleamed in Philip's eyes. 'Excellent! You're just the type of person whose vote we'll need in two years' time –'

'What "type of person" is that?' asked Freya.

He paused, not expecting the question. 'Well . . . um, an ordinary person.'

Freya pulled back her chin at that, and trying to sound amused, said, 'Does anyone really think of themselves as an "ordinary person"?'

Nancy caught her tone, and understood. 'Philip, it's worth bearing something in mind when you start on the campaign –

every voter is an individual. Freya, whom I'm sure you didn't mean to offend, is the *least* ordinary person you'll ever meet. In fact, there is no one else like her.'

Philip, embarrassed, started to back-pedal frantically. He hadn't meant 'ordinary' in the sense of – that is, he didn't wish to seem in any way – if he had somehow – Nancy cut him short.

'I wonder if you'd be a dear and fetch us both a drink?'

He coloured, aware of his being dismissed. 'Of course,' he said, and with a little nod slunk away.

As they watched him go, Nancy said quietly, 'Oh dear, I hope I wasn't rude.' But there was a lightness in her remorse, and it came into its own as a genial self-assurance that had, Freya realised, grown mightily in her absence. 'Let me look at you,' Nancy said now, taking a half-step back as though to frame her. A tiny flicker of surprise flared in her eyes and vanished into a smile. 'I can hardly believe you're here, in front of me. The years!'

Freya laughed. 'Nor can I. How are you?'

'Oh . . .' She waved the question away. 'I'd much rather talk about you. I do love your hair. It makes you look –'

'Like a boy?'

Nancy narrowed her eyes. 'Like a gorgeous elf. How is it, being back in London? Have you seen anyone?'

'I've seen Nat a few times. He's living high on the hog in Albany – enjoying the bachelor life now Pandora's gone.'

'Yes, I'd heard that was over. Is he all right? I'm afraid I still haven't seen *The Hot Number*.'

Freya pulled an ambiguous expression. 'It was fine, though hardly worthy of Nat. He said the best parts didn't make the final cut. I can tell you who was decidedly *not* impressed . . .'

'Who?'

'Remember Jimmy Erskine?'

458

'Oh, that name takes me back!' cried Nancy. 'The Oxford Union, wasn't it? – I remember afterwards how excited you were about him agreeing to help get you started at the *Chronicle*. Jimmy Erskine . . . he must be *ancient*. Is he still writing?'

Freya nodded. 'He's eighty-five – just published his second volume of memoirs, *Echoes of Homer* – Christ! I mean, *Ecce Homo*.'

Nancy raised her eyebrows. 'That's sailing rather close to the wind . . .'

'That's what I thought . . . I felt a bit sorry for him. He's fallen into neglect. I thought I might try to whip up a little revival for him.'

'Nice of you.'

'He said something quite interesting, actually. We'd been talking about luxury – you know he was a great collector and bon viveur in his day. He must be the only man in London who still wears spats! Well, I asked him what he thought the greatest luxury of all was, expecting him to name some car, or vintage wine, or what have you. D'you know what he said?'

Nancy shook her head.

'"Time." He said the greatest fallacy of all is that you can buy time – but you can't. "It is ineffable and ungraspable,"' she said, slipping into an imitation of the Erskine drawl, '"and yet, most mysterious of all, it is free. And those who spend it properly are the richest people of all."'

Nancy smiled and nodded slowly. 'He's absolutely right. The luxury of time. To think of how much we waste just in –'

Their eyes met, and held. She had made the remark innocently, but its pertinence was too close for them to ignore. The interval of years had suddenly obtruded itself and silenced them – not time wasted, but time they had chosen to live absent from each other. It was not something they could easily talk their way around.

After some moments Nancy said, 'Have you seen him yet?'

Freya nodded. 'He was friendly, and I'm afraid I didn't answer him in kind. I still find it difficult, I'm sorry –'

'You don't have to apologise,' Nancy said, frowning. 'I realise I should have been – I don't know –'

The sentence hung there, unresolved. Freya waited, and then said, 'I'm glad I ran into him, though, at the Corsair. We might have gone another eight years without talking if I hadn't.'

'Oh, to think!' said Nancy, averting her gaze.

Freya, touched by this exclamation of fright, hurried on. 'There's another thing. Actually, two things. I wanted to tell you how much I enjoyed your new book. I think it's your best. And to thank you for what you wrote – I mean, for the dedication.'

'As I said in my letter, I put it there in the hope you'd find it one day.'

'Well, it was nice. No – I mean, it was lovely. Nat was rather envious. He's never had one, so I had to promise that if I ever wrote a book I'd dedicate it to him.'

Nancy threw her head back and laughed. It gave a glimpse of the inside of her mouth, of her neat white teeth, and Freya realised that this, even this, was something she had missed about her. She thought again of the years that had intervened, years that suddenly, in front of Nancy, seemed a delusion – a wilful spurning that had hurt no one more than herself.

She took a sip of her drink, and when she looked up Nancy was gazing at her. She said, without warning, 'D'you mind if I ask you something? Are you pregnant?'

The surprise of this direct hit must have registered on her face, because it bounced right back onto Nancy's. For a

460

second Freya thought of denying it, but couldn't gather the strength. 'How did you – is it obvious?'

Nancy seemed almost stricken by her own surmise. 'No, no – though the moment I saw you I did wonder, perhaps . . .'

Freya stared at her. 'It was a mistake. I'm not in touch with –' How could she begin to explain? It would make her sound so feckless. But Nancy was a step ahead of her.

'You're not going to keep it, are you?' Her voice was low, and the shock of it was that she said it not as a question but a prediction.

'Are you a fucking *witch* or something?' Nancy had drawn out her secret just by studying her face. It was uncanny.

'Oh God, Freya,' she said, grasping her hands. 'I'm sorry. How far along are you?'

She looked round at the other guests to check that nobody was earwigging. 'Twenty-one weeks, thereabouts,' she said in an undertone. 'I'm getting – I have an "appointment" for this Monday.'

Nancy's brow was creased with concern. She seemed to be taking the news almost personally. 'Do you need – would you like me to come with you?'

Freya, touched, felt she mustn't give way, not here. She had arrived at the house only an hour before with her defences up, bristling, and yet Nancy had just hurdled them, first with an astonishing leap of intuition, and then by the simple tenderness of her tone. She covered her hesitation with a brave little laugh. 'Thanks, but I'll manage.'

Any further discussion of the matter was firmly checked by the interruption of Robert, in company with Bruce Haddon, thus doubling Freya's inclination to make herself scarce. But, perhaps eager to batten on the goodwill his wife had been re-establishing with their guest, Robert had planted himself before her in such a way that blocked escape. He introduced Haddon, who gave Freya a nod before saying, without charm, 'We've already met.'

'So, now you're back, Freya, can we hope to see you more often?' Robert, emboldened by his political success of yesterday, seemed to be trusting in its extension to the social sphere today.

For Nancy's sake she decided to keep a civil tongue. 'I don't know. It looks like you're going to be the busy one – your secretary was just telling us about the big push for the next election.'

'Well, we always have time for friends, don't we?' he said, looking to Nancy, who, arms folded, returned a supportive smile. 'We should have a dinner for you, a sort of welcome home. Bruce here seems to know the manager of every posh restaurant in London.'

Haddon gave a twitch of a smile. 'At your service.'

Freya, goaded by mischief, said, 'Maybe we could all meet up again at the Corsair, with Chrissie.'

Nancy tucked in her chin, puzzled. 'Chrissie Effingham? Do you know her?'

Freya shook her head. 'Not well. We've met a couple of times.' She glanced at Robert, who seemed rather put out by the conversation's turn: her instinct had been right, though she couldn't tell why.

Bruce, staring at her, said, 'I heard you two'd met the other week. She just took off in the car one morning without telling me.'

'Does she have to tell you? – I mean, is it in her contract?'

Haddon didn't rise to the bait. He spread his hands outward in a gesture of reasonableness. 'She's my client. I worry about her.' He drew in Robert and Nancy with his gaze. 'She's a twenty-year-old girl, and a bit naive. She'd think nothing about talking to a hack off the record. It's my business to protect her against personal intrusion.'

Freya shrugged. 'I'd be surprised if Chrissie thinks of me as an intruder – if she bothers to think of me at all. And she's twenty-one, by the way.'

Nancy started to ask something about Chrissie, but Haddon cut her off. He was still buzzing with curiosity about Freya's unscheduled meeting with his 'client'.

'So you and Chrissie – what did you talk about?'

Freya gave an objecting half-laugh. 'I really *don't* think that's in the contract. But since you ask, we chatted about knitting, about Bromley, about her dog – a Jack Russell, is it?'

Haddon nodded, listening intently. 'Is that all?' he said bluntly. Now he was annoying her. His tone was at once officious and condescending. She had been polite, and he was addressing her as if she were some two-bit gossip columnist.

Without adjusting her tone she said, 'Actually, we talked mostly about the size of your cock. Quite small, we imagined.'

Haddon stared at her for a disbelieving moment. Nancy snorted a laugh behind her hand, while Robert shook his head in the manner of a schoolteacher who's had enough of the disruptive kid on the back row. 'Freya . . .' He sounded wearily reproachful. But Haddon looked as though he had swallowed a wasp.

'You think you're so smart, don't you?' he said, his mouth in an ugly sneer.

'In your company I feel like a bloody genius,' Freya replied. They stood toe-to-toe, like duellists.

'I knew your type the moment I saw you with that jumped-up poof Fane. You people make me sick –'

'Bruce, really,' said Robert in a low calming voice.

'*You people*?!' Freya echoed, turning to Nancy. 'He doesn't like Nat because Nat called him a cretin, though I'm not sure he knew what it meant –'

'You fucking bitch, how about I give you a –'

'All right, that's enough,' said Robert, placing his hand on Haddon's shoulder and pushing him away. Other guests were looking round, alerted by their raised voices. But Haddon still wasn't done; narrowing his eyes he almost hissed at her: 'I'm gonna make sure you never talk to Chrissie again. That's a promise.'

Nancy stepped across Freya's eyeline, perhaps to prevent her firing a parting shot and inflaming the mood further. But Freya, her blood up, felt constrained by the circumstances: this was not how a reunion with her friend ought to go. She wasn't going to apologise, all the same. Nancy had pulled a face, widening her eyes in humorous complicity.

'Would you like to meet some other people?' she said, lightly steering her back into the house.

Freya smiled at her tact. Robert (she noticed) had guided Bruce Haddon to the far edge of the lawn, his head bobbing as he poured conciliatory words in his guest's offended ear. She wondered why he, a Shadow Cabinet minister, should be so eager to appease such a man. Or did Haddon command more respect than she assumed? Inside, Nancy introduced her to one of their neighbours, a waveringly tall, bespectacled man who turned out to be a critic and essayist of some note – in fact, as Freya admitted, Jimmy Erskine had talked about him *en passant* the previous week. The man twinkled at the mention, and they proceeded to chat about 'the old boy'. Freya thought how pleased Jimmy would be to know that his name in London drawing rooms had not been wholly forgotten. They were joined a few minutes later by Barry Rusk, his antennae twitching from the 'unpleasantness' in the garden. He gave a sideways wag of his head.

'What was that all about?'

She dismissed it with a snort. 'Nothing. Chrissie Effingham's manager, being an arsehole.'

When Barry pressed her for his name, he raised his eyebrows on hearing. 'I've heard about him. He's got some form.'

'Has he?'

Freya's interest was piqued, but the essayist neighbour chose that moment to shunt this promising line of gossip into a siding: instead he wanted to know about Chrissie Effingham, wasn't she the girl in the bread advert? – and was she *terribly* famous . . . ? Barry began a patient account of her to the man, while Freya silently cursed this dozy diversion into a subject he should already have known about. She waited for a pause to wrest the talk back to Haddon's 'form', but agonisingly the thread was being pulled further away by the two men. She glanced at her watch, and saw that it was later than she'd thought. Excusing herself, she did a once-around the party in search of Nancy before turning into the hall, where she saw her at the foot of the stairs.

'I'd better be going,' she said. 'But before I do, will you show me where you write?'

Nancy smiled. 'Of course. Come on.' And they started up the staircase. The Morris wallpaper of the hallway changed as they reached the first landing into a buttery yellow with pale green fleur-de-lys. The patterned runner on the stair looked affably worn. On the second floor Freya peeked into the bedrooms – for a moment she wondered if the small one belonged to a child, except she'd heard that they didn't have children.

'Does someone else live here?'

Nancy nodded. 'Our lodger, Marian. She's a student at King's. We like having her around, and it's a bit of extra money.'

Her study was the back room at the top of the house. It was narrow but orderly, with a strangely expectant air, as if the desk and the typewriter and the telephone were obedi-ently awaiting their owner's return. An oak swivel chair with a buttoned leather back was the only pompous touch ('Robert bought me that,' said Nancy). The sash window looked onto the backs of houses, clustered and clotted against the encroaching dark. Bookcases had been fitted on either side of the desk, and as she gazed on the serried volumes – the ones Nancy had read earnestly at school and Oxford, mixed in with the wild multiplication of paperbacks devoured in London – they seemed to her like rings of grain in a tree, marking the years. And there, placed at eye level, was another tender relic, the devotional portrait of Francis de Sales, patron saint of writers. Freya picked it up for a closer look.

'He's done you proud.' They both laughed.

Nancy moved around her, leaning her weight back on the edge of the desk. They faced each other in the diminishing light.

'I wondered about when you might come back – *if* you might. It seemed quite possible that you never would.'

Freya nodded faintly, and looked out again at the curving backs of the houses beyond, moved by the everyday wonder of bricks and chimneys and gutters and windows that furnished a shelter – a home.

After a moment she said, 'D'you ever think about Great James Street?'

'Oh, often,' Nancy replied. 'Remember how cold it was? It's the only time I've ever had chilblains.'

'Yes, I have an image of us sitting on the sofa, muffled in our winter coats and eating fish and chips. And –' She was about to mention her getting into bed with Nancy on those freezing mornings, but it felt too sudden and intimate a reminiscence for her to bring up: they were still, at some level, strangers. Nancy had waited for a moment, and then pushed herself off the desk with purpose. From a run of uniform spines she plucked out a copy of *The Hours and Times*.

'I know you've read it but I want to sign one for you,' she said. 'I would have sent you it if I'd known where you lived.'

She switched on her table lamp and cracked open the book to the title page. Freya, watching as Nancy uncapped her fountain pen, was in two minds about what she was going to say next; she had a question, and knew there was a strong chance that she might not like the answer. It would be wiser to let it lie. But curiosity trumped wisdom every time.

'May I ask you something? The character of Stella –'

Nancy, finishing her signature with a flourish, looked up. 'Ah, she's the one they all ask about.' She offered a smile of encouragement.

'I wondered about her – is it me?'

She laughed – a little nervously, Freya thought. 'What made you think that?'

'Actually I wouldn't have done, until the end, when I came across a description of Stella – I can't remember the exact words – but it tipped me the wink.'

Nancy nodded, seemingly relieved. 'I didn't quite realise it myself. I've never based a character wholly on someone I know. But I suppose there are strong correspondences between the two of you.'

Freya stared at her. 'So that's how you see me?'

Nancy flinched. 'What d'you mean?'

'I mean – this impossible, demanding, egotistical freak who almost destroys an entire family, *this* is the woman you base on me?'

'I just told you, my characters aren't based –'

'– on real people, yeah, right, except in this case you admit that there are correspondences – *strong* correspondences – between me and Stella.'

'Yes! And I'm amazed you could even think of taking offence. Stella – she's the most interesting character I've ever created. Even the reviews said so. You say she's a "freak" – to me she's a funny, headstrong, vulnerable woman. And the best parts of her I took, well, from *you*.'

467

Oh God, she thought, replaying in her head those scenes involving Stella and her awful abrasive treatment of the people she was supposed to love. Her witty but careless put-downs, her wilful misprisions, her pathetic efforts to make amends that only got her in deeper – these were passages in the novel that Freya had tutted and cringed through. The best you could say of Stella was that she spoke her mind, and it brought down chaos and misery around her. Do other people think of me like that? Freya wondered.

'I have to go,' she said.

'Oh, Freya, not like this – don't.' There was pleading in her voice. But Freya, having heard the truth, was feeling sick. She turned for the door, but Nancy darted in front, blocking her way. 'Please. Could we just talk?'

'We just did. There's nothing more to say.'

She brushed past her and took the stairs, feeling her stomach lurch with every step. She couldn't tell whether she felt queasy because of this horrible revelation or because she was pregnant. Three days to go before she went off to – another fucking ordeal. (At least the doctor wouldn't know she was the model for Stella.) She heard Nancy's footsteps in her wake as she reached the door.

Collecting herself, she said, with stiff courtesy, 'Goodnight. Thank you for inviting me.'

Nancy opened the door for her, looking at her but not speaking. She assumed this hurt silence was her reply, but as she went down the steps and onto the pavement Nancy trailed behind her. The trees screening the terrace struck wide postures of alarm against the purplish evening sky. Lamplight leaked a thin, yellowish illumination.

Still she heard Nancy a few steps behind her. Was she going to follow her all the way to the car?

'What do you want?' she said, halting.

She shook her head in disbelief. 'To be your friend again of course! To start making up for lost time.'

'You should have thought of that before you skewered me in your book. Enjoy your revenge.' It was as if someone else – someone she loathed – had spoken the words before she could stop them coming out of her mouth.

Nancy gasped, took a step back. 'Revenge? What are you talking about – ?'

'Look, Nancy, I feel tired and sick. I have to go.'

'You always quit,' she said, so quietly that Freya had to lean forward to hear. 'You leave things – people – behind, you push them away even when you need them. You did it with me.' She inclined her head towards Freya's stomach; their eyes met for a moment. 'That's how I knew what you were going to do about that.'

It took Freya a moment to find her voice, so winded was she. 'Fuck you,' she said, at a gasp, and walked away down the terrace. It wasn't until she got to the car that she realised she was still holding Nancy's book.

The call came early on Sunday morning. She'd been dreaming about being trapped – nearly all of her dreams at the moment were about that. She was trying to find her way out of a dark warehouse that was essentially a labyrinth, except the direction of her struggle was not horizontal but vertical: as eagerly as she clambered upwards to some notional point of exit, her path to the light kept turning up blind alleys.

She had recently taken the precaution of putting the telephone on the floor next to her bed. Blearily she swam into consciousness and reached down to quell its dreary ring.

'Hullo?' she droned, sleep-stunned.

'Freya. It's Nat.'

'Hnngh? Oh.' It didn't sound like Nat. It sounded like a dead sober eighty-year-old impersonating Nat.

'Are you listening? I've some news. Bad news.'

That did it. She hauled herself up in bed. 'What? What is it?'

She could hear him take a breath. 'It's Chrissie. She's dead. They found her at her flat this morning. Chrissie Effingham's dead.'

29

Chrissie Effingham, who died in the early hours of Sunday morning, had the world at her Bally-shod feet. Signed up by an agency at eighteen, she was the highest paid model in the country at nineteen and a bona fide star at twenty. In London this spring one could hardly pass a billboard that didn't have her face on it. People wanted to meet her, or just be seen with her. There is a photograph from the Royal Variety Show last year in which she is shaking hands with the Queen, and you can't tell which of them looks more impressed. Last week *Vogue* hit the news-stands with Chrissie's face staring out from it – her first cover, and now her last. It captures in that doe-eyed gaze the twin poles of her attraction, both the erotic allure and the unassuming girl-next-door homeliness. The picture is cropped, showing her from the waist up wearing a flower-print Quant dress and twirling a small Chanel handbag, the epitome of cosmopolitan glamour. But you can bet that below the camera's eye she wasn't wearing

Bally, or any other fancy-named shoe: more likely she was in plimsolls, or simply barefoot, as she preferred to be. It is a beautiful cover that has accidentally, and tragically, become a memento mori.

Her face, with its milk-soft skin, retroussé nose and heavy fringe, still had the look of a schoolgirl. Her voluptuous five-foot-ten frame, though, was very much a woman's, and the moment her agency released pictures of her the advertisers came flocking. She herself had no inkling of why the world of fashion had taken to her. 'They hand me the clothes and I put them on, and they look all right. I don't have a clue about "poise" – that's just a word they use.' It's true that for a model she was rather gawky, and sometimes looked ill at ease under the spotlight. Yet there was an unknowing gracefulness of manner that singled her out: one saw no contradiction in her being both coltish and a thoroughbred. As a person she was, in a word, adorable. She suffered from shyness, which she camouflaged with her natural qualities of enthusiasm, good humour and spontaneity. She wanted to know about things, like jazz and painting and food, which her schooling at a Bromley secondary modern had failed to supply.

She could not bear to see anyone in discomfort or distress. When I happened to tell her that I'd been sleeping badly she took me in hand with maternal solicitude, drawing up a list of herbal remedies and infusions I should prepare. No stranger herself to insomnia, she favoured more serious medication in the struggle for a night's sleep. She had prescriptions for barbiturates. That she had been taking them for a while ought to have set off alarm bells. Early reports issuing from the coroner's office suggest her blood contained dangerous levels of the drugs; she freely admitted to taking more than the recommended dose.

A sleeping disorder is a physiological misfortune. It can happen to anyone, like cancer, or heart disease. Chrissie bore her condition uncomplainingly. But she fell prey to a different ill luck, the sort that should have been avoidable. It emerged in the choice – or perhaps rather the imposition on her – of the people paid to look after her interests. The famous attract hangers-on in the way a coat picks up burrs. Chrissie hadn't been famous for long but she had somehow accumulated a retinue of people larger than the neediest showbiz veteran's. I had evidence of this when Nat Fane introduced me to her at Television Centre. She was surrounded, as I initially thought, by friends, who turned out mostly to be hired 'assistants' of one stripe or another. A manager, Bruce Haddon, orchestrated this party like Count Dracula with his brides, always sniffing the air for their next feed. Accountants, agents, public relations executives, and – for all I know – food tasters and soothsayers milled around, claws out, a squadron of winged Furies ready to pounce on anyone daring to approach their mistress. The only employee one saw doing a demonstrably useful job was Ken, her driver, who also happened to be the least self-important of all her staff.

473

Chrissie did have real friends, of course, most of them from school. One must remember how recent those schooldays were – the dew of youth was still on her. She had been born in December 1940, in Bromley, at a time when its citizens would have been among the first to hear the drone of the Luftwaffe's bombers approaching London. The youngest of three daughters, doted upon by her parents Reg and Sonia, she grew up in an unlyrical neighbourhood with unexceptional prospects. She was working in a cafe on the high street when a talent agent spotted her: he must have thought it the find of his life. If such a discovery had occurred in 1950 fame might have come calling, but it would have taken its time. In 1960, with television colonising so many living rooms, Chrissie Effingham went from unknown to face of the moment almost overnight. As well as portrait stills in magazines she was being beamed into people's homes, initially in teen-aged ensembles, then spectacularly in an advertising campaign for a well-known brand of bread. In a matter of days she became 'That Girl'.

After the evening at Television Centre I met her once more. We had a fry-up breakfast at a cafe in Islington, where she had reverted, without effort, to the girl next door: she wore a sweater and ski pants, her face barely made up. None of the clientele recognised her. She chatted about her parents (she had plans to buy them a house), her friends back in Bromley, her dog Alfie. There was talk of her going to work in New York, and the whisper of a film role at Ealing. She had much to live for. A week later I ran into her manager, who was furious about this 'unscheduled' meeting with Chrissie, or, as he called her, 'my client'. It seemed that he expected his permission to be sought for any social engagement, even one that meant just dropping in on someone – as Chrissie had on me. And yet this self-appointed custodian of her time had the last laugh. Following a heated exchange between us he vowed that I'd 'never see Chrissie again'. On that score, it grieves me to say, he kept his word.

She will be mourned, as the loss of any promising young woman might be. One suspects that more will come to light about the circumstances surrounding her death. For now, I want to remember not That Girl on the TV but that girl who, in Nat Fane's words, 'simply cheered you up by walking into the room'. I want to remember her here, in the flat where I write this, performing a little shimmy to Dexter Gordon's 'I Was Doing All Right'. The expression on her face was eager, poised on the verge of a smile. She was happy. She was doing all right.

Freya Wyley

Freya watched Nat, cross-legged in an armchair, hand over his brow as he read the piece. She had finished it in the ash-grey light of dawn and later telephoned him at Albany; he agreed to come over. It was now late on Monday morning, and the papers, scattered on her floor, were exultant with shock. MODEL FOUND DEAD IN MAYFAIR FLAT.

Most of them had used the stock photograph of her hurrying down a street wearing a thin stone-coloured mackintosh, looking away from the camera.

Nat nodded, gazing at the typed pages. 'It's strong stuff . . . "Brides of Dracula"? They'll spit feathers when they read it at Haddon Management.'

Freya stared at him. 'But is that all? I wanted it to say something about her, and how lovely she was.'

'And you do, it's very tender,' he said, thoughtful still. 'I'm glad you mention me . . . but wouldn't you like a quote of mine with a little more *sparkle*?'

'The piece isn't about you, Nat. And I like what you said anyway – it's just how I felt about her.'

Nat tipped his head in acquiescence. They had met each other on the doorstep in a mood of forlorn bewilderment. Nat's agent had telephoned him with the news. Apparently the concierge in Chrissie's building had heard her dog whining inside her flat and gone to investigate at about four in the morning. Having received no reply to his knock he let himself in, and found her lying lifeless on her bed. The police had been called, and an ambulance soon followed. An array of prescription drugs was found on her bedside table.

'The signs are that she took an accidental overdose,' said Nat.

'So they don't think that she –'

Nat took her meaning with a heavy shrug. 'We must hope not. But one can never be sure. The autopsy report should clear it up.'

A gloomy silence intervened. They had talked about her to a standstill. Freya rolled a cigarette and lit it. Nat, glancing at his watch, said, 'Shouldn't you be at work?'

She blew smoke from the side of her mouth. 'I had a doctor's appointment this morning, which I cancelled. I couldn't face it after all this.'

'Oh?'

'Just a touch of anaemia.'

'Hmm. You are looking a little peaky.' He got up and stood at the window, gazing out. 'Extraordinary place you've chosen to live . . .'

'We can't all afford Albany.'

'I swear to you, on my way here I saw a chimney sweep and his boy, sooty faces and all. Merry Islington! I know you deplore the modern craze for building, but this place – it's like Dickens still lives.'

'I like it,' she shrugged. 'It's a good neighbourhood for writers, this square in particular, as I was saying at the Cosways' only the other night . . .'

'Ah, yes, the grand reunion. And how were your long-lost friends?'

'Friend – singular. Nancy was . . . the same girl I always knew. Same warmth, same smile. We talked, and the years between just melted away. And then I fucked the whole evening up.'

'Oh . . . what did you do?' Nat looked eagerly amused.

She sighed, and recounted their argument about Stella in *The Hours and Times*, and the unpleasant note on which it had ended. As she listened to herself talking she sensed how prickly she must have sounded, and how ungrateful after all that Nancy had done to repair things.

Nat eyed her narrowly. 'I'm surprised you should have taken offence.'

'Why? You've read the book – Stella's a bitch.'

'That is your view of her. I take a different one – and I dare say Nancy does, too. But in any case, aren't you forgetting something?'

'What?'

He looked incredulous. 'The book is *dedicated* to you, for heaven's sake! What more proof of her regard do you need – blood?'

477

Freya looked away; she didn't really have the heart to defend herself, but she had one more go anyway: 'That may only have been a decoy, to cover for the harsh truths about my character.'

Nat's expression had become pitying. 'I don't for a moment think you believe that. She wants to be friends again, and for some reason you're making it as difficult as possible.' He paused, then went on. 'And what of him – did you speak?'

'Briefly. He knows that I detest him.'

'I wonder how he's taken the news – he and Chrissie were rather close. Regular dance partners at the Corsair, I'm told.'

Freya stared into the middle distance. 'Isn't it strange and terrible to be talking about her as someone *in the past*? This girl, so full of life, just – snatched away.'

Nat turned back to the window; after a long moment of brooding he murmured something, so softly she almost didn't hear it. 'She should have died hereafter.'

When she had telephoned the abortion doctor that morning he had asked her whether she wished to make another appointment. She had dithered for a moment, and said no, she would call back later. Her head was in such disarray with the news of Chrissie that she felt herself incapable of making a decision on the spot. She would leave it for a day or two: once the shock to her system had worn off she would know what to do.

When she arrived at the *Journal* on Tuesday she had a quick scour of the paper, and was puzzled. There were news stories and opinion pieces about Chrissie's death, with photographs of her looking sad and thin and doomed. But her own piece wasn't among them. She knocked at Ivan Brock's door, which was open, and entered.

'My Chrissie Effingham obit isn't in.'

'I know,' he said neutrally.

478

'So it's being held over till tomorrow?'

He leaned back in his chair and fixed her with a look. 'No, it's not. I'm not running it.'

'What? You're joking.'

''Sfunny, they were the very words that came to mind when I finished reading it. "She must be joking if she thinks she can get away with this."'

'What's wrong with it?' She felt a sudden heat bloom in her face.

Brock pulled a disbelieving frown. 'It's defamation! First you accuse Haddon and his staff of being bloodsuckers. Then they're "a squadron of winged Furies" –'

'It's a classical reference.'

'I don't care what it is. But that's not even the worst –' He reached into his tray and plucked out the typewritten pages, flicking through them. 'Here: "Haddon vowed that I'd never see Chrissie again . . . on that score he kept his word." You've practically accused him of doing away with the girl! He'll have his lawyers on to us like *that*, and I wouldn't blame him.'

'All I said was Haddon kept his promise that I wouldn't see Chrissie again – I didn't say "see Chrissie *alive* again".'

'But you implied it, and he'd sue. We're not going to get involved in a court case just so you can have cheap shots at a perfectly respectable bloke.'

Freya couldn't tell which she felt more – incredulous or furious. 'Cheap shots? What the f— If you'd met Haddon –'

'I *have* met him.'

'Then I'm amazed you can't tell that he's a creep. You seem more interested in defending him than you do supporting one of your own writers. Excuse me if I find that hard to understand.'

Brock shrugged. 'No editor in his right mind would run that piece.'

'I can think of one or two who would – I might try them.'

'I'd look at the small print in your contract first,' he advised.

That tore it. She couldn't take it elsewhere and risk losing her job; it would be another mark against her as 'a volatile commodity', in Barry Rusk's words. She decided to be conciliatory. 'All right, then. I'll take out all the references to Haddon and his crew – it will be a straight tribute to Chrissie, which is after all the point.'

But Brock was shaking his head. 'We've got people working on it now. I'm disappointed with this. It's too personal, too mixed up with your own feelings about her. There's no detachment.' He tossed the pages back onto his tray.

She stared at him. 'I don't *fucking believe* this,' she almost shrieked, ignoring his moue of distaste at the expletive. 'I brought you the idea about doing Chrissie weeks ago, and you said, in this very office, that it was a good one and you'd make sure nobody took it off me. Now you've not only spiked my piece but you're doing exactly what you said you wouldn't.'

'I think you should calm down,' said Brock sternly.

'No, I won't calm down. You made me a promise, and you've broken it. What gives you the right to behave like that?'

'Lower your voice. I made no promises, nor would I. If you'd been professional about it and written a proper obituary of Chrissie, as instructed, we wouldn't need to have this conversation. And what gives me the right? Take a look there –' He pointed to the open door and its stencilled sign: EDITOR. 'What does it say?'

Was he really going to make her recite it, like a fucking tutor? He was waiting, arms folded. She let out a gasp of disgust. '*You* say it. A pity you don't know how to act like one.'

She walked out, pulling the door behind her.

480

She half expected him to give her the sack after that, and during the next few days she braced herself for a summons to his office. None came. This leniency did nothing to improve her mood, however. She brooded about his betrayal, and his removal of her from a story she had considered her own. It was doubly sickening because she knew that, had Chrissie lived, she would have been kept writing fluff about her clothes, her celebrity, her latest ad campaign. With her dead, Chrissie was suddenly a bigger proposition, so Brock set his news lieutenants – all men – on the saga, even sending one to the funeral in spite of the family asking for privacy. The autopsy report put a new wrinkle in the mystery: as well as barbiturates, alcohol had been found in Chrissie's blood, though it was well known that she didn't drink. An inquest had been called.

Meanwhile, there was the small matter of her pregnancy. Whereas her first three months had presented no outward signs, now she was beginning to show. Twenty-three, twenty-four weeks had gone; still she couldn't bring herself to telephone for the euphemistic 'arrangement', and she knew that with every day that passed the opportunity was narrowing. Partly it was complicated by the shock of Chrissie. She hadn't known the girl well enough to feel she could wallow in the dam burst of bereavement. Whenever she was caught on the verge of tears she would reprove herself, even out loud: *You hardly knew her, for God's sake*. Yet she couldn't erase Chrissie's look of hurt that morning at the cafe when she realised that Freya positively didn't want a child.

But she was also still smarting from the barb Nancy had fired with such accuracy the night of the party, when they argued outside her house. It was true, by any reckoning, that Freya had always left things – school, college, jobs, men – when they didn't suit her. Her most dramatic desertion, hitherto, was that of eight years ago, when she had packed her bags to leave London, and Nancy, behind. It was a rupture she had hoped would heal, in time, though of course she expected Nancy to do the patching up. And her expectation had been met.

That she, Freya, had contrived to upset the apple cart again was ostensibly down to a wilful misreading of a novel. But there was something else she had to come to terms with – something she could barely admit to herself. It was the possibility that she might be envious of her old friend. It wasn't envy of her success, exactly. She admired Nancy's writing and was pleased for her continuing acclaim, though it was slightly galling that her career should have advanced in a way that her own had not, baulked as it had been by bosses and colleagues, of whom Brock had proved to be the latest perfidious example. But no, it wasn't that. It was more to do with an inkling that the balance of power in their friendship had decisively shifted. She had felt it the moment she and Nancy had come face-to-face with one another. What had taken her aback was Nancy's poise, her self-confidence as hostess among other self-confident and influential people. This, the woman who had once despaired of being published and of getting a man. She had done both, while Freya had nothing but a child she wanted rid of.

She was half listening to the wireless one evening when the song came on. It was slow-paced, with a shimmering guitar and piano to the fore, allied to a ghostly doo-wop chorus. It didn't register at first, but once the singer picked up the refrain she knew it for sure.

Are the stars out tonight?
I don't know if it's cloudy or bright,
'Cause I only have eyes for you, dear.

She'd never heard it done like this before, like a fugue, the harmonising voices – black, male, American – crooning

482

through the lyric and lifting it into the ether, where it floated and glimmered, iridescent, like a soap bubble about to pop. It had been a while since she'd thought of the song – she hadn't played it since that night at Kay's place in Fiesole, the holiday when Nancy heard that her novel had been accepted. 'Their' song, since VE night. She had a sudden longing to bring this new version to Nancy's notice.

She opened the drawer of her desk and took out a sheet of writing paper. It had been so long since she'd written to Nancy she felt almost shy of starting again.

5 Canonbury Sq., N1

Dear Nancy,

I've been meaning to write and thank you for inviting me to your party a few weeks ago. I was so pleased to see you again after all these years, and I'm only sorry that I managed to ruin the night with my tactless and petulant behaviour. As usual it has taken me a while to realise something that would appear obvious to almost anyone else. My prickliness about Stella was misplaced, I see now, and far from creating a fuss I ought to have thanked you for that lovely dedication you made in the book. Nat Fane gave me a rap on the knuckles about that – well earned!

Regarding my 'condition', I have been through intensities of dithering you wouldn't believe over these last weeks. I won't trouble you with a full account, but certain events conspired to decide me in favour of going through with it. I can't say that I'm overjoyed at the prospect of being a mother, and in fact I still have moments of blind panic, but in the end the thought of getting rid of it (it?) felt more terrible than the long slog of bringing it forth. I hope I'm not making an awful mistake. You are the first person I've told.

With that in mind, I feel an urgent incentive to put my house in order, and I don't just mean getting my front doorbell fixed. First, and most important, I want to make a proper apology to you, in person. I could cook dinner for us, only the kitchen here is a bit poky, and the oven a bit nasty. So we could dine out in town, or else – the thought has just occurred – I could drive us out to the country somewhere and we could find a pub. (Did I tell you that Nat has lent me his sports car?) Of course I realise that you may prefer not to see me after those horrible words outside your house the other night. I could make an excuse of the volatile nature of a pregnant woman. Or I could just admit what a <u>bitch</u> I am! But I hope I can appeal to your great reserves of forbearance and forgiveness. You've always been better at that than I have.

With much love,

Freya

There was a little record and hi-fi shop she knew, off Wardour Street. A couple of skinny youths were absorbed in flicking through the long stacks of sleeved vinyl. The air was sour with patchouli, cigarettes and dust. One wall was a scruffy patchwork of flyers announcing concerts and adverts for new releases. The floor and front window were shaking to a heavily amplified song brash with twanging guitars. Freya approached the counter: behind it a man in his middle twenties was examining the inner label of a long player, holding its edges lightly on his fingertips. He flipped it suavely to look at the reverse. His unkempt black hair and bottle-end spectacles could not wholly conceal a certain pleasantness of face.

'Would you mind –' she began, and he canted his head towards her, as if she needed to speak up – 'would you mind turning the volume down, please?' *Christ*, that sounded old, she thought. He stared at her for a moment, before

484

reaching beneath the counter: the noise dropped a few decibels. On his checked shirt he wore a button badge urging BAN THE BOMB.

'I'm looking for something by the Flamingos. Heard of them?'

'Yeah . . . doo-wop, isn't it? Pretty sure I got nothin' in by them.'

She told him the song's title and asked whether he could get hold of it from somewhere. He gave an absent nod and picked up a well-thumbed paperback catalogue, which he briefly riffled through. 'Mm. "I Only Have Eyes For You". Single. 1959.'

'Right . . .'

'Take two weeks. Maybe three.'

'What?'

He shrugged. 'Have to order it, from the distributors. It'll be the same anywhere else.'

With a heavy sigh she gave him her name and telephone number, which he noted in biro on the order form. He'd give her a call when it came in, he said. She saw that he had written her name down as F. Y. Lee.

Outside on the street she was about to get into the car when a tall, tousled-haired figure ambled by. In his air of preoccupation he hadn't seen her, so she could have let him pass unbothered.

'Ossie,' she said, and he started on hearing his name. The eyes spoke of someone surprised in a furtive act, or a criminal one, which in his case was not that unlikely. He stared for a few moments, seemingly unable to place her. Then he said, 'Oh. It's you.'

She knew better than to expect courtesy of Ossian Blackler. He wore a fawn-coloured suit with a tie loose at his collar. His hard, gaunt face had not changed much in the years since she had last seen him, though the prices his paintings now fetched had. Despite his burgeoning wealth he remained loyal to the wild side of Soho – the only loyalty he was known for – and stories of his gambling debts and scrapes with loan sharks still did the rounds. His dark gaze, feral and quick, had taken her in.

'Up the stick, then,' he said without preamble.

She nodded. 'Is it that obvious?'

He gave a half-laugh. 'Well, I've never seen you with tits before.'

'I think the last time I saw you was that evening at Nat Fane's house. You were with a young girl –'

'Was I?' he shrugged, as though he couldn't be expected to remember a particular evening, or a particular girl. 'I heard you and Fane were – not his, is it?' he said, nodding at her stomach.

'No. And we never *were*, by the way. Have you seen Jerry Dicks?'

Ossie made a regretful little noise at the side of his mouth. 'He's back in the sanatorium. Got TB, emphysema, jaundice. He's fallin' apart, poor fucker. I'm going to visit him next week . . .'

'May I go with you?'

He looked at her, disbelieving. 'You don't wanna see him, not in his state. And he won't wanna see you, either. He only agrees to have *me* there cos I bring him a bottle of vodka and a sleeve of fags.'

'What – in a sanatorium?'

'I smuggle 'em in. If I didn't he'd lose the will to live – what little he has left.'

'Oh God,' she muttered. 'Poor Jerry . . . I wonder if – if there's something you could give him from me?'

'What is this? Jerry's been sick for years –'

'And I've been away for years. He once – I was in a terrible jam, and he helped me out, though he didn't have to. And I never managed to thank him.'

486

Ossie twitched his chin. 'He probably wouldn't remember.' He was staring at her again, but in a more speculative way, as though he'd just noticed something new about her. 'Tell you what – if there's something you want me to give old Jer' you can bring it over to the house. Call me Friday or Saturday.'

'I don't have your number,' she said.

'Nobody does!' He laughed his old laugh – *ha ha ha*, each syllable mirthlessly enunciated – and without warning he clasped her arm and shoved up the sleeve of her cardigan, exposing her bare flesh. From his jacket pocket he took out a marker pen and plucked off its cap with his teeth. Very carefully, on the inside of her forearm, he inscribed *SLO 2211*, and then drew a fancy picture frame around it. He pulled her sleeve down. 'There – you got my phone number and your own Blackler limited edition, too. Don't pass it on.'

He held her gaze for another moment, and walked off up the street. As she got into the car she chuckled to herself. Ossie really hadn't changed. He hadn't said hullo, and he didn't say goodbye.

30

At the inquest into the death of Chrissie Effingham the verdict was out. The deceased had been found with lethal quantities of barbiturates and alcohol in her blood. The coroner did note the anomaly that the young woman was said to be teetotal, so the fact she had been drinking at all must be counted as 'mysterious'. However, he ruled out the possibility of suicide. The deceased was known to be taking medication for insomnia, but the weight of evidence from those who knew her suggested there was no predisposition to overdose. The probability was that in the unfamiliar state of inebriation she had accidentally taken a higher dosage of sleeping tablets than was advisable. Thus: death by misadventure.

From the gallery Freya watched as reporters hurried out of the courtroom to the row of expectant telephone boxes. She ought to have been one of them. Brock's treachery still rankled, though her stirrings of homicidal intent had been quelled; now she only wanted to punch his face. Outside the day was warm, the air drowsy with pollen. Early summer had sidled into the city. She walked on to Fleet Street, where buses and taxis grumbled along its length. Newspaper stalls stood in readiness; the late edition would gobble up the verdict. By the time she got back to the *Journal* she was sweating. She felt – she hated the word as much as the condition – *blobby*.

Late in the afternoon, just as she was packing up for the day, her phone rang.

'Is that – Freya Wyley?'

She confirmed that it was.

'This is Ava.'

'Er, who's that?'

'Ava Dunning. I'm – I was a friend of Chrissie's. We met once at the Corsair.'

'Yes, of course . . .'

The black girl with the beautiful sloping cheekbones. She said she had just read in the *Standard* about the inquest. 'I remembered you worked for a newspaper, so I thought you might want to know, but . . .'

'Want to know what?'

There was a moment's hesitation. 'Could I – can we meet? I'd rather tell you this in person.'

She invited her to come to the flat, but Ava said that her work would make that difficult: would it be all right for her to suggest somewhere? Freya took down the details, and after a few moments they ended the call.

At an old-fashioned tobacconist's in Holborn she found something for Jerry Dicks. She recalled that when she knew him he used to smoke Turkish cigarettes, but in his present condition such a gift might seem irresponsible, and Ossie Blackler was already keeping him in supplies. In one of the glass display cases she spotted an art deco ebony cigarette-holder. This felt to her a decent compromise between something he might like to have and the habit that was slowly killing him.

Ossie had described his house in a lane off Cadogan Square, since there was no number on the door. On the phone he'd been very particular in laying down the procedure on arriving: three distinctly spaced knocks, and then wait – 'as long as it takes' – for him to answer. She presumed this was his safety measure against the unscheduled calls of coppers and gangsters. Though it was getting on for nine in the evening she knew he was probably still at work; he talked about his 'night paintings' as if they were a genre of their own. She had knocked, and taken a step back to survey the tall stucco-fronted house, its windows opaque to the world. A few moments passed before a low buzzing sounded at the door lock, like a trapped wasp; she pushed through into a musty, darkened hallway. She almost tripped on the rubbish – a mound of unopened post, old newspapers, coats, a broken bicycle. You could scarcely move for it.

Having navigated a path to the foot of the stairs she called up: 'Ossie? Could you switch on a light?'

No word of reply came. A scratching, scurrying noise from the far end of the hall indicated mice. She felt for a light switch and clicked: it was dead. Had she not just been admitted she would have assumed the building to be derelict. A faint illumination from above beckoned her on. She took the staircase, carpeted with old leaves and rags, rags everywhere, splotched with paint and stinking of turps. Neglect coated everything; even the banisters were velvety with dust. She had been inside a few artists' houses in her time, with Stephen, and they weren't always quite clean: but she had never encountered squalor on this level before. As she approached the second-floor landing she saw that the paltry light was decanted from a glass cupola in the roof. It seemed to be a house ill-lit by moonlight.

She called his name again, and this time it brought Ossie's voice, from a room on the left. 'Door's open.' It was a relief, she felt, to hear any voice at all. She walked across the bare-boarded landing and through the door, adjusting her eyes to a different gloom, where a single gas lamp burned on the floor. The sight that met her provoked a laugh of surprise. Ossie stood a foot away from his easel, knife in one hand, smeared palette in the other, cigarette at his lips: he was

490

completely naked but for the unlaced boots on his feet. The lamp cast one half of him in glare, so that she could see flecks of paint spattered the length of his lean body, from his neck and shoulders down through his torso, pendulous cock and balls, to his scribble-haired legs. Yet nearly as remarkable was the absolute lack of self-consciousness he displayed in his undress. Indeed, he might have forgotten he was naked at all. He seemed to her in this moment less a painter than some wild creature – a satyr, perhaps – whose lair she had stumbled upon.

'Found it all right, then,' he said. His long vulpine face stared at her through the murk.

She nodded, and looked around the room. It was as scruffy as the rest of the house, paint peeling off the walls, uncurtained windows, with only a disused fireplace to hint at its erstwhile elegance. Of furniture it had but two items: one was an armchair with a wide cracked leather seat, the other a mattress, reduced to its striped and stained ticking. He waved an arm towards the window ledge, where alongside tubes of pigment stood an opened bottle of Lynch-Bages and a couple of cloudy glasses.

'Help yourself. I've just got to finish this,' he said, and scraped up a gobbet of paint onto his knife. For the next few minutes he was absorbed again in his canvas. She had a sense that he didn't appreciate chat while he worked, so she poured a glass of the claret and folded herself into the armchair to wait. Ossie looked somewhat sinister, standing there, his great forked shadow looming against the bare wall. There was something highly 'painterly' in the scene, for which she pondered a title: 'Ossie by Gaslight', perhaps, or 'In the Altogether'. She rolled a cigarette, and asked him for a light.

'On the bed,' he said absently.

She found his cigarettes there, and a book of matches – from the Corsair. Her quiet groan of dismay caused him to look round.

491

'What?'

'Nothing,' she said. 'This place – I was once there with Chrissie Effingham. I attended the inquest this morning.'

'Oh yeah? I met her a few times. I'd like to have –' a choked snigger – 'painted her.'

'I'm sure you would.' It was useless to reprove Ossie on grounds of delicacy: he wouldn't understand.

Still daubing away, he mused, 'Though it sounds like she was busy enough already –'

'What d'you mean?'

He shot her a disbelieving glance. 'You think a girl like that got anywhere without opening her legs?'

'Not everyone's as cynical as you. From what I knew of her she preferred knitting and a cup of tea.'

But Ossie was warming to his theme. 'Any time you saw her she was surrounded by men. That fucking manager of hers. And the actor, Tarrant –'

'Queer, according to her.'

'What about the MP? You're not telling me he never gave her a portion.'

'Who – Robert Cosway?'

Ossie had come over to the bed, on which she had been idling. He kneeled down in front of her and began stroking her legs. He murmured, almost to himself, 'Don't understand women wearing trousers.' She assumed he meant 'instead of a skirt', though it may have been a more general point about them wearing anything on their lower half at all.

His hand had reached her thigh, and she knew that now was the moment for evasive action. Sitting up, she placed his bony, bespattered hand to one side and, with humorous tolerance, said, 'Not really in the mood, I'm afraid, Ossie.'

She had a fleeting image of him clambering on top of her, and having to deal a swift knee to his unprotected groin. But he backed off without complaint, perhaps accepting

492

that, even with his powerful naked allure, refusal was one of those unfathomable hazards.

'You'd be offended if I didn't try,' he said, shrugging, and she returned a sweetly non-committal smile. 'But take your clothes off anyway – I should at least like to draw you.'

She narrowed her eyes. 'Have you forgotten I'm – ?' She gestured at her stomach.

'Not at all. I find pregnant women the most satisfying of all – like Rubens.'

She wondered if this might be another stratagem to get his leg over, but in fact Ossie had got up off the bed and padded across the floor to fetch a loose-leaf pad and his charcoal stick. He was ready to return to work. 'Painting and fucking' – she remembered someone say it – these were the only things he cared about.

'To be honest, I only came by to drop this off,' she said, indicating the cigarette-holder she had wrapped up for Jerry.

But Ossie wouldn't be refused twice: '– which I'm taking round to poor old Jerry on his sickbed. So wouldn't you say one good turn deserves another?'

'I'm no great model,' she said, running out of objections.

'Doesn't matter – I'm a great painter.'

That made her laugh. He had opened a window, and the air stirred a little. A distant church clock struck the hour. She asked him if he had any kif, which he did, and she smoked a joint while she slowly pulled off her sandals, then her T-shirt and trousers. In a reflex she folded her arms across her narrow braless chest, but Ossie wasn't even looking at her. She stepped out of her knickers.

'Where d'you want me?' she said, momentarily blindsided by the strength of the cannabis. A small detonation had made her brain wobble. Ossie had settled himself on a camp stool. He pointed to the mattress.

'Resting back on your elbows . . . that's it. Legs apart. Turn your head a bit –'

493

Within a minute he had re-entered his trance of concentration, making marks on the paper. He muttered to himself as he worked, while she let herself swim in the rubbery intoxicating fumes of the kif.

At one point (she recalled later) Ossie had tipped his head appraisingly. 'I always thought you'd have a nice cunt,' he said.

She laughed again. It was the closest she had ever heard him come to paying her a compliment.

Having picked up the Flamingos record from the shop she had taken it home and spent the evening playing it to death. The echo on the singer's voice, the drowsy hypnotic piano figure, the backing chorus and their harmonies – she couldn't get them out of her head.

You are here and so am I
Maybe millions of people go by
But they all disappear from view . . .

It was on perhaps its tenth repeat when the telephone rang.

'Freya, is that you? It's Nancy.'

'Nance!' She felt her heart do a flip. 'I was hoping you'd – did you get my letter?'

'I did. I was very touched.'

'Oh . . . so you've forgiven me?'

'I don't see anything to forgive. A small tiff. You surely didn't imagine I'd let another eight years go by, did you?'

'Nance, please never let us argue again – please? I don't think I could stand it.' Oh Christ, here it comes, she thought, as tears sprang to her eyes. Why am I crying when everything's all right again?

'Freya, darling, are you OK?'

'I will be in a sec,' she replied, knuckling her eyes. 'Ever since I knew I was . . . I've become this *quivering jelly*. I

494

don't know what on earth has got into me. Or rather, I know too damned well what has – I can feel it kicking.'

Her tone was rueful, and yet she almost swooned with pleasure on hearing Nancy's voice. Her tears were wrung from relief as much as emotional giddiness; she knew there *had* been something to forgive, despite Nancy making light of it. It was true, she had been a quitter, but not any more.

'What's that noise?' Nancy was asking.

'Oh, just a record,' she replied, only now aware of the volume at which it was playing. Freya pictured her there, sitting in her study, half smiling as she strained to hear the faint, tinny-sounding melody emanating from the Dansette. They talked on for a while. Nancy wanted to know how she was 'coping', and Freya felt grateful that she didn't say the dread word out loud. Nobody understood her like Nancy did.

'I'm finally telling my dad tomorrow. Diana's cooking dinner at Tite Street.' She paused. 'I wish you were coming with me.'

Nancy gave a little laugh. 'Well, if you really want me to . . .'

'No, no, I wouldn't put you through that.'

There was a slight hesitation before Nancy replied. 'It's meant to be something *joyful*, you know.'

Her gentle tone carried, she thought, a hint of wistfulness. She wanted to know why Nancy hadn't had any herself, but sensed it wasn't the moment to ask. They were still feeling their way back into friendship.

'I know, you're right. Joy will be unconfined. It's just – I'm still waiting for the moment when I feel it too.'

'All right, all right, that's enough of that,' she said, disengaging herself from Diana's tearful embrace.

'Darling, it's just – we're just –' She dabbed her streaming eyes with the handkerchief Stephen had slipped her.

'We're rather overwhelmed,' he said, beaming at her. 'It's a wonderful surprise.'

'It was a bloody surprise to me, I can tell you,' she said, taking another long swig of her Martini. Stephen had opened a bottle of champagne, but she had felt in need of something purely alcoholic.

'And what does Daniele make of this?' asked Diana.

Freya looked at her. 'What d'you mean?'

Diana laughed nervously, and with a glance at Stephen said, 'Well, I – you've surely told him about it?'

'No, I haven't. In fact I haven't had any communication with him since I got back home.'

'*Oh* . . .' In her confusion she looked again to Stephen for support.

'Don't you think you ought to tell him?' he said.

She gave an impatient sigh. 'I told you – it was over between us, even before I left Italy.'

'Yes, but doesn't this rather change things?'

She had anticipated this response, of course. Stephen was very far from being a hidebound patriarch. His own past, with its trail of affairs and a divorce, had never let him presume to tell his daughter how she ought to behave – and he knew her intractable nature too well to try. His concern, she knew, sprang from a practical, not a moral, instinct.

'It doesn't change anything. Until a couple of weeks ago I had actually been planning to get rid of it. Since then I've been too busy or too panicked to think about Daniele. And I can pretty much guarantee that he hasn't been thinking about me.'

She shrugged, and a brief silence intervened while they absorbed this sudden bump on the road to familial happiness.

'What changed your mind?' asked Diana.

'I don't know . . . Crazy as it sounds, it may have been something to do with Chrissie Effingham. I met her, not long before she died – she happened to drop by on the very morning I'd found out from the doctor. I was so upset I let it slip. Something about her, the way she looked at me . . . Then her dying just –'

She didn't really understand the connection herself, and from their puzzled looks they didn't either.

'Darling, he deserves to know,' said Stephen. 'Obviously no one can force you, but I think it would be the decent thing – the right thing – to do.'

Freya shook her head, and took another swallow of her drink. 'From your point of view it may look that way. But I know him, and believe me, he won't thank me for the news. All Dani cares about is his motorbike, his clothes and getting home for meatballs at his mama's. He isn't a grown-up, really, and he wouldn't be ready for fatherhood *in any way*.'

'I thought Italians loved children,' said Diana rather pleadingly.

'Maybe he does. But not at the moment, and not one of mine. Now may I please have another one of these excellent Martinis?'

She felt that she had let them down, pouring out cold hard facts to douse the cosy fire of congratulation. She knew she was right about Dani, though it didn't help resolve her own anxieties. She could hardly rejoice at the idea of bringing up a child on her own. What if she forgot to feed it – Christ, she had to stop saying that – or accidentally dropped the thing on its head? She had heard horrific stories: the new mother who slept with her baby next to her and woke to find she had rolled on top of it in the night, crushing it to death.

Seeking to restore the happy mood she suddenly said, 'I have bett— I mean, some other good news. I finally met Nancy again.'

Stephen, brightening, said, 'At last! I always wondered when you two were going to make up. You were pretty cagey about it last time I mentioned her.'

'She invited me to a party at her house, a few weeks ago. And as soon as we started talking I realised what a lot of time I'd wasted being mad at her.'

'I never quite got why you *were* so mad at her. Wasn't it *him* you fell out with?'

'Yes. He made himself my enemy. I suppose what riled me was the fact Nancy couldn't tell what sort of man Robert was – presumably she still can't. But in every other way she's the person I always knew and loved.'

'It's a pity about him – Cosway, I mean,' said Diana. 'He seems rather dashing in his photographs.'

Freya wrinkled her nose. 'He's always been plausible. He has a lot of front. The first time we met – I must have told you – I was visiting Dad's old staircase at Balliol. He came out of a bathroom stark bollock naked . . .'

'Oh!' drawled Diana, lifting her brow saucily.

Freya smiled back. 'He's not as impressive as he thinks he is. Apply that verdict as you wish.'

The sky was a sullen grey lid pressing down on the warm afternoon. Dust flew up behind the buses as they trundled along Kilburn High Road, whose exhausted pavements drummed to the footsteps of children in uniform. It was nearly four, and school was out. Freya, who had been waiting for twenty minutes, couldn't understand why Ava Dunning had chosen this bus stop as their rendezvous. Two 31s had already carried off eager squawking presses of schoolchildren, and more were quickly replenishing the vacated stop.

Freya, leaning back against the brick wall, studied them. She was mesmerised by their complete absorption in their own world, and their utter indifference – nearly a blindness – to the actual one moving around them. Pedestrians had to sidestep, or pause, or say 'excuse me', just to get through the jostling throng, which barely registered the passing stranger's inconvenience. They would be different, more noticing, when they were alone. When she tried to remember being a child herself she could recover only the feelings of boredom. She had been waiting, longing, to be an adult.

Another bus had just arrived when she heard her name called. The voice came, startlingly, from the open platform of the bus itself. She looked up, screwing her eyes, and realised that the black girl, momentarily unfamiliar in her bus conductor's uniform, was Ava herself. She was animatedly beckoning her forward, and held off the pack of kids scrambling to come aboard ('Oi! Wait your turn!') to let Freya on first.

'Go upstairs, I'll be there in a minute,' she said, as the tide of schoolkids finally burst around her.

On the upper deck she found a seat near the front, half listening to the hoots and cries of the adolescent zoo behind. The bus wheezed onwards, its stops announced by a ping of the bell and, from down below, a cry of 'Hold tight'. They were in the thick of Westbourne Grove by the time Ava found a spare moment to say hullo. She rested the back of her head against a chrome rail.

'Sorry, I couldn't find another time to see you. Madness round here.'

Freya's smile took in her uniform, neat as a new pin. 'I didn't realise you . . .'

'What – had a job?'

'Well, when I saw you with Chrissie, at the club that night –'

The mention of her name made a brief unspoken communion between them; then Ava said, 'Most of her friends weren't models. We came from school.'

'I know. She told me. She talked a lot about you, actually.'

Ava nodded, silent. They held each other's gaze for a moment. The bus had halted. Craning forward to check the mirror on the downstairs platform, Ava pulled the bell string twice, and they were off again.

'We get to White City in about twenty minutes. You got time for a cuppa?'

'Of course.'

Ava had started back down the swaying deck when Freya caught her sleeve. 'Aren't you going to take my fare?'

She had never seen the girl smile properly before. Her teeth were shapely and white and even but for a tiny gap between the front two. 'This one's on me.'

The bus pulled into the terminus, and Freya was coming down the curved staircase with the remaining passengers when she saw three blazered youths crowding just behind Ava. As the last boy passed he whipped off her conductor's cap and gave her head a quick, vigorous rub. He jumped from the platform, laughing with his mates as they ran off.

'What was that?' asked Freya.

Ava, stoically, picked up her hat and tossed it onto the tartan moquette bench seat. 'They think it's good luck to touch your hair – "gollywog's hair". Used to happen all the time when I first started. Some people still rub my hands to see if it's dirt that made me black.'

'Really?' She felt faintly appalled.

Ava's languid shrug said that it was no matter, since it would happen whether she liked it or not. She lifted the straps of the metal ticket machine from her shoulders and loosened her tie. They stepped off the bus, and Freya watched as she exchanged a few words with the driver, who was also black. After she had divested herself of the machine and her satchel of change at the office, she rejoined Freya and with her eyes indicated the way. Outside the depot they crossed the road and found a cafe whose patrons included a handful of bus workers. Ava nodded to this or that one as they settled themselves at a scratched Formica table and gave a waitress their order.

Ava's gaze had dropped to Freya's midriff. 'So you're, erm . . . ?'

'Yes. "In the family way."'

'Chrissie told me.'

'She happened to call round the very morning I found out. Something a bit motherly about her.'

Ava smiled. 'That's what she was like. The modelling didn't change her. The money and the hotels and having her photograph everywhere – she really didn't care about it. The clothes she had . . .'

'I remember that amazing orange minidress you wore that night –'

'She gave me that! I couldn't afford it.'

Freya smiled. 'I don't know if she told you, but at the cafe she didn't have any money, so I paid – which was fine. But to make up for it she sent me a television set.'

'That's what she was like,' Ava said again more quietly.

Freya reached for her handbag, and took out a paper napkin. She opened it to show a telephone number, written in biro:

MAYfair 6098 Chrissie x

'I never called – I wrote a postcard to her instead. It's odd, but I find I look at this thing more often than I do the TV.'

Touching the edge of the napkin, Ava dipped her head. When she looked up again tears were standing in her eyes.

Freya reached over and gently put her hand on hers. 'I'm sorry, I didn't mean to –'

Ava used her other hand to shield her brow. 'It's just . . . seeing her handwriting. Like she's still alive somewhere.'

Freya nodded, pained and simultaneously struck by how beautiful the girl looked. She waited a few moments for her to regain her composure. The waitress had just arrived with their tea, and she asked her for one of the glazed pastries that had been imploring her from the stand on the counter.

When she had gone, Freya leaned forward and began, carefully, 'You said, when you telephoned, there was something I might want to know – about Chrissie, I think.'

Ava made a little movement of her neck before she began. 'What they said about her in the paper, at the inquest, well – it wasn't true.'

'What wasn't?'

'They said the caretaker found her at about four o'clock. That's not right. It was me who found her.'

She had just finished a shift, she said, about half past midnight. Chrissie had asked her to telephone, because she thought there might be a 'late one' at the flat. This meant that Bruce Haddon was bringing over some of his cronies from the Corsair, business types who didn't much interest her. She would usually ask Ava to come round, since she was the only one of her friends who would be up that late and still in town. But when Ava rang that night to confirm, Chrissie didn't answer. It was a woman, Frances – they all knew her from the Corsair – who picked up the phone. There was something odd about this.

'She said Chrissie was really upset cos Bruce had been "at her" about something. Said it was all a bit tense there, and that it might be best not to come round. I could hear Bruce shouting in the background, that was how he got sometimes, and I thought, well, what's the point?'

'So you didn't go?'

'I was done in anyway, being on me feet all day, so I got a night bus going south. We'd got to Victoria when I changed my mind – I thought, if Chrissie really is upset she'd want a friend with her, so I hopped off and caught another bus going to Park Lane. I must have arrived at Curzon Street about half past one, maybe a bit later. I could hear Alfie, her dog, whining and pawing at the door inside, but nobody answered my knock. I went down to the porter and asked him if he could let me in. The flat seemed empty, which didn't feel right. I went into the bedroom, and there she was, lying on the bed. At first –' she took a deep breath, composing herself – 'I thought she was asleep. I called her name. Nothing. I sat on the bed and tried to wake her. She didn't move. I asked the porter to come in. He looked at her, then got a mirror to hold near her mouth. He just said, "She's dead."'

Freya let the silence lengthen a beat before she spoke. 'What about Bruce and the others? Where were they?'

Ava lifted her thin shoulders. 'That's just it. When I phoned it sounded like a party was going on – I could hear music. Now it was like they'd never been there. Someone must have cleared up pretty quickly, cos all the ashtrays had been emptied, bottles and glasses had gone.'

'When you found her, on the bed, was she clothed?'

Ava nodded.

'What did you do then?'

'The porter went to phone the police. But before they came Bruce arrived, looking like a ghost. It was like . . . like he already knew. He said to me – "You don't wanna get involved in this, there'll be all sorts of publicity, the papers will be after your family."'

She fell silent then, seeming troubled by what she had to say. Freya, with a tiny movement of her brow, encouraged her to go on.

'I asked him about the police, and he said he'd deal with them. I knew there were drugs, which would make things . . . To be honest, I was so upset at that point I wanted to go anyway, and he could tell. He gave me twenty pounds, I think just to make sure I didn't . . . say anything.'

'Twenty quid's a lot. I wonder what he thought he was paying you not to say.'

Ava was tracing her finger around a pattern on the table. 'I shouldn't have taken it – should I? I should have stayed and talked to the police. Then they wouldn't have just claimed it was an overdose.'

'What do you think it was?' said Freya, scrutinising her. 'Why was he so eager to get you out of there?'

'I don't know. The idea she'd been drinking was crazy – she just *didn't*. I have this awful feeling, you know, if I'd been able to talk to her on the phone, or if I'd gone to her flat straight away I could have – done something. Saved her, maybe.'

'You can't know that. She may already have been dead.'

Ava looked away, her eyes closed. It seemed she was in a struggle with delayed feelings of remorse. Freya wasn't sure what she had got hold of. There was something fishy about that night, not least the abrupt dispersal of the gathering at Chrissie's flat. Bruce Haddon's fortuitous reappearance just after Ava discovered the body looked even more suspect, as did the hush money he handed to her. *It was like he already knew*, she said.

'These late-night parties at Chrissie's place – how many people would turn up?'

'Twenty, twenty-five, I suppose. You'd see the same faces.'

'The woman who answered the phone – Frances? – do you know anything about her – where she lives?'

Ava shook her head. 'She was a good-time girl, you know – wore a lot of fur, always nicely made up.'

'And she was friends with Chrissie?'

'Well . . . I'm not sure how well Chrissie knew her. She was a bit older than us. We used to see her around the Corsair.'

They drank more tea, and for a while talked of other things. Now and then Ava would favour someone in the grey serge of London Transport with a smile, or just a lift of her chin. The fellowship of the route.

Ava, aware of herself being studied, said, 'What's the matter?'

'Nothing. When I was writing Chrissie's obituary it occurred to me that I hardly knew this girl, and yet I felt such a strong connection to her. I couldn't understand it.'

Ava looked off into the distance. After a pause she said, 'I sometimes find myself talking to her out loud. I keep thinking I'll hear her voice, she feels that close. But I never do.'

31

The summer was stretching out, and day by day the uproar over the death of Chrissie Effingham dwindled, became fainter. With no fresh gossip to feed on the papers lost interest and, quietly, like a bad conscience, they dropped her. The *Vogue* cover by necessity hung around, but then gave way to a new issue, and a new face. Freya continued her search for the elusive Frances, looking through photographs of Haddon and his cronies in the paper's picture library, hunting for the woman Ava had described: mid-twenties, dark-haired, petite, a bit 'brassy'. She found one or two likely candidates, but when she checked the names no 'Frances' came up.

Her friend Fosh, who had done stints as a smudger outside the Corsair, had promised to look through his recent photographs for possible sightings, but so far he too had drawn a blank. Nor did she get much change out of Ivan Brock, who considered the story done with once the coroner's report was published. She had told him about the new information relating to the discovery of the corpse, and the oddity of the flat so suddenly emptied in the hours before. Someone, probably Bruce Haddon, had been quick to eliminate any traces of the party going on that night. What did he think of that? Brock, in fact, didn't think much of it at all. She had the unsubstantiated story of an unnamed 'friend' of Chrissie's, who may have had her own reasons to 'kick up a fuss'. She had no evidence of Haddon's involvement in a cover-up, no evidence of wrongdoing, and no evidence that contradicted the coroner's findings. The girl – even her name was a reach for him now – had died of an overdose. Sad, but there it was.

Freya had half expected this lack of enthusiasm on the editor's part. When Brock had spiked her obituary of Chrissie that morning he had admitted to knowing Haddon, and dismissed her characterisation of him as 'a creep'. Now she recalled them talking to one another at the Cosways' party that evening, perhaps they'd been introduced by their mutual friend Robert. She supposed vested interests were at work, editor and agent trading favours in private to maintain the smooth running of their own offices. She would have to be a bit craftier in her dealings with Brock, she realised, given his reluctance to challenge the official line or cause Bruce Haddon any discomfort.

She drove them over Magdalen Bridge just as a party of students were hurrying across, their black gowns flapping like ravens' wings. Oxford basked in a heat haze, its high windows glinting gold from the low flat sunlight. The spires and towers yearned against the sharp blue sky, and the college stone seemed to glow with secretive delight. Freya glanced at Nancy in the passenger seat.

'I don't remember it looking this pretty when *we* were here, do you?'

Nancy looked about her, smiling, as the shops on the high street slid by. 'It's looking more prosperous than it used to. You saw the place at its lowest ebb, really.'

Freya hadn't been back in more than a decade. They were making a stop here on the way to the Chilterns, where they would stay at a cottage for the weekend courtesy of a friend of Stephen's. Nancy had suggested the detour, and to her

evident surprise Freya had agreed. The fires of her resentment towards the place had burnt out, and she felt only
curiosity as to how it would look in the long perspective.
Along the high, students lately out of schools were making
merry, tearing off their subfusc and swigging from wine
bottles. Freya, never having taken an exam here, laughed
bemusedly at their abandon.

They scooted over the cobbles of Radcliffe Square and onto
the Broad – her favourite street in Oxford – where they parked.
They both wore sunglasses against the glare of the day. Freya,
in drawstring slacks and T-shirt, almost had to lift herself out
of the car, such was the unwieldiness of her bump.

Nancy, smoothing down her navy summer dress, said,
'You look amazing – like you're glowing from within.'

'Really? Feels more like sweating than glowing. Have you
noticed how I've started to *waddle*? Talking of which –' She
walked a halting circle around the Morgan.

Nancy looked at her. 'What did you do that for?'

'Oh, just a little superstition I picked up from my dad.
You walk a witch's circle around the car to make sure you
don't get a parking ticket.'

'But . . . why not just park in a place where you know
you won't get a ticket?'

'I suppose that would be the sensible thing.'

They walked up St Giles and called in at the Eagle and
Child, where they took a table by the window. Motes of
dust danced in the slanting light. They clinked their gin and
tonics, and Nancy said, 'To the old place.' Freya had thought
there might be a significance in her wanting to come back:
they had met in London, but they had become friends in
Oxford. Even then they had been through some precarious
times. But when Nancy next spoke it turned out she wasn't
thinking along nostalgic lines after all.

'How far ahead have you thought about –' she nodded
at the bump – 'I mean, once it's older?'

508

'Well, I'm not going to give up *work*,' said Freya, with a touch more defiance than was necessary.

Nancy raised her hands in defence. 'I never for a moment thought you would. It's just – how will they deal with you at the *Journal*?'

'Badly, knowing them.'

'Won't they hold the job over for you?'

She shook her head. 'Not a hope. I don't think the editor likes me much anyway – this will just give him the chance to get rid of me.'

Nancy looked puzzled, so she recounted her set-to with Brock over the obituary of Chrissie Effingham, and his reneging on the promise to let her pursue the story. She rolled herself a cigarette as she talked, while Nancy responded with clucks of sympathetic protest.

'Brock was at your party, of course. I wasn't aware he knew Robert that well.'

'They met when they were at the *Envoy*. They like to keep in with one another – especially now that Robert's getting a name for himself.'

'Pity he can't put a good word in for me,' she said with a rueful laugh. 'At your party Barry Rusk was kind enough to remind me of my "reputation" on the Street – "a volatile commodity". It's held me back. That – and being a woman.'

'Soon to be a mother . . .'

'Christ, it's hard to believe, isn't it? I always vowed I'd never be one of those women who'd get in pod at the drop of a –'

'Cap?' supplied Nancy, and they both laughed.

Freya, sensing the moment, ventured: 'Have you ever . . . ?'

'We wanted to, but we can't. Perhaps it's for the best. Robert's hardly at home in any case, with his work, and I've got my writing to keep me occupied. A child would be . . .' Her shrug was brave, and Freya supposed she was

509

going to say "an encumbrance"; but she discerned something wistful in her face, and was moved. Before she could say anything Nancy continued. 'Have you thought of names yet?'

'Mm. If it's a girl, "Ella" – after my grandmother. Stephen's mother.'

'That's nice. And for a boy?'

'Not sure. I hardly need tell you who's suggested "Nathaniel". I think he meant it, too. I've considered "László" . . .'

'*László*? Whatever for?'

'He was someone my dad once knew. I was reminded when I saw his portrait at Jimmy Erskine's place a while ago. He was an awfully sweet little man.'

'Well, it's unusual . . .'

On leaving the pub they decided to walk on, the sun still pasting the noble fawn stone of the walls. They headed east to the Parks, where a cricket match was under way. They stopped to watch for a few moments, soothed by the languid movement of young men in whites, though neither of them had a clue about the game. The small crowd, most of them in deckchairs, were now and then roused to applaud.

They sauntered around the pitch, where other spectators had also chosen to perambulate. It reminded Freya of a ritual she missed from Italy.

'This is like a little *passeggiata*,' she said.

'Shades of Florence,' smiled Nancy. 'D'you ever hear from Kay?'

'Yes, we still write –' She fell abruptly silent as a man and woman were passing: a face from the long-ago had surprised her. The man considered her momentarily before his gaze straightened and moved on. Nancy looked round to ask what was the matter.

'Keep walking,' muttered Freya. 'I've just seen someone, from way back.'

510

'Who?'

But before Freya had time to answer they heard her name being called, and turned to find the man hurrying after them. He was short, neatly dressed, with a beard he hadn't had in earlier days. But the petulant set to his mouth hadn't changed.

'It's Dr Melvern, isn't it?' she said.

'Professor now,' he corrected her. He had left the woman to wait on her own. Melvern's adenoidal voice hadn't changed either, nor his marked resemblance to an elf. It transpired he was now at All Souls, and about to publish an anthology of twentieth-century British poetry. Freya, unable to resist, asked him, 'Will any of your own poems be included?'

Melvern smiled thinly. 'I thought it seemly to keep the roles of editor and poet separate.' There was a small hesitation as he switched the focus of attention. 'I used to see your name in the newspapers. Are you still writing?'

'Oh, most of the time,' Freya replied. 'I was working abroad for a few years, then came back to London. I'm at the *Journal*.'

He was looking at her curiously. 'I recall something you once said, at our very first meeting, in fact. I think we must have been talking about which novelists you admired, and you said that you didn't read much modern literature, because you'd prefer to write it. It struck me at the time.'

Freya laughed, despite herself. 'What arrogance I must have had! I'm afraid my literary promise remains unfulfilled. But this is someone who does write – my friend Nancy Holdaway.'

Melvern's eyes widened in momentary surprise. 'Ah. A name I know. I – I had assumed from reading your work that you'd be older.'

Nancy smiled, and shrugged. 'I'm thirty-five, which seems quite old enough.'

'You were fooled by the maturity of her writing,' Freya observed.

Melvern, whose frown implied a resistance to being fooled by anything, only said, 'Well, well.' His professorial minimum had been discharged, and he seemed to have no small talk. Freya, who thought he might at least have remarked on her convex gut, gestured with her eyes to his loitering companion.

'Your wife?'

He nodded. 'Yes, we like to stroll about here on a weekend. The Parks make an agreeable prospect.'

This is hard work, she thought. 'And she's also in academia?'

'Yes. She teaches at Somerville.'

'Ah, my old college,' she said, giving him an opportunity to introduce her. But Melvern was either deaf to the cue or else unwilling to extend the scope of their talk. It was strange, she thought, that he had bothered to hail her at all if he was so ill at ease in company. Or was he merely uninterested? He hadn't even asked her what she was doing in Oxford.

The silence threatened to continue until she said, 'Well, it was nice to see you after all these years.'

He murmured a goodbye, but he didn't offer his hand.

They walked on, and once safely out of earshot Freya said, 'God, that was strange. He wanted to talk and yet seemed to have nothing to say.'

'Isn't that pretty typical of a don?' said Nancy. 'Once they're outside the study or the lecture hall they always seem a bit . . . helpless.'

'My failure to turn up at schools infuriated him – at our last meeting he really tore me off a strip, I remember. Said I was lazy and arrogant. Which wasn't wide of the mark, I suppose. Maybe that's why he wouldn't introduce the wife – fear of contamination.'

Nancy, with a glance back over her shoulder, said, 'And yet, remarkably, he *has* a wife.'

'To leave her just *standing* there, though.'

'In my experience of marriage that's not so . . . unusual.'

Freya turned to her, incredulous. 'You mean –'

'No, no, I mean in my *observation* of marriage,' Nancy corrected herself quickly. 'There's a certain type of man who doesn't like anything to divert attention from himself for a moment – which may include the inconvenient baggage of a spouse. They resent them, or feel embarrassed by them. You see that a fair bit among the people we know.'

Freya nodded, and wondered if Nancy had inadvertently let slip a secret of her own, for the attention-hogging egotist she had just described sounded to her very like Robert. Or was that the old antipathy warping her view? In the brief time she had witnessed Nancy with Robert at their party they seemed perfectly content with one another. Who knew? What went on behind the closed doors of a marriage was a mystery to those on the outside – perhaps to those on the inside, too.

The cottage, a twenty-minute drive from Oxford, surprised them. Neither of them had dared to hope it might be even half so picturesque. Its secluded position on the edge of a wood, with a view over the rolls and dips of the Chiltern Hills, made it feel a long way from London. A Tudor facade had been all but erased by a Georgian one of burnt-orange brick and flint. Gables swept low over leaded windows, the tiled roof described a pleasingly crooked line from front to back, and a weathervane stood at an enquiring angle to the cluster of chimneys.

Inside, the low-ceilinged rooms were either panelled like a hunting lodge or white-plastered with exposed oak beams. In the living room a grand fireplace looked benignly upon Persian rugs prostrated on the wooden floor. An affably

513

rumpled sofa and armchairs crowded about a long treacle-dark coffee table loaded with magazines. At the back a creeper-walled garden ended in a little brook, beyond which could be seen a meadow, and sheep.

'Golly!' breathed Nancy. 'Who owns this place?'

'Oh, some rich broker friend of my dad's. You can tell from the way the books have leather bindings. The rest of us make do with Penguins.'

In the kitchen stood another fireplace and a round dining table. Copper pans hung on hooks either side of the central worktop. Freya went about opening cupboards until she found what she wanted.

'Here we are,' she said, reaching for a bottle of Tanqueray. 'Ah, and Vermouth. They must have known we were coming.'

As she began to mix a jug of Martinis she felt a brief stomach cramp, not the first she'd had that week. At her last check-up the doctor had said this was normal; it was the uterus expanding to accommodate the baby. Or something. If only she could just pop the thing out and get on with her life.

'Are you all right?' asked Nancy, looking up from the table where she'd been slicing a lemon.

'Yeah. Just a cramp. Nothing to worry about.'

Because Nancy was interested, she explained what it felt like, being pregnant. For something so common it was the weirdest thing imaginable; walking (waddling) about with your stomach like a cauldron, inside which you sensed something brewing, stirring – becoming. After nearly thirty-eight years of living as one person it was alarming to be suddenly living as *two*.

'And rather wonderful?' said Nancy encouragingly.

'Mm, I suppose . . . But you're talking to the wrong person. Until a few weeks ago I wasn't going to have it at all. I hardly feel ready for it now.'

514

Nancy pulled a face. 'You're going to be fine. And I bet the child will adore you.'

Freya gave an objecting laugh, though she felt secretly grateful to Nancy for these assurances.

Nancy said, in a changed tone, 'You know you asked me about being a godparent –'

'Oh no! You're having second thoughts –'

'Of course not. I'm just – if there's a ceremony, it would be difficult, I mean with Robert. You might have to . . .'

'I know,' Freya said, pouring another Martini from the jug. It had been on her mind, long before she had thought to ask her to be godmother. In the end she would have to compromise if she wanted Nancy back in her life. Impossible that she could like Robert; but she would find a way to tolerate him.

They returned to the subject over dinner. They'd bought glossy fillets of plaice and green beans in the covered market before leaving Oxford. Freya had found a bottle of white burgundy in the fridge and was topping up their glasses.

'I'm sure we can rub along together, Robert and I. It shouldn't be so hard.'

Nancy, perhaps hearing the effort in her words, said, 'He's always been good company, whatever else you may think of him.'

'Yes, that's true,' Freya agreed. 'Even when we argued he used to make me laugh. Cosway's Theory of Attraction, for instance.'

'What's that?' said Nancy, who flinched before she smiled.

'Did he never – ?' Freya looked at her, and in the same instant wished she'd not mentioned it. 'Oh, it was just a bit of nonsense.'

'But what was it? Tell me.' She was still smiling, but Freya had a feeling she might not be once she heard it. Could she pretend to have forgotten? No. Nancy knew her too well.

'First of all, this was eight years ago he told me, when he was in the middle of his divorce. He said attraction goes in three upward stages, beginning in the groin, then travels to the heart, and finally to the head, "the HQ", where you eventually decide whether to stick or – twist.'

Nancy, having listened, nodded. 'That sounds very like Robert.'

Freya, aware of seeming to undermine Robert behind his back, said in mitigation, 'He insisted it was just a theory, I remember. We disagreed on the sequential nature of it. I thought the elements of attraction more likely worked in concert – the sexual and the romantic and the cerebral, all co-dependent on one another.'

'That's because you're a woman,' said Nancy. 'A man would see it as a series of doors to go through. But a woman – she'd see it as three parts of the same door.'

'Exactly! With the knob in the middle,' Freya added, and they collapsed in laughter. On recovering herself she found Nancy gazing at her. She sensed the moment had broken a long-held barrier of reticence between them.

Nancy, chin resting on her cupped hands, began, 'You know, I never really did understand . . .'

'Understand what?'

'Why you ever left. I know how furious you were with him, and with the *Envoy*. I could see why you'd quit *that*. But the country? It felt so . . . out of proportion.'

Freya paused before answering. Her tongue had been loosened by drink. She had already got away with it once; Nancy's question was inviting her again. The confidential mood between them was so like it was in the old days. 'I suppose – I don't know – the real reason was that I couldn't bear the fact you preferred him to me.'

Nancy, with a look of fond puzzlement, said, 'But that doesn't make sense! It wasn't a matter of preferring one of

516

you to the other. Robert was my boyfriend, and you were my *best* friend. Why would you make it a choice?'

She hadn't understood. She couldn't. And she never would, unless Freya chose to be direct with her. But how could she do so without the risk of scaring her off? At times she had wondered if Nancy had suspected – in a look, a glance – and then dismissed it. Impossible for her to guess something that Freya herself had barely come to understand after all these years. My God, she was sweating just to think about it.

'Darling, you've gone awfully pale,' said Nancy, leaning forward across the dinner table.

'Have I?' She was feeling a bit strange, come to think of it. 'There wasn't anything wrong with that fish, was there?'

'I don't think so. It tasted fine to me.' Nancy came round the table and held her hand gently on Freya's forehead. 'Maybe you've had too much sun today.'

She nodded, and drank off the rest of her wine. The sun *had* been fierce, and with the car's hood down the whole time . . . 'I think I might have an early night. Sleep it off.'

'Good idea. I'll bring you a glass of water and an aspirin.'

But she didn't drop off for ages, despite the astonishing quiet outside her bedroom window. She heard the distant hooting of an owl, but nothing else – no cars, no traffic of any kind, pierced the velvety black night. She switched on her bedside light and read a few pages of her book, which calmed her for a while. It had been a long day: a good one . . .

Next thing she knew she was waking groggily from sleep, the bedside light still on. Nancy, in shadow, was lifting the splayed book off the pillow.

'Must have dozed off,' she slurred. 'What time is it?'

'Just after midnight,' Nancy whispered, holding up the book to squint at. '*In a Summer Season*. Is it good?'

517

'Very. Though nothing to compare with *The Hours and Times*.'

Nancy laughed softly, and stroked Freya's hair. 'How are you feeling?'

'Not so wonderful. My stomach's sending out distress signals.'

'Could it be – ?'

She shook her head. 'I don't think so. It's been fine so far.'

Nancy, on the edge of the bed, got up to leave, but Freya said, 'Would you – not go just yet? Is that OK?'

'Of course. I'll lie here next to you.'

She felt Nancy's weight settle behind her, and then took her hand in hers to rest across her stomach. She thought, as she often did, of those raw mornings at Great James Street when they pressed themselves together in bed, for warmth. Her head was still buzzing with the things she had meant to say when they'd been talking downstairs. Another time. Another time.

She felt better in the morning, and opened the curtains to let in a flood of peachy sunlight. She couldn't help marvelling at the stillness of the place. They weren't far, she gathered, from the new motorway and yet all she could hear outside the window was birdsong. In the bathroom she examined her reflection and found some of the colour restored to her cheeks. She palpated the mound of her stomach, and found nothing amiss after the ominous roilings of last night.

Down in the kitchen Nancy was already dressed and making breakfast.

'Morning! They really *did* know we were coming – there's coffee and butter and everything. Would you like eggs?'

'No thanks. Just a slice of that toast.'

They talked about what they might do with the morning. Freya was game for a walk despite her discomfort the day before, and in a drawer Nancy had found maps of the neighbourhood. On the drive from Oxford they'd seen one or two decent-looking pubs they might stop at.

'You're sure you feel up to it?' Nancy asked, searching Freya's face.

'Of course. I'm only pregnant, you know – not crippled.'

An hour later she was dressed and ready, while Nancy outlined the route they'd be taking. Nothing too strenuous, she said, and had pointed out a village on the map, towards which they'd be walking. Freya nodded, not really taking any notice. She had only ever lived in big cities, and while she liked the idea of the countryside she had no feel for the country. If she wanted to go somewhere she'd get a bus, or a train, or drive.

The sight of Nancy with walking boots and rucksack made her determined to muck in, however. The sun was out again, though it was relieved this morning by a fresh little breeze. Their stride soon hit a rhythm, and she found the roll of the hills calling her onwards. The ground had a dry, tussocky feel underfoot, and when they passed by woods she could hear the branches creak like leather. Nancy had insisted on her taking a thumb stick, which helped her gain a little purchase as she walked. Across the horizon woolly clouds bumbled, refusing to be hurried.

They had been out for half an hour when Nancy stopped and pointed upwards. Freya, lifting her gaze, at first saw only a faint dark flake, like a screw of charred paper rising from a bonfire. But then it resolved itself into something winged – a hawk, hovering, whirling, almost dancing. It seemed to juggle the air. As they stood there, Freya felt a sudden bolt of burning pain through her abdomen that almost doubled her over.

Nancy stooped at her side. 'Darling, what's the matter?'

At first it was too disabling even to speak. She felt herself gripping Nancy's hand, waiting for it to pass. 'I feel – like I've been – fucking stabbed – in the gut.' When at last she raised herself upright again she said, 'I think I might have to go back, Nance.'

'Of course – we must,' said Nancy immediately. 'Do you think you'll be able to walk?'

Freya nodded, though she knew they had no choice in the matter. Even without having to consult the map she sensed they were approximately nowhere. They hadn't been near an actual road for twenty minutes. She took Nancy's arm, like an invalid, as they began to retrace their steps. The stabbing inside kept on, like terrible period pains, causing her to stop and take deep breaths. Gently, Nancy asked if there was anything she could do, but Freya shook her head.

'Just keep talking. Tell me about your new book.'

There was comfort in the feel of Nancy's arm in hers, in being helped and guided. Nancy began to explain the novel she had started writing a few months ago, describing the characters, the setting, the outline of the plot which she hadn't quite fixed yet. It was her first go at a historical novel, London society in the 1870s, and what did she think of that? Her voice was tender, reassuring; it would not panic, it would maintain its steady lilt even when her listener wanted to cry out against the agonising turmoil within. It would help her keep going – keep going.

When they came within sight of the cottage Nancy said, 'Right, you can rest your bones on the couch while I call for a doctor.'

'Oh no,' said Freya, palm to her forehead in frantic dismay. 'There's no telephone here. I remember Dad telling me. They've got leather-tooled books and a wine cellar but no *bloody phone*!'

'In that case,' said Nancy, 'I'll have to borrow your car. There's a village a few miles west – they'll know of a doctor in the neighbourhood.'

They had settled that crisis when, at the very door to the cottage, Freya was overtaken by a new emergency. It came first as a warmth, then a trickling down her leg; she thought she had wet herself, but a glance at the crotch of her trousers told otherwise. The stain was spreading dark, and reddish.

'Nance . . . what's happening to me?'

She looked up to see Nancy's face, dumbstruck, appalled.

'Let's get you inside,' she said, sounding shaken, and Freya realised for sure what trouble she was in. She made it to the bathroom and rolled down her trousers. The V of her white knickers had crimsoned, and blood was dribbling down the inside of her leg. Nancy plucked a sanitary towel from her make-up bag and helped her onto the toilet seat. The molten pain inside her gut no longer seemed round in shape but elongated. She felt nauseous, and her stomach heaved once, twice, but only bile came up. And just as abruptly she was calm again, and had command of herself. She took the sanitary towel, and glancing up said, 'Just try to find a doctor, will you.'

Nancy nodded, and kissed the top of her head. 'I'll be as quick as I can.'

As Freya heard her hurry down the stairs she called out: 'The keys to the car – I think they're on the kitchen table.'

She wasn't sure if Nancy had heard, but a minute or so later she heard the growl of the Morgan's engine and a brief racking of the gears before she was off. Left alone, she felt the accelerated beating of her heart. What if the pain got so bad she couldn't move? She felt sweat pricking on her face and brow, and wiped them with her sleeve. Blood, sweat, tears: every part of her was oozing something. Slowly, she stood up and turned to examine the lavatory bowl. The sides were streaked red; the water was a witchy stir of red and purplish black. She pulled the chain, and the bowl was nearly clean again. Standing up had made her dizzy, though, and she felt herself leaking again from between her legs – more freely now. The sanitary towel was a sodden mess, and she threw it in the bowl; the guest towels were pale, the colour of butter, but that couldn't be helped. She grabbed one from the rail and her hands, slippery with blood, made a vivid imprint, like the dumb clue in a pulp crime novel.

The dreadful ache had started up again in her abdomen, and as she lowered herself onto the side of the bath she began to sob, such quiet and childish sobs that the sadness of them made her weep more openly. Something terrible was happening to her. Was there anything she could do to stop it? Perhaps if she held herself very still the flow of the blood might slow. But then another wave of nausea crashed through her, and she gasped out her distress. Sitting was no better than standing; she noticed that the bathroom floor was spattered with blood, already turning to brown on the pinkish carpet. She'd have to give the place a good scrub before they left. The floor, though . . . If she could lie down on the floor that would surely stop the bleeding. Gingerly she lowered herself onto the carpet, carefully folding the towel beneath her as a sponge. There, that was better, even if the pain hadn't really abated.

She tilted her head back until it touched the carpet. She was staring up at the curved porcelain underside of the tub, a free-standing Victorian thing with wrought-iron feet. It was more soothing to look there than at her own underside. The pain was still shrieking away, and she remembered something Nat once told her, about his obsession with being beaten. He said it wasn't the pain itself he enjoyed, that was awful; no one who shared his habit had ever admitted to relishing the violent impact of cane or crop. What he loved, what he craved, was the *apprehension* of pain, the threat of it. So too the warmth afterwards, and the sight of the marks on your arse. It had baffled her. How, she asked him, could he experience pleasure in anticipating something he knew would hurt him? He shrugged in his lordly way, and said, laughing, that there used to be an ointment for sale that deadened the skin: it was much sought after by masochists. But the *pain*, she repeated, how could he stand it? 'Pain is merely the price demanded for the pleasure that precedes and follows it.'

She had distracted herself for a few minutes. If she'd known how to pray she would have done. (Nancy would know the right saint to petition; Catholics seemed to have one for every eventuality.) The hot tarry coil that had been elongating inside her: it was coming. An unholy tumult was swaying up to the boil, burning, burning through her innards and slithering out between her thighs in an unstoppable viscous rush. The last thing she remembered before blacking out was the strange sensation of emptying herself while lying down.

She woke to the sound of Nancy at the bathroom door with a man – the doctor? – and her smothered exclamation of dismay, 'Oh! . . .' Freya looked down to find herself bathed in blood, buckets of it, and still coming. She watched the doctor kneel down and take something that looked like a tiny pink doll from the floor; he wrapped it in the sopping bloody rag that had been a towel.

Nancy was kneeling at her side, holding her slippery hand between hers. Confusingly, she seemed to be covered in blood, too. Then Freya realised it must be *her* blood, getting everywhere.

'Is it dead?' she heard herself say in a broken voice.

Nancy's face was close to hers. She was crying, taking deep gulps, unable to speak.

And so Freya knew it was.

32

She had ended up back at Oxford, almost back at Somerville, in a room at the Radcliffe Infirmary. The view from her window, over lines of uneven rooftops, was familiar from years ago, and she lost herself for minutes just gazing out at it. Lives were going on beneath those gables, behind those walls; whenever she saw a face at a distant window she would stare at it, fixedly, until it moved away.

It puzzled her that she should spend quite so much time crying for something she hadn't even known she wanted. Before visiting hours she composed herself, which fooled most of them: she had never been one to 'give way' in public.

'Just think – back in your own backyard, right next to the alma mater,' Stephen had said brightly, looking from that same window a few hours earlier. He and Diana had come loaded with flowers, which she had no sooner put in vases than she broke down again. Her imagination refused such a beautiful sight.

Stephen, holding her as she hid her face, waited until her shoulders had stopped heaving, and said, 'You really wanted chocolates instead, didn't you?'

'Stephen!' cried Diana in sharp reproof, but Freya could laugh through her tears.

They could all laugh now, just about, with tragedy eluded by a whisker. It was fortunate that a local GP had been at the village pub Nancy had entered in such panic that Saturday afternoon. Fortunate, too, that he had a nippy motor hard by, and knew the quickest route to an emergency department. Freya had lost so much blood she was almost white by the time they arrived. Nancy told her, in a shocked undertone, that the bathroom had looked like 'a murder scene'. She had continued bleeding all over the back seat of the doctor's car while Nancy held her, shivering piteously beneath a blanket. Christ, she had never felt so cold! She remembered being carried from the car to a stretcher and then wheeled hurriedly down corridors, half listening to the babble of urgent voices: then a needle in her arm delivered her to sweet oblivion.

Nancy was there when she woke. She was at her bedside every day, having taken a room at a hotel nearby. It transpired that Freya had suffered a placental abruption, a complication of late pregnancy most commonly found in older women. The placenta would detach itself from the uterus to cause internal and then external bleeding. In most cases the foetus would be stillborn; sometimes a severe complication might be fatal to the mother also. They didn't know why it had happened to her in particular, it wasn't anything she'd done that had caused it; just a case of bad luck.

One evening, when Freya had woken from a doze, Nancy said, in a voice brittle with nerves, 'Darling, there's been something on my mind, and I want to ask you about it in case – well, in case you blame me in some way.'

'What are you talking about?'

'It was that night of the party, at our place – I said the most dreadful thing.'

'I don't remember,' she replied, though of course she did.

Nancy paused, and swallowed. 'I said that you always abandoned things, and people. And I indicated that I could tell you were going to –'

'Oh yes,' said Freya, jumping in to save her, 'abort the baby. I prefer to put that down to your amazing intuition.'

'It was horribly unfeeling of me. And I just hope I didn't provoke you –'

'Into going through with it? Of course not. Is that what you've been worrying about?'

She nodded, and Freya gave a sad little laugh. 'Don't. I mean it. I was in such a state at the time I hardly knew what I wanted. The thing that actually tipped it was Chrissie Effingham. Her death unnerved me, and what I intended to do – well, I just couldn't any more.'

Nancy looked thoughtful. 'I think Robert was quite shocked . . .'

'Did he know her well?'

'I think so. He meets a lot of people in that world.'

Freya waited for her to say more, but Nancy didn't continue. She rose from her bed and took out from the cupboard a round tin. Inside it was a cake.

'From my mother. Lemon sponge. Will you have some?'

She cut them each a slice. Nancy, her mouth full, offered an appreciative humming sound. 'How was your mother?'

'Strangely sympathetic – managed to refrain from mentioning her dashed hopes of being a grandmother.'

'I should hope so,' said Nancy.

'As well as the cake, she brought *Gerald*.'

Nancy laughed. 'I love the Lady Bracknell-ish way you say that name. What was he like?'

'Oh, perfectly agreeable, had a small moustache, knows about sport and not much else – the doggishly loyal type, I suspect, which is probably what she wanted after Dad.'

She watched Nancy as she said this, wondering what sort of loyalty she got from Robert, who wasn't that type of dog. There was danger in prying, though, and she feared putting her foot in it. She was picking crumbs off the bed when she said, casually, 'What you were saying about

526

Robert and "that world". You must meet these people, too?'

'A few. He's out more often than I am.'

'But you didn't meet Chrissie?'

Nancy looked at her curiously. 'No. Why d'you ask?'

'Oh, no reason. I've been writing a piece about her, and I wondered what someone like Robert thought of her. You wouldn't imagine politicians and models had that much in common.'

Nancy blinked, considering. 'You'd have to ask Robert,' she said with a glance at Freya, who realised from that unlikely projection that the subject was closed.

Though still sore and swollen she hated to mope in a hospital room, and at the end of the week she checked herself out of the place. Nancy drove them back to London; Freya sat numbly in the passenger seat, sunglasses shading her red-rimmed eyes. They had set off from London only days before in giddy high spirits, and were returning exhausted and hollowed out with grief. Freya felt as though she had aged in years, not days. And yet somehow their living through this trauma had secured a bond between them stronger than one that could ever have derived from contentment. When Nancy was preparing to leave her at Canonbury Square, having carried her bags up to the flat, they stood in the darkened hallway holding on to one another like survivors of a hurricane.

She took sick leave from work, and then found herself unable to settle to anything at home. It was difficult to concentrate on a book for five minutes at a time. She watched television, without much interest; it all seemed so tinny and frictionless. She busied herself around the flat, finding distraction in chores. She covered everything with dust sheets and painted the walls white, then decided it looked too antiseptic and started again, choosing duck-egg blue.

527

One night she woke in violent alarm, remembering the appalling mess – 'the murder scene' – she had left in the bathroom at that cottage, and telephoned her father. Stephen, woken from sleep (it was 2 a.m.), blearily explained that it had all been taken care of, they'd got cleaners in, and the owner had been more than understanding about it . . .

Her face at night in the bathroom mirror had a wary, chastened look, like the mugshot of a convicted criminal. The ripeness that had filled out her chest and stomach would fade; she would return to her old skinny self. She had briefly been two; now she was alone again. For the first time she saw something precarious in her beauty. Though men and women had always been attracted to her she had no great gift for companionship. She had been too proud – unforgiving. Whenever people had got close she had withdrawn from them; she thought she could afford to refuse. A moment of carelessness had led to disaster. She knew an effort would be required to avoid a solitary life; but she didn't know if she could make it. Or even if she wanted to.

This haze of self-interrogation was broken when Fosh telephoned her from the office one morning. He had just developed a roll of film he had taken at the Corsair, the last of the photos to feature Chrissie and her court of hangers-on. He thought he might have found what Freya was looking for.

'The woman who'd been at Chrissie's flat – Frances? – dark-haired, petite, thirtyish. This one's a dead ringer. Only thing is, I asked this copper friend of mine to have a look. He recognised her all right, but thought her name was *Bridget*, not Frances.'

'Damn. So it's not our woman?'

'Well, not unless she's changed her name recently. Vickery, my mate at the Yard, said she looked very like someone he knew called Bridget.'

Freya sighed. 'I'd like to see them anyway.'

'Right. When are you coming in? I can leave them on your desk here –'

'No! For Christ's sake, don't. I'm pretty sure someone's been snooping around there, checking up on me.'

'You're kidding.'

'I wish I was. Ever since Brock spiked my Chrissie obit there's been something funny going on. Stuff has gone missing from my desk. I'll give you odds that if you leave those photos around they'll have disappeared by tomorrow.'

There was a pause at the end of the line. *He thinks I've gone nuts*, she told herself. Fosh's voice came back: 'All right. I'll meet you somewhere.'

The cafe by the Shepherd's Bush bus depot was busier than the last time she'd been there. She and Fosh were among the few not wearing the grey-and-black livery of London Transport workers. Fosh gazed around at the uniformed patrons taking their leisure, smoking, reading the paper. A couple at the next table were playing a listless game of dominoes.

'There's a lot of stoical faces in this room,' observed Fosh, dropping his voice.

'Driving a bus in London would probably incline you to stoicism,' said Freya, looking towards the door. 'There she is.'

She waved across to Ava, who acknowledged her with a characteristic lift of her chin, and began making her way past the tables. Fosh, having taken a look at her, glanced back at Freya with his eyebrows hoisted to a level of candid interest. Before Ava sat down she tipped her head this way and that in an exercise to relieve her neck.

'Long day?' asked Freya.

Ava nodded, and took off her cap. 'I'm back on at six.'

Freya introduced her to Fosh, who raised his hand in wordless salutation. Once they'd ordered tea she opened the envelope of photographs and drew them out. They were all black and white, ten by eights. Freya watched Ava inspecting them one after another. About halfway through the pack she stopped, and her face creased into a sad smile: she held up a photograph of Chrissie, stepping, almost hopping, across the threshold of the Corsair and offering a little wave as she went. Her hair swung in a curtain, blurrily, behind her.

'That's the pick of 'em,' said Fosh, also watching her.

Ava only nodded, and continued to flip through the photos, which made a sucking noise as each one was slid off the pack. Her even pace, and the little noise, became so monotonous that Freya began to wonder if Ava had forgotten why she was looking through the pictures at all. Her expression never flickered, like a croupier dealing out cards. Hosts of faces that Fosh had caught on film were examined, impassively, and discarded. Until she stopped at one, and without hesitation put her finger over it.

'That's her. That's Frances.'

Fosh looked at it, and then at Freya. 'Same woman,' he said with a bemused frown.

Freya tapped the photograph. 'Ava, listen. Someone else picked out this woman, but reckoned her name was Bridget – might you have been mistaken?'

She shook her head. 'All I know is, I met her a few times an' she called herself Frances.'

A conundrum: two people had separately recognised the same woman but couldn't agree on her name. Freya thought the best thing for it was to talk to the copper and clear up the confusion. Fosh supplied her with his phone number; she took some change from her purse and told them she'd not be long. The telephone box, baking in the sun, reeked of burnt dust and piss.

DI Vickery from the Met answered on the third ring. Yes, Fosh had told him to expect a call from her, about the Corsair photos . . .

530

'To be honest,' she said, 'we're stumped. I've just been talking to a friend who said she'd met the woman you identified as Bridget –'

'Bridget Lockwood.'

'Right. She said she knew her as Frances –'

'Oh yeah . . . ?' She could hear him riffling through papers – bored, possibly – and then joining in a facetious conversation with colleagues at his end. A minute or so later he had refocused his attention. 'So there's a confusion over the name. Not unusual with these women.'

'What d'you mean, "these women"?'

Vickery said, 'Well, when they're on the game they often use aliases – more than one.'

Freya paused. 'You mean to say this woman's a prostitute?'

'Yeah. Known to be. Didn't Fosh tell you?'

Before ringing off she asked him if he had an address for Frances/Bridget. He didn't, though he knew that she often frequented a coffee-and-pie stall just by Embankment Tube station. 'The night shift,' he added with a dry chuckle.

Back in the cafe, Fosh disclaimed all knowledge of the lady's profession. 'I think Vickery takes me for more a man of the world than I am.'

It was plain from Ava's expression that she'd had no idea, either. 'I thought she was a friend of Bruce's,' she said to Freya, who now wondered what sort of 'fixer' Bruce Haddon really was.

They talked for a while longer. Ava had to clock on again, but before she went she asked Freya how the pregnancy was going.

'Oh, you know . . .' she smiled.

Ava stretched across the table and gave her hand a friendly squeeze. 'Look after yourself, yeah?'

They watched her as she weaved back through the tables, and out the door.

'Why didn't you tell her?' asked Fosh.

Freya shrugged. 'I don't know. I thought it might upset her.'

She sensed Fosh taking this in, though it didn't affect him unduly, for his next utterance had quite a different tone about it. 'Most beautiful bus conductor *I've* ever seen.'

The amber sodium lights made a necklace of illumination along the Embankment. The coffee stall opened for business just before eleven in the evening and closed around two. Its windows carried a hand-painted price list (*tea, mug, 4d.*) with a claim that their pies were 'the best around'. Having staked out the place all week Freya had the measure of the clientele, a mixture of night workers from the Tube, closing-time flotsam, cabbies, vagrants and street walkers, the last tending to clot in groups between midnight and one. Ignored at her post on a bench and sipping a coffee so hot it would burn the tip of her tongue, she was able to monitor them at close quarters; she watched as cars idled near the kerb and the women casually dipped their heads to the unseen driver's window. Now and then one of them would climb in, and the car pulled away, its tail lights blushing.

Freya at first resisted the temptation to ask around; if the girl knew she was being sought it might scare her away. But when a fifth night disclosed no sighting of her she decided to be more direct. A girl wearing a beehive hairdo and leopard-print coat wandered over to the bench and asked her for a light, Freya gave her a smile along with a book of matches.

The match flared within the girl's cupped hand as she sparked up. 'Slow tonight, isnit?' she said, exhaling a jet of smoke. 'You 'ad any luck?'

Freya half laughed at the girl's cheerful misapprehension. 'No, I'm –' she began, and changed tack. 'Yeah, it is slow – though actually I'm looking for . . . I think she's called Bridget.'

The girl looked at her. 'Bridget? She's right there,' she said, pointing to a group of her sisters huddling across the road. The girl put two fingers in her mouth and unloosed a piercing whistle. ''ERE! Bridget!'

From the cluster one of them detached herself and approached from across the road; she was short, clad in a miniskirt and thigh boots. She was also blonde, and Freya was about to make an apology when the play of the street lamp picked out something familiar in the girl's face. Her short-sightedness, and the girl's newly peroxided hair, might have fooled her indefinitely. She had a swagger about her as she stepped up to Freya, who said, 'Are you Bridget Lockwood?'

The girl tipped her head enquiringly. 'Who wants to know?'

Freya introduced herself. 'You knew Chrissie Effingham, right?'

Bridget made a backing-off motion with her hands. 'I'm not talkin' to the papers, love – only get me into trouble.'

'I don't want to make trouble. I just want to ask you a few things.'

But she gave only a slow shake of her head. Freya, thinking on her feet, said, 'I won't name you. And whatever Haddon paid, I'll double it.'

'How d'you know he paid me?'

'Because he was desperate.' She could see Bridget calculating what sort of money she could get. Freya dropped her voice low. 'I've got twenty quid in my purse, right here.'

Bridget's expression didn't change, but a movement of her neck gave her away: twenty was way more than double Haddon's hush money. She also took up Freya's offer of a drink, and they moved with their coffees to a shadowed bench by the railings. Close up Freya saw how pretty she was, a heart-shaped face with neat features that became animated in talk. Only the contrast of her dark eyebrows

533

and peroxide-yellow hair hinted at disrepute. On hearing that Detective Inspector Vickery had passed on her name, Bridget said, with a lewd wink, 'We do each other favours now and then.'

It transpired that Haddon would sometimes hire her for nights when he was entertaining clients at the Corsair. She didn't ask who they were, and she wasn't interested in any case: they were punters, and she got paid by the hour. By degrees Freya shifted the conversation around to that night. She knew Chrissie only slightly, she said, and hadn't been to her flat before.

'Everything had been fine till Bruce told me to join them in her bedroom. Chrissie got in a right fit – she liked things as it was, just her and her feller –'

'Sorry – her feller?'

'Friend of Bruce's. He called him "Mr Hooper", that's all I knew about him.'

'Why did you answer the phone that night, when Ava rang?'

''Cos no one else would! Chrissie had told us to get out, she was crying and shouting at Bruce, *you bloody pimp*. Ava wanted to know if she should come over – I said, well, she could, but the way things were goin' . . .'

'Ava did go over, but by that time the flat was empty. Except for Chrissie, and she was dead.'

Bridget shook her head: as she recalled, the party was going strong when all of a sudden Bruce was tearing through the flat, telling everyone to get out. 'I had *no idea* what was up. I seen Chrissie's feller come out of her bedroom –'

'On his own?'

She nodded. 'Oh, he looked white as a sheet! I don't know why he come over to me. Maybe he was grateful I didn't make a fuss or nothin' – Chrissie had said *Whatja need this tart for when you've got me*. I could understand it, really. Two's company an' that . . .'

'So you all got out?'

'Yeah, like there'd been a fire alarm. It was only later I wondered what had 'appened.'

'And this man – Mr Hooper – can you describe him?'

'Oh . . . early thirties, dark hair. Handsome. He was one of Bruce's clients.' She stared into the distance for a moment, frowning. 'One thing he said stuck with me, though, when we was getting taxis outside the flat. That scene with Chrissie must have been on his mind, cos he gives me a fiver and says, "Sorry about that back there – *you behaved like a right good chap*."'

Freya realised she must have shivered, because Bridget looked at her curiously then. She felt herself speaking quite mechanically. 'They were his actual words?'

'Yeah – a right good chap! Funny thing to say. Here,' she said, squinting, 'are you all right?'

She got back to Canonbury Square just before two in the morning. After leaving Bridget she had driven around the darkened streets for a while, trying to fit the pieces together in her head. Truth wasn't stranger than fiction; it was just more grotesque, and upsetting. She could have guessed that Bruce Haddon had put his squalid touch on the events of that night. Chrissie had guessed it, too. *You bloody pimp*. If she hadn't known before, she rumbled him that night. And yet neither was Chrissie the innocent Freya had thought her. The girl from Bromley whose wide doe eyes seemed to glisten with incorruptible purity and youthful cheer . . . Of all the men – of all the married men – she could have had, she had to pick *him*. It was beyond understanding, except that, in some obscure vault of her heart, Freya understood quite well. If the girl had let the secret slip, she could have set her straight, told her what manner of being he was. And maybe that wouldn't have made one bit of difference, either.

She waited until ten the next morning before she picked up the telephone. She felt in her nerve endings an impatience that was almost sensual.

A secretary had asked her to hold the line. A click, and then his voice, puzzled yet pleased. 'Freya?'

'Robert.'

'To what do I owe the pleasure?'

'I need to speak to you.'

'OK . . . I'll have to consult my diary –'

'I'm afraid this can't wait.'

She heard a choked-back laugh at his end. 'Honestly, I've got meetings all day –'

'Cancel them. I'm serious. I found Bridget Lockwood.'

In the silence she could almost hear him thinking. When he spoke again his tone was cool and urbane. 'What's this about?'

'You know what it's about.'

This time the pause was longer, and before he could reply she named a time and a place. She half expected him to object, to bluster, like a cornered politician would, but instead he came quietly. 'All right,' he said and rang off.

He entered the square from the Serle Street side. She was sitting at the bench that had once been her favourite, in front of the wrought-iron screen facing the chapel. The morning was warm, though the sky looked sullen and dimly threatening. A crocodile of capped and blazered schoolboys were filing towards the gatehouse, and Robert checked his step to let them pass.

He twitched a greeting with his eyes as he sat down, not quite next to her. He was wearing a dark narrow-lapelled suit with a crested tie. Surveying their surroundings he said, 'I get the irony, of course.'

She looked at him. 'What d'you mean?'

'Your choosing an Inn of Court for this . . . rendezvous. A good place to dispense justice.'

536

'That's not why I chose it,' she replied. 'It was somewhere I used to come when I was at the *Envoy*. I once ran into Alex McAndrew here.'

Robert gave a mirthless little laugh and looked away. 'Well, I thought there'd be an irony *some*where. By the way, I'm sorry about your – Nancy told me. I gather it was –'

'Pretty grim,' she said crisply. 'But I was lucky. If Nancy hadn't been there I might have just bled out, alone, in a stranger's bathroom.'

There was a pause between them, like gunfighters poised to draw. When a little dust had settled on her last remark she began: 'A lonely death . . . When I was in hospital I wondered what it had been like for Chrissie. I still can't believe she meant to do it. I suspect she was so depressed, and drunk, that she forgot how many Tuinal she'd taken. And she drank because, well – the man she loved, or thought she loved, had just invited a prostitute into her bedroom.'

'Wasn't my idea. Bruce organised the whole thing. I don't know why. I think he was annoyed with Chrissie for some reason, wanted to punish her. So he told the girl, Frances – Bridget, whatever her name was – to join us in bed.'

'Why didn't you just tell her to piss off?'

Robert slowly rubbed his face in his palms. 'I couldn't see the harm in it. She was an attractive girl . . .'

'But you could see that Chrissie was upset, surely?'

'Not until later. She took off out of the room, Frances and I were left there –' He laughed miserably, recalling. 'Next thing I know, Bruce stalks in, tells me Chrissie's in the other bedroom – in a fucking coma.'

'Why didn't you call an ambulance?'

'I thought Bruce had. When I saw her lying there I tried to . . . revive her. She was limp, a rag doll. I thought there was still a chance –'

'The ambulance didn't come because Haddon didn't call one. But I'll never be able to prove it. Ava Dunning found her two hours later, dead.'

'I didn't know. Really. I see how bad it looks now. But to be found there would have finished me – everything. Bruce was shouting in my ear, *you've got to get out of here*. So I did.'

Passive to a fault, she thought. As long as she had known him Robert could not face up to things – two-timing her at Oxford; a divorce he delayed and bodged; now girls arranged through a pimp. Strange that he could be so decisive in professional life – the campaigner, the coming man – and so cowardly in private. She sometimes felt she had spent all her life arguing with men, refusing to be bullied by them, demanding her due. It had left some bruises. But at least in an argument you could make sure you were taken seriously. Robert's disfiguring flaw was that he wriggled out of confrontation, hoping that others would sort out the mess. Not any more.

'I don't understand you. I don't understand how you refuse to deal with people – how you can pretend they don't have feelings.'

Robert, who'd been staring dead ahead, turned to face her. 'I'm selfish. Most people are, I find.'

'That's not good enough,' she said, shaking her head. 'You've had such advantages – Oxford, a successful career, marriage to a brilliant woman. You've lived among sensitive, educated people your whole life. You've read *Middlemarch*.'

'What's that got to do with it?'

'I don't know. Everything. It's unfathomable to me how someone who's read *Middlemarch* could behave the way you have.'

He looked at her askance. 'You have a very odd idea about the value of fiction. It's just storytelling, you know, not a primer in morality.'

'Is that all you think of Nancy's books – just stories? Do they not have any more meaning than that?'

'They earn her a living. That's enough "meaning" for me.'

He leaned forward on the bench, elbows resting on his knees. He seemed pensive, when she had expected him to dissolve in a puddle of remorse. When he spoke again his tone had become musing. '*Comeuppance*. Always liked that word! Slightly afraid of it, too. Like it's coming for you.'

'Is that what you think this is?'

'Well, it'll make a fine front page. An MP in a scandal of sex *and* death – this one'll run. It's funny, you know. Some people think I'm a hero. You ask any West Indian, who's been their main defender in Parliament, they'll say my name.'

'And you think that should save you?'

Robert gave a shrug. 'Immigration will be an even bigger issue in two years. It could help win us the election. I didn't mean to become a spokesman for them, but that's the way it turned out.'

It was an oblique plea for mercy, but she heard nothing of humility in it. 'You're no hero, Robert, whatever they say. That you should try to save your hide like this only shows what kind of man you are.'

He reverted to brooding. Freya half attended to the people passing through the cobbled square: a bespectacled gent wheeled a bicycle, trouser clips throttling his ankles; two young women deep in a lunch-hour conversation; bowler-hatted City men, students, clerkish types.

After a long minute he said, 'So there's no appeal I can make to you – to spare me?'

'What, like you did with Alex? There's no earthly reason why I should think of sparing you.'

'There's one,' he said quietly. 'Your best friend.'

She stared at him. 'You think Nancy would want me to do that – for you?'

539

'As a matter of fact I do. She knows my faults, better than anyone, but she has found it in her to forgive.'

'There's the mystery. It's nagged away at me all these years. Why has she been so loyal to you when you're so *utterly* unworthy of her?'

Robert flinched, and tried to cover it with a dismissive laugh. 'Maybe *Middlemarch* did it. And she's always had a tender heart. She'd hate to see me dragged into the stocks and pelted, for all my sins.'

Freya shook her head, disbelieving. 'Let me ask you something. If you had the goods on someone – someone you had cause to loathe – and the story was big enough to make headlines and your own name along with it, what would you do?'

'I think you already know the answer to that. Fortunately, not everyone's as ruthless as I am. Some have a conscience about what they do.'

She stood up, despising the charm of his self-reproach and yet swayed by it, reluctantly. Perhaps, at bottom, he did know himself. But why should that earn him a reprieve? For some people admitting the fault was a subtle means of excusing themselves from the blame.

'I'm going,' she said.

Robert rose from the bench, his eyes fixed on the ground. 'Why did you ask me here? You've already got the story. I can only think it was to gloat.'

She considered a moment. 'Maybe it was. I was interested in how you'd react. I wondered if you'd beg.'

'I see . . .'

She turned to leave, and Robert took a sudden step forward.

'Freya, wait. I'm ready to, if that's what you want. Beg, I mean.'

She stared at him. 'Don't bother.'

'All right. I'm begging you.' It was as if he hadn't heard her. His voice was low and urgent. 'Please don't do this. I'd offer you money but I know you'd despise me even more.'

'You're right.'

'So I'm appealing to your good nature. Please. However disgusting you think me now, you did like me once, years ago. Think of that naive galumphing chap back in Oxford, the one you knew before his – before all of this. The one who read *Middlemarch*. Something of him survives, I swear it.'

'A right good chap,' she murmured.

'What?'

'Nothing. I'm sorry, I shouldn't have asked you here. I just wanted to look you in the eye.'

'But – why?'

She gave a little squint. 'To convince myself I could still hate you this much.'

With a nod she turned and walked away. She didn't look back in case the sight of him standing there alone moved her, again, to pity.

She drove up Chancery Lane and into the maze of Bloomsbury. Confused by the area's remodelling, she made a couple of wrong turns and had to retrace her route. The old Georgian streets had been knocked about badly, first by the Blitz, then by the bulldozers of the university. Whole terraces had tumbled since she was last here. She made it eventually to the threshold of Euston Road and waited at the lights, indicating right, back to Islington in the east. Across the way a colossal void gaped: the vast and trunkless legs of the Euston Arch were gone, and the breakers with them. *Nothing beside remains* . . . Cars and buses swished past, unconcerned by the bare, boundless space. We shall obliterate all that we love, and then live on.

541

The lights changed to green, and, in a split-second decision, she hung a left, heading west. She felt not quite in possession of herself. Life was running things with a logic of its own, invitingly, like the outline of a drawing she was merely required to shade and fill. As cars shoaled and bunched around the junction of Great Portland Street and Marylebone Road she turned north to skirt the perimeter of Regent's Park. The stately Nash houses looked on, their windows vibrating thinly to traffic that was once all hooves and carriage wheels. The temperature was still muggy; the sky wore a stubborn mouse-grey colour.

When she reached the top of Parkway she began to slow. She wasn't sure where she was going, except that it seemed she knew the way. Her eyes in the rear-view mirror looked wary, underscored with violet crescents. She found a space to park and pulled up the Morgan's hood, anticipating rain. Their terrace looked shabbier in daylight, the pavement flags cracked and veined with weeds. It only occurred to her as she tapped the door knocker that she might not be in.

She had taken a step back when the door opened and Nancy stood there, blinking her surprise. 'Hullo? What are you – come in!'

She followed her down the hall into the kitchen, Nancy chattering on about the warm weather and its encouragement to indolence. She seemed in a good mood, and Freya, watching from the table as she made them tea, felt the weight of what she had to say like a concealed weapon. She hadn't prepared anything in her head; it would have to come spontaneously or not at all.

'I've just seen Robert,' she began, taking a breath.

Nancy's back straightened as she turned from the sink. 'Robert? You mean, by chance?'

'No. I arranged for us to meet.'

542

She stopped what she was doing and looked at her. 'What on earth for?' She was smiling, uncertainly.

'You need to sit down first.'

The smile died. Without a word she took the chair opposite. She tilted her head in a way that invited her to start.

'I'm afraid this is going to upset you. What's worse, I have a feeling you're going to hate me for telling you.'

Nancy was staring fixedly at her. 'You'd better tell me.'

'Robert was having an affair with Chrissie Effingham. He was with her the night she died. Bruce Haddon had been pimping for him – there was another woman involved, and Chrissie became upset. She may have had a problem with barbiturates already, but after a row with him it tipped her over the edge. They found her in a coma. Bruce said he'd called an ambulance, but it looks like he didn't. Robert scarpered, in any case.'

Nancy held herself very still as she listened. Then she said, 'I see. I assume you've told me to pre-empt the report I'll read in tomorrow's paper.'

Freya scrutinised her. 'You don't seem all that . . . surprised.'

She looked away. 'I've known, over the years, how susceptible he is. Robert tends to take what he wants, and he's never been very good at hiding things. The first time I caught him was with a student lodger of ours, here, in the house. There've been others that I've known about, and – evidently – one or two I haven't.'

'Why don't you throw him out?'

'I suppose . . . because I don't think he can help it. And because he needs me.'

'He has an odd way of showing it.'

'I thought there might be something going on with the girl – Chrissie. She was very beautiful, wasn't she?'

Freya nodded. 'She also had the kindest heart.'

543

'I'm sorry. I know you liked her,' she said softly. Then her tone took on a note of bravado. 'So – retribution has come round at last. Robert brought down Alex, and now you bring down Robert. Poetic justice. How did he take it?'

'Pretty well, in the circumstances. But he did try to bargain with me. In fact, he asked me to spare him for *your* sake – said that you wouldn't want to see him disgraced, "for all his sins". Would that be true?'

Nancy sighed heavily. 'Just do what you've got to do, Freya. Don't drag it out.'

Freya stood up and walked to the kitchen worktop, where the tea had been brewing, forgotten. She poured them each a cup and carried them back to the table. 'You know, I'd never understood that old line "be careful what you wish for". Among the things I wished for was a headline scoop that would make my name, and for Robert to get what he calls his "comeuppance". I couldn't have imagined the luck of getting both at once. And yet I find I can't enjoy either of them.'

'Why not?'

'Well, running the story will finish Robert's career in politics. But it will also finish us.'

'I don't see that it should.'

'You can say that, but it will. I'd always be a figure of Nemesis. The bringer of doom. That's why I'm handing the story over – my gift to you. You can tell Robert you know about it or not. Maybe you think he deserves a second chance, or a third, or however many he's had.'

Nancy looked taken aback. 'Why are you doing this – really?'

Freya's gaze fell. 'I'm not sure you'd believe me if I told you.'

'I'd rather you did.'

Here it was. Time had been nudging her insistently towards this crisis, and she knew she must find its voice or have it choke her forever. Nancy's green eyes had become brilliant in intensity. Freya stood up and extended her hand – the gesture was almost courtly – which Nancy took, puzzled, and rose; they stood facing one another. It was like the moment you paused before you began to dance. With the fright and exhilaration of leaping into a pool, Freya stepped forward and pressed her mouth firmly against Nancy's. Surprised, Nancy yielded for a few moments, perhaps bemused by the sudden strangeness of being kissed by a woman – this woman. Then she pulled away, and Freya was left leaning into space.

'What are you doing?'

'You asked me why I'm sparing your husband. This is me telling you. It's not because I pity him, but because I love you. It's important that you understand that.'

'You . . . love me? – but I already knew that.'

'No, not like that. I mean, like a man would love you. I've spent years, *years*, wondering if it could be true, and telling myself it couldn't be. But it never went away, and I realised that however much I kept hiding from it, this love would be there, not moving. When I think of romance, I'm thinking of you. Your face. Your body. Isn't that the oddest thing?'

Nancy stared at her, half disbelieving. She began to say something, and stopped – then began again. 'How can you be? It's only men you've ever – How can you suddenly have changed?'

'It's *not* sudden, I just told you. I've felt like this for years. Yes, I'm attracted to men, but I'm excited by women. I know it must be hard to understand. It took me most of my life.'

'So have you ever . . . with a woman before . . . ?'

'Now and then. There'd been flirtations when I was in the Wrens, schoolgirl stuff. The first proper experience was with Hetty – you remember her, Ossie Blackler's friend?

545

That was when I first felt that being with a woman could thrill me as much as being with a man. Maybe more. It was frightening, in a way. But also wonderful, because something in me had been freed.'

Nancy nodded, but her expression was troubled, and she turned away to face the kitchen window. Her arms were crossed over her chest. The clock on the wall ticked out the silence between them. There was a strain in her voice when she spoke again. 'Thank you for not punishing Robert. I know what a sacrifice you've made, professionally *and* personally –'

'Nance, please. I don't give a fiddler's fuck about sacrifices, or about Robert. I want to know what you think about *this*.'

She blushed now. 'I – I hardly know what to think. I think you must be mistaken about me, you can't be in love with someone who's –'

'Married?' she said in a mocking voice.

'Yes, married! It's more than one kind of obstacle. And talk about a bolt from the blue. You didn't speak to me for eight years. Now, within three months of meeting again, you're telling me you – It's too ridiculous. I think you're still in shock from what happened with the baby. It's quite understandable, you've been through a trauma and it's unsettled your reason –'

'Stop trying to sound like a doctor. This has got nothing to do with the baby. I understand my sexual feelings perfectly well, thanks. I'm sorry if this has embarrassed you, but circumstances have made it necessary. If I'd said I was doing Robert a favour from the kindness of my heart you'd never have believed me. He should count himself lucky, in any case, because the only person on earth who could have stopped me exposing his contemptible character is you.'

'And I'm grateful –'

'Oh, fuck off, Nancy. You're not listening! I don't want your gratitude. I'm offering you something. You have my heart in your hands.'

Nancy had looked away, shunning her gaze. She said quietly, 'I have listened. And whether you care to hear it or not, I *am* grateful – more than I could ever say. But what you're "offering" – it's not something I can accept. I don't feel that way about you. I'm sorry.'

Freya stared hard at her, hoping to draw her eyes to hers. But Nancy wouldn't look at her. She waited, in silence, until she knew there was nothing more to say. As she left she trailed her hand lightly across Nancy's back. She had felt those last words like a wrecking ball to the walls of her life. *I don't feel that way about you.* There was an end of it. It seemed a long walk from the kitchen down the hallway to the front door, but she got there, and she didn't slam the door when she let herself out.

33

'I'll miss her, of course,' she said thoughtfully. 'She'd become rather a friend.'

'Please, stop!' cried Nat. 'I can't bear it. I feel like a brute to be separating you.'

'Well, you gave me fair warning. I'm reconciled to the loss.'

She fished the keys from her bag and put them on the windowsill. Nat had come to collect the Morgan. His accountant had been 'doing the sums', and it seemed he wasn't quite so rich as he thought he was. Certain assets would have to be sacrificed, starting with two of his three cars.

'Will you have to quit Albany?' she asked.

Nat raised his eyes heavenwards. 'The accountant pushed for it, but I dug my heels in. My financial position hasn't dropped to the Micawber line of indigence – yet.'

'What about another screenplay?'

'God spare me. Demeaning oneself before people who wouldn't know good writing if it thwacked them smartly on the arse. Pardon the image. To be honest, I'd like a break from writing altogether.'

'To do what?'

'Nothing! Truly – I'm sure there's an art to doing nothing. I simply need to find the gallery that will pay me for it.'

Their voices echoed in the untenanted house. The floors had been stripped to the boards, and not a stick of furniture except a sofa and mattress had been carried in. They stood on the first-floor front overlooking the square. Nat, having turned up with a bottle of champagne, had to go straight out again to buy glasses. It was characteristic of him that he bought a set of Victorian crystal flutes from an antique shop on Upper Street. A house-warming present, he announced.

'I suppose moving in next door saves you the expense of Pickford's.'

'Next door but one. And I'll be needing them anyway for the stuff I've had in storage.'

After all the years of renting it was hard to believe she was a homeowner. She had heard that number 7 was going up for sale back in July, and thought nothing of it. It was Stephen who had suggested she ought to consider buying it. She'd laughed, and asked him where he supposed she might raise that sort of money. The bank? Not a chance. Very well then – *he* could lend it to her. It looked like a good investment; that sort of property would only appreciate in value, and the area seemed (a brief hesitation) fine. She had dismissed the idea, but it must have wormed its way inside her head because every time she stood on the street she imagined herself living there. A few days later Stephen had handed over a cheque, with its disconcerting vapour trail of zeros.

And you really believe I'll pay you this back? she'd said.

Nat's thoughts were still running on pecuniary matters. He had been advised to open an account at another bank so that Coutts didn't have to bear the entire load of his debts. 'There I was, the very model of a modern major playwright, shaking hands with my new branch manager, in his office. He asked me to take a seat. Can you guess what his first question was? "So, Mr Fane, and what do you do for a living?"'

Freya spluttered champagne down her nose in laughter. 'Oh, what I wouldn't *give* to have seen your face at that moment.'

Nat shook his head wonderingly. 'Odd, isn't it? We're all sorts of leading characters to ourselves, whereas other people comprehensively haven't heard of us. So much for "Nathaniel Fame" . . .'

Freya smiled at him. 'That's the most humble thing I've ever heard you say. Actually, the *only* humble thing I've ever heard you say.'

He shrugged, brushing off the modified compliment. 'Am I to see the rest of the house?'

'Of course. Bring your glass with you,' she said, and they took the staircase, discoloured and denuded of carpet. Fronds of ancient wallpaper curled off the walls. They entered the duplicate of the room below, where the mattress lay rumpled from her night's occupancy. 'Sorry, it's in disarray. I'm sort of camping here at the moment.'

Nat had paused to examine pencil marks on the jamb of the doorway. 'Look, this was once a children's bedroom – they've marked off their heights.'

He shot a sideways look at Freya, who had come over to inspect it. She felt a sudden ripple of embarrassment in the space between them, for he had said the wrong thing, and knew it. He had kept away from her when the news of her stillbirth got out.

'You got my letter, didn't you, about – ?'

Freya nodded, and patted his arm in thanks, and in pardon. Nat was never at his best around illness, or bereavement, or anything that required a show of deep sympathy. He was beset by a dread of speaking sincerely. The only use he had for other people's tragedies was to put them, disguised, into his plays. It was a failure of feeling that had, she knew, lost him friends. She sensed that he was grateful to her for not minding.

550

With a chastened air he said, 'Talking of which, I got a letter myself the other week, forwarded by the BBC. From Sonia Effingham – Chrissie's mother. She'd seen my interview with Chrissie on television, and wanted to thank me for being "such a gentleman" to her. She and Reg had been so proud to watch their girl on the screen; after what they'd been through it was a comfort to see her looking so happy, and they'd had a good cry afterwards . . .' Nat looked stricken as he was recounting it. 'Oh, Freya, the pity of it –'

He faltered to a stop. His eyes had brimmed, and he looked away. It seems I've got him wrong, she thought; it's not the feeling he lacks, just the means to convey it. A very English trait. Nat straightened, shaking off his fit of grief, and pasted a brave smile to his face. 'What happened to the piece you were writing about her?' he asked.

'It's done. I sent it to Barry Rusk at the *Chronicle*. He said he'll run it in the next few weeks.' It was an admission that the story was no longer urgent.

'Did you find anything? Last time we talked you said you were meeting with Chrissie's friend, the black girl.'

'Ava. Yes, we talked. I heard rumours . . . but nothing I could substantiate. It won't surprise you to hear that Bruce Haddon is a creep – and a pimp.'

'I heard something about a *tendresse* between Chrissie and Robert Cosway . . .'

'Hm. I heard that, too,' she said neutrally.

Nat stared at her, waiting for more. Silent, she held his gaze. 'I suppose, even if it were true, his influential friends would have closed ranks to keep his name out of the papers. But I felt certain you'd dig up something on him.'

'Someone once told me that in politics luck counts for more than ambition. Robert's got both, it seems.'

Nat looked askance at her evasion. 'Given the righteous fury you poured into that obituary of Chrissie, I'd have expected something more. He didn't get to you, did he?'

She narrowed her eyes at him. 'Come on.'

But Nat still wanted the last word. After another appraising look he said, 'Thou wilt be condemned into everlasting redemption for this.'

She laughed. 'And I have no idea what that means. Here, have some more of this –' She replenished his glass, and they clinked. 'Care to see the top floor?'

The final ascent brought them to rooms of attic-like dimensions which from the back offered a long view towards the east. The sky, a washed-out blue, had flossy little clouds stuck to it, like a sky painted on a ceiling. Tower blocks had sprouted amid the jumble of terraces. They speculated as to what distant part of the city they might be looking on.

'Isn't it somewhere like . . . Poplar?' said Nat, squinting.

'You make every place outside Piccadilly sound like it's the Andes. We're still in London, you know.'

'Thank God we are! The idea of living anywhere else is insupportable,' he sniffed.

'But you grew up in the suburbs.'

'Which is why I never want to go back there. I'm still haunted by the exquisite tedium of Sunday afternoons when my parents would take us for a drive in the country – *another* frightful place, by the way.'

Freya shook her head, smiling. 'That reminds me. Did I ever tell you about the first time I made my dad laugh? I mean *really* laugh, not the fake "aren't kids crazy" sort. We'd been on a Sunday drive somewhere in the country and stopped off at a pub. I suppose I was nine, or ten. Mum took Rowan into the back garden and I followed Dad into the lounge. I think he must have forgotten I was there, because he stood at the bar in this chummy way, like men do, and asked for two halves of bitter. So I looked up at him and said, in a perfectly serious voice, "Aren't you going to get something for Mum as well?" He just fell about laughing.'

'I can almost hear you saying it,' said Nat.

They had ambled through to the front, stuffy from the warmth of the early afternoon. It was the first week of September. Nat hauled the sash window open with a clack and leaned out to look over the square. At this height you could hear the topmost leaves shiver on the trees. The summer was holding steady, but there came a winnowing breeze, like a warning. He was still resting his elbows on the ledge when she saw his attention diverted by something below.

'I believe you have a visitor,' he said with a sly turn of his head. He leaned forward to shout 'Ahoy!' and waved. 'I'll go down and let her in.'

He was past her and bounding down the stairs before she could even ask him. Craning her head out she looked down to the raised pavement. Two doors along Nancy was looking up, perhaps bemused as to why a person she hadn't expected had hailed her from a house she hadn't even knocked at. Freya held up her hand in welcome, and Nancy offered a tentative mirroring. They hadn't seen or talked to one another since the encounter at her house several weeks ago. She watched Nat appear on the pavement, and the dumbshow of greeting. She ducked back into the room, feeling an inward flurry of nerves at this unscheduled visit. She heard their voices climbing the stairs, like a duet, Nat's drawling tenor against Nancy's unassuming alto.

She came out onto the landing just as Nancy, at the turn of the stairs, looked up. Her expression was uncertain, and Freya thought, Well, she would be uncertain, finding herself in a house that had been unoccupied for months, undecorated for years. But she had come. Her hair was pinned up, in a primly attractive way, showing her milk-pale neck.

'I thought you were at 5,' Nancy said. 'I kept ringing the bell . . .'

'I was at 5. Just moved, to 7. I'm going up in the world.'

Nat had retreated a floor to fetch another glass, and was now filling them up from what remained of the bottle. He cleared his throat theatrically.

'Shall I make the toast? May bliss reign upon this house, and upon its new owner –' he paused, and beamed – 'our dearest Freya. May she, like Mrs Proudie, live forever.'

Freya, with a sideways wag of her head, thanked him. 'But may I just say, I don't want to live forever.'

'Oh, but you must,' he replied, frowning. 'Who else should keep me company through the dreary wastes of my immortality?'

'Nice to hear you're making provision,' she said, and looked to Nancy. 'What about you – d'you fancy living forever?'

Nancy dropped her gaze, considering. 'I'm not sure I feel equipped for it, to be honest. I couldn't face making the same mistakes over and over again.'

Nat shook his head, suddenly enthused by his vision. 'But that's the beauty of it, we'd have whole lifetimes to correct the mistakes. An infinity of lifetimes!'

'That sounds terribly bleak,' said Freya. 'A *single* lifetime is more than some can bear. I'm sorry, Nat, no takers here. You'll have to look elsewhere for your companion in eternity.'

He gave a philosophical shrug. 'Looks like I must recruit Mrs Proudie after all. Though I'd prefer Emma Woodhouse, or even Emma Bovary. It's funny how some characters, mere figments on the page, never really die in our heads, or hearts. We think about them even after we've clapped shut the book. Nancy, you must have thought about this. Will the characters in your novels live on?'

Nancy pulled a face. 'I suppose that's what every writer hopes. That somewhere they'll be talked about a hundred years on, like we're doing with Mrs P. But unfortunately we won't be around to enjoy it.'

Nat nodded slowly, with the pleased air of someone conducting a debate. This is all very fascinating, thought Freya, but I do wish he'd go. Nat ran on, however, with further cogitations on immortality, which he somehow managed to incorporate into a quite detailed preview of his next play. He was becoming one of those people who addressed even his friends in the slightly overloud way of a public speaker. Freya watched Nancy listening, her expression governed possibly more by politeness than enthusiasm. She, too, it seemed, had her mind on other things.

Only when he caught her sneaking a look at her watch did Nat realise he might have overrun his time. With a knowing look he said, 'I have delighted you long enough. And I've just remembered I have a piece to write for one of the Sundays. "The Twenty Greatest Plays Since 1945". An impossible task for me, I'm afraid. I have written only five.'

He looked satisfied by their laughter, and at last he took his leave.

'Nat, the car keys are on the sill, first floor,' she called down the staircase after him. They heard his footsteps grow fainter, and then the slam of the door. She walked to the window, listening, until she heard him start the Morgan's engine. Nancy was looking at her, waiting.

'I know it's only a car. I shouldn't really feel so sad about it.'

'But look – you've got a house instead.'

'I'm glad you're here. I'm not sure *why* you're here.'

Nancy's gaze had misted. 'You remember when we were racing to the hospital, with you bleeding everywhere in the back of the car, and me thinking you might, um – ?'

'Snuff it,' she said, and Nancy winced.

'I never knew I could feel so desperate about someone – I mean, wanting them *so badly* to live. It frightened me, actually.'

'I must have lost so much blood I hardly knew if I was living or dying.'

'They said at the hospital it was a very close thing. I made a vow to myself, anyway, that if you lived I'd make sure you'd be in my life, always, no matter what.'

'"No matter what,"' Freya echoed archly.

Nancy spread her hands in a helpless gesture of appeal. 'I'm sorry about that day. I wasn't ready for what you . . . said to me.'

Freya gave a half-laugh. 'It was rather a bombshell, wasn't it?'

Nancy nodded, and her expression struggled with a sudden access of pain. 'I've left Robert. We had it out, that night, when he got home. I told him I knew what had happened, with Chrissie, and with the – other girl. He didn't try to lie about it. I was grateful at least for that.'

'What did he say?' Freya's voice came out at a whisper.

She waited some moments before replying. 'He started to tell me about Chrissie, and broke down. He seemed almost to age in front of my eyes. He hadn't known how vulnerable she was – though he ought to have. I asked him if he had been in love with her. He said "yes". But it was what he said next that really shocked me. He said, "Please don't ask me to resign." It hadn't been foremost in my mind, but of course that's what Robert most dreaded – not that he might lose me, but that he might be thwarted of his destiny.'

'He knows you have something over him, though. You could make him do what you like.'

'What would be the point? I'm not going to hold him to ransom. He wouldn't have forgiven me if I'd made him resign. And I couldn't live with him knowing that he wouldn't.'

'Do you blame me for telling you?' said Freya.

'No, I don't blame you. I blame myself for – holding it all in. I think he must have despised me a little, knowing I'd forgive him – keep forgiving him. We didn't have a future any more. Perhaps we never did.'

'He loved you, Nance.'

'But not enough. He was driven by something else, that wasn't love. It's the way it is. What one person must have, another doesn't need.'

They had sat down on the floor, each leaning against a wall. A silence lengthened as they waited for the atmosphere, stirred by revelation, to settle. When Freya eventually caught her eye, Nancy smiled in a weary sort of way. She had stayed with a couple of friends in the immediate aftermath; for the last few weeks she'd been minding another house while the family were on holiday. She'd start looking for a place soon.

Freya looked at her. 'Come and stay here. For as long as you need. You may have noticed I'm not lacking for room.'

Nancy's face made a rueful objection. 'That's nice of you, really, but I couldn't –'

'Why not? Because of what I said to you?'

'No, no . . .'

'Nance, listen. I think I'd be able to keep my hands off you, irresistible as you are. Honestly. You'd have your own bedroom. And your own study.'

Nancy, blushing, laughing, leaned her head against her upraised knees. Her face was momentarily hidden. *Oh bloody say yes*, thought Freya, though she would never plead. She was much too proud for that. She waited, refusing to say one more thing, until Nancy raised her head again.

'For a little while? You could let me help with the mortgage.'

Freya smiled, at last. 'Whatever you like.' She lifted the bottle and found it empty. 'I was going to say we should drink to it, but Nat's Moët has all gone. I could nip to the caff round the corner and get us some tea, what d'you say?'

'I'd say it's an excellent idea.'

Freya hauled herself upright and brushed the dust off her trousers. She held up a finger to Nancy: *wait there*. On her way down the stairs she stopped at her bedroom and

557

knelt before the Dansette she'd installed in the corner. The record was already on the turntable, and as she dropped the needle onto its rim she lifted the armature so it would play on repeat. The piano slinked in, followed by the high ghostly doo-wops of the backing chorus.

You are here and so am I,
Maybe millions of people go by
But they all disappear from view . . .

She turned the volume high, grabbed her keys and took the rest of the stairs at a skip. Outside, she stopped and stared up at the house. She loved these sooty Regency bricks, the reassuring steadiness of them. They were old, older even than Mrs Proudie. How many occupants had they outlived? She pictured Nancy on the top floor, her head back against the wall, while the song drifted up the echoing house, keeping time. She wondered how long it would take her to recognise it.

Acknowledgements

Thank you: Dan Franklin, Rachel Cugnoni, Joe Pickering, Victoria Murray-Browne, Clare Bullock, Michal Shavit, Richard Cable, Suzanne Dean, Lily Richards, Katherine Fry, Beth Coates, Anna Webber.

Bless you: Catherine Smith, Elizabeth Day, Doug Taylor, Peter Quinn.

Praise you: David Kynaston for his brilliant ongoing social history of post-war Britain, *Tales of a New Jerusalem*; Katharine Whitehorn for *Selective Memory*; Joan Wyndham for *Love is Blue*; Ariel Levy for her *New Yorker* essay 'Thanksgiving in Mongolia'; Kenneth Tynan for Letters and Diaries; James Agate for *Ego* Vols I-IX; Françoise Hardy for her amazing photograph.

Love you: Rachel Cooke, for unstinting support and encouragement, and for her inspirational book *Her Brilliant Career: Ten Extraordinary Women of the Fifties*.

DRUGS, DANGER, DEBAUCHERY AS LONDON SWINGS
IN THE SUMMER OF '67.

EUREKA

A NOVEL

ANTHONY QUINN

THE BRAND NEW NOVEL